"Putting this one down is a near impossibility. The descriptions of the work, the prejudice, fear, and bittersweet success of becoming a female pilot seemed so real I felt as if I were sharing every step with Velva Jean."
—Nancy E. Turner, award-winning author of *These Is My Words*

"From the ballads of the Grand Ole Opry to the magnificent women of Avenger Field, Jennifer Niven spins a tall tale that is utterly heartfelt and rings true."
—Sherri L. Smith, author of *Flygirl*

Praise for *Velva Jean Learns to Drive*

"A touching read, funny and wise, like a crazy blend of Loretta Lynn, Dolly Parton, a less morose Flannery O'Connor, and maybe a shot of Hank Williams . . . Niven makes some memorable moonspun magic in her rich fiction debut."
—*Publishers Weekly* (starred review)

"In this story Jennifer Niven creates a world long gone, a mountain past where people suffer failure, loss, and betrayal, as well as the strength and joy of connection and deep love. *Velva Jean Learns to Drive* takes us far into this soaring, emotional country, the place where our best music comes from."
—Robert Morgan, author of *Gap Creek*

"A fluid storyteller."
—*Wall Street Journal*

"Velva Jean learns to . . . not only drive, but to soar. This beautifully written coming-of-age story captivated me, and I recommend it to anyone who has ever longed to 'live out there.'"
—Ann B. Ross, author of the bestselling *Miss Julia* novels

"Spirited."
—*Parade*

A PLUME BOOK

VELVA JEAN LEARNS TO FLY

JENNIFER NIVEN's first novel, *Velva Jean Learns to Drive*, was published to wide acclaim and was chosen as an Indie Reader's Group "Top Ten" Pick. *Velva Jean Learns to Fly* is her second novel. Niven has also written three nonfiction books. *The Ice Master* was named one of the top ten nonfiction books of the year by *Entertainment Weekly*, has been translated into eight languages, has been the subject of several documentaries, and received Italy's Gambrinus Giuseppe Mazzotti Prize. *Ada Blackjack* was a Book Sense "Top Ten" Pick and has been optioned for the movies and translated into Chinese, French, and Estonian. *The Aqua-Net Diaries*, a memoir about her high school experiences, was optioned by Warner Bros. as a television series. Niven has conducted numerous writing seminars and addressed audiences around the world. She lives in Los Angeles. For more information, visit jenniferniven.com or follow her on Facebook.

Praise for *Velva Jean Learns to Fly*

"An endearing portrait of a young woman with a big heart—*Velva Jean Learns to Fly* illuminates the power of going after a dream and the courage it takes to never let go."
　　—Beth Hoffman, bestselling author of *Saving CeeCee Honeycutt*

"Velva Jean's story delves into the contributions made by amazing women during World War II and tells a compassionate story about adventure, love, and war. This is a wonderful book—very hard to put down." —Ann Howard Creel, author of *The Magic of Ordinary Days*

"I devoured *Velva Jean Learns to Fly* and immediately began spreading the word: This one is not to be missed!"
　　—Cassandra King, author of *The Same Sweet Girls*

DISCARDED FROM
GARFIELD COUNTY PUBLIC
LIBRARY SYSTEM

"For any who have ever chased a dream, for any who have ever risked it all, for any who have ever stumbled and risen and brushed the grit from their palms, for any who have ever grieved and mended, fallen in and out of love, wished to fly and then flown, there is Velva Jean, the fearless, wide-eyed, big-hearted heroine of Jennifer Niven's second novel, a sweeping adventure that takes the reader from the streets of Nashville to the belly of a WWII bomber."

—Benjamin Percy, award-winning author of
The Wilding and *Refresh, Refresh*

"In this fun, fast-paced, heartwarming sequel to *Velva Jean Learns to Drive*, we follow the beloved young heroine from her mountain home to Nashville. But soon after Pearl Harbor is attacked, Velva Jean begins singing a new song—one full of patriotism, courage, and feisty independence. The perfect read for any girl of any age who yearns to soar beyond her dreams."

—Susan Gregg Gilmore, author of *The Improper Life of Bezellia Grove* and *Looking for Salvation at the Dairy Queen*

"God Bless Southern women, their dreams, energy, and courage. Jennifer Niven and her heroine Velva Jean have those in spades."

—Beth Grant, award-winning actress from
Little Miss Sunshine and *No Country for Old Men*

"Who would have thought that a young woman's adventures in World War II would capture my attention—and keep it? Velva Jean pulled me into her story and wouldn't let me go, from her comical and sometimes humiliating trip to Nashville, the city of her dreams, to the first time she grabs the throttle of a plane and soars. We see her get her wings and fly through wartime danger, intrigue, suspense, and even sabotage. This gripping, heartwarming action-adventure tale stays with you long after you turn the last page."

—James Earl Jones, Tony Award–winning,
Emmy Award–winning actor

GARFIELD COUNTY PUBLIC
LIBRARY SYSTEM

JENNIFER NIVEN

Velva Jean Learns to Fly

Garfield County Libraries
Parachute Branch Library
244 Grand Valley Way
Parachute, CO 81635
(970) 285-9870 • Fax (970) 285-7477
www.GCPLD.org

A PLUME BOOK

PLUME
Published by the Penguin Group
Penguin Group (USA) Inc., 375 Hudson Street, New York, New York 10014, U.S.A. •
Penguin Group (Canada), 90 Eglinton Avenue East, Suite 700, Toronto, Ontario, Canada
M4P 2Y3 (a division of Pearson Penguin Canada Inc.) • Penguin Books Ltd., 80 Strand,
London WC2R 0RL, England • Penguin Ireland, 25 St. Stephen's Green, Dublin 2, Ireland
(a division of Penguin Books Ltd.) • Penguin Group (Australia), 250 Camberwell Road,
Camberwell, Victoria 3124, Australia (a division of Pearson Australia Group Pty. Ltd.) •
Penguin Books India Pvt. Ltd., 11 Community Centre, Panchsheel Park, New Delhi – 110
017, India • Penguin Group (NZ), 67 Apollo Drive, Rosedale, Auckland 0632, New Zealand
(a division of Pearson New Zealand Ltd.) • Penguin Books (South Africa) (Pty.) Ltd., 24
Sturdee Avenue, Rosebank, Johannesburg 2196, South Africa

Penguin Books Ltd., Registered Offices: 80 Strand, London WC2R 0RL, England

First published by Plume, a member of Penguin Group (USA) Inc.

First Printing, September 2011
10 9 8 7 6 5 4 3 2 1

Copyright © Jennifer Niven, 2011
All rights reserved

Grateful acknowledgment is made for permission to reprint an excerpt from "I'll Fly Away"
by Albert E. Brumley. Copyright © 1932 in "Wonderful Message" by Hartford Music Co.
Renewed 1960 by Albert E. Brumley & Sons/SESAC (admin by ClearBox Rights). All rights
reserved. Used by permission.

Ⓟ REGISTERED TRADEMARK—MARCA REGISTRADA

LIBRARY OF CONGRESS CATALOGING-IN-PUBLICATION DATA
Niven, Jennifer.
    Velva Jean learns to fly / Jennifer Niven.
        p. cm.
    ISBN 978-0-452-29740-1 (pbk. : alk. paper)   1. Young women—Appalachian Region,
Southern—Fiction.   2. Nashville (Tenn.)—Fiction.   3. Airplanes—Piloting—Fiction.
4. Women air pilots—Fiction.   I. Title.
    PS3614.I94V46 2011
813'.6—dc22   2011015887

Printed in the United States of America
Set in Granjon • Designed by Eve L. Kirch

Without limiting the rights under copyright reserved above, no part of this publication may
be reproduced, stored in or introduced into a retrieval system, or transmitted, in any form, or
by any means (electronic, mechanical, photocopying, recording, or otherwise), without the
prior written permission of both the copyright owner and the above publisher of this book.

PUBLISHER'S NOTE
This is a work of fiction. Names, characters, places, and incidents are either the product of the
author's imagination or are used fictitiously, and any resemblance to actual persons, living or
dead, business establishments, events, or locales is entirely coincidental.

The scanning, uploading, and distribution of this book via the Internet or via any other means
without the permission of the publisher is illegal and punishable by law. Please purchase only
authorized electronic editions, and do not participate in or encourage electronic piracy of copy-
righted materials. Your support of the author's rights is appreciated.

BOOKS ARE AVAILABLE AT QUANTITY DISCOUNTS WHEN USED TO PROMOTE PRODUCTS OR SERVICES.
FOR INFORMATION PLEASE WRITE TO PREMIUM MARKETING DIVISION, PENGUIN GROUP (USA) INC.,
375 HUDSON STREET, NEW YORK, NEW YORK 10014.

For John Ware,
who helped give Velva Jean her wings,
and who always encourages me to fly
And for Mom, as ever
And in memory of Mabel Rawlinson,
Betty Taylor Wood, and the thirty-six
other WASP who lost their lives
in the line of duty

I was happiest in the sky . . .
Think of me there and remember me.

—Cornelia Fort, January 1942

Acknowledgments

People often ask if I ever get lonely while writing a book, to which I reply, "Even when I am sitting alone at my desk, I'm surrounded by people who are a part of the journey." My dynamite agent and friend John Ware has been on that journey from the start, as wise as the Wood Carver, as funny as Johnny Clay, as encouraging and supportive as Daddy Hoyt. As usual, I could not have done this without him. My brilliant editor, Carolyn Carlson, has my eternal gratitude for believing in Velva Jean, not once, but twice now, and for helping to shape and hone and strengthen her story with her magical and insightful editorial notes. Deepest thanks to her and to all the wonderful folks at Plume—Clare Ferraro, Kathryn Court, John Fagan, Liz Keenan, Amanda Brower, Katie Hurley, Milena Brown, Eve Kirch, and the terrific sales team—who have been a part of this story. And thank you to Melissa Jacoby for once again creating the perfect cover.

Enormous thanks and gratitude to my first readers: Penelope Niven, Scott Boyer, and Valerie Frey. Their thoughts and feedback were invaluable. Extra special thanks, as always, to my dear mama, Penelope Niven, who is not only a wonderful editor but my very best friend in the world. She was the person—along with my father, Jack F. McJunkin—who first taught me to fly and who has, ever since that first lesson, encouraged me to keep flying. Thanks to my sacred circle for love, laughter, silliness, and support: Joe Kraemer, Lisa Brucker, Angelo Surmelis, Christos Sourmelis, Ed Baran, Dan and Magda Dillon (and Daniel too), and last, but in no way least, Louis Kapeleris, who may have arrived late in the process, but who has been such a part of it just the same, filling my days with love and sunshine and dreams come true (as well as sage feedback and a rock star author photo), and who has given me the happiest writing space I've ever known. And thanks to my wonderful family and friends: all my McJunkin and Niven kin, Lynn Duval Clark, Judy Kessler, Beth Shea, Binnings Bent, Vanessa Vaughn, Tate Whitney Parker, Fred Tyler, John Hreno, Brian Stone, Tabitha Marsden, Jamal Farley, Jack Meggers (for teaching me that rattlesnakes like ragtime), Ian Fraser, Jan Ricci, Shawn Kowaleski, and Lynda Boyer, for making me feel so welcome at Ruth's Oasis, where so much good writing was done.

Thanks again to my mom, who is not only a brilliant writer of books but a brilliant writer of songs. Velva Jean and Butch Dawkins are both indebted to her skills. Heartfelt thanks to Curtis Duncan (and his family), a boy I once loved who died too soon, for writing me a song called "You Make Me Happy" before he went away.

As always, I could not have written this book without the devoted and energetic help of literary kitties Satchmo (who diligently protected the house so no stray cats could get in and disturb me while I was writing), Rumi (who purred at and around me constantly, stopping only to attack each page as it was printed), and Lulu (who insisted on sitting on my lap while I wrote and oftentimes on the computer itself).

I'm grateful to the National WASP World War II Museum in Sweetwater, Texas; Nancy Parrish and WASP on the Web (wingsacross america.us); Texas Woman's University; the Palm Springs Air Museum (where I toured a B-17!); the Marietta Aeronautical Museum and Education Center; the Kennesaw State University Oral History Project; Marion Stegeman Hodgson and Edward Hodgson for romantic inspiration (anyone craving a great adventure/love story should read Marion's book *Winning My Wings*); and to Bernice "Bee" Haydu and Jean T. McCreery and all the other brave and daring members of the Women Airforce Service Pilots. How I wish I could have been one of you.

Finally, I couldn't have written the book without Carole Lombard, *Supernatural*, the Jonas Brothers, Bootcamp LA, *Rescue Me*, the Silver Lake Reservoir, Robeks, *90210*, the ArcLight, Mind-Body Fitness, Mark

Wahlberg, Griffith Park, Vitaminwater, *The Bachelorette*, Liberation Yoga, Palermo Ristorante Italiano, the BigFoot Lodge, and Ryan Bingham. I created Butch Dawkins before I knew who Ryan Bingham was, but it's like he walked off the page—right down to that face, that hair, the tattoos, those songs, and the whiskey-and-cigarettes voice. Mercy.

Last of all, thanks to the loved ones who are no longer here but who live on in my heart and, in part, on these pages: my grandmothers Eleanor Niven and Cleo McJunkin (who together make Granny); my grandfathers Olin Niven (Daddy Hoyt) and Jack McJunkin Sr. (Johnny Clay); Charlie Kelly; Charles McGee; Phil Clark; Mary Martin; Mary Ellen Boyer; literary kitties George and Percy; and, most of all, my father.

Contents

~ 1941 ~

When the shadows of this life have gone,
I'll fly away.
Like a bird from these prison walls, I'll fly,
I'll fly away.

—"I'll Fly Away"

ONE

*E*ver since I was a little girl, I knew that singing at the Grand Ole Opry was my life's dream. Now I was driving myself from Alluvial, North Carolina, to Nashville, Tennessee, in my old yellow truck and I was planning to sing the whole way. I began with "The Unclouded Day" and from there ran through my favorite hymns before I started in on the mountain folk songs I was raised on and, finally, songs I'd written myself.

> *Yellow truck coming,*
> *bringing me home again.*
> *Yellow truck going,*
> *I'm on my way . . .*

I'd decided that when I got to Nashville I was going to drive straight to the Opry before I went anywhere else, before I even found a room to rent or a place to work. I wanted to touch the building where Roy Acuff and the Smoky Mountain Boys had been discovered, and where I knew I would sing someday. I might even kiss the building, depending on how dirty it was.

> *On my way to tomorrow*
> *and dreams come true,*
> *leaving my yesterday . . .*

The day was bright and blue, and the sun beamed down on the old yellow truck and on my arm hanging out the window. I'd kicked my shoes off long ago. I wanted to feel the pedals under my feet.

I'm driving this truck to Nashville,
home of dreams come true . . .

I was writing a new song as I drove with one eye on the road, the other on the rearview mirror. The mountains—my mountains, the ones where I was born, where I was raised, the one named for my mama's people, the one where I'd lived with Harley Bright after we got married, the ones I'd just up and left hours before—were slipping away.

where I'll wear a suit of rhinestones
and play a guitar made of jewels . . .

Just east of Sylva, I turned off the Scenic and onto Route 23, and I saw the first sign for the Balsam Mountain Springs Hotel a mile or so later. I tried not to remember my honeymoon, back when I was sixteen and had never been anywhere and had to rely on Harley Bright to take me places. I tried not to think about an orchestra under the moonlight, about the night Harley made me a woman, and the morning after when I looked at myself in the mirror and decided I really didn't look any different after all.

I tried not to think about Harley coming home tonight from the Little White Church, expecting his supper, expecting me. I tried not to picture him walking in the door and not finding me—that first moment when he realized I was gone really and truly, and not just to my sister's or to Granny's. I tried not to think about what might happen if he found out where I was and decided to come looking for me.

It was August 22, and the air was still heavy with summer. In my rearview mirror, the mountains were full and green. I sang till I almost couldn't see them anymore, till I was surrounded by new mountains, strange mountains, ones I didn't recognize. And then, just before the very tip of Fair Mountain disappeared, I pulled that truck over to the side of the road and got out. I left the engine running because I wanted to hear the rumble of it while I stood there with my back to it, looking off toward home.

I stood with my hands on my hips and stared at Fair Mountain and tried to imagine what everyone was doing at this very minute. It was still morning, but barely. Granny would be out on Mad Maggie, her mule, off to deliver a baby or tend to a new mother. My granddaddy, Daddy Hoyt, would be gathering plants for his healings. Ruby Poole, my sister-in-law, would be fussing over baby Russell and giving him his morning feeding. My oldest brother, Linc, would be rounding up the cattle or working in the barn. Sweet Fern, the oldest of all of us, would be cooking something and shouting at Corrina to stop teasing her brothers. Harley would be at the Little White Church.

My other brothers, Johnny Clay and Beachard, were off somewhere, just like me. Beachard was working on the Blue Ridge Parkway—we called it the Scenic—the new road that stretched across the mountaintops from Virginia to North Carolina, right up to the border of Tennessee. But Johnny Clay could be anywhere. He might be in California by now. He might even be in Mexico, running far, far away from home and the man he almost killed.

I stood there and blinked at the mountains. A stranger would have thought they all looked the same, but I could tell them apart from here: Devil's Courthouse, Witch Mountain, Bone Mountain, Blood Mountain, Fair Mountain. Fair Mountain was mine.

I stood there a long time, very still. I almost stopped breathing. I felt myself start to fade into the air, into the road. I lost track of my feet and legs and arms and hands.

Suddenly I could hear that truck. It was saying, "Get back in, Velva Jean. Come on. Let's keep going."

Yellow truck coming,
bringing me home again.
Yellow truck going,
I'm on my way . . .

I turned around and walked to the truck and climbed back inside. I pulled out into the road, and as I started on toward Nashville, I didn't look in the rearview mirror again. I just stared straight ahead till I could breathe.

By the time I crossed the Tennessee state line, I'd stopped singing. I felt like I'd been driving for days, but it had only been hours, and I still had miles to go. I thought I would never get to Nashville, not in five years.

I pulled into an Esso station in Calderwood. The attendant shuffled when he walked and went slow as could be, as if he had all the time in the world. He looked at me funny and then leaned past me and kind of peered in the cab of the truck like he was looking for something or someone. He said, "Afternoon, ma'am."

"Afternoon. Could you fill it up please?" I counted out my money from the coin purse that held every penny I had in the world—$121.11. It suddenly didn't seem like much.

"Yes'm. Sure thing." He frowned, looked past me at the empty seat, and then shuffled over to the gas pump.

As he filled up the tank and then cleaned the windows, I pulled out the map and looked at the line I'd drawn from Devil's Kitchen— which wasn't even a dot on the page—to Nashville. It was a long line. It was miles and miles long. Why hadn't I noticed how far it was when I was setting out?

I thought, Velva Jean, maybe you should just turn back, girl. You got no business being on this road by yourself. You're a married woman. You got a home and family. What are you doing out here in this great big world?

I sat there for a moment and really thought about this. The attendant said, "Where you headed?"

I said, "Nashville."

"Where you coming from?"

"Up near Waynesville." I picked a town he might know. "Over in North Carolina." I felt a stabbing in my heart as I said it. For the first time in my life, I was in another state. I was in Tennessee. I was getting farther and farther from home and from everyone I knew in this world.

He narrowed his eyes, and then he nodded. "Well," he said. "You got a long way to go."

I passed the hitchhiker east of Loudon. He was young and dusty with a crew cut and a bag over one shoulder. He held his thumb out like he expected everyone in the world to stop, like that was all it took. He waved at me as I drove on past, turning to stare at him. I wondered if he was a murderer or a thief or a person in search of his destiny, like me. I tried to picture myself hitchhiking, thumb out, suitcase and hatbox at my feet, waving to everyone going past.

There wasn't another soul on the road for a mile or two, but I rolled up my window just the same. I wondered if there were thieves who hid in the bushes, waiting to jump out at single lady travelers. I hoped I didn't see another person till Nashville.

I drove till just after seven o'clock, and then I pulled into a town called Sparta and found a motel. In an hour the sun would set and the sky would turn black, and I wanted to be off the road before then. The motel parking lot was empty except for my truck, which made me feel like the only person in the world, next to the manager, who asked me to fill out a card and pay cash up front before he handed me the key.

I went into the room and turned on all the lights, every single one, because it made me feel less alone. I carried in my suitcase and my hatbox, and then I stretched myself out on the bed and opened the Esso map and figured out how much farther I had left to go.

Afterward I got out the little card Darlon C. Reynolds had given me—the one with his address and telephone number—back when I recorded my songs for him in Waynesville the time Johnny Clay and me went to audition. By now I knew those numbers by heart. Then I unpacked my framed picture of the Opry.

There was a telephone in the lobby of the motel. The man at the desk said I could use it as long as I paid him for the call. I stared at it for the longest time, and then I picked up the phone and asked for a long-distance operator. When she came on the line she said, "Where are you calling to?" Her accent was thicker than mine.

I said, "Deal's General Store in Alluvial, North Carolina."

She said, "Asheville?"

I said, "Alluvial."

She said, "What's your name, please?"

"Velva Jean Hart." I left off the Bright without thinking.

She was quiet for a minute, though I could hear a shuffling of papers. And then she said, "Hold, please, dear."

The word "dear" was enough to do me in right then and there. I couldn't even think about Nashville and all that lay ahead to do—finding a job, a place to live. What if Darlon C. Reynolds didn't remember me? What if the Opry didn't want girl singers who also played mandolin and had run away from their husbands without a word of good-bye? I blinked the tears back in.

In a moment there was a flat, loud ringing on the line. It rang five times, and then a voice, thin and crackly, on the other end said, "Deal's."

The tears sprang back. The operator said, "Velva Jean Hart calling from Sparta, Tennessee."

"Velva Jean!" It was Coyle, the oldest Deal boy. He said to someone, "It's Velva Jean!"

I started crying then and couldn't stop. I said, "Coyle?"

He said, "Velva Jean, is it really you? Where you at, girl?"

I said, "Tennessee! I'm in Tennessee."

Coyle whistled. Suddenly the phone crackled and I heard a woman's voice. "Velva Jean?"

"Sweet Fern?"

Sweet Fern was my sister, ten years older, who'd been left to raise me and my brothers after Mama died and Daddy went away.

"Where are you?"

Even though Sweet Fern and I never did get on well, the homesick feeling I'd been swallowing ever since I left rose up again and made my throat freeze so that I could barely say "Sparta, Tennessee."

She said, "Why didn't you say good-bye?"

I said, "Because I never would have left."

Sweet Fern got quiet at this, and then she said, "You be safe, Velva Jean." And I could hear the tug in her voice. Then Mr. Deal was on the line, and then Jessup Deal—the youngest of the Deal boys—and then Hink Lowe's daddy, and finally Ruby Poole, who'd just walked in with baby Russell. She said, "Velva Jean, are you wearing your lipstick?"

I said, "Every day."

She said, "Listen, you be careful and just know that all of us up here are rooting for you. We can't wait to see what you're going to do."

I said good-bye then and hung up the telephone and paid for the call and went on back to my room. I lay down on the bed and looked at my Opry picture. I imagined all the songs I'd sing, and then I started in on them, one by one, until I sang myself to sleep.

~

I wasn't far past Watertown, where Highway 26 got ready to merge with Highway 70, when the truck started wobbling. I drove on, hanging tight to the wheel, and suddenly the truck veered off toward the roadside, and I had no choice but to bring it to a stop under some trees. I was shaking as I sat there, checking all my windows and the rearview mirror for hitchhikers.

I took a breath and got out of the cab. The truck was leaning over to the right, looking as worn out as Elderly Jones—the old Negro who lived in Alluvial—without his cane. That front tire was flat as a quarter. I stood there in my bare feet and said all the bad words Johnny Clay had taught me. Then I sat down on the side of the road and said, "Well, Jesus, I hope you're happy."

Jesus and me hadn't been on good terms for years, ever since he took my mama away, made my daddy leave, and got me tangled up with Harley Bright, my husband—moonshiner's son, tent preacher, and the most unspeakable man I ever did meet.

I sat there, dust in my hair, gravel poking me about the legs and bottom like mean little pinches, and told Jesus exactly what I thought of him for letting this happen. I said, "Lord, all I asked from you when

I started on this trip was that I make it to Nashville safe. I didn't ask for a recording contract once I get there. I didn't ask for a job or money past what I got saved up. I didn't even ask you to help me find a decent place to sleep. All I asked—the only thing, after all we been through, and good gracious knows that's a lot—is that you let me get there without anything happening to this truck."

The more I talked, the madder I got. I felt a slow burning under the collar of my dress that was growing right up the sides of my face. I felt mad at everyone who was driving a car that wasn't giving them trouble.

From nearby a voice said, "Are you all right there, honey?"

A car had pulled off to the side. A man was behind the wheel, and a woman—I guessed it must be his wife—leaned out the window. They were my daddy's age. The man wore a hat, and the woman wore glasses and white gloves.

I said, "No, ma'am, I'm not."

The woman said, "Are you out here by yourself?"

"Yes'm."

She said something to her husband, and then he leaned around her and stared at me. The woman smiled a smile so kind it nearly started me to crying again. She got out of the car, unfolding herself as stiff and careful as a paper fan. I heard a door slam, and her husband walked around the car to stand beside her. He said, "Let's take a look at that tire."

We watched as he kneeled down beside it, shaking his head. The woman said, "I'm Myrna Dover, and that's my husband, Franklin."

"I'm Velva Jean."

"That's an unusual name, but pretty."

"Thank you."

She said, "Do you have a husband, Velva Jean?"

I was surprised at the question but tried not to show it. I wiped my nose and smiled my most polite smile. "Not with me."

Her face clouded up, and I could tell she thought he had died. She took my hand and looked up toward heaven and said, "You poor dear."

I said, "Oh he's not dead. He's in North Carolina."

Her mouth popped open. She looked like she was deciding how

she felt about this. "What are you doing out here by yourself?" Her voice took on a hard tone. I thought she sounded just like Sweet Fern.

I said, "I'm going to Nashville to be a singer."

She glanced behind me, to the truck, her eyes going from my suitcase to my hatbox to the map, which was still unfolded and lying across the seat. She said, "How wonderful." But her mouth pursed up a little, like she had just sucked a lemon, and she looked at her husband as if by looking at him she could hurry him along.

He sat back then, resting his wrists on his knees, and said, "You got a spare?"

I shook my head. Johnny Clay or Danny Deal must have used it long ago and never replaced it, if the truck had even come with one in the first place. Why hadn't I thought to get a spare? In all my planning and checking of oil and lights and brakes, I never once considered it.

He said, "I don't think ours would last you very long." We all looked at the car and the tires, which were smaller than the tires on the truck.

We drove for a mile before we saw a service station. It rose up along the side of the road, the only building except for a couple of tiny houses set off nearby. I had put my shoes back on, and now I wiggled my toes, which felt boxed up and hot.

Franklin Dover got out and talked to the station attendant, gesturing with his hands so that I knew he was describing my truck and what was needed. Mrs. Dover and I sat in silence. At some point she said, "You need to be careful out there." She was looking straight ahead, through the window, out at the trees and the road.

"Ma'am?"

She said, "You probably got folks worrying about you." It was a question.

"Yes."

There was a fat little smack against the windshield. And another. Rain.

She said, "Well, make them worry as little as you can. There are hitchhikers and strangers and all sorts of hooligans who might not be so kind. You let your folks know you're safe by staying safe."

"Yes, ma'am."

It started raining harder—an end-of-summer storm, the kind that came in fast and left fast, washing everything clean.

We sat, not talking, the rest of the time we waited. Mr. Dover came over to the car and tapped on the window. Mrs. Dover leaned over me to roll it down. He said, "It'll be seven dollars for the tire."

I opened my coin purse and counted the money. He turned around and handed it to the attendant, and then I watched the attendant count my money that I'd worked so hard for. I thought, I should buy a spare tire while I'm at it. What if another tire goes flat? What if I'm out there on the road, all by myself, far away from a service station or anyone that can help me, and something goes wrong? Seven dollars was a lot of money. If I handed over seven more dollars for another tire, I might as well just hand over my entire life savings.

Then I thought, Dammit! I can take care of this myself. And as I thought it, I suddenly believed it. I could take care of it myself. Hadn't I been doing everything myself for the past few months? Not just the cooking and the cleaning and the looking after my husband's daddy and my own husband, but teaching myself how to drive and how to learn an engine, and writing songs and even recording two of them. When Harley nearly died in the Terrible Creek train wreck and then stopped his preaching, it was me that kept us fed, with help from his daddy, and it was me that had to get Harley up off the settee and make him start working again.

I thought: I need to get out of this car. I need to get back to my truck. I am going to change that tire.

I looked in the side mirror and back down the road we'd just driven. You couldn't see the truck anymore but it was back there, and suddenly I was desperate to get to it. In my head I heard a voice—faraway but firm: "I need to do this on my own." And when I heard it, I felt the truth of it down in my bones. I didn't need Harley or anyone else to help me change a tire. I could do it myself.

I opened the car door. Mrs. Dover turned to look at me. I got out and shut the door and leaned in the open window. I said, "Thank you, ma'am. Y'all have been awful kind."

Then I turned to Mr. Dover and said, "If it's all the same, I'll be taking my tire. I've troubled you enough, and I can take care of this from here on out."

The attendant said, "Looky here, you need a jack and a lug wrench?"

I wasn't about to tell him that I didn't know what either of those things was. "No, sir," I said. "I do not."

And that was how I found myself walking in the late-summer rain, down a gravel road, just a few miles east of Nashville, somewhere near a place called Watertown, chin up, mountains fading in the distance, wheeling a tire I'd bought with some of the money I'd earned and saved myself so that I could keep on going.

The truck manual didn't say anything about where the jack and the lug wrench were kept. I went over every inch of that truck until I pushed the seat forward and found them behind it, slid underneath. The jack looked like an enormous black bird. It was heavy and shaped like a strange, flattened S. The lug wrench was a steel lever bent at each end—one going up, the other going down. There was a funny-shaped, six-sided hole the size of a quarter at one of the ends.

It's like a puzzle, I told myself. I was good at puzzles. Didn't I almost beat Johnny Clay at putting together a puzzle once, back when I was eight and he was ten and Mama was still alive? I came so close to beating him that afterward he didn't speak to me for a week.

I lay the jack and the lug wrench down on the ground by the tire, and then I dug through my hatbox until I found *How to Drive* and *Man and the Motor Car*, the books I learned to drive by. I read through, page after page, until I figured out that the jack needed to be placed under the front axle. I put it just where I thought that was, and just where it needed to be, but it didn't look right compared to the picture in *How to Drive*. I got down on my knees and moved it forward an inch and then back an inch and then right back to where I'd had it in the first place. Then I stuck the jack handle into the "rotary mechanism" at the bottom of the jack. All that time the rain came down, down, down.

Next I studied the tire—the wheels were wire, the yellow paint chipped, the hubcaps scuffed and dented. My poor old truck. It looked like I felt—banged up here and there, scraped and scarred, but still running strong.

The book said something about removable hubcaps. I pulled, gentle as my mama's touch, at the hubcap, afraid to break it. When it wouldn't come off, I sat down and yanked at it with all my might. It flew off and sent me backward into the dirt, which was now turning into mud.

There were five lug nuts underneath where the hubcap had been. I picked up the lug wrench and fit the hole over one of the nuts. I turned it hard as I could until I felt it give a little. Then a little more, a little more, a little more—until I had all five off.

The old tire practically fell in on itself then. I pulled it off and threw it aside, and then I rolled the new one over and lifted it into place. One by one, I screwed in the lug nuts, and then I popped the hubcap back on and cranked the jack until the truck was all the way on the ground again.

I sat back—hands and face muddy, hair wild and wet from the breeze and the rain, fingers aching, arms scratched—admiring my new front tire, which was now, thanks to me, attached to the truck. An automobile drove by and honked its horn. I thought, What a sight I must be. I wished Berletta Snow or Oderay Swan—who Harley called "good Christian women, close in touch with the Lord"—could see me right this minute, sitting in the mud like a wild mountain heathen, just like one of the Lowes, who were always filthy and ridden with mites.

I stood up then, brushing myself off, and picked up the old tire and dropped it into the bed of the truck with a thud. Then I swung back up behind the wheel and looked at myself in the mirror. There was dirt on my cheeks and a leaf in my hair, which dripped water like I'd just gone swimming in Three Gum River. My face and dress were wet. My lips were their own dull pink color again. I threw the leaf out the window and rubbed at the smudges on my face and patted some of the rain off as best I could. Then I opened my hatbox and pulled out a shiny gold tube, shaped just like a bullet. I painted my lips as neat as I would paint a picture. Magnet Red—"very new, it's very red. A dashing red."

In my new life I was going to wear lipstick all the time.

TWO

On Saturday, August 23, I drove into Nashville. Right away it was the biggest, noisiest city I'd ever seen. I said out loud, "You done it, Velva Jean. You got yourself all the way here."

I stopped at the first filling station I came to and sat there catching my breath. When the serviceman walked up, I rolled down the window and smoothed my hair. I said, "Can you tell me how to get to the Grand Ole Opry?"

He stared at me like I'd been blown in on a windstorm, which was probably exactly what I looked like. He said, "Where you comin' from, miss?"

I said, "North Carolina. I just drove 346 miles."

He slapped the side of the truck, not too hard, but like he was clapping. He said, "Congratulations."

I said, "Thank you."

He said, "Welcome to Nashville."

I said, "Thank you. It's awful good to be here."

The Grand Ole Opry broadcast out of the War Memorial Auditorium, just next to the state capitol, downtown. It looked, with its six fat columns, like it should have been someplace far away and exotic, like Greece. It was the dressiest place I'd ever seen—like something on a postcard.

Nashville itself was fancy. The buildings were tall and grand and joined together side by side, all the way down Church Street, as far as the eye could see. There were red-and-white and green-and-white striped awnings at every storefront and streetlamps that already glowed a little even though the sun hadn't set. The sidewalks were filled with people. Trolley cars rattled past. There were men preaching outside taverns and music halls, and men and women standing on curbs or up on truck beds, playing the guitar, the banjo, the fiddle. Most everyone was singing. Music was everywhere. All those years of dreaming of Nashville, and I realized I couldn't have thought up this place if I'd tried.

I parked the truck on Third Street and walked past all the places I'd read about in magazines and heard tales of: Shacklett's Cafeteria; Candy's Inc., with its windows full of sweets; the old Princess Theatre, which showed movies and a vaudeville stage show; Harveys department store; the Tulane Hotel. There were jewelry stores—glittering with gems of all shapes and sizes, and not rough uncut gems from the mountains but shiny ones set in rings or necklaces—sandwich shops, bakeries, eye doctors, a hat cleaner. Krystal, where they made cake doughnuts in the front window. La Vogue Beauty Salon, where the women from the Opry got their hair done. I stood at the corner of Fifth and Church—called St. Cloud's Corner because of St. Cloud House, a hotel that had been there since the Civil War—and breathed it all in.

Then I walked over to the War Memorial Auditorium and the Grand Ole Opry. I pushed through all the people going this way and that and walked right up to the Opry building and pressed my hand against the side of it. The stone was cool and smooth beneath my palm. It had a heartbeat. I could feel the life in it, feel it breathing, or maybe it was my own pulse.

I'd just driven all those miles in a truck I'd learned to drive without any help from anyone. I'd pumped my own gas and changed my own tire and smiled at the things folks said about me being on my own, without a husband. I thought coming here was either the foolhardiest thing I'd ever done or the best.

I leaned up against the building and closed my eyes and felt the stone pressing into my skin, holding me up. I was all alone in this world—no mama, no daddy, no husband. I didn't know where my brother was, and I'd left my family far behind. I didn't have anything but an old yellow truck, a suitcase, a hatbox, and a mandolin. But here was the Opry, right where I could touch it.

There was a sign on the door of the War Memorial Auditorium that said: "Tickets now required: twenty-five cents." This was because the show was so popular that everyone wanted to see it. Even as I stood there, folks were walking up, pushing past each other and me, going inside, dressed in pretty clothes, clean clothes—the men wearing hats and starched shirts, the women wearing hats and dresses, nicely pressed. I noticed a smart-looking girl hurrying through the crowd. She wore red, red lipstick, and she was hatless. Her brown hair was cut in a bob that hugged her chin, and she carried a purse the color of tomatoes. She was a giant girl, fat as Harley's mama, but pretty. She looked like she must be from Atlanta or New York. She walked by me and dropped a fifty-cent piece in my hand.

I stared at it and then started laughing. That girl thought I was some sort of less fortunate, a down-and-out in need of help. Granny had told me the cities were full of them. I held that coin tight in my fist and then opened the door and followed everyone inside. I walked up to the box office and bought one ticket. My hair was a mess, my dress was dirty, my shoes were making squish-squish sounds as I walked, like they might come off my feet and stick right to the floor. But my lips were painted bright as rubies.

I sat straight up during the show, rigid as a post, and listened to every word, every note. Down on the stage, all the musical acts I'd grown up hearing on Saturday nights on the radio—Pee Wee King's Golden West Cowboys, Bill Monroe, the Possum Hunters, Minnie Pearl, the Missouri Mountaineers—stood around the WSM radio microphone playing their most famous songs.

The auditorium was beautiful, with a grand, high ceiling that looked like an enormous gold-and-white checkerboard and a chandelier that hung down in the center. I sat up in the left balcony, but what I really wanted to do was to climb down into the audience and jump onto the stage and sing my heart out.

And the stage—that was something else. It was a ten-foot circle of dark wood that looked like magic to me. Even from the balcony, you could feel the history of it, like everyone who'd stood there had left a piece of themselves behind.

When Judge George D. Hay, dressed in a black suit and black hat, cigar hanging out of one corner of his mouth, said into the microphone, "Now put your hands together for Roy Acuff and the Smoky Mountain Boys," I felt a thrill going through me from my feet to the top of my head. Judge Hay was the program director of the Opry. On the air he was called the Solemn Old Judge, and he chose everyone who sang on the show.

I wondered if just seeing Roy Acuff, even from way up here in the balcony, would send me into a swoon like some woman from a movie or an old-timey novel like the ones Ruby Poole read when Linc wasn't around. I leaned forward and rested my arms on the railing. I wondered if Roy Acuff might see me in the audience, seated up here above the stage, just like Harley Bright had noticed me in the congregation of that first revival, the one he preached on the banks of Three Gum River, when I knew that one day I would marry him, when I thought I'd just been saved for the second time. Just in case, I sat up straight and tried my best to look regal in spite of my matted hair and dirty face. I was hoping Roy Acuff would see past the dirt and see the Velva Jean who could be clean and shiny and pretty in spite of freckles and too-wavy hair.

Roy Acuff was as tall as Harley. He sang "The Wabash Cannonball," "The Precious Jewel," and then "The Great Speckled Bird," which was my favorite. He was skinny and handsome, with thick and wavy black hair and a sweet face that looked like he'd just scrubbed it with soap and water. It was the kind of face that seemed to be smiling even if he wasn't. I wanted to kiss him, and just the thought of wanting to do such a thing made me clap my hand over my mouth and laugh like someone who had lost all sense.

This was one of the nicest moments I had ever had. I had done so much to get here, to this seat up in the balcony. I didn't know where I was going to sleep or how I was going to earn money. I didn't know the first thing about starting my new life as a singer. I missed my family. I missed Fair Mountain. But at this moment I didn't miss Harley. Instead I sat there and thought about all the things I had done to get there, to that very seat. It was funny what you could do in twenty-four hours. You could start the day in one place, married to a man you sometimes liked but most of the time didn't, and you could end the next day in another place, far away, a single woman chasing her dreams. I thought there was some kind of miracle in that.

After Roy Acuff finished his last song, Judge Hay shuffled back to the microphone. As the Smoky Mountain Boys started playing soft in the background, the judge—around his cigar—said:

> *Nothing to breathe but air,*
> *Quick as a flash 'tis gone;*
> *Nothing to fall but off, nowhere to stand but on . . .*

> *Nothing to sing but songs,*
> *Ah well, alas! alack!*
> *Nowhere to go but out, nowhere to come but back.*

I sat there for a long time, until the auditorium cleared out and one of the ushers told me to go. He was an itty-bitty boy with bright red freckles. I said, "I'd like to speak to Judge Hay, please." I stood up and I was taller than the boy by half a foot.

He said, "Sister, you and about a thousand other people."

I thought, Really? Well that's fine, but he'll see me, just you watch.

Outside the night was alive and bright, the streetlamps glowing like lightning bugs, the people talking and singing and walking arm in arm, the streetcars jangling up and down. I stepped out into the middle of it.

I decided to walk around back of the building because maybe Judge Hay wouldn't want to be in this crowd with so many people wanting to talk to him, and maybe there was a door back there that he could leave from. The building was a long way around but I followed it, over the sidewalk and then, when that ran out, the grass and the dirt. There were men standing out back, smoking cigarettes, and talking in low voices. Every now and then one would laugh, a great booming sound.

I walked up and said, "I'd like to see Judge Hay, please." I tried to look like I knew what I was doing. I stuck out my jaw a little, just like Johnny Clay always did when he meant business.

They stared at me like I was a haint. I could tell they didn't know whether to be rude or nice. Finally one of them said, "He's already gone on home, little lady."

I said, "Are you sure he ain't in there?"

He smiled at this, but only on one side of his mouth. He said, "I'm sure."

One of the other men said, "On his mama's grave."

The first man said, "Shut up, Otis." But he didn't say it mean.

I thought their accents were funny—like ours but not as thick. Maybe a little more twangy, like an out-of-tune guitar string. I stared hard at the back door, like I could see through it—like maybe I could see if Judge Hay was really in there or not.

The first man said to me, "Honest, honey. He's really gone on home."

I said, "Thank you." As I turned away, they stayed quiet, and I knew they were watching me or watching each other till I went away. Just before I rounded the building, they started talking again.

Back out front, I lost myself in the crowd. I thought I would walk along for a bit and pretend I was on my way somewhere, to someone, that somebody was waiting for me, that I knew where I was going. The night was clear and warm, and it felt good to be a part of something.

Even if I hadn't got to talk to Judge Hay, I was in such a good mood from the Opry that I felt bad over scolding Jesus about the flat tire. As I walked down Church Street, I thought: *Dear Lord, I'm sorry for getting so mad. It's just that things are hard and I'm out here alone in this world, and it was tough enough leaving home for here without something happening to my truck.* I wished for maybe the ten thousandth time that I had the patience of my mama or Daddy Hoyt.

I told myself I'd walk the length of Church Street—down one whole side and then back the other—looking for a rooming house or hotel, somewhere I could sleep just for that night. Folks were walking in and out of soda shops, five-and-ten-cent stores, and movie theaters.

They all looked fine and handsome, the men wearing hats, the women wearing hats. At the corner of Church and College Street, I saw the smart-looking girl from the Opry—the girl that had given me the fifty-cent piece—hurrying through the crowd.

I followed her, thinking I would give her money back. She was probably my age, maybe a few years older, and she wasn't wearing a wedding ring. Other than me, she was the only girl walking by herself, and there was something about her that seemed brave and free. She was exactly who I wanted to be in my new life.

I lost sight of her now and then, only to find her again seconds later. Two old men stood on the sidewalk playing the banjo and the guitar. Just past them a short lady in overalls was singing her heart out, a hat at her feet. Every now and then someone would throw money into it as they walked by. I tried to stay closer to the girl with the purse. Two blocks later she turned down Fifth Avenue.

She walked faster than me, and I knew how to walk fast because Johnny Clay had the longest legs and practically ran when he walked, and I always tried to keep up with him or even beat him. This girl was taller than I was, but my legs were almost as long.

Fifth Avenue was just as busy as Church Street. People talked and laughed and ate popcorn and peanuts out of bags. I thought that it seemed almost like a carnival. I passed a hat shop, a dress shop, a shoe store. I expected the girl with the purse to stop at one of them. We passed a tobacco shop, the Orange Bar, Rex Theatre, the Fifth Avenue Theatre, and the Arcade, which was majestic and beautiful and full of shops and restaurants. I almost forgot about the girl and turned in, but I kept going.

Suddenly the girl stopped. She pulled a cigarette from her purse and lit it with a lighter that gleamed silver in the dark. She stood there, the cigarette to her lips, inhaling and blowing out delicate rings of smoke. I pulled up short in front of her, and before I could say a word, she said, "Why are you following me?" She sounded like Katharine Hepburn.

I took fifty cents out of my change purse. "I wanted to pay you back."

"No offense, honey, but you look like you could use it more than me."

I stared down at my clothes. I looked just like one of Hink Lowe's sisters, the ones Sweet Fern called mountain trash. I said, "It's money I earned myself. I've got more. Please take it."

She threw the cigarette on the ground and crushed it with her heel. She took the fifty cents from me, dropped it into her purse, and then pulled out a stick of gum and tore the wrapper off. She stuck it in her mouth, and then she offered me one. I took it from her without opening it.

She said, "Where're you from?"

"North Carolina. I just got here. I left home yesterday."

"What are you doing here?"

"I'm a singer."

"Where are you staying?"

"I don't know yet."

She blew a bubble and then sucked it right back in. She said, "Come on, then." She marched off through the crowd, and I followed her until we stopped suddenly outside a place called the Lovelorn Café. The downstairs windows were bright and warm—inside, customers sat in booths or at the counter. Upstairs there were four or five more levels and the windows were smaller, more narrow. It was a great big house, right there in the middle of the city. She marched on in through the front door.

I stood there on the street, studying the house—there was music coming from inside. I walked up to the window and looked in. Suddenly I felt all alone again. I thought, if someone saw me standing here, staring in this window, they might think I was a beggar needing some food. I thought "lovelorn" was the perfect word for how I was feeling.

The door to the café swung open, and the girl stood there chomping her gum. She said, "Well, come on. You don't want to sleep out there, do you?"

Inside there was an oriental woman, soft as a dumpling, clearing tables, and a man with a trim black beard tipping back on a chair, writing things on a pad of paper.

The girl said, "Look what I found." She turned to me. "Meet Nori and Crow Lovelorn." She turned back to the Lovelorns. "Mind if she stays with me?"

The man set his chair legs back on the floor. He had a wide, beaming smile. He said, "As long as she can stand you."

The woman kept on stacking plates. Her hair was shiny black in the light. She said, "You look like you could use a bath. Gossie will show you where it is."

Back through the kitchen of the Lovelorn Café there was a staircase leading up and then up again and up, up, up. The girl was already huffing her way up them, two at a time.

I climbed up the first flight of stairs and passed a parlor with a piano and a sitting room right across from it. The second flight of stairs took us to a small landing, the size of a closet. There were two doors on either side, right across from each other. A light shone out from underneath one of the doors, and this was the one the girl pushed open.

The apartment was tiny but warm. The girl went on in and sat down on the settee, which was worn and old but comfortable. She took up a cigarette and lit it and stuck her chewing gum in an ashtray. There were movie magazines spread over the coffee table, a rifle propped against one wall, and the head of a buffalo hanging between the two narrow windows that looked down on the street.

When she saw me in the light, the girl said, "Jesus H. Christ. You look like you've been run over and back again. You shouldn't be walking around Nashville at night."

I said, "My truck is parked up there on Church Street."

She said, "It'll be all right till morning. What's your name?"

"Velva Jean Hart."

She nodded like she thought this was fine. "I'm Beryl Goss. But please don't you dare call me Beryl. My mother played a cruel joke naming me after her father. Can you imagine? At least I wasn't named after my father's father, or I would be Virgil Bartholomew. Call me Gossie."

For a big girl, she moved fast and talked fast. She got up and poured herself a drink from a bottle of gin. She poured me one too and handed it to me before I could say no. "It'll warm you up." I stared at the glass and she laughed. "Oh, come on. Don't tell me you've never taken a drink."

I remembered the time Johnny Clay and me stole the moonshine from Harley's own daddy—the moonshiner—back when we were little, after Mama died and Daddy left us with Sweet Fern, and we were running wild and doing every bad thing we could think of. I could still feel the burn of the liquor on my throat.

I said, "Once."

She laughed at this and said, "Well sit down and tell me everything. You can drink it or not, it's up to you."

I sat on a rickety antique chair with a round red cushion and balanced the glass on my knee. I said, "What do you want to know?"

She said, "Start with why you look like this and what you're doing here."

So I did. I told her the whole story, trying to shorten it up so she wouldn't have to sit there for hours. I told her about Mama dying and Daddy leaving and the Scenic being built right through our mountains, and Harley the delinquent and Harley the preacher and Harley the husband, and how he turned on me and so many others, and Johnny Clay running away and my dreams of Nashville and the Opry, and Danny Deal and the train wreck that killed him and the yellow truck he left behind and how I taught myself to drive it, and how one morning I just got in that truck and drove away.

Afterward I took a drink, a small one at first and then a bigger one. The gin burned going down but not as much as the moonshine. I sat there blinking the tears—tears from the sting of the alcohol and the sting of my story—out of my eyes.

Gossie let out a long, low whistle and lit another cigarette, her fifth since I'd been talking. She said, "Sweet Mother of Jesus, girl. You've been through it."

I said, "Yes." The tears were gone. I took another drink.

"Your freedom's hard won."

I liked the way that sounded. I thought it sounded just right.

She said, "Mine is too."

I waited for her to tell me her story, but when she didn't I looked around the room. I said, "This is a nice apartment."

She said, "It's pretty ugly actually. But it's home." Then she stood up and stretched her back and said, "There's a second bedroom, but it's no bigger than a drunkard's wallet. I've got a bunch of stuff stored in there but we can move it."

I said, "I can just sleep here on the settee."

"For tonight maybe, but you're going to need a room."

Then she was already in that second bedroom, talking to herself and moving things around. She started singing "Happiness Is a Thing Called Joe" at the top of her lungs. She couldn't carry a tune in a bucket, as Granny would say, but it didn't seem to matter. She came out of the room, her arms filled with books, clothes, a large pair of rain boots, a helmet, a fishing rod, and said, "Well, come on in here, Mary Lou, and grab an armful."

I said, "My name's Velva Jean."

She said, "I know that. But everyone needs a nickname," and then she went back in and kept singing.

August 24, 1941

Dear family,

This is just a note to let you know that I made it to Nashville safe and sound. I'll write more soon, to tell you about how I went to the Grand Ole Opry already to hear Roy Acuff sing and how I made a friend. Her name is Beryl Goss, but she goes by Gossie, and she's twenty-six years old. I'm going to be her roommate in an apartment above the Lovelorn Café. This morning I parked my truck right outside the front door, where I can keep an eye on it, but Gossie says as far as big cities go Nashville isn't dangerous— not like Boston, where she comes from.

I miss you all like crazy. I'm happy to be here, but you're too far away.

I love you,

Velva Jean

THREE

*G*ossie worked as a salesgirl selling women's scarves and handbags at Gorman and Rattlebaum, a department store on the corner of Fifth and Union. She said, "Everyone calls it Gorman's. The pay's not bad, but it could be better."

Gossie was from a rich Boston family. She'd moved to Nashville eight months ago, after her daddy turned her out for not only refusing to marry a boy named Bertram R. Shelby, the heir to an oil fortune, but for eloping with the gardener. Her daddy cut her off without a penny, she and the gardener came to Nashville so that he could play guitar, and then he ran off with a girl who played banjo. After all that, the last place Gossie wanted to be was home, so she stayed in Nashville. She said the only people that were nice to her back then were Nori and Crow Lovelorn. She said that in this city full of strangers and folks coming to chase their dreams, the Lovelorns believed in helping people, in taking them in. This was something they lived by, and one of the rules of living under their roof was "do unto others." It was one reason Gossie was nice to me—because she knew what it felt like to come to a strange city and be completely alone.

She said now, "But the men you meet . . ." She whistled. "Coming in to buy scarves for their sisters, mothers, wives."

I said, "You wouldn't date a married man?"

She said, "Only if he was happy. The ones you don't want are the ones that hang around all the time, wanting to marry you."

I thought this was one of the most shocking things I'd ever heard, but I pretended it didn't shock me, because this was my new life, in my new city, where people probably dated married people all the time. I was already trying not to be shocked by the way Gossie swore almost as much as Johnny Clay and the way she drank a lot of gin. She said on a good day she and God were barely on speaking terms, but on a bad day she wasn't sure she believed in him at all. Every night she washed her hose and underthings in the sink and hung them out the window to dry because she liked the way they smelled of fresh air afterward. Her brassieres and girdles were big as circus tents, and they just hung out there, blowing in the breeze, for all the world to see.

Gossie said, "I'm saving up for my next adventure. I'm going to China to capture a snow leopard, one of the most exotic animals in the world."

"You're not going to kill it?"

She waved her hand just like she was shooing a fly. "The National Zoo will pay me a hooker's ransom to bring them one." Then she said, "We need to find you a job. What can you do?"

I said, "I can sing and play guitar and mandolin. I can write songs." I remembered writing songs with Johnny Clay's friend Butch Dawkins, how he helped me find the melody, how he taught me the blues. I felt the pang that I always got when I thought about him—the medicine beads he wore around his neck, the "Bluesman" tattoo, the gap between his front teeth, his crooked smile. I said, "That's why I came here. I'm going to be a singer." I remembered something Butch had said: "I figured if my destiny wasn't coming to me, I would go to it." I pulled out Darlon C. Reynolds's little white card from where I carried it in my pocket. I said, "This man wants to make records with me. We already made one, back when he was in Waynesville looking for singers."

Gossie took the card and gave it a good, hard look. She said, "Do you have a contract with him?"

"I have his card."

She handed it back to me. "I see that, but did you sign something with him? Something that says he'll record you again?"

I said, "He told me to get in touch with him when I got to Nashville."

And then we'll make another record and he can send it to Judge Hay at the Opry, and Judge Hay will bring me in to sing on stage and try me out, and then I'll join the Opry cast. This was the way I'd pictured it happening ever since Darlon C. Reynolds handed me his card back in Waynesville.

Gossie said, "Oh, Mary Lou." She shook her head. "You can sing. I'm sure. But so can every two-bit hick in this town."

I was starting to get mad. I said, "But I've wanted this since I was little. This is what I was made to do."

She said, "I'm sure, I'm sure. But wanting it and getting it are two different things." She lit a cigarette. "Look, I'm not trying to rain on your parade, Mary Lou, but I don't want you to go out there and expect one thing and get another. Maybe all you have to do is go see this man and just like that"—she snapped her fingers—"he'll make you a deal, but most of the time it doesn't happen that way."

I remembered Sweet Fern, back when I was twelve, telling me, "It's nice to dream, but you can't dream too big." Of course I wasn't the only one in Nashville with a dream. There were lots of folks who dreamed of this town and the Opry and who might be more talented than me. But that didn't mean I couldn't make it anyway.

I said, "You'll see." I would go out right now and show her. I would call up Darlon C. Reynolds himself and ask to meet him. I would take him all the songs I'd been writing since I last saw him.

Gossie said, "All right. But you know that even after you sell something it's going to take a while for them to pay you. You might have to do something while you're waiting." I couldn't tell if she was teasing me or not. Her face looked serious, but I didn't know her well enough to know what her tone meant. She said, "What else can you do?"

I said, "Well . . . Cook a little. Clean a little. I got real good at serving Harley his meals." This was meant funny, but she sat up straighter when I said it.

"You could work in a restaurant maybe. You could try Woolworth's, Marchetti's, the T & K Sandwich Shop, Krystal, the Tulane Hotel. Hey, maybe you could work in an office—be a file clerk or secretary. Answer phones. A doctor's office maybe, or insurance. You know, just until you get your recording money. I'll draw you a downtown map, or you can just go right out and start looking, but either way I have to get to work." She reached for her red purse and then handed me a key. "It's the big city, so we lock our doors. Take mine till we get you one of your own. I get off work at four thirty, so be back by quarter to five to let me in. We'll do dinner somewhere fun. My treat."

I took the key. "Thanks, Gossie."

She said, "Don't mention it." She winked and walked past me to the door. Then she turned and must have seen how everything was crowding in on me all at once—the newness of her, of the place, having to find myself a job, being so far from home, realizing that I wasn't the only person in this town with a voice and a dream. She said, "Knock 'em dead, Velva Jean. I think compared to all you've gone through, getting a record contract might be the easiest thing you've done all year."

After she left I sat there for a few minutes, wondering if I had it in me, after such a long trip, after everything, to get up and get myself dressed and go out there on the streets of Nashville and find Darlon C. Reynolds and maybe get myself a job. Just thinking of it all made me tired. I wanted to lie back down and sleep.

Somewhere, far off, I could hear my mama: "Live out there. That's where you belong, Velva Jean." I could see her face fading into the pillow, feel her hand in mine. And then, because I didn't travel all those miles just to sit inside an apartment and think of all the things I dreamed of doing, I decided to get dressed.

I walked into my room—my own room. I'd never had a room of my own before, not with Harley, not at Mama's house, not when I was a little bitty girl. I'd always shared with someone—Sweet Fern or Johnny Clay or Sweet Fern's babies or my husband. I opened my suitcase and pulled out the suit with the bolero jacket—the one Harley had bought me years ago. It was wrinkled from the trip, so I laid it on the bed and smoothed out the skirt, and then I set my brush and comb next to it, and then my Magnet Red lipstick, Mama's little Bakelite hair combs, and her wedding ring. I slipped the ring on my finger for luck. Then I turned myself around in front of the framed picture of the Opry. The sun was hitting it just so, lighting up the microphone. And then I pulled off Gossie's nightgown and got myself ready.

I took out the little white card Darlon C. Reynolds had given me and walked to the Warner Building on the corner of Sixth Avenue and Church Street. I only had to stop twice to ask for directions. According to his card, Darlon C. Reynolds had an office on the sixth floor. I stood in the elevator and went up, the elevator stopping at each floor to let someone off. I'd never been in an elevator before, and I thought it was the most wonderful thing. I stood right in the center of it and felt myself whoosh up, up, up. It was almost like flying.

On the sixth floor, the elevator man pulled open the door.

"Thank you, sir," I said.

"Happy good day, miss," he said.

Happy good day. I liked the sound of that.

I walked off the elevator and passed one office after another until I came to one that said "Cyclone Records." I pushed the door and went in.

There were chairs along two of the walls and photos hung up above of Roy Acuff and the Possum Hunters and some other people I didn't recognize, but there was also one of Darlon C. Reynolds smoking a cigar and laughing off into the distance.

At one end of the room was a desk. The girl behind it was on the telephone, and as I walked over she waved at me not to speak. She said into the receiver, "As soon as he's in the union . . . No . . . No . . . Yes . . . That's right . . . No." And then she hung up. She wrote something down on a pad of paper and then looked up at me. She had a sharp, bad-tempered face, like some sort of animal thrown out into the sun too soon after a winter's sleep. She said, "Yes?"

I showed her the little white card. I said, "Mr. Darlon C. Reynolds came to North Carolina a year ago to record songs, and he gave me this card. He said to look him up when I came here, so we could record more."

She said, "Mr. Reynolds is in New York City. He spends most of his time at our office there."

I said, "I recorded 'Yellow Truck Coming, Yellow Truck Going' for him, and the back side was 'Old Red Ghost.' My brother Johnny Clay played guitar and sang on 'Old Red Ghost,' but he's not here. It's just me."

She was looking at me like she didn't have the first idea what I was saying. She said, "Okay."

"Mr. Reynolds wanted to record more songs of mine back then, but I had to get on home."

"He's in New York right now."

I said, "Do you know when he'll be in Nashville again?"

She said, "No."

I wasn't sure what to do, so finally I said, "Please tell him Velva Jean Hart came to see him."

She didn't write it down. She said, "I will."

I said, "I'm living in Nashville now."

She blinked at me.

I said, "It sounds like *heart* but it's really Hart, without the *e*. H-a-r-t."

She said, "Got it."

I stood there wondering if I should tell her to write it down on her pad, for saints' sake, but then I decided to just leave it alone. I told myself I would come back when someone else was working at the desk. I would come back again and again till Darlon C. Reynolds was in town and could see me himself.

That night Gossie and I went to supper at Mario's, which was a little Italian place with plastic tablecloths and big red booths. I ordered spaghetti, and Gossie ordered chicken Parmesan, which was fried chicken with cheese and tomato sauce. I wished I'd ordered it myself, because it looked fancy and like the kind of thing you should order when you lived in a city.

Gossie said, "How did it go today?" She was drinking red wine.

I said, "Great." I was drinking sweet tea.

"Did you find Darlon C. Reynolds?"

"He's in New York City right now."

"I see." She took a dainty bite of chicken and then dabbed her mouth with a napkin. I waited for her to say something more but she didn't.

That night, after Gossie went into her bedroom and shut the door, I picked the newspaper out of the trash bin, and then I searched around until I found the telephone directory at the bottom of a stack of books lying underneath the coffee table. I went into my room and sat at my little desk and spread open the newspaper. I searched through it until I found the names and addresses of every record company in town. And then I searched the telephone directory, doing the same. I pulled out a piece of paper from the little pile I kept for writing my songs and I made a list.

The next morning I put on my dress with the bolero jacket and took that list and went to each studio, one by one. This time I took my record with me, the one I'd made for Darlon C. Reynolds. I figured I could play it for the record producers, so they could hear how I sounded on a recording and so that they could see what I'd already done.

At every place, I waited in a long line of people wanting someone to hear their songs. These were people of all ages—young and old and in between. There were men and women and boys and girls and even some children. They carried banjos and guitars and fiddles and dulcimers—anything you could play a tune on. They were handsome and pretty and plain and short and fat and skinny and weathered.

It was the same everywhere—the receptionist would write down our names and tell us someone would be in touch, which I was starting not to believe for a minute. I never once got to sing for anyone or play them my record.

I thought about Waynesville, back when I first went to see Darlon C. Reynolds, who was looking to record hillbillies down from the mountains, and how all those people stood in line for hours, burning up in the hot sun, just waiting to be heard. And then Johnny Clay made me go around back and sneak up the stairs and go through the balcony, and that was how Darlon C. Reynolds heard me sing. I'd made two records for him that day, and I knew I was going to have to do something like that again—go around back and sneak up the stairs—if I ever wanted a chance.

At the very last place, I thanked the receptionist and turned to leave, and the person behind me stepped up to give her his name. I thought, There's got to be a better way than this. As I walked out onto the street, I wished for Johnny Clay because he was brave and always knew exactly how to get the things he wanted and what the right way was for going about something, even if it was an up-the-back-stairs-and-through-the-balcony kind of way.

Outside on the street was a girl I recognized from waiting in line. She was standing on the corner, guitar case open, playing and singing for passersby. Every now and then someone would throw a quarter or a fifty-cent piece into the case and keep on walking. She nodded at them when they did, and kept on singing her heart out.

The song was a good one—pretty words, catchy tune. It made me want to hum along. She was young and fresh looking, and her voice was clear and bright and strong. I thought she sounded as good as I did, maybe even better, and here she stood on a Nashville street, singing for strangers just like she was a down-and-out.

That night, before bed, I shut the door to my room and dug in my hatbox for my Nashville money: $101.65. It was all the money I had in the world. Out of it I had to pay for food and gas and my room here at the Lovelorn Café and anything else I might need. I tried to figure how long it would last me.

If I didn't make a record by the end of three weeks, I decided, I'd be in a pickle. I wondered how quick they would pay you at these recording studios. I should have asked them when I was there. I thought I'd go back the next day, and if they didn't want to make a record with me, maybe they would buy my songs. I would take all the ones I had with me and see if anyone was interested. If that didn't work, I would tell them I'd be willing to sing backup on a record or two and maybe play mandolin or guitar just till they wanted to record me on my own.

It was good to have a plan. I would get a contract and then that would show Gossie. She would say, "I'm sorry for ever thinking you couldn't do it, Mary Lou." If there was one thing I hated in this world, it was folks who told you that you couldn't do something. That was worse than being told you shouldn't do it. I knew she meant well, but a person had to believe in herself even when no one else did.

FOUR

The woman looked down her nose at me, blinked three times, and then leaned forward. The sign over her desk read: "Insurance Company of North America: Your fire-insurance policy is a price tag on your house!"

The office itself was dark like a cave—dark-brown carpet, dark-brown chairs, dark-brown desk. The receptionist had fat orange-red curls all over her head and glasses that sat on the end of her nose. There was a mole beside her left eyebrow and another one on her right cheek. They looked painted on. She wore a navy-blue suit that was so crisp and clean that it must have been brand new. She smiled the kind of smile that didn't leave her mouth. She said, "Can you type?"

"No, ma'am."

"Have you had any experience working in an office—filing, answering telephones, sorting mail, things like that?"

I hated to disappoint her again. She looked so worn down, and I wanted more than anything to surprise her by saying "yes, ma'am. I know how to do all those things."

I said, "No, ma'am."

She shifted a little, refolding her hands. She said, "What kind of experience do you have?"

I said, "I can sing." And milk cows and gather eggs and make soup and a few other things, although not very well. I can write songs and play the mandolin and the guitar a little. I can sit still like a statue for hours while people preach and carry on. I can hide my feelings and sometimes be a good wife and sometimes a bad one. I can run fast and spy on murderers and read a map and drive. I can drive and drive.

The woman sighed so deep and long that I thought all the breath had gone out of her forever. When she was finally done she said, "I'm sorry, but there's nothing for you here."

The same thing happened at the Princess Theatre, the Knickerbocker Theatre, and the Paramount Theatre. It happened at the Cain-Sloan Company and the Family Booterie and Castner-Knott Dry Goods. It happened at the Peanut Shop, Cato's Malt Shop, Woolworth's, and the B & W Cafeteria. Gossie had told me to lie, to say I'd waited tables before and that I knew how to type, but when they asked me if I had any experience I didn't know what to say, except "No, ma'am" or "No, sir."

I couldn't believe I wasn't even able to find a regular job. Two weeks after I'd knocked on the door of every record studio in Nashville—three or four or five times each and in the case of Darlon C. Reynolds's Cyclone Records six or seven—I was now knocking on the doors of restaurants and dress shops and insurance agencies and doctors' offices. I spent six dollars on a new dress—navy with a skirt that twirled—so I'd look professional, but no one wanted my singing and no one wanted me to work for them, not even to wash dishes or sell gloves or answer telephones.

Most of the places were run by men, and not only that but men who didn't seem to think women should be working. One of them, at the Tulane Hotel, said, "Why you want to work, honey? Wouldn't you rather find a nice man instead?" The way he said it was like we were best friends and I could tell him anything, even secrets.

I said, "No, thank you." What I didn't say was that I had had it with men, nice or not.

The Tulane Hotel was a red-brick building that sat on the corner of Eighth Avenue and Church, the front of it actually narrowing into a point at the corner so that it looked like a giant triangle or a wedge of cheese. There were six floors, and the lobby was wide and long, with high ceilings and fireplaces at either end. There were potted palms and large chairs that people were sitting in, reading and drinking cocktails. I was on my way through, trying to look like I belonged there and like I wasn't staring at everything and everyone, when I heard a banjo and the sound of someone singing.

I followed the music and there, off the lobby, was a door with a sign on it that said "Castle Recording Studios." There was a little window in the door—a narrow square—and I stood looking in, so close that my breath fogged up the glass.

It was just one room divided by a window the size of a wall. On one side of the window were two men talking to each other, arms crossed, nodding, one of them working a panel of controls. On the other side was Eddy Arnold. *The* Eddy Arnold. The Tennessee Plowboy. I'd never seen him, only heard him on the radio, and he was the kind of man you might see behind a plow or hoeing a field. He looked so great and big that it was hard to imagine how he fit into that little space, especially with that giant voice of his.

Chills were starting in my toes, the way they did when I heard something truly wonderful. I pressed my nose against the window and tried to see better. I pressed my cheek against the glass and closed my eyes, listening.

All of a sudden there was a rap on the window, and I jumped ten feet. One of the men from the other room—the one behind the controls—was standing just inches from me. He said, "Get on now. Go."

I knew without seeing my face that it turned ten shades of pink. Eddy Arnold was kind of craning his neck around to see who it was that was interrupting him. I waved and smiled like "I'm so sorry. Don't mind me," and then I turned around and ran.

I ran all the way back to the Lovelorn Café, just like they were chasing me—which they weren't. My feet were sore and pinched in my shoes with the bow on top, heels going clatter-clatter on the sidewalk. I pushed my way through the crowds, past the street preachers and street musicians, past the trolley car creaking up and down Church Street. The city was so loud it hurt my ears. It was like a wild party that made me want to dance and sing and shout because it stirred me up way deep down. Even without a job or a record contract and with all my money running out, I loved the loudness. I wanted to sleep right there on the sidewalk, right in the middle of it. I wanted to bottle it up like an orange Nehi and drink it fast until it made my head spin from the bubbles and the cold.

The sky started to cloud over, and somewhere in the distance was the sound of thunder. One fat raindrop landed on my head, then one on my arm, my cheek, my shoe. I ran faster and faster down the street and up another street and turned a corner and stood waiting for the trolley to pass, and as I waited I looked in the shop window behind me. It was filled with books and a chalkboard and there, at the very front, was an old typewriter. The trolley car creaked past, but instead of crossing the street I walked into the shop.

When I walked out again, I was carrying the typewriter, all packed away in a beat-up black case. I bought it for three dollars, and when I told the man who sold it to me why I wanted it—to teach myself to type so that I could get my very first job—he gave me a book called *How to Type* and also a Gregg shorthand book so I could teach myself shorthand. I walked down that Nashville street, swinging the little black case back and forth. I thought of all the things I was going to type on this typewriter. I thought I might even use it to write down my songs.

The Lovelorn Café was as noisy as the street outside. The booths were filled with families having supper, drinking milk shakes, eating country ham and biscuits or chocolate pie with whipped cream on top, or the fried chicken that made the Lovelorn famous. Sometimes folks waited in line for an hour or two just to get a taste of the fried chicken and biscuits. Couples and teenagers and single men and women sat at the counter, leaning over their meals, spinning on the stools, tapping their fingers to the jukebox.

Nori Lovelorn was behind the counter. When she saw me come in, she pointed to an empty seat. I sank down onto the stool and caught my breath. I kicked my shoes off, and they fell with a smack onto the floor, and I set the typewriter and books on the seat next to me. I said, "Could I get a chocolate milk shake please?"

Nori said, "Hold one minute, darlin'." She touched my hand and looked toward the kitchen like she was waiting for something.

The jukebox stopped, and suddenly Crow came out from the kitchen, strumming his guitar, and two of the waitresses wove their way through the restaurant, plates in hand, singing a song. I sat back, forgetting all about my feet and the fact that I didn't have a job and the fact that the money it took me years and years to save was flying out the window faster than kudzu growing up the trees. I just sat there letting that music cover me like a big, cozy blanket.

They sang "Pocketful of Dreams," and if ever I needed to hear a song like that, this was the time. I thought about how sometimes God sent you reminders and signs of things that you needed to think about. These were like the messages my brother Beachard carved into trees and chiseled into rocks. Sometimes it was hard to remember yourself until you got reminded.

After the song stopped, Nori patted my hand and said, "Now what was it you wanted?"

I said, "Why were they singing?"

"Crow's idea. When we opened this diner, he said, 'We got to give folks a break. So many talented musicians come to Nashville all the time and can't get heard.' He said we should do our part."

I said, "I can sing."

"I'm sorry?"

"I can sing. Better than those girls, even though they sing pretty and I don't mean anything against them. But I've got just about the best voice I ever heard." I didn't know where this was coming from. I sat there bragging like Harley or Johnny Clay when he got full of himself. I sounded just like someone I usually couldn't stand, only it was me saying these things about my own self.

Nori squinted up her eyes like she was taking me in, and then she folded her arms, her mouth crooked up, and hollered, "Crow!"

He came out from the kitchen, still holding his guitar. "What's that?"

Nori said to me, "Sing, then."

I opened my mouth, right there at the counter, and started singing in front of everybody, not just the Lovelorns. I sang "Yellow Truck Coming, Yellow Truck Going." I sang the whole song, and when I was finished everyone in the café started clapping. Crow slapped me so hard across the back that I nearly fell off my stool.

Nori said, "We can show you how to wait tables, but no one can teach anyone to sing like that. We can pay you fourteen dollars a week. You're hired."

In my room that night, I sat down with *How to Type* and read it cover to cover. Now that I had a job at the café, I thought maybe I should take the typewriter back. But I liked the idea of having a stack of songs all typed up, just like I was a professional. I thought maybe I could type up the words to all my songs and then give copies to Darlon C. Reynolds and Judge Hay at the Opry and those men who recorded Eddy Arnold.

I took the typewriter out of its case and set it on my desk, and I ran my fingers over the keys, over and over, until I got the feel of them. I liked the feel of the keys on my fingertips—cool and smooth—and I pretended to type something, just like I was in an office and had two moles on my face that looked painted on.

Afterward I sat on my bed, balancing a book against my knees, and wrote a letter to my family, using the book like a desk. One day, I thought, I'll be able to write a letter on the typewriter. One day I'll be able to type my songs up and not just scratch them down on paper like a chicken.

Now I wrote: "Dear Daddy Hoyt, Granny, Linc, Ruby Poole, Sweet Fern, Aunt Zona, Celia Faye, and Clover." In the end I added Beachard's name too because he might be home and he might still be gone, but just in case he had drifted home I didn't want him to feel left out. It seemed strange not adding Johnny Clay, but I knew he was long gone, maybe somewhere in California or Texas.

I wrote all about my trip, even the flat tire, and then I told them about Nashville and the Lovelorn Café and my new job as a singing waitress and my typewriter and Roy Acuff and Eddy Arnold and the Opry. Then I told them all about Gossie—how she came from Boston and was the only daughter of one of the biggest real estate tycoons on the East Coast. How she eloped with the gardener just to make her daddy angry, and then divorced him when he left her for another girl. And how she sometimes traveled the world, bringing back souvenirs like a buffalo head from South Dakota and a lion's head from the Serengeti, sometimes sending them to museums and sometimes keeping them for herself.

I gave them my address at the Lovelorn and the telephone number of the café, just in case they needed me. At the end I wrote: "I am happy in my new life, but I miss you all. I wish you were here, but I don't wish I was there anymore. I hope you understand that. I love you more than words," which was something Daddy Hoyt always said. "Always, your Velva Jean."

I sat there a minute, reading it over. I didn't want the letter to end, because while I was writing it I was with my family in my mind. It was almost like they were sitting on my bed with me, in this tiny room that was all my own, all around me. But there was only so much room on the paper, and I'd filled up all the space. I folded the letter and slid it into the envelope, a long, smooth white rectangle.

Then I pulled the letter back out and unfolded it. "P.S.," I wrote up the side. "I haven't made a record yet, but I'm working on it."

FIVE

*N*ori was Japanese, born in Nashville. She had five older brothers who also lived in Nashville and drove trucks. None of them had ever been to Japan. Only her parents, who were supposed to be very, very old, had been there and left long before Nori was born. At sixteen she met Crow, when she was working as a hand model at one of the local department stores—modeling gloves and jewelry and hand lotion for customers—and Crow had walked past her and then turned right around and come back. He bought five pairs of ladies' gloves from her, even though he didn't have a mother or sisters or a wife. He later gave them to strangers he saw walking down the street, folks who needed something to keep them warm because they didn't have a house or winter clothing. He was twenty-two years old then and from Oklahoma. He'd come to Nashville to be a guitar player before he and Nori decided to open the Lovelorn Café.

I was awful at waiting tables. At least once a day, sometimes twice, I dropped a dish or a cup. Crow said, "At this rate we're going to have to start using paper plates." I only ever once dropped something on a customer though. I was proud of that. It was a man with gray hair and a big soft belly. I tripped over my own feet and sent his Coca-Cola flying so it ended up all over his shirt and pants. He stared down at his wet legs and arms, and then he started laughing. Before he left he gave me a two-dollar tip, and Crow said if I had to spill a Coca-Cola, I'd certainly picked the right man to spill it on.

What I liked was the singing. I lived for the moment when I got to stop waiting tables and sing with the other girls. Every now and then, I'd sing a solo while the girls sang harmony. They were nice girls, a few years older than me: Marvina and Tommie Lou. Marvina was from Kansas City, and Tommie Lou was from Alabama.

Tommie Lou was six feet tall. She was the biggest girl I'd ever seen, but she talked so low you could barely hear her because, she said, she always worried about overwhelming people. She'd come to Nashville five years ago to be a singer, and every day she said she was going back to Alabama, that she'd had it with Nashville for good.

Marvina wore her bright blonde hair cut short and styled big. She was trashy, but she loved to read, even though she was all the time asking what this or that word meant. Every morning she came to work with a different book. Her favorites were the ones about prisons and damsels in distress. She said that one day a man was going to save her from everything, just like Tom Buccaneer, her favorite fictional hero, who was always rescuing girls by throwing them onto the back of his horse.

Besides Tommie Lou and Marvina, there was Stump Mitchell, who was eighteen years old and the skinniest person I ever saw. His real name was Harold Lee, but he'd been called Stump ever since he was a baby because both of his thumbs stopped at the knuckle. It was the way he was born, and Gossie told me everyone said it was because his mama was a loose woman. Even without thumbs, Stump was a good banjo player. He'd come from Louisville, Kentucky, six months ago, with the idea that he was going to be the next Eddie Peabody, who was known as King of the Banjo.

When Stump talked, his Adam's apple bobbed up and down so hard you could barely listen to what he was saying. He washed dishes and ran errands and every day he wrote me a poem. Sometimes he handed them to me on napkins and sometimes he told them to me: "Velva Jean, you are a queen, prettiest dern girl that I ever seen. Will you be mine? I'd like it fine. I'd love you for the rest of time." The only thing that saved Stump's bad poetry was that he was funny. He would sing those poems to me in his wheezy, off-key voice, his Adam's apple going like a motor, and make me laugh.

At the end of each day, my feet hurt like I'd been running barefoot through the woods back home. The café stayed open till eleven o'clock every night, but it closed at five o'clock on Sundays, which was my day off. If I worked late, I'd drag myself upstairs and lie on the settee in our apartment and prop my feet up on the arm. Gossie was a night owl, and she would pour gin for her and ginger ale for me, and we would talk about our days. She would complain about the spoiled women who came into Gorman's and tried on every scarf and then didn't buy a one. "The things you see when you don't have a gun," she'd say.

Afterward I would get up and go to my room and practice my typing for an hour, till the clock at the corner of Church and Fifth chimed one. And then I would write a song or maybe even two. I couldn't write fast enough these days. I thought this was probably because of leaving Harley and being in Nashville where everyone was writing songs and dreaming of singing at the Opry, just like me. I thought there was something in the air here, and also something in me that made the words and music come easy.

When I couldn't write anymore or when it was too late to keep going, I would get into my bed and lie there, tired and worn out, and think how nice it was to have a best friend to talk to at the end of the day—like I used to do with Johnny Clay and for a while with Harley— and how good it felt to be earning my own way in this world.

~

The first letter from Harley came at the beginning of October. I didn't know how he got my address. I couldn't think of anyone in the family who would give it to him except Sweet Fern. I went into my room and closed the door and sat on my bed and looked at Harley's handwriting on the envelope. I thought his writing looked wild and proper all at once and just the slightest bit accusing. I turned the envelope over in my hand and slid my finger under the edge of the flap on the back. I started to rip it open, but then I stopped myself. I couldn't think of a single thing I wanted to hear from Harley Bright.

I dropped the letter into the trash basket and left the room. I washed the dishes Gossie had stacked in the sink, and then I straightened the living room, emptying ashtrays and collecting glasses and stacking up newspapers. Then I sat on the settee and flipped through a movie magazine, and all the while I thought of the time it must have taken Harley to write that letter. What if he decided to come find me now that he knew where I was? What if he came all the way to Nashville and tried to make me go home with him?

I went back into my room and pulled the envelope out of the trash. I thought that even if I wasn't going to read it, I shouldn't just throw it away. So I stuffed it into my old suitcase and went to bed.

One week later, I got another letter. I put it away in my suitcase with the first one, and every time I got another letter I stacked it, unopened, with the others and slid the suitcase under the bed, pushing it all the way back against the wall, as far as it would go.

November 5, 1941

Dear Velva Jean,

I'm writing on behalf of all of us here to wish you a happy birthday, because it's not every day a girl turns nineteen. I hope this new year of yours brings you everything you ever want. Everyone up here is listening to the radio and asking Mr. Deal to order your records from the city. I don't think even Roy Acuff has so many fans. I've been trying to explain that it don't just happen like that, that you only been in Nashville for a couple of months and that sometimes it takes years to get your big break, but they're all too excited. You got us all stirred up here, honeybee.

And you are going to make it, sure as I'm writing this. But just know you're going to have some rough days and that this is okay. Everyone who ever had a dream and chased it has had to go through it. I just hope you'll read the story about Myrna Loy in the *Picturegoer* I sent. You can read it for yourself, but her daddy died when she was young, and she had to leave school to help with the family, and she worked for years as a dancer and playing orientals in tiny roles in bad movies before anyone ever discovered she was so funny and put her in *The Thin Man*. The rest, as they say, is history.

The biggest news from here is that Sweet Fern and Coyle Deal were married Sunday in the living room of Daddy Hoyt's house. Dan Presley was best man and Corrina was the flower girl. Reverend Broomfield did the ceremony, and afterward we sat outside and ate fried pies and drank cider.

I can't wait to read an article about you someday. Before we know it.

Love,

Ruby Poole

SIX

For my birthday, Gossie and I walked over to the War Memorial Auditorium, where Carole Lombard and some other Hollywood stars were holding a rally, right there on the front steps, to sell war bonds. There were over a thousand people standing on the sidewalks and on the grass, and Carole Lombard told us that if we wanted to win this war, each and every one of us needed to do our part. She said, "The war is costing over two hundred fifty million dollars a day. We may not be in this war officially, but we are in it just the same, so it's up to us to sacrifice, save, and serve!"

The spotlight caught the blonde of Carole Lombard's hair and turned it into white gold. I am nineteen years old in Nashville, Tennessee, I told myself. I couldn't believe I was so old already, nearly the same age as Sweet Fern when our mama died.

In bed that night, I lay there thinking about how I wasn't getting any younger. I got up early the next day and on my lunch break—and every lunch break that week—I went back to each recording studio on my list and waited in line again and gave my name to the receptionists.

On Friday, November 21, I stopped in at Cyclone Records, and this time there was a different woman behind the desk. She was blonde and wore glasses and a green suit, and I remembered that I had seen her before in Waynesville, back when I made the record for Darlon C. Reynolds.

She smiled and said, "May I help you?"

I said, "My name is Velva Jean Hart. You probably don't remember

me, but I met you last June when my brother and me recorded two
songs for Darlon C. Reynolds in Waynesville, North Carolina, back
when he was auditioning hillbilly acts." I hated the word "hillbilly,"
but it was the word Darlon C. Reynolds himself had used.

She said, "Velva Jean Hart. Of course I remember. You sang that
wonderful song about the yellow truck."

I stood up straighter. My heart started thumping fast in my chest. I
said, "Yes, ma'am."

She said, "Honey, he's not in today, but can you come in tomorrow
afternoon at three?"

I was so surprised I couldn't speak for fifteen seconds. Finally I
said, "Of course."

"Good," she said. "I know he'll be glad to see you again."

I floated back to the café, through the kitchen, and up the stairs to
the apartment. When Gossie got home, I told her, "I'm singing tomorrow for Darlon C. Reynolds at Cyclone Records."

She said, "The same man you made the records for back in North
Carolina?"

"Yes." I was fidgeting like Hink Lowe at Sunday meeting. I wanted
to dance all over the living room.

"Look at you, Mary Lou." I could tell she was impressed. "You
don't mess around, do you?"

"Of course not," I said. "This is why I came here."

That night I hung out the window and practiced my songs because
I didn't want to wake up Gossie by singing in the living room or inside
my bedroom. I just leaned right out into the cold, dark air. I was going
to sing a brand-new song, one I wrote about coming to Nashville. I
called it "On My Way to Now." If Darlon C. Reynolds wanted to hear
another song after that, I could sing him the one I'd written about a
girl with no parents, who went to live on the moon.

Darlon C. Reynolds looked just like I remembered him—he was
short and round, with glasses and thin brown hair that barely covered
a head so shiny it could have been rubbed with a cloth. He shook my
hand and said, "Velva Jean Hart. I wasn't sure I'd ever see you again."

I said, "I wasn't sure I'd ever see you again either."

He laughed, and then he led me back into the studio itself, into a room with a microphone on one side of a glass wall and controls on the other. There was a stool in front of the microphone, and he said, "Why don't you take a seat, and I'll see you on the other side."

I wasn't sure what he meant by this, but I sat down on the stool and watched as he walked into the glass booth and shut the door. He sat down behind all those controls, and while he got himself settled I looked around at the walls of the studio. There were pictures of some people I recognized and some I didn't.

His voice came into the room, over the speaker, and he said, "Anytime you're ready."

I wished I had a Hawaiian steel guitar instead of my daddy's old mandolin. I decided right then and there that as soon as I made money from a record I was going to buy myself one.

"Miss Hart?"

I thought, Boy wouldn't Harley die if he could see this! Then I wondered what Harley Bright was doing right then. He was probably writing a sermon or yelling at some sinner or trying to save someone's soul. I wondered if he'd forgiven me, if he ever would, or if he would hate me forever. I thanked Jesus, for about the thousandth time since I'd left home, that I was here and not there, trapped in Li'l Dean's house up in Devil's Kitchen.

"Miss Hart? Any time you're ready."

I looked at the other side of the glass, and there was Darlon C. Reynolds, sitting there staring at me. I thought: How long have I been sitting here thinking things to myself?

I started to play "On My Way to Now," strumming my mandolin. I was so grateful and relieved it was in tune that I forgot to sing, and then I forgot the melody—it just walked right out of my head. I pretended the intro was longer and started playing "Yellow Truck Coming, Yellow Truck Going" because it was the song I knew the best, even though Darlon C. Reynolds had already heard it before.

Only, I couldn't remember how the song started, so I jumped right in to the second verse.

Over in Asheville
there lived a man
struck down by the Mean Devil Blues . . .

Oh damn. The Mean Devil Blues. That's what I forgot. The first verse was all about the Mean Devil Blues being the worst kind of blues, the kind that won't leave you alone.

There was nothing to do at this point but keep going.

He drove a dark truck
and dressed all in black
from his hat down to his shoes.

What came next? Something about the Mean Devil Blues again. Where had I even got that phrase to begin with? Daddy Hoyt, I guessed. He had names for all sorts of blues. The Gentle and Wholesome Blues. The Sacrifice Blues. The Peculiar Blues.

The Mean Devil Blues
had him down on his knees
out of fun, out of luck, out of hope.
"I've gotta change something
or die," he said,
"I'll just start with this old truck."

Well, that wasn't right. "Hope" didn't rhyme with "truck," and then I realized I'd switched them around. It was supposed to be "out of fun, out of hope, out of luck."

Dammit. While I was thinking about what I'd got wrong, I forgot to sing the next lines. Oh hell, I thought. And then I just started in on the chorus, even though it wasn't due for nine more verses.

Yellow truck coming,
bringing me home again.
Yellow truck going,

I'm on my way—
on my way to tomorrow
and dreams come true,
leaving my yesterday.

Like hell you are, I told myself. You're on your way home because you can't even remember the words to your own song. You should just go back to the Lovelorn and pack up your bag and let that yellow truck take you on your way all the way home to Fair Mountain.

My one chance, the chance I'd been waiting for ever since Darlon C. Reynolds handed me his card and told me he wanted to make more records with me, and I was acting like someone who'd never sung a note.

I kind of fizzled to an end then, somehow getting through a few more verses, two in the wrong order, and one more round of the chorus before I stopped.

Darlon C. Reynolds didn't ask me for another song. Instead he came out of the glass booth and pulled up a stool so that he was sitting across from me, the microphone in between us.

"You got one hell of a pretty voice, Velva Jean. Can I call you Velva Jean?"

"Yes, sir."

"One hell of a pretty voice. And you know I love that song or I never would have recorded it."

I was trying to think of a Cherokee witch spell that I could put on myself so I might disappear. I said, "Sir, I butchered that song like I was working for the grocer down in Hamlet's Mill. That's not even the song I meant to sing you."

He smiled at this, and then he folded his arms across his chest. "I'm guessing you got more songs just like that one and like the other one we recorded in Waynesville."

"Yes, sir. Lots of them."

"Good, good. Here's the thing." By his tone, I thought, uh-oh. "It's important to have a style of your own and be really good at it. I mean, with Roy Acuff, Eddy Arnold, Bill Monroe—any of the greats—you know what you're going to get from them. You know the kind of thing you're going to hear. People want that. It's reliable. It makes them feel good. But before you find that style and settle on it, I always recommend getting as much musical experience as you can get. All different kinds. Try them all or at least hear them all. You ever been to a juke joint?"

"No, sir." I didn't know what a juke joint was, but it sounded like a dark and dangerous sort of place.

"You should go. Go to a honky-tonk. Go to an opera. Let yourself feel and experience different kinds of music, and then come back to me and sing me that same song. You may not change a note, but I guarantee there'll be something else about it, something deeper, something in the background that will make you stand out even more. That's what I'm looking for."

I suddenly felt my limbs growing heavy. It was the feeling of being tired and worn out and burdened. I thought, I did my very best. I can't sing much better than I just did, so what am I supposed to do if that isn't good enough? Why can't I just be happy waiting tables at the Lovelorn? Why on earth do I want to do something so hard?

I said, "Mr. Reynolds, I want to sing more than anything I've ever wanted to do in this world. But I'm beginning to see that it's not as easy as just wanting to sing and being good at it. Is there anything else I can do to be better?" I heard Gossie's words: "wanting it and getting it are two different things."

He cupped his chin, his arms still folded, and then he said, "I'd join the musicians' union if you can. If you want folks here to take you seriously, that's the first step."

~

The office of the musicians' union was on the sixth floor of the Warner Building, near Cyclone Records. Union membership cost twenty-eight dollars, which took almost all the money I'd saved up from working at the Lovelorn. But joining the musicians' union meant bands could hire me to sing with them and give concerts at the local restaurants or hotels. It also meant that record studios might be more willing to look at me.

The problem was that anyone who wasn't twenty-one needed a parent to sign a sheet giving them permission to join. I figured I was done in then, but that's when the Lovelorns stepped up and walked with me to the union office and offered to sign the sheet as my landlords and unofficial Nashville guardians. Afterward I handed the money to Mr. Bob Payne, who was the secretary-treasurer and spoke so soft you almost couldn't hear him. Then he gave me my union card, and I almost floated the whole way back to the Lovelorn, with Nori and Crow walking on either side of me. "That girl's not even using her feet," Crow said to Nori. "She's going to fly all the way home."

Before bed that night, I said to Gossie, "That was a nice thing Crow and Nori did for me." I was sitting on the floor, with my back to one of the chairs and the typewriter on the coffee table in front of me, typing up one of my songs. I thought I might write a song for the Lovelorns. I was far away from home and practically an orphan, and it felt good to have two kind people acting like parents.

Gossie lay on the settee, blowing smoke rings at the ceiling. She looked at me out of the corner of her eye. "You know that Crow sang at the Opry?"

I stopped typing. "When?"

She blew three rings. "About twelve, fifteen years ago. You've heard him play, but have you ever heard him sing? He's good. Damn good. That man can sing and play like a house afire."

I thought of Crow down in the kitchen making fried chicken and pot roast and chocolate cream pie. I pictured him washing dishes and stacking plates. I said, "What happened?"

She said, "Just because you sing at the Opry once doesn't mean you keep singing there."

I said, "Why not?" I couldn't imagine a thing in this world that would keep me from singing at the Opry over and over once I got my chance.

She blew two, three, four more rings and then she sat up and brushed the ashes off her lap. Gossie was the messiest person I knew.

She said, "Oh, Mary Lou. You got so much to learn. Crow's good, but so are a lot of people in this town. Most of it comes down to luck."

I said, "Johnny Clay says I'm the luckiest person he knows. He says I'm charmed."

Gossie stubbed out her cigarette and lit another. She didn't blow rings this time, just took two puffs and then stubbed this one out too. "That's a good thing, then," she said.

SEVEN

*A*ccording to Granny, there were three things to do if you saw a mad dog: climb up a tree, crawl into a ditch, or stand perfectly still and hold your breath. There was no use running, she said, because a mad dog could smell you and would be on your heels in an instant. Johnny Clay and me used to take turns playing the mad dog and the prey, one of us growling by, foaming at the mouth, or crouching behind a bush, and the other trying to hurl himself at the nearest tree or ditch. I used to practice on my own too, trying to see how long I could stand still and not breathe. From what Granny said, being bit by a mad dog was the worst thing that could happen to you. She said it only took nine days to go completely mad yourself, and then you just dropped dead.

On the afternoon of December 6, 1941, Tommie Lou was standing at the corner of Church and Fifth Streets, waiting to cross, when a mad dog wandered up and bit her right on her behind. At first, she didn't think anything of it—the dog wasn't drooling or growling. She just told it to shoo and then she hugged her purse to her chest and walked over to the other side of the street. Because mad dogs don't make a habit of roaming the Nashville streets, she figured it was just a regular dog that belonged to someone who lived nearby and probably forgot to tie it up.

But the next morning she started feeling poorly, and when Nori went upstairs to check on her and find out why she hadn't come to work she found Tommie Lou chattering away to herself like a crazy person. Nori ran downstairs and immediately called Dr. Hewitt Clark, who had taken care of Nori's daddy when he got sick with influenza and somehow nursed him back to health, even when half the city was dying. Dr. Hew, as we called him, was a nice old man with a kind, wrinkly face. He had his doctor's degree from the University of Tennessee, but he was also part medicine man. He had grown up in the mountains, learning secrets from the Indians just like Daddy Hoyt.

When he got to the café, I asked if he needed a nurse.

He said, "I won't know till I see how bad off she is."

Tommie Lou lay on her belly, strapped to her bed. I wore rubber gloves and fed her water with a spoon because she wouldn't drink a drop although she said she was thirsty.

"Don't get too close to her," Dr. Hew said. "She'll bite you."

Dr. Hew showed me how to hold the spoon and feed her from a distance, but I was still scared to death of being bitten. I was worried I might turn mad too or maybe change into a werewolf. Johnny Clay had told me once about a man in Swain County who turned into a wolf with every full moon and had to be tied to a tree so he didn't kill anyone.

"Don't let me bite you," Tommie Lou kept saying over and over again. "Please don't let me bite you."

Dr. Hew had been soaking a madstone in milk for twenty minutes and now he set it on the bite. Suddenly Tommie Lou began to cry, and I backed away, dripping water all over the floor.

"It needs to sit there till it falls off," said Dr. Hew.

"What happens when it falls off?" I asked, suddenly wishing Gossie was there, because her arms were longer. "Please don't let me bite you," Tommie Lou kept saying, even though she looked like that was exactly what she wanted to do.

"It falls off when it's sucked out the disease."

We sat there in silence, watching Tommie Lou. Dr. Hew was not a man who spent time discussing things like the weather or the latest Opry broadcast.

When the fever broke and Tommie Lou fell into a quiet sleep, Dr. Hew and I went downstairs to the café to get a drink. As soon as we walked in the door the hairs on the back of my neck stood up. Something was wrong. Women were crying. Men were swearing at each other. Babies were being bounced on knees to keep them still. One old man kept cursing the "dirty Japs" over and over again.

Nori and Crow stood behind the counter. He had his arms around her.

I said, "What's going on here?"

Crow said, "The Japanese have blown up a place called Pearl Harbor. It's in Hawaii." He pronounced it *Ha-why-a*. "It happened this morning. They think hundreds, maybe thousands, of our boys was killed."

Dr. Hew sank onto a stool. "Dear God," was all he said.

Crow said, "The president don't have a choice. We're going to have to get in this war."

I blinked fast and tried to concentrate. I was breathless, like I'd been hit in the stomach or been spun very fast, yet I felt far away from everyone and even from myself, like I was separated from my own body. I could see my hands and feet way down below and feel the tightness in my throat—so tight I couldn't swallow.

I had heard about war from Mama, Daddy Hoyt, Granny, and Levi Bright. I had read history books and learned all the dates and names in school, and I had seen war in moving pictures like *Wings* and *Hell's Angels*. I'd watched the newsreels and heard the reports on the radio, but this war had seemed such a far way off and so separate from America and everything or everyone I knew. I'd been worrying about it but not worrying about it for a long time. Now what would happen? And where was Jesus in all of this, and what would he do to help?

I looked at Nori, my friend, who was Japanese, even though she'd been born here and never been to Japan once, not even to visit. I wondered how long it would be till folks started looking at her funny, just like when Harley got everyone in the mountains stirred up about outlanders, rounding them up and sending them back to where they came from.

Tommie Lou would recover. But instead of feeling relieved and thanking the Lord for sparing her, I went upstairs to my room to wait for Gossie, feeling worse than if I'd been bit by a mad dog. Why would God spare Tommie Lou Tyson but send all those boys to their deaths?

Over two thousand people died at Pearl Harbor, and by Tuesday, December 9, they were still counting the dead. I suddenly forgot all about the recording studios that weren't calling me back and the juke joints and operas I was supposed to be going to. I even forgot about the Grand Ole Opry.

The president said, "It will not only be a long war, it will be a hard war." Mr. Roosevelt called it a privilege and not a sacrifice to serve the country. He was asking all able-bodied men to enlist. "We are going to win the war, and we are going to win the peace that follows."

One thought kept going round and round in my head: Johnny Clay. I didn't know where on this earth my brother was, but I knew him well enough to know that he would be first in line at the nearest recruiting office. He could already be at training camp. He could be leaving soon for Europe or the Pacific. I might never see him again.

On the night of December 9, Gossie and I sat up and talked till four in the morning. Outside the windows, I could see lights in the building across the street. Voices came up from down below and there was the sound of shouting and cheering and automobiles passing and streetcars clattering. Nashville was awake but even more than normal. It had been wide awake since the bombing.

I sat on the floor by Gossie's feet, with my knees tucked under my chin. Gossie was winding my hair in pin curls like I'd seen in a magazine. She said this would help direct the wave and make it less wild. I was all the time, every day of my life, trying to keep my hair from being wild. She was drinking gin, and this time I was too. I held the glass and sipped at it, and the warmth of it going down made me feel grown-up and fearless, like an Indian warrior.

I said, "I should go home." I handed her a bobby pin. The comic book Gossie had given me for my birthday sat on the coffee table— *Flyin' Jenny*, about a young woman named Jenny Dare who was a beautiful and courageous pilot. I was right in the middle of reading about her being captured by spies after her plane went down near a place called Shark Island.

Gossie said, "Back to Devil's Hole?"

I didn't bother correcting her. "Back to Fair Mountain."

She said, "You've come too far to go back, Velva Jean."

Gossie was fascinated by Harley and my marriage. She all the time wanted to know when I was getting divorced. She wanted me to talk to the lawyer in Boston who helped her get a Mexican divorce so I could start figuring out a way to earn my freedom once and for all. She said the more she knew me, the less she could see me as someone's little wife, cooking and cleaning and going to church. And the more time that got between my being here and my being there, the less I could see it too. Sometimes being Mrs. Harley Bright seemed like something that happened long ago to someone else.

Gossie said the very best thing that ever happened to her was her divorce. The truth was I wasn't sure how I felt about having one of my own. I didn't know anyone that had a divorce except some woman in Civility who was run over by a car just a week after she got hers. Although they didn't say it, I knew some people believed it was her punishment, that that's what she got for getting divorced. I knew this wasn't true, but *divorce* was still an ugly word, the kind that followed you around forever, making people look at you funny and with pity and maybe a little meanness. It was kind of like the way they looked at you when you told them your mama was dead and that your daddy'd left when you were ten. Folks never seemed to have any patience for something so unfortunate, even if it wasn't your fault.

Now I handed Gossie the bobby pins one by one. I took another drink, a bigger one this time. I said, "I guess I should go home." But I didn't want to go home, and just thinking about going put a great big lump in my throat that took up all the space.

Gossie said, "You can't go back."

I thought: She's right. I can't. There's no going back now.

December 14, 1941

Dear Velva Jean,

I hope you are safe and happy as a person can be right now in this world. Up here on Fair Mountain we can't believe what's happening. Linc and the Deal boys went down to Hamlet's Mill to the recruiting office today. Beach showed up just in time to go with them. He'd been over at Cherokee, down by Big Witch Gap, working on the Scenic, and we hadn't seen him since you were here last. Coyle enlisted in the navy and Sweet Fern is beside herself.

Linc and Beach wanted to enlist as paratroopers, but they won't take married men because it's too dangerous, so Linc signed up for the infantry instead. Married men don't have to enlist, but we both thought he should. We stayed up all last night talking about it.

Linc's worried about Russell and me, but I told him we got plenty of folks to look after us. I told him his country needs him more. They said it would be weeks before they called him. They don't have enough training camps to hold everyone.

We all love you and miss you, honey. I can't wait to buy all your records when you're ready to make them. You take good care and let me hear from you.

Ruby

P.S. Beach joined the marines. He's going to be a medic. We haven't heard a word from Johnny Clay.

EIGHT

One week after Pearl Harbor, I stood in the recruitment office on the corner of Church and Seventh Streets blinking at the chaos. When Stump said he was planning to go down there, I asked if I could go with him. He said, "Why you want to do that, Velva Jean?"

I said, "I don't know. I'm going to support you."

He shrugged and said, "Okay, then."

I didn't tell him that something was making me want to go down there but I didn't know what. I wanted to see what was happening. I wanted to see if there was anything a girl like me could do for the cause.

In 1934, the year after Mama died, when I was eleven going on twelve, a do-gooder man had come to Alluvial to talk to women about voting. Only four women signed up—saying later they were afraid not to and just did it to be polite—but only Granny made the trip to Hamlet's Mill on voting day. She and I rode down on Mad Maggie. We hitched that mule up outside in the street, and then Granny took my hand and marched into the building.

"Why you want to vote?" I asked her all the way down the mountain.

"Because I can," Granny said. "I reckon my vote is worth as much as anybody's."

She had voted just that one time and never felt the need to do it again. On every election day that came after, when Daddy Hoyt asked if Granny didn't want to go down the mountain with him to vote, she just shook her head. "I had my say." And she would smile at him, smug as a cat, like she knew something he didn't.

Harold Lee and I stood at the edge of the room, watching. There were young boys signing up, but there were also old men and men my daddy's age. It seemed like every man in this world was there, and I wondered if my own father would ever do something so sacrificing.

Stump said, "What do you think? Air corps or navy?"

I said, "Golly, Harold Lee, I don't know."

He said, "Which do you think's more romantic?" He waggled his eyebrows at me. His Adam's apple waggled too.

I said, "Staying right here and not getting yourself killed." I was all of a sudden mad at him and all these other boys signing up, making their families worry. I was maddest of all at Johnny Clay, who I hadn't heard from since he left North Carolina, just before me. For all I knew he was dead somewhere, already shot down by the Germans or the Japanese.

Stump said, "I'm joining the navy. The next Jap that tries to bomb us will be sorry. I'll blow him out of the sky."

I said, "Good luck."

As he walked away I read the signs on the other tables—Army Air Forces, infantry, navy, marines, paratroopers, Red Cross, WAAC. I'd never heard of this last one, but there were women in uniform on the posters and a real one standing behind the table. She waved at me, and I walked over to her.

"Hello there." She was tall and narrow, her silver-black hair pulled back at her neck. Her face was as smooth as ivory and she had a warm smile. "I'm Ellen Tillman." She held out her hand and I shook it. "Are you here to sign up?"

"Yes, ma'am," I said. I thought, Velva Jean, you have lost your mind.

The posters that hung over the table said: "It's a Woman's War Too! Join the WAAC—Your Country Needs You Now!" and "This Is My War Too! Women's Army Auxiliary Corps, United States Army."

"Wonderful." She was beaming at me. "Can I answer any questions?"

I wanted to ask, What is the WAAC? Where did you come from? What do you do? Why are you wearing uniforms? Are they sending women to fight? Is this really our war too?

When I didn't say anything, she said, "By joining up you free a man to fight. The WAAC trains women to do noncombat jobs that are currently held by army soldiers. We're the first women, other than nurses, to serve in the army."

"But you don't actually go to war."

"Not overseas, not yet, but we're doing important war work. Some of the women are even flying planes."

This sounded like something she was making up.

Ellen Tillman tilted her head to one side. "The First Lady said this is not a time when women should be patient. 'We are in a war and we need to fight it with all our ability and every weapon possible. Women pilots . . . are a weapon waiting to be used.'"

I thought about flying, which seemed exciting but dangerous.

I said, "Maybe I'll just take some information from you for now." Ellen Tillman handed me some papers and then I walked away fast.

I could feel her eyes on me so I told Stump I'd wait for him outside. I went all the way out to the sidewalk before I let myself breathe again. Women fighting and flying. It was too thrilling. I thought about how confident the woman named Ellen Tillman had looked, like Carole Lombard or Flyin' Jenny or Constance Kurridge, pilot and spy, who I used to read about in the comic pages of the newspaper. What would Harley say? Just what would he say to this? "Velva Jean's gone and joined the war." I laughed just thinking of it.

~ *1942* ~

Forward to battle go . . .
Vict'ry is ours we know . . .

—"Forward to Battle"

NINE

On May 21, I was collecting empty cans of Hunt's tomato sauce, Dole pineapple juice, and Chicken of the Sea fancy tuna and stacking them on the counter in the café. The Arcade had turned into a collection depot for tin cans—tops and bottoms with paper labels cut off, washed and flattened. The cans were picked up weekly and carted to the loading docks of trucking companies, and from there they were sent to Colorado to a central depot. The president said we needed to save all our tin and metal so that we could build airplanes and make bullets.

I was trying to imagine one of these cans all the way in Colorado, when Gossie came in from work and sat down at the counter. She used the big toe of each foot to push the shoe off the other. She said, "I'm sick of selling handbags." While the customers watched, she pulled off her nylons and said, "I'm doing my part. I'm donating my stockings. I'm tired of wearing them. I'm never going to wear them again." The government needed nylons for making medical supplies, parachutes, powder bags for artillery pieces, and tow ropes for gliders. "Do you think they can use them even if they're runny?"

I said, "I don't see why not." I couldn't stop thinking about all the sacrificing we were doing and about women everywhere working and fighting for freedom, like Carole Lombard who was killed on January 16 when her plane crashed into a Nevada mountainside. She had been flying back to California from Indiana, where she was selling war bonds at a rally. There were twenty-two people on board the plane, including Carole Lombard and her mama, and every single one of them died instantly.

I was starting to feel worn down by the war, by people dying, by Nashville, by my life dreams. I'd been to every recording studio in town more times than I could count. I'd started writing letters to Judge Hay at the Opry—a letter a week—hoping he might want to audition me, but I hadn't heard a word from him. I'd been to one opera and a Sacred Harp singing and a bluegrass show and I even went to the colored church on the edge of town, way out past the airport, to hear the gospel music. I was trying to educate myself, just like Darlon C. Reynolds said, and that also meant going to the Opry whenever I could.

The truth was, no matter how many kinds of music I listened to or how many times I left my name at studios, no one wanted me. Ever since February I'd been working on a good case of the blues. I hate the blues because they aren't like the measles—you don't just have them once and then you're done with them forever. Daddy Hoyt said he'd had them so many times in his life that he thought he must have worn them out, when there they would come back all dressed up, fresher than ever, to throw him down, choke him, and dare him to tell it. I've always wondered where they come from and where they go off to once they leave you.

Right now I had the kind he called the Gentle and Wholesome Blues—not the type, like the Mean Devil Blues, that made you kick the door or break someone's window. The Gentle ones were quieter, but they were just about the worst kind because they sat around you and on you and in you, just like a headache or a bad winter cold, and wouldn't leave you alone.

After I stacked the cans, I soaped down the counters and rubbed at a stubborn bit of food and then wiped them clean. I could feel those blues gathering right over my head. I could feel my mind growing dark as a thundercloud.

Gossie said, "What's wrong with you, Mary Lou? I've never seen you look so blue." She laughed. "Hey, look at me writing a song. You should turn that into something."

I said, "Maybe," which meant I wouldn't. Ever since Pearl Harbor, my songs had been drying up. After I was done with work for the day, I sat down at my typewriter, and I just stared at the blank sheet of paper. Sometimes I typed a few words, but none of them made sense. They felt outside me, like I was standing far away from myself and trying to write instead of writing from the inside.

Lately I'd been thinking I might just give up music for a while and sign up to be a WAAC. To be a WAAC you had to be between twenty-one and forty-five, at least five feet tall, and weigh at least one hundred pounds. The girls who joined up worked as file clerks, radio operators and repairers, sheet-metal workers, typists, control-tower operators, weather observers, and bombsight maintenance specialists.

Gossie said, "You and the girls should sing something. Sing something right now. That always makes you feel better."

I said, "Maybe. I'm going to take these plates back to Crow." I picked them up and walked into the kitchen. As I did, the bells on the door jangled, which meant someone came in or went out.

Crow was frying chicken, his face red and wet from the heat. He said, "What do you know, Velva Jean?"

I said, "Not much." I dropped the dishes one by one into the soapy water of the sink and watched the bubbles rise up to the surface, just like the dishes were taking in one last breath. There was a kind of hazy film on the top of the water, and I could see part of myself in it—a blur of lips and one eye and curling hair. I looked up at Crow and watched him wipe his face. He shook the chicken in the fryer and hummed to himself. I tried to picture him on stage at the Opry. I thought, There I'll be, twenty years from now, just like Crow, frying up chicken right here at the Lovelorn.

Marvina burst in from the café and said, "Lordy, you should see what just rolled in. Tom Buccaneer in the flesh." She grabbed her handbag from the cubby where we stored things and flipped open her compact. She took out her tube of lipstick and painted her mouth even though it didn't need it.

She went out and Gossie came in then, wading in her bare feet. Crow said, "You better have shoes on, Gossie. This is a place of business. This is a restaurant, for God's sake."

She didn't pay him one bit of attention. She said, "Mary Lou, you better get on out here. I've got a surprise for you."

I said, "I'm busy." I swished the dishes around in the sink. My reflection went away. All I wanted was to be left alone for even a minute or two.

Gossie grabbed my arm and started pulling me, and so I kind of half walked and was half carried out of the kitchen, my hands dripping water all over the floor. There was Marvina standing just behind the counter, looking back and forth between me and this tall man that was standing on the other side, bag slung over one wide shoulder, skin the color of gold dust, hair cut short like a soldier. Marvina had a wild grin on her face and her head was just whipping around on her neck. Now big old Tommie Lou was lining up, smiling like a fool. She was herself again, good as new. You never would have known she'd been bit by a mad dog.

Gossie pushed me forward, and the man said, "Great holy Moses, girl. I hardly even know you." And then he whistled long and loud.

My hands went clammy and my heart jumped right up into my throat and I ran up and threw my arms around him so tight I could hear him trying to get his breath.

"Velva Jean, you're going to strangle me."

I said, "I hope so. I hope I do." It was too impossible and wonderful to believe. I couldn't let go of him. Somehow he got out of my grip and dropped his bag and picked me up and swung me round and then he hugged me tight. I was crying by then, even though everyone in the Lovelorn Café was staring. I said, "Johnny Clay Hart, where in the Sam Hill have you been?"

Johnny Clay had been everywhere, up and down the country, heading west. Gossie took over my shift, waiting on tables in her bare feet, while he and I went out onto the Nashville streets and walked and walked and walked. He'd grown about three inches since last summer and he looked as pleased with himself as I'd ever seen him. Every girl we walked by turned to look at him and I thought, Heaven help us all.

He said, "How many records you made, girl?"

I said, "None yet." I didn't tell him that nobody would hear me sing except for Darlon C. Reynolds, and now he would probably never want to hear me again after the audition I gave him.

Before Johnny Clay could ask me why I hadn't made it yet or what exactly I'd been doing with myself since I'd been in Nashville, I said, "Start with when you left Fair Mountain. I want to know everywhere you been and what you been doing." I wondered if this would make him think about Lucinda Sink and the man that tried to hurt her, the one he nearly killed, which was why he had to run away in the first place. If it did, he didn't let on.

He winked at some girl going past in too-high heels and too-bright lipstick. She was staring at him so hard she walked into a streetlamp.

He said, "I jumped the train out of Alluvial and just rode. I rode till I got to South Carolina and then I jumped another train to Georgia, another one to Alabama, and then another to Mississippi. I bummed a ride down to Gulfport and then another to New Orleans, where I tried to look up Butch Dawkins." Butch Dawkins was Johnny Clay's friend, half-Choctaw, half-Creole, who'd taught me to play the blues. My brother didn't say anything for a moment, like he was letting this sink in just to see what I'd do. I kept my face still but I felt my heart speed up.

I said, "Oh? Did you find him?" I tried to sound like I didn't care two bits if he found him or not.

He said, "Nah. No one knows where he's got to. Said they hadn't seen him since he left to find his destiny. Thought he was up in Chicago by now or Kentucky. So I went on. I hitched another ride, this time to Monroe, Louisiana, then another to Shreveport. I jumped a train to Dallas, but that was about the worst damn place I ever saw, Velva Jean, so I got out quick and went right up to Oklahoma, over to Tulsa, where I stopped to rope steers. I like Tulsa. It's as different as can be from Fair Mountain—ugly and flat and brown as far as the eye can see—but the folks there're honest and they work hard. I got a job on a ranch and rode horses. I stayed there a month, and then it got too cold and I walked out to the road and found a man driving all the way to California."

It was all too much to bear. I wanted to ask about each place, but he was talking too fast and I had too many questions. He told me about New Mexico, Arizona, and then California. He said, "Where do you think I went, Velva Jean? I went all the way to Los Angeles."

I said, "No you didn't."

He said, "Yes, I sure did. You know how I always said I was going out to ride horses in the movies? And that I was going to find William S. Hart because maybe he's related to us?"

I said, "Yes."

He said, "He's done making pictures and now he lives up in a place called Newhall. It's just like the Old West. Like Jesse James and outlaws and shit. I went up there to find him."

"No you didn't, Johnny Clay."

"Yes, I sure did. I went up there to find him, and it took some doing to get there, but I met a fella on the train who said he knew his son, Will Jr. So we get out there and there he is, this grouchy old bastard, sitting on top of a horse at nearly eighty years old—William S. Hart, not the horse—just as straight in the saddle as he was in his pictures. He said, 'Are you a cowboy?' And I said, 'No, sir, I'm a gold miner,' and he said, 'What's your name?' and I said, 'Johnny Clay Hart, spelled just like yours.'"

Johnny Clay said he stayed for supper, and it was the worst food he ever had—goat or some such—but he didn't care because William S. Hart had always been one of his heroes. Afterward he and his friend headed back to Los Angeles, where Johnny Clay figured he'd get himself discovered for the movies even though William S. Hart told him not to waste his time.

I said, "So is he our kin or not?"

"I don't know, Velva Jean. We couldn't figure it out, but I'm sure he is."

I said, "They have gold in California. Did you go panning?"

Johnny Clay waved his hand at this. "I ain't interested in California gold, Velva Jean." He said it like the idea was insulting. Then he said, "I tell you what though. I sat next to Joan Blondell at Chasen's, and she said, 'You're too good-looking to stand. You should be doing what I'm doing.' She said, 'I want you to come over to Warner Brothers with me tomorrow and meet Jack Warner.' I said, 'I'm busy tomorrow. How's Monday?' She just laughed. That was Friday, December 5. Two days later the Japs bombed the devil out of Pearl Harbor, and instead of going to Warner Brothers I started heading east. And this time I rode on troop trains—that's what they call them now because the only ones riding them these days is soldiers. We had to stand five deep."

We walked for almost a block without saying anything. Then I said, "You know, Linc and Beach and the Deal boys signed up." I held my breath. I thought, Don't you tell me you've signed up too, Johnny Clay Hart. I looked up at his hair, which was cut just like a soldier's.

He said, "What about the great Reverend Harley Bright?"

"I don't know." I didn't tell him about all the letters from Harley that were still coming every couple of weeks—less often now—hidden away, unopened and unread, under my bed in Mama's old suitcase.

Johnny Clay was staring at me out of the corner of his eye. "You did the right thing by leaving. I mean, in some ways I can't believe you actually left him, Velva Jean. But in some ways, I can't believe you stayed with him so long. I'm pretty goddamned proud of you, little sister. That took some real guts to do what you did." He shoved his hands in his pockets and looked around. "Hell, to do what you're doing. You got yourself a job. You got yourself a place to live. You got yourself some friends." He whistled. "Yes, sir."

I didn't say anything because I couldn't. It was hard to think of how far I'd come when I still had so far to go. I almost never could see it for myself. I didn't think I'd done a single thing yet that earned my leaving. We walked for a while like that, both of us looking ahead, not talking, me trying not to cry, him whistling a song.

Then he said, "Everyone's signing up, Velva Jean." My chest got tight because I knew what was coming. He took my arm and put it through his, trying to make us best friends again. He held tight to it so that I couldn't get away. He said, "The day after Pearl Harbor, when I was supposed to be at Warner Brothers, I went to the recruiting office in downtown Los Angeles and I mean to tell you the place was jumping. The only table without a line was the one for the paratroopers.

There was this man in uniform standing by himself. Sergeant Briggs. Behind him was a poster of a paratrooper jumping out of a plane with his parachute open. 'Swoop Down on the Enemy like a Falcon from Above,' it said. 'Don't Walk into the Fight—Jump!'"

I wished I could close my ears because I didn't want to hear what he had to say.

"I saw this article in *Life* magazine that said paratroopers are the toughest. Briggs said being one ain't for sissies. It's only for the bravest men. Before you're even allowed to jump, you go to ground school where they train you to jump, and after you've learned to jump they train you to fight when you're on the ground. The pay is good—fifty dollars more a month than anyone else."

He stopped then and looked around him. He said, "Hey now. Where's the Opry?"

I pointed off in the direction of the War Memorial. My finger was shaking.

He said, "Let's see it. I guess you've already been."

I nodded but didn't say anything about Roy Acuff or what it felt like to be there after all these years, because he would want to hear all those things and I was mad at him.

He said, "I want to see the show while I'm here."

I said, "It's twenty-five cents for a ticket." I thought: Who cares, Velva Jean? What does it matter?

He said, "I'll tell you something else I want to do while I'm here, and that's learn to fly an airplane. I can't stand this waiting around. I'm going to make the most of my time till they call me up for training camp. I figure I'll learn to fly, and then after I do I'll learn to jump, and by the time they call me up I'll be ahead of everyone."

We started for the Opry, crossing the street just in time to miss the trolley car, which almost ran us over. We raced out of its way like wild rabbits, Johnny Clay laughing, and then he pulled me back up on the sidewalk. He said, "Did you know that when a human body falls out of an airplane it takes eight and a half seconds to hit the ground? If you count to four and your regular parachute don't open, you pull the rip cord on the emergency parachute strapped to your chest. It should open in two seconds—giving you two and a half seconds before you die."

I said, "Johnny Clay Hart!" I was so upset I could barely walk.

He went on. "I signed my name to papers that said I agreed to jump out of planes and that I knew all the dangers. Then I joined a group of fellas who also signed, and they made us jump on and off a desk over and over. Afterward Sergeant Briggs told us to go home and wait to be called. When I walked out of there, I could feel the weight of my wallet in my back pocket and the picture that was in there—this one here." He stopped on the sidewalk and opened up his wallet, pulling out a photograph, all bent and creased. "It's the one I tore out from *Life*." The picture showed a paratrooper making a jump and landing standing up. Johnny Clay looked at the picture a good long minute, and then he folded it up and put it back in his wallet. We started walking again. "I'm going to be like the man in that picture. I'm going to be one of those that lands on my feet."

I said, "When do you go?" My throat was so dry I couldn't swallow.

He said, "I got to report to training at Toccoa, Georgia, in September."

I said, "How long are you staying here?"

"A couple weeks. Maybe more. Depends on how long you'll have me."

I was suddenly so happy and so sad and so angry and so relieved, all at once. When I could talk again, I said, "Johnny Clay Hart, you're going to get yourself killed." By this time we were almost in front of the War Memorial Auditorium, in front of the Opry. I said, "What about me? What about Daddy Hoyt and Granny and the rest of us?"

He said, "Maybe I'll get myself killed. Maybe I won't." I'd never heard his voice so serious. It hit me then that he was a man, not a boy. I thought about me being nineteen years old. That would make Johnny Clay twenty-one. "But at least I'll know I was doing something good, Velva Jean, something better than sitting around and waiting. Waiting for what? I'm going to die one way or the other one day, and I figure I might as well do some good before I do." We stopped in front of the Opry, and my brother looked down at me and grinned that wicked grin that hadn't changed a bit since he was twelve, except that it was maybe a little sad now around the edges. "Better late than never, right?"

Then he turned around and took in the Grand Ole Opry. He placed his hand against the side of it just like I had that very first time. He breathed it in. Then he said, "Tell me straight. What's going on with your singing?"

"Nothing," I said. "I can't get an audition to save my life. The only one I got I messed up. Remember Darlon C. Reynolds? The man we met in Waynesville? He told me I needed to learn more about music, different kinds. He told me to go to a juke joint and a honky-tonk. He said I have to go and do that before I come back to see him. I'm thinking I might just join the army myself."

He had his listening face on, which meant he was staring hard at me and then staring hard at the sky. He still had his hand against the Opry. "You'll show 'em, Velva Jean," he said. Then he closed his eyes and I knew he was soaking it up, making a memory. I wanted to cry right then and there because he was so young and beautiful and good, when it came down to it, in spite of it all, and so much like me and so much like himself, and he was the most important person in the world to me and I didn't want him to ever die.

TEN

*J*ohnny Clay slept in the empty room across the hall, and during the day he helped out in the café, clearing tables, lifting boxes, organizing the storeroom for Crow. When he wasn't working, he sat at the counter, picking his guitar, or he went off on his own to explore the city, or he just stood outside in the daylight, staring up at the sun like you weren't supposed to, like he'd never seen anything like it.

Gossie and Johnny Clay got on like a house afire. They stayed up late at night and talked about their adventures, while I sat there thinking that I'd only really had one adventure in my life, not counting the panther attacking me, and that was driving to Nashville. It didn't seem like much when I listened to the two of them talk about shooting lions in Africa or hitching rides across country and almost becoming movie stars or getting a Mexican divorce or jumping out of airplanes to fight the enemy. When Gossie asked Johnny Clay why he'd left home, he told her he almost killed a man, but he didn't say why. He hadn't said one word about Lucinda Sink since he'd come to Nashville.

Later Gossie asked me, "It was over a girl, wasn't it?"

I said, "Yes, but don't you say anything to him about it. We don't mention her."

She said, "I knew it," and then she had a million questions: Who was the girl? Did he love her? Did she love him back? Was she worthy of him? But Gossie never brought it up to Johnny Clay. She was always good as her word. She said, "Honestly. The way girls lose their heads over your brother. I've never seen anything like it. What he needs is a friend in this world. Thank God he has you, Mary Lou. Now he has me too."

On the morning of May 29, Johnny Clay walked back into the café from outside and said, "Velva Jean, if you're really serious about this singing business, we got to teach you something other than hillbilly tunes. You want to be the best singer you can be, right? Then you're going to have to do what Darlon C. Reynolds said and learn about all kinds of music."

I said, "I went to an opera and a bluegrass show and a colored church where they sang gospel."

He waved his hand at this and looked like he wanted to spit. He said, "That's not the kind of music I'm talking about."

I said okay because I knew he was right and because, when it came down to it, I didn't want to be Crow or Marvina or Tommie Lou or Stump, working for years at the Lovelorn Café while my dreams dried up like leaves.

That night we got all dressed up and drove way out into the country in my yellow truck. It was me and Johnny Clay and Gossie, and I was driving. I said, "Where are we going?" I thought all the music you could ever want was right there in downtown Nashville.

Johnny Clay said, "You'll see." He was telling me to turn here and turn there. He had the window down and his arm was hanging out of it, cigarette glowing in the dark. He was suntanned and happy, the freckles on his nose fading away into gold. Every now and then he ran his cigarette hand over his short hair, back and forth like he was trying to get used to it. His profile was straight and strong, high Cherokee cheekbones, full mouth. He was always laughing.

He said, "Turn here, Velva Jean."

I turned onto a narrow dirt road that was just a thin slice out of the night. It was so dark—sky, trees, land—that I couldn't see more than three feet in front of me.

He said, "Pull over." He leaned forward and pointed with his ciga-rette. "Right over there."

I stopped the truck, but there was nothing but trees and dirt and a little house, actually a shack—metal roof, boards pieced together to make walls, raised up off the ground on stacks of bricks, rickety wood stairs climbing up to the front door. The shack looked like it was crumbling down into the earth, like it might fall down at any time. There was a sign over the door that said: "Ice-Cold Jax—Ale, Beer, Stout: The Drinks of Friendship."

The door swung open then, and out came the music—like nothing I'd ever heard before. Colored people spilled outside. Men in suits and ties and hats, and women in dresses as bright as bird feathers.

Johnny Clay was already out of the truck. He threw his cigarette onto the ground and stamped it out. He said, "Come on."

Gossie and I climbed down from the truck and started walking after him. I felt just like I was in the fog or the smoke that would roll in over the mountains where I used to live, hiding every house and tree.

The music was beating, beating. I felt it in my pulse, in my hands and arms and veins and chest, and mostly way deep down in my heart. It was wild and free and loud. It was all the colors of the women's dresses, only even brighter, even more. I walked like a dazed person, like someone out of her mind, up the steps and into the juke joint where there was only smoke and dancing and twirling, swirling energy. Laughing. Talking. Shouting. Just like they'd never heard of Pearl Harbor. Just like we weren't at war. Feet stamping. Hands clapping. Music beating, beating until I thought I would faint right there.

Johnny Clay took my hand and dragged me forward into the middle of it. The place was dusty and cramped, no bigger than a shoebox. Couples were dancing together, and men and women were dancing by themselves. Up on stage there was a band—drums, guitar, piano, stand-up bass. The men were beautiful, young and old. Written on the wall behind them was: "Blues for the body, food for the soul."

Johnny Clay found a spot by the bar, and we stood with our backs against it and watched.

Gossie said, "I want to marry a colored man. Look how gorgeous they are, Mary Lou."

I didn't say anything, but I was thinking: When I die, I want to come back as a colored person. Granny, who was half-Cherokee, believed that your spirit sometimes came back to earth after you were dead and gone. She thought you could become part of the sea or sky or dirt or tree roots, but I thought I would rather be one of these women in a scarlet dress, dancing like I couldn't help myself, like it was all I could do on this earth.

Just then a man walked over. He was black as could be, and I thought he looked like some exotic prince or king and not someone who should be in a juke joint. He shouted over the music, "Either of you ladies care to dance?" He was looking at me.

Gossie took his hand and said, "Try to keep up."

He laughed, and they started to dance, Gossie shaking all over, up and down. I laughed at the sight of her. Gossie had rhythm, but she took up a good part of the dance floor.

I felt a tap on my shoulder, and there stood a boy, probably no more than sixteen or seventeen. He didn't say a word, just held out his hand. I thought that I had never held a colored boy's hand before. The only colored person I knew was Elderly Jones, who lived in Alluvial, just across from Deal's General Store, and was at least one hundred, and who usually stayed on his porch, watching people go by. The boy's hand was warm and strong, and he pulled me close and then spun me out and then pulled me back in again. I could see Johnny Clay watching us, keeping his eyes on that boy.

And then I didn't think about anything except the music. There was music you thought about and music you felt, and this was music you felt. It was like something Butch Dawkins would have played on his steel guitar—burning and churning and searing like a hot poker. You felt it down in your feet and up to the hair on your head. It wasn't at all polite or sweet or something you might sing in a little white church on top of a mountainside.

Hours later the three of us sat outside, looking up at the moon. It was full and round and orange and hung low in the sky. A witch's moon, Granny called it. The music was still humming and beating. I was tired and my feet hurt from dancing. I'd never danced so much in my life. I tried to think of the war that was coming, that was already here, but it felt too far away to keep in my mind for long.

I said, "I think I'll write a juke-joint tune. Something loud and fast and bluesy." One was already spinning through my head, something about a beautiful boy who never said a word, but who danced everything he had to say. I closed my eyes and tried to hear the melody.

Johnny Clay yawned and lit a cigarette. He crooked his mouth to the side to blow out the smoke. He said, "Just you wait, Velva Jean. You ain't seen nothing."

The next night I went to my first honky-tonk, a place called Bootsy's Striped Dog, which was squeezed into Printer's Alley, between Third and Fourth Avenues, narrow and dark with a crowd of tables and a tiny stage set up at the end of the room by the bar. The place was thick with smoke and mostly men, tattooed and blue jeaned, staring into their whiskey glasses. The air was electric, like the way it felt just before a tornado. There was the feeling of something coming, something building, of something exciting just around the corner getting ready to hit hard and knock down some trees.

The windows of Bootsy's were covered with posters of the famous people who'd sung there, most of them Grand Ole Opry stars. All Nashville seemed to be packed inside, dancing on the uneven woodplank floor. A sign hung over the tiny stage: "Talent Night! Every Thursday!" In a shop just next door there was a photo booth where you could take a picture of yourself and wait five minutes, and it would develop right there in the machine, and then you could walk away with it. Every inch of Bootsy's, floor to ceiling, was covered with pictures. Everyone from Roy Acuff to Eddy Arnold to Maybelle Carter was up there. This was what they called the Wall of Fame, even though the photos were everywhere.

Bootsy herself was greeting folks as they came in. She was a short woman, round as a summer hen, wearing glasses and a housecoat. She looked like she'd just wandered in from the market, and not like a woman who ran one of the most famous honky-tonks in Nashville. Her hair was teased into curls that were gathered up high on her head, and she sat on a stool, holding the door open, greeting each of us like we were long-lost family. As Johnny Clay and me walked by, she reached up and squeezed his cheek. She said, "Mercy, look at you."

Up on the stage there was a band playing the rowdiest country music I ever heard. The singer and guitar player was a man named Travelin' Jones, who was lean and lanky, with hair the color of a dusty road and a face stubbly from not shaving. He had tattoos up and down his arms and creeping out from the collar of his shirt. He looked like he had seen a lot and lived a lot, but he couldn't have been more than thirty. He wore a cowboy hat pulled low and his hair tied back in a ponytail, with blond pieces wisping out here and there. Every now and then he tucked one behind his ear. He played the guitar like no one I'd ever heard, except for Butch Dawkins. He kind of talk-sang, but sometimes he just sang, and his voice was as clear and pure as water.

The other men played fiddle, stand-up bass, and drums. In between songs, Travelin' Jones told stories about the places he'd been and seen. He said he'd set foot in every one of the forty-eight states and had been to twelve foreign countries. This made Johnny Clay bristle. I knew he didn't like the idea of anyone traveling more than him, especially now that he'd seen some places other than home.

I couldn't even think of twelve countries, but listening to Travelin' Jones I was filled with a green envy that made it almost impossible to listen to him and even more impossible not to. He sang a song that had to do with each place he'd traveled. My favorite was called "Dead Woman's Crossing," about a bridge in Oklahoma that was haunted by a woman and her daughter, killed by a whore-lady.

There were two girls next to us who were leaning forward so far in Travelin' Jones's direction that I thought they were going to fall off their chairs.

I said, "God, he's good."

Johnny Clay was staring at Travelin' Jones like he wasn't sure about him. He said, "He's okay."

After the song was over, Travelin' Jones said, "I'm looking for a singer to join my band on this Fourth of July. As some of you know, I got an orchestra on the side, and we're playing at the Tulane Hotel. Anyone wanting to audition better get up here right now."

I sat up straight. I looked at Johnny Clay. I said, "I'm a member of the musicians' union—maybe I should go up there." I tried to think what on earth I could sing. Travelin' Jones would want me to sing something he already knew, something he and his band could play along with, which was just as well because I hadn't written anything new since Pearl Harbor. Sometimes I could hear music in my head, but the words fought each other, or else they wouldn't come at all and I just sat there thinking in blank lines. Every now and then I got out the words to "Yellow Truck Coming, Yellow Truck Going" and marveled at them just like they were written by someone else. The song felt outside me and far away, like something that came from off somewhere. I wondered if Travelin' Jones ever had this problem or if maybe there were too many words in his head for him to ever write them down.

Johnny Clay said, "Maybe."

I said, "What do you mean, 'maybe'?"

He said, "I don't like the looks of him."

I rolled my eyes. Johnny Clay couldn't stand any man that took the spotlight away from him, especially if he could sing and play good.

One by one people went up on stage and sang a song with the band. Travelin' Jones stood off to the side, playing guitar, watching them.

My hands were growing hot because I was going up on that stage too. I thought of every song I knew the words to, but they seemed silly here—too country, too hillbilly. I looked around at the men and their tattoos, drinking their whiskey, smoking their cigarettes. I wanted to sing something dangerous.

Travelin' Jones said, "Anyone else? Best get on up here before Bootsy chases us out."

Before I could think too much about it, I stood. Men looked up from their whiskey glasses and Travelin' Jones looked at me from the stage. Johnny Clay tugged at the back of my dress, just like when I was ten and he was twelve and he was trying to keep me from answering the altar call at camp meeting, back when I wanted to get myself saved.

I kicked him, just like I'd done then, and I brushed my hair back over my shoulders and walked up to the stage and said, "Do you know 'Pretty Polly'?" This was a song I'd learned from my mama years ago. It was about as dangerous a song as I'd ever heard, about a girl who got murdered by the man she loved, and then he buried her.

Travelin' Jones said, "I think we can figure it out." He counted off the band, and they started playing and then I stepped up to the microphone and sang. Travelin' Jones watched me for the whole last verse of the song, and I tried not to look at him because I knew it would only make me forget the words, and after I'd forgot the words to my very own song in front of Darlon C. Reynolds this was the last thing I wanted to do.

After I finished the song, I sat down beside Johnny Clay, my face hot as a poker, my legs wobbly. He said, "You did good, Velva Jean," but I could tell it killed him to say it.

Travelin' Jones said, "Listen here, thank y'all for coming. We'll be posting our choice tomorrow, right here at Bootsy's."

Then he and the boys played a song. It sounded like "John Hardy," only wilder and louder and wide open. Travelin' Jones scooted around the stage, doing some rough but fancy dance steps, and that's when it happened—he looked up from under his hat, just for a second, just a flash, and he was smiling. It was like quicksilver. One minute it was there, the next it was gone, but it was too late—I felt myself falling from some great height like Old Widow's Peak up on Fair Mountain or the courthouse itself on Devil's Courthouse. I thought: Uh-oh. I hadn't felt my stomach drop like that since Harley came preaching in Alluvial, all those years ago.

On the way home, Johnny Clay said, "I didn't like the way he was looking at you."

I said, "How was he looking at me?" I wanted to hear it from my brother, just to make sure I wasn't imagining things. Johnny Clay didn't answer. I said, "How was he looking at me?"

He shrugged, shoving his hands in his pockets. "Like I should punch him in the jaw."

I said, "Don't you dare, Johnny Clay." But my thoughts were racing. I was replaying that smile over and over in my mind.

When we got to the café, we found Crow in the kitchen by himself, stacking the clean dishes into a neat pile. Johnny Clay went on upstairs, but I got myself a Coca-Cola and then stood there watching Crow. I said, "Do you ever miss playing music?"

He turned and looked at me, his arms full of plates. He said, "I still play music."

I said, "I know, but I mean on stage. Like around town. At the Opry."

He said, "I only played the Opry once." He was as smiling and easy as ever, like we were talking about the weather or tomorrow's menu. He stacked the rest of the plates and then began putting them away in the cupboards. "Don't get me wrong, it was a thrill to end all thrills, Velva Jean, but I did it and they never asked me back and that was enough for me."

I tried to imagine being happy with playing the Opry only once. I said, "Didn't you ever want to record songs? Make records?"

He said, "I did make records. I made two records, and they were good ones. Not great ones, or maybe I wouldn't be standing here." He waved his hands at his apron, at the kitchen itself. "But I ain't too upset about where I am either." And then he went back to work, wiping down the counters.

I said, "Did you know since you were little that you wanted to sing?" I wanted to keep at him, to make him talk about this, to explain to me how he could be okay with making meat loaf and fried chicken when he'd once played at the Opry.

He was rolling up his sleeves, pushing them higher over his elbows. He plunged his hands into the sink water, starting in on the dirty dishes. He said, "Velva Jean, sometimes dreams change, either because they have to or because life has something else in mind for you. You'll realize that as you get older."

I thought, I hope not. It was the very worst thing I could imagine.

ELEVEN

I met with Travelin' Jones and his orchestra every day until the Fourth of July. Johnny Clay made sure to tag along, saying he wanted to spend all the time he could with me now that he was here in Nashville and before he left again, but I knew he was really just trying to keep an eye on things.

He didn't have to worry, though, because Travelin' Jones was nothing but a gentleman. We met at Bootsy's, and sometimes Bootsy was there too. I showed up to work and we practiced our set and then afterward he stayed on stage with the band and told me I could go on home, that they had things to work out—instrumental numbers and ones he sang himself—that they didn't need me for.

On the last day of rehearsal, as we were getting ready to go to Bootsy's, Crow asked Johnny Clay to help him with a delivery, and before Johnny Clay could say anything I ran right off without him. My heart was pounding when I got there, from running and from leaving my brother behind. I knew he'd be mad as a snake when I got back, but I didn't care. I wanted to see what Travelin' Jones might do if Johnny Clay wasn't around.

We ran through the set and when we were done, Travelin' Jones said, "How about I buy you a drink?"

I said, "Ginger ale, please."

He smiled at this and said, "All right, then." He ordered me a ginger ale and then got himself one too, even though I knew he'd probably rather have whiskey. We sat at a little table right by the jukebox, and it was so small that my knee kept bumping his under the table. Every time it did an electric shock went right through me.

He said, "How old are you, Velva Jean?"

I said, "Nineteen."

He said, "You don't mind me asking?"

"I don't care. You can ask me anything. How old are you?"

"Twenty-seven."

I thought he looked at least thirty but didn't say so. I tried not to imagine all the things he'd done in his life to make him look older than he was.

He said, "You're one hell of a singer."

I said, "Thank you."

We sat there drinking our ginger ale, and he took his hat off and set it on the table. He ran his hand through his hair and scratched his beard, and the whole time I tried not to look at his tattoos.

I said, "Why do you have two bands?"

He picked up his glass and swirled it around, just like I'd seen people do with whiskey. He took a drink and said, "One represents one side of me, and one represents the other. The orchestra's for business. It makes me money. But I also like that kind of music. It makes me feel romantic, and I don't always feel that way." My knee bumped his again and I moved it away fast.

He said, "The Travelin' Jones Band is my own raw self, though, with all the bad habits and bruises and scars. The two together tell my whole story."

He put his hat back on, brushing wisps of hair out of the way, off his face, back behind his ears. He said, "Any other questions?" His knee bumped mine under the table and stayed pressed against it. This time I didn't move away.

I said, "What's your real name?"

"Charlie," he said.

On the Fourth of July, Charlie Jones and me played the Tulane Hotel with his orchestra. Johnny Clay said that for his part he didn't trust a man with two names and two bands, but I was so excited I could hardly stand myself. I wrote to everyone back home and told them what I was doing. "You are on your way, Velva Jean," Ruby Poole wrote back. I wore a dress Gossie had borrowed from Gorman's—a strapless gold dress that glittered in the light. It was the most beautiful dress I had ever seen in person or anywhere. I promised not to eat or drink while wearing it so we could give it back to the store in perfect condition. She never would tell me if Gorman's knew she was borrowing it or if she'd taken it without asking.

We went on at eight o'clock that night, standing on a stage in the Tulane's ballroom, which was enormous and painted white. The floor was a dark wood, almost black, and there were palm trees sitting in great, fat pots in the corners. People danced or sat at tables with starched white tablecloths, and everyone but me was eating and drinking.

Johnny Clay, Gossie, Nori, Crow, Tommie Lou, and Marvina came and also Harold Lee, all dressed in a suit that he had already outgrown. I sang five songs with the band: "You Are My Sunshine," "And the Angels Sing," "Over the Rainbow," "I've Got My Love to Keep Me Warm," and "God Bless America." Charlie Jones sang the other songs himself, the ones that had words, and it was strange to hear him singing something that wasn't about murdered prostitutes or whiskey.

At nine o'clock we played "In the Mood" and everyone danced. Then we all went up to the roof to watch the fireworks over the river. Men and women shouted and clapped and kissed whether they knew each other or not. I thought it was the war that was making everyone so patriotic. I looked around and it hit me that I didn't have anyone to kiss, not in Nashville and not in this world. I thought of Harley and wondered what he was doing at just this moment. I pictured him sitting at home, working in his mud room, while Levi snored upstairs.

It was 1942. We were at war. I was far away from almost everyone I knew and loved. I was still a married woman, but I didn't feel like it. I'd just sung my first concert. Across the roof I could see Gossie and the girls, their arms linked through my brother's, and instead of making me feel less alone, the sight of them made me feel small and far away.

"You were good tonight." I looked up and there was Charlie Jones. I said, "Thank you." I had to shout it over the fireworks and the noise.

A waiter in a white tuxedo passed by with a tray of champagne. Charlie Jones took two glasses and handed me one. I drank, careful not to spill a drop. The champagne went right to my head. I drank more.

He finished his glass and said, "Maybe we can play together again."

I looked at his straight nose, the blond-brown hair that was circling his cheek, the cupid's bow mouth underneath the beard, and I tried not to fall in love with him. Charlie Jones looked rough and talked rough, but he was smart and he knew who he was. He could also be nice, but deep down I wasn't sure he was nice. And that made me like him even more.

I said, "I'd like to."

He said, "Why don't you come to Bootsy's next week and sit in with the band?"

"Okay." I finished my champagne in one long, burning gulp. The fireworks were cracking and popping and booming, and everyone around me was laughing and kissing and clapping their hands. I felt like I was suddenly on a carnival ride I couldn't get off, like when Johnny Clay and I would push each other down Fair Mountain inside an old tire—going faster and faster—and halfway down I would wonder why in the world I ever wanted to do it in the first place, especially when I knew I was only going to crash at the bottom.

I thought: This man is like being inside a tire going too fast down a hill. This man is every bit as dangerous as Harley. What is it with you, Velva Jean? What is it about this kind of man?

There was a cold panic rising in me and the roof was spinning. I could smell Charlie Jones, and he smelled sweet but deadly—fresh like spring with a kind of muskiness underneath that made me want to run.

Suddenly I felt his lips on mine, and there was a jolt like a lightning bolt and I felt my feet go out from under me, only they didn't. Somehow I was still standing. I hadn't kissed a man since Harley. I hadn't ever kissed a man but Harley. Charlie Jones was the second man I'd ever kissed in my life.

I said, "I have to go." I ran back inside the hotel, down and down and down the stairs and through the ballroom. I didn't stop running till I got back to the café.

~

For weeks after the concert, I jumped every time the door to the café opened or the telephone rang, hoping it would be Darlon C. Reynolds or some other record producer come to find me and offer me a contract. The most that happened, though, was that I sang one more show—this time at Bootsy's—with Charlie Jones. He didn't try to kiss me again. On July 22 he signed up with the Marine Corps and the next day he left Nashville. On July 24 Tommie Lou and Marvina joined the Red Cross and said they'd be shipping out in August.

The next evening Johnny Clay and I went to the Opry. He'd been here for a while already, and I held my breath all the time, afraid I would wake up and he would tell me it was time for him to go. I told myself to make the most of it, not to waste time missing him when he was still here.

Johnny Clay and I walked to the Opry and stood watching the people going in. It was a cool, clear Saturday night. The sky was turning a dark, deep blue, the color of the very best marbles. It had been a cloudy day, but the clouds were starting to go away and now you could see the moon and the stars.

I said, "Do you ever write to her?" I knew he'd know who I was talking about without me even saying her name.

He said, "No."

"Not even once?"

"No."

"She might want to hear from you and know you're okay."

"If she wanted to hear from me, she would've married me when I asked her."

He looked so closed away and silent then that I told myself I wouldn't bring Lucinda Sink up again, so I changed the subject fast as

I could and asked him to see that picture in his wallet, the one of the paratrooper. And then I asked him a hundred and one questions about jumping out of airplanes and what kind of training would he have to do and whether he was scared or just excited. I knew this would make him happy and make him forget I'd asked anything, even if I hated like the devil to hear it.

Suddenly we heard a distant roar, and there was a flash of silver across the sky. Everyone froze and stared upward, trying to see what kind of plane it was—was it the Japanese? The Germans?

President Roosevelt and the government had started sending out warnings about spies. They said that spies might be among us—German spies, Italian spies, Japanese spies—and to keep our eyes open for suspicious behavior. Johnny Clay and I had always loved playing spies and so we'd been practicing all the things we needed to know if we were going to spy on the enemy. Spies were never supposed to write anything down, so we memorized people on sight. Johnny Clay said we had to learn to think like con men because that was the only way to catch them.

"It's one of ours," Johnny Clay said now. He said it again, louder, so that the people around us could hear. After a moment everybody nodded and breathed and started talking and walking just like they'd been doing before.

The two of us stood there, side by side, staring up at the airplane. Johnny Clay had an admiring look on his face like he was proud and awed at the same time, like he had something to do with that plane. I knew he was thinking about how he was going to fly one for the war and also jump out of them. For me, I was picturing myself up there, just like Flyin' Jenny, hair blowing out the window, singing loud and free, something like "Silver Plane Coming, Silver Plane Going."

Carole Lombard was killed in a plane. She was flying in one just like that, sitting in her seat, talking to her mama. She was going home to Clark Gable. She didn't have any idea she was going to die. She was only thirty-three years old. Look away, Velva Jean, I told myself. Look away.

Johnny Clay said, "We're going to be late." But he was still watching.

I said, "Imagine being up there, high above the earth, flying like a bird, the whole world stretching away from you."

I heard a voice in my head: "Women pilots are a weapon waiting to be used."

Johnny Clay said, "I can't wait to jump out of one."

We watched the plane till it disappeared behind a cloud, into the dark. I said, "I think the thought of it is the most terrifying thought in the world. I hope I never set foot in a plane as long as I live." I didn't want to crash into a mountain like Carole Lombard. But at the same time, I couldn't help it—I wondered what it would be like to be a part of the sky.

Johnny Clay didn't say a word during the Opry show. He sat with his chin in his hands and his face blank and serious, and I knew he was taking everything in. The only time he was ever this still was when he was gold panning.

Afterward he stayed in his seat while everyone else stood up and walked out, buzzing, humming, chattering, singing. He stared at the stage and looked like he was in a fog, like maybe he was somewhere far away.

I stood up and touched his sleeve. I said, "Cat got your tongue?"

He said, "That's where you'll be one day, Velva Jean. Don't you forget it. Just like that framed picture I gave you. You're going to be right up there with the rest of them. It may not be now and it may not be soon and you may have to wait for a while, at least till this war's over. Maybe longer." He paused. "But you'll be there, Velva Jean."

I looked down at the chill bumps on my arms. There was a touch of the sixth sense about all of Mama's children.

I said, "Really?" It came out a whisper. I sat back down. I'd been writing Judge Hay every week since January and so far I hadn't heard a word from him or anyone at the Opry.

Johnny Clay said, "Sure as I'm sitting here."

We looked at the stage, both of us picturing me up there in my satin and rhinestones. I could almost feel the wood of the stage below my feet. I could almost hear the first song I would sing . . . something about a little girl from a little place who taught herself to drive a yellow truck so that she could go to the Opry.

TWELVE

On Sunday, July 26, Johnny Clay knocked on the door to my room and said, "Velva Jean, get up."

I was lying in bed with my eyes closed, trying to stay asleep. I said, "Go away."

He said, "Get up now. We got somewhere to be."

I said, "It's Sunday, Johnny Clay. I don't have to work today. It's my one day to sleep. Go away."

Johnny Clay threw the door open and the light poured in behind him. I could see Gossie just past him on the settee, drinking her coffee. She waved her little finger at me. Johnny Clay said, "Time's a wastin', girl. Come on."

I looked at him and thought how sad I'd be when he was gone to Georgia for training, even if he was getting on my last nerve right now. I couldn't think about what came after that—Europe, the Pacific, the war. I sat up and rubbed my eyes and said, "Where are we going?"

Johnny Clay said, "You'll see. Bring your keys because we're taking the truck."

Johnny Clay wanted to drive, but I said, "No, it's my truck and I'm going to drive it." He sat beside me, feet propped against the dashboard, staring out the window at the trees and whistling. We'd left downtown and were headed out into the country, past little houses and farms and every now and then a filling station. But mostly there were just trees and trees and more trees.

I said, "Where are we going?"

He said, "You'll see when we get there." He was giving me directions. I turned onto a flat country road, and he said, "Now stay on this for a while." Then he started singing—it was a song we used to sing when we were little. It was called "Old Maid's Last Hope" and it was what we sang when we wanted to drive Sweet Fern crazy. It was about a burglar man that went to rob a house, and when he heard the woman who lived there come in the door he hid himself under the bed.

Johnny Clay sang: "She took out her teeth and her big glass eye, and the hair right off of her head. That burglar man had nineteen fits, and he rolled out from under her bed."

When he sang the part about the old maid taking out a revolver and pointing it at the burglar man and telling him he had to marry her or she'd blow off his head, I couldn't help it—I started laughing. And then I joined him for the last verse: "He looked at the teeth and the big glass eye, and he had no place to scoot. He looked back at the bald-headed miss and said, 'Woman, for Lord's sake, shoot.'"

Johnny Clay and I just laughed and laughed. It was the best kind of laugh—the kind that I only shared with my family and with Johnny Clay especially. It was like being home, no matter where you were on earth.

I looked out the window and we were passing another farm, another field. As far as I could tell this was the hundredth farm we'd seen since leaving downtown. But this time Johnny Clay told me to turn off onto the dusty dirt road that cut through the farm. I rolled up the window so the dust wouldn't choke me. I said, "What on earth?"

We drove down that dirt road till we came to a tiny little building—just a white square that looked like a cracker tin. Next to it was something that looked like a barn but wasn't exactly a barn. And stretching away to the horizon was a flat field of grass, as wide as twenty trucks bumper to bumper.

I stopped the yellow truck and Johnny Clay got out. He kind of stretched this way and that, raising his arms up over his head and then out in front of him. He looked back at me over his shoulder. "Well, come on."

I got out of the truck and slammed the door and said, "What on earth?"

He started walking toward the little cracker-tin building. I followed after him, saying, "Johnny Clay? Johnny Clay!" I followed him into the building, which was just one room. It smelled like pipe smoke and musty old books. There was a desk on one wall stacked with papers and magazines, and a tiny table where two stooped-over men with white hair and wrinkled faces sat playing a card game and shouting at each other.

One of them said, "That was the day I shot down the Fokker D. VII. And I did it after losing an engine!"

The other man snorted. "You think that's something? I shot down thirteen Fokker D. VIIs, four other German fighters, five observation balloons, and four reconnaissance planes. And I did it flying blind!"

"That wasn't you. That was Eddie Rickenbacker!"

"Rickenbacker!" The old man spat on the floor. "Rickenbacker was a woman!"

Johnny Clay said, "Either of you Duke Norris?"

They looked up at us, and one of them shouted, "*What?*"

Johnny Clay hollered, "Either of you Duke Norris?"

The man said, "Out there!" He crooked his thumb at the barn.

Johnny Clay said, "Thank you, sir," and then he ducked out of the building and headed, long legs moving, for the barn. I thanked the men, but they didn't hear me because they were back to fighting over Eddie Rickenbacker, and then I ran after my brother.

The barn wasn't really a barn because instead of a hayloft there was open space from floor to ceiling, and instead of doors there was just a big gap where a wall and doors should be. Inside was the littlest airplane you ever saw, painted bright yellow—not the yellow of my truck, which was the deep gold-yellow of mustard or goldenrod or birch leaves in the fall, but more like the sweet, new yellow of daffodils. The plane was oil splattered and rickety and looked like it was held together with rubber bands and hairpins.

Johnny Clay stood there, grinning like a fool.

I said, "Where are we, Johnny Clay?"

Parachutes were stacked high in a corner, covered in dust, and engine parts were scattered here and there along the walls. There was a gas pump and farm equipment and part of an old car rusting in one corner, and a sign propped up on its side that said "John Deere Quality Farm Implements."

He said, "I thought we'd learn to fly."

I stood there looking at him like he'd just sprouted wings and danced a jig. I said, "What in Sam Hill are you talking about?" I thought about Carole Lombard. My heart started to thump hard and fast in my chest.

"Ever since I got here, I been looking and looking for a good teacher, but they either cost too much or they don't know what the hell they're doing. A man out at the airport told me about this guy, said he's supposed to be the very best in Nashville, though he don't fly much anymore."

I said, "Johnny Clay Hart. I told you I never wanted to set foot in a plane ever in my life." Then I suddenly thought of the old men yelling at each other over their cards. I said, "Who's going to teach us?"

Just then a man appeared, walking toward us, carrying two bags of seed, which he dropped against one wall. He wiped his hands and said, "You the Harts?"

"Yes, sir." Johnny Clay shook his hand. "Johnny Clay, and this is my sister Velva Jean."

The man said, "Duke Norris." He was just my height and wiry. His skin was burned brown from the sun and he had hair that wasn't blond or red but was somewhere in between. He had a scar on his nose that was shaped like a star. I thought he was probably my daddy's age and that, nice as he seemed, he didn't look like the very best pilot in Nashville.

He said, "Pleasure." He looked at me. "This for both of you or just you?" He said this to Johnny Clay.

I said, "Both of us." I felt a thrill saying it. I thought: What are you doing, Velva Jean? What are you saying? You're not actually going to do this.

The man nodded like this was no big deal, like he taught women to fly all the time. He said, "Who wants to go first?"

I said, "He can," because my palms had gone clammy and the back of my neck was hot and sticky like when I had a fever.

Johnny Clay crooked his eyebrow at me, which meant "are you sure?"

I said, "Go on. I want to watch you." I hoped he couldn't tell how jittery I was.

I looked on as Duke showed my brother how to climb into the plane, into the passenger's seat, which was just behind the pilot's seat. Johnny Clay hopped right in like he'd been getting in and out of planes all his life. Then Duke swung himself up, and he was graceful, like a dancer. They put on their seat belts and goggles and helmets, and Johnny Clay gave me a thumbs-up as Duke started the engine and steered the plane out toward the flat field of grass.

At the sound of the engine, the old men tottered out of the cracker box, cards in hand, and shaded their eyes from the sun. One of them hollered, "Flight of the angels, Duke!"

I held my breath as the plane went up, afraid it would fall to pieces in front of my eyes, but it rattled and shook as it climbed, and suddenly it evened out and it was smooth as could be, just like a bird. I thought it was maybe the most beautiful thing I'd ever seen.

From the sky, Johnny Clay waved down at me, and I could tell he was laughing. Suddenly I wanted them to come down right away so I could take my turn. Duke did twirls and spins and loops and I swore I could hear Johnny Clay yelling. They spun by me, and my brother waved again and he had that fool's grin on his face, and I thought right then and there that I didn't want to sit where he was sitting. I wanted to sit where Duke was.

When they finally came down, Johnny Clay waited till he got the okay and then he jumped out and ran for me. He said, "Velva Jean, you won't believe it. I almost hate I'm going to have to jump out of them, because they're too damn fun to ride in." He went on and on, breathing hard and talking fast.

Duke walked up, slow and steady. He looked at me and said, "Ready?" I suddenly felt weak at the knees. I wanted to run back to my truck. I said, "Why don't I wait till next week?"

Duke looked at me, calm and patient as could be, but Johnny Clay said, "You have lost your mind, Velva Jean." And he started pushing me toward the plane like a wheelbarrow.

I could hear the old men laughing. I said, "Johnny Clay, stop that this minute."

Johnny Clay said, "You're as chicken as Sweet Fern. You're worse than the old True sisters."

Duke said, "She don't have to go up if she don't want to."

Something about the way he said it made me smack Johnny Clay's arm and march over to the plane. My heart was beating hard in my chest, so hard I was sure those old men could hear it, deaf as they were. But I swung myself up into the passenger's seat and waited. I sat there thinking that I'd got myself into this plane just like someone who'd been doing it all her life, and I felt proud. I thought: To hell with you, Johnny Clay. To hell with you, old men. To hell with you, Harley Bright. I'm doing this thing right now. I'm going to fly. Just watch me.

Duke came up the side and leaned in and snapped my safety belt tight around me. Then he handed me my goggles and helmet. He stared me square in the face and said, "You sure?" His tone was kind.

I felt the anger slip away. I said, "Yes, sir." But I knew I didn't sound sure.

He said, "I'll tell you something about flying, young lady. It's a little like driving, only up in the sky instead of on the ground." He looked over his shoulder at my yellow truck. "Your brother told me you taught yourself to drive."

I said, "Yes, sir."

"Well this is going to be easier because I'm going to teach you to fly. You ain't going to have to learn all by yourself. But I got a feeling if you know how to drive you already know a bit about flying. That feeling you got when you first put your foot on the clutch and your hands on the wheel? That feeling that made you decide you could do that? That you wanted to do that? That's all you need to fly."

I remembered what the Wood Carver told me once about how the figures he made were already in the wood, just waiting for him to find them and carve them out.

I said, "Like I've known how all along and it's just waiting for me?" This was what singing was like for me, and also driving.

"Yes." He gave my belt another tug, just to make sure it was latched. I thought about how his face seemed to look sad no matter what he was saying. When I thought about people, I always pictured them the way they looked when they didn't know anyone was watching them. Johnny Clay had a grin that meant wickedness. Sweet Fern frowned in a way that meant she didn't approve of things. Granny's eyes always danced like she was thinking up mischief. Daddy Hoyt was peaceful. Ruby Poole sparkled like a firecracker. Linc looked serious as an undertaker. Beachard's eyes were far away as the moon. Mama had been sunshine. Our daddy's face was always changing, just like Harley Bright's. But Duke wore a sad face, even when he smiled.

"You'll have to help me get the plane started," he said. "While I swing the propeller, I want you to stamp hard on the brakes and pull the stick back into your lap so I don't get run over."

I said, "Where are the brakes?"

"Those little knobs under the rudder pedals."

His feet hit the ground and he disappeared around the front of the plane. I waited a minute, nervous that I'd stamp on the brakes too early or too late. I strained to see what Duke was doing but lost sight of him. Then Johnny Clay was waving at me, so I stamped down as hard as I could and pulled the stick back into my lap. I thought that the very last thing I wanted to do was kill my flying teacher before I'd even gone up in the air.

I could feel the rumble in my whole body, from my feet to my head. I wanted to scream and jump out, but it was too thrilling and I wanted to keep feeling it. I thought, Oh dear Jesus, keep me safe. Duke reappeared then and shouted, "Good job, Velva Jean!" Then he lowered himself into the pilot's seat.

I held my breath as we rattled down the grass runway, the plane shaking and quaking, and just when we got to the end, just when I thought we would drive straight into the high green grass, the nose of the plane rose up, and Duke pulled up sharp, and I felt the tail leave the ground. My ears popped and my head went light and spinny, and as the plane climbed higher and higher into the blue of the sky I dug my nails into the seat and shouted prayers to Jesus that I would make it back to earth.

At first I stared hard at the back of Duke's head, at the little gold-red hairs on his neck, at the flecks of gray here and there, at the freckles coming out of his shirt collar. After a while I forgot to hold on to the seat, and I glanced, quick as I could, out at the sky. I couldn't believe it. We were higher than any building. We were as high as the sun.

Duke flew the plane steady, no dips or spins this time. I breathed a little easier. Then I looked out over the earth and at the water and the mountains far in the distance, at the blue of the sky and the rays of the sun that cut the sky into shining, glowing stripes, and I felt the wind in my face and the stinging in my eyes. I thought of Carole Lombard again and then I pushed the thought away. Up here there was no looming mountainside to crash into. There wasn't any sadness or loss or even death. There was no guilt over Harley, no lost daddy, no dead mama, no faraway family, no worries, no fear. There was only sky and sun and wind and the earth spread out beneath me

I touched the controls once or twice, trying to get a feel for them, pretending I knew what to do and what they meant and how to fly this plane. I let my hands rest on the different switches and levers, hoping that something would come over me and suddenly I would start flying, like I'd known how to all along.

In the truck all the way back to the Lovelorn, I could still feel the light of the sky on my face, on my arms, in my chest. Johnny Clay talked and talked about what it felt like going up and how he couldn't wait to do it again and to one day jump out of planes bigger than that one. I listened to him just like I would if he was far away and I couldn't make out every word. I didn't say anything, just let him talk on and on, but I couldn't sit still. I kept hearing Ellen Tillman's voice: "Women pilots are a weapon waiting to be used."

In my mind I knew exactly how to use those controls. I was flying dangerous missions in the dark of night and rescuing soldiers that were dying or wounded or taken prisoner by the Germans.

THIRTEEN

*D*uke Norris chain-smoked Camels, his fingers stained brown from the tobacco, and he always seemed to be looking through us at something else, as if expecting to see someone come walking over the horizon. He never said much, but there was a kindness in his eyes underneath the shadow of dark circles and the sadness, and I decided he wasn't bad looking, in a faded, tired sort of way.

He could fly loops, barrel rolls, and spins in his yellow Aeronca Defender biplane. At our second lesson, one of the old men said that Duke's wife had died after stepping into the propeller on their honeymoon. He said Duke had become a full-time farmer then and that he shut the plane away in his barn. Sometime later—no one knew why—Duke started barnstorming, stunt flying, and air racing. He seemed to be daring the plane, punishing it, pushing himself to fly higher and faster and wilder. But he never had an accident. I wondered if he'd wanted to, if maybe he wanted to die just like his wife. The old man said Duke wanted to teach but no one would take lessons with him because they said he was cursed. I didn't know if he was cursed or not, but I thought he was romantic, and Johnny Clay thought it had just been some damn bad luck.

The Aeronca used gasoline from a car, and there were things about it that Johnny Clay said weren't allowed on new airplanes anymore—external wire braces, fabric construction, single-ignition engine, and no airspeed indicator. It had a 65-horsepower Continental engine, and the rear seat sat up higher than the front seat so you could see over the head of the pilot. You could also fly the plane from either position, front or back. Duke said it was almost impossible to make a rough landing in the Aeronca because it was a glider. Even if the ride itself was bumpy, coming down was smooth as could be.

The second time I went up, I took my turn before Johnny Clay. I sat behind Duke with my feet on the rudders, one hand on the throttle, and my other hand on the stick. Duke told me to follow his every move, and I did my best. The Aeronca bounced along the grass runway, propeller spinning, until suddenly it roared up into the air, banked to the left, and then swept into the deep blue of a clear August sky.

Just like before, the world opened up and I could see the green of Nashville spread out below like a blanket. We practiced level flight, climbing turns, and gliding, which all seemed pretty easy except that I couldn't keep my mind and eyes away from the earth. It was a different world up there—a world of blues and whites, gold streaks of sun bouncing off the propeller, color everywhere. I thought that the world looked different now that I'd been up there. I thought that maybe the world would always look different now, even when I was back on the ground.

At night I lay in my bed and pretended it was an airplane and that there was nothing below me but sky and earth and the green, flat grass of the runway. I closed my eyes and thought hard on it. I thought so hard that I could almost feel the wind on my face, the rumble and rattle of the engine, the pressure of the altitude closing in on my head, the shake of the throttle in my hand, and the cold metal of the wheel. I thought so hard that I could see the old men and Duke and Johnny Clay watching me from way down below, so far below that I couldn't make out the details of their faces. From the clouds, I waved at them, knowing I was only a speck to them—a yellow, zooming blur—just like they were only specks to me. And then I started to sing.

From that time on I practiced once a week, depending on the weather. Summer in Nashville was hot and rainy, which meant that more than once we had to sit inside with the old men, waiting for the

rain to let up and the sky to clear. Sometimes we played cards and
sometimes we just sat and listened to them talk about the Great War.
Lessons were three dollars an hour, and this took a good bit of my
earnings from the café, but even with that Johnny Clay and me spent
every Sunday at the airfield. Johnny Clay loved talking to the old men.
He asked them a million questions about their time in the war, and
they told us tale after tale about their adventures. He was learning to
fly himself, but Duke wouldn't let him jump from the Aeronca no
matter how much he pestered.

Because I was working most days, Johnny Clay went out to Duke's
some mornings to take lessons on his own. This meant that he earned
his solo time before I did—you had to have eight hours up in the air
with Duke before you could fly by yourself. I was mad and jealous, but
the one good thing about it was that Johnny Clay and I could now go
up in the Aeronca together, him flying and me sitting in the seat
behind.

At first he flew just like Duke had taught him—no spins or dives
or loops. Just gliding nice and peaceful over Duke's farm, and then
back around and down to the landing strip, steady as you please. Duke
stood on the ground, hands shoved in his pockets or on his hips, and
watched us with that gaze of his that didn't flinch or blink, no matter
what.

But about the third time up with just the two of us, Johnny Clay
decided to let loose. You could tell he just couldn't hold himself in
anymore. The first thing he did was fly off the regular path and take
us over the main road leading to Duke's and then beyond that to the
farms that spread out wide around it. He swooped down low over the
ground like a bird hunting for prey, and just when I thought he was
going to crash us headfirst into the earth he pulled up sharp and we
were back in the sky.

I let go of the stick and the throttle long enough to pinch his neck
hard. I hoped it left a bruise. Just for that, he took the plane into a
loop—first one, then another, then another, then another, until I
thought I was going to be sick on my stomach. I started yelling at him:
"Johnny Clay Hart! Dammit, Johnny Clay!"

He just laughed. And then he took the plane into a dive, and I leaned up to his ear and I yelled, "So help me Jesus, you better stop it right now."

He shouted, "I can't!"

"What do you mean, you can't?" I caught sight of his face, the part I could see from the side, and he looked scared. This terrified me because Johnny Clay was never scared in his life. I shouted, "Bring us up!"

He said, "I can't!"

Then I saw the fuel gauge. I pinched him again. "We're out of gas!" We were losing altitude fast. The little plane seemed to be picking up speed as it headed down, down, down.

He was pulling on the throttle, pulling on the wheel. He said, "What do I do? Shit, Velva Jean. Shit, shit, shit!"

I held on tight to the sides of the seat and leaned into the glass so that I could see the ground. Farms everywhere. Corn and high grass and barns and silos. I'd lost sight of Duke and the old men and the barn where he kept the airplane and the little cracker-tin building. And then, just ahead and to the right, I saw a pasture full of cows grazing. I shouted, "There! Take it down there! Can you land it?"

He peered to the right, and I knew he'd seen the pasture. He said, "Goddamn cows."

"Can you land it?!"

"Dammit, Velva Jean!" And then he swore a blue streak—words I'd never heard before, not even from my daddy when he'd had too much to drink. The nose of the plane was pointed straight down toward the ground, and I could tell Johnny Clay was freezing up, not sure what to do. Without thinking, I gripped hold of my controls and pumped the rudders and slammed the throttle and did my best to level her off. I felt like my arms were going to rip out of my sockets, but I held on hard as I could, leaning back into the seat with all my strength. I gritted my teeth so hard that I saw stars and I could taste blood where I'd bitten the inside of my cheek. Suddenly the nose of the plane started to inch upward, just like it was going through swamp water, and then it inched up a little more, a little more. We were still free-falling, but she was getting more level.

I steered us toward the pasture. We were coming down hard and fast, and I wondered if this was what it felt like to jump from a plane. I heard my brother's words: "Did you know that when a human body falls out of an airplane it takes eight and a half seconds to hit the ground?"

Eight and a half seconds . . . eight and a half seconds . . .

I shouted, "Hold on!" And I thought, What a stupid thing to say. Of course he was holding on. We were both holding on for life. As I struggled to land that little plane, I was thinking about everything that had happened to me so far—from Mama dying to Daddy leaving to the panther cat to Harley Bright to the Wood Carver to Butch Dawkins to learning to drive to recording my songs to leaving home and coming to Nashville. My whole life was going by like a newsreel only faster and faster, gathering speed, until the images were blurred and fuzzy.

The ground came toward us hard and fast, and I started praying. *Dear Jesus, please don't let us die. I don't want to die. Not like this. Not smashed against a pasture full of cows. I've got too much to do in this world. Please help me land this plane safe and, so help me, I will earn my leaving home.*

We bumped and bounced through the air, and I held on for dear life and kept up my prayers. And then suddenly—we were floating. For a second, I wondered if I was dead, and then I saw that we were just over the pasture and the plane was gliding fast, skimming the top of green, but we were smooth and steady. The cows scattered in a hundred directions, and then I felt the landing gear touch the ground once, twice, three times, and we were coasting fast through the pasture, wheels on the earth.

I thought about crying and then I slapped the back of Johnny Clay's head instead. I shouted, "Don't you ever do that again!"

Then I climbed out of the plane and nearly fell on my face because I was so mad and grateful to be alive and my legs didn't work. Johnny Clay jumped down, and I could tell he was a little wobbly, but he was grinning at me the same way he did after the panther got my leg—with admiration. He said, "Velva Jean, you just flew that plane."

I said, "Don't you even talk to me."

I kept the cows off the Aeronca while Johnny Clay hitched to the nearest farmhouse to beg for gasoline. "Shoo, cow, shoo." Every time I waved one away, another would come wandering up. They seemed to like the yellow of the plane. They stood there chewing grass and staring at me with their sad brown eyes and then they'd try to climb up on the wings. It was something to see, but we couldn't have a cow on the plane, so I ran round and round, hollering at them to stay back.

After about an hour, Johnny Clay came sauntering back, gas can in hand, whistling a tune. That was the thing about my brother. You couldn't rush him. You couldn't make him do anything he didn't want to do, even after we'd almost died.

As he poured the gasoline into the tank, he said, "We had ourselves an adventure, Velva Jean."

I didn't say anything because I still wasn't speaking to him.

He said, "Yes, sir. Feels good, don't it? After all this time? Good for the soul. Like running away from home and hopping the train and being chased by the panther cat. We was nearly killed but we weren't." He finished emptying the gas can and then he leaned back against the plane and ran one hand over his hair. He said, "Yes, sir." He closed his eyes and took in the sun.

I looked at him hard then and wanted to say something about how the last thing that was good for my soul was nearly dying in a field of cows, but he looked so gold and happy and peaceful, and suddenly I had a flash of him in uniform, jumping out of an airplane bigger than this one, carrying a gun, being shot at in some strange place by men that didn't even speak English. And I couldn't help it—I felt my heart go soft at the center. And then I thought: I flew an airplane. I landed an airplane. I saved our lives.

I said, "I'm glad you're here, Johnny Clay."

He opened one eye and said, "Don't you get sentimental on me." Then he went loping off toward the farmhouse, swinging the empty gas can. "Be right back," he hollered.

It was August 23—one year to the day since I arrived in Nashville—and getting close to time for him to go. We didn't talk about it, but I knew he didn't have much longer before he had to report for training. Every time I went up in the Aeronca I pretended he was in my plane, getting ready to jump out of it, and that I was making it my duty to know that plane as good as I could so that nothing at all could ever go wrong.

One of the cows shuffled up to me and stood, not blinking, just chewing and watching my face. I said, "Shoo, cow." We stood there looking at each other and finally I said, "I don't know what I'd do if anything happened to him." The cow just chewed and stared. As I stood there staring back, a great heaviness gathered around me till I wondered if that little plane would be able to even get off the ground to carry us back to Duke's.

FOURTEEN

On Saturday August 29, Gossie and Marvina and Harold Lee and Johnny Clay and me went to Bootsy's to hear Travelin' Jones's band, only now that he was gone to war one of the other men was leading it. I sat there feeling blue over Johnny Clay leaving soon and also blue over Charlie Jones being off to war. I touched my lips, remembering when he kissed me.

Tommie Lou had left for the Red Cross on Wednesday, but Marvina wasn't going till the next week. She was leaning in close to Johnny Clay, swinging her crossed leg in his direction, every now and then bumping him with her foot. Harold Lee had a stack of napkins and he was writing down lyrics and passing them to me. Gossie was looking around at the Wall of Fame and pointing out all the people up there that we didn't recognize. She said, "Each one has a story, and just think of all those stories we'll never know."

Marvina perked up at this because she loved stories. She said, "Let's make up a story for everyone."

And she and Gossie started doing that very thing. "Unwed mother. From Topeka. Left her baby to come out here and chase her dream. Stayed two years, but went back home after getting her heart broke and only recording one song. Now works in a bank." Or: "Oldest of twelve. Never had anything for himself. Was barefoot when he first got here, but someone heard him singing on Church Street, trying to earn money enough for shoes, and that someone recorded his first record."

The whole time the band played and they talked and Marvina swung her foot and Harold Lee wrote on napkins, Johnny Clay sat looking up at the pictures. Suddenly he grabbed my hand and pulled me up and said, "Come on, Velva Jean." The girls and Stump were staring.

I said, "Where are we going?"

He said, "You'll see."

And with a wink at Bootsy herself, he dragged me outside the lounge and into the street and next door to where the photo booth was, in an old musty-smelling store that sold cigars and headache powder.

He said, "We're going to take a picture before I go."

I felt my heart clinch up. I said, "When are you going?" And I was sorry I asked it because I didn't want to hear the answer.

He waved my question away with his hand. "We need something to remember us, Velva Jean."

We sat down side by side in the photo booth and tried to figure out how to work it. There were some buttons and a lever and a place to put money. Johnny Clay pulled out his wallet and when he dug for money, I saw the paratrooper picture from *Life* magazine still folded and tucked away. He shoved his wallet back into his pocket and then he slid a quarter into the machine and there was a clicking and then a flashing bright light. He threw his arm around me, and we bent our heads together so they were touching, and he said, "Smile, Velva Jean."

The light flashed and then popped, and I was nearly blind. Then it was over and we sat there waiting for the photograph to develop. I thought, What would Granny say if she could see this?

I said, "I don't believe it."

Johnny Clay said, "Just you watch."

About five minutes later there was a spitting and a whirring and a grinding—like the booth was gearing itself up to run away—and then out came our picture.

I'd never seen a picture of myself before. It was good of both of us—Johnny Clay looked big as life, handsome and laughing, a little bit blurred, and just like Daddy around the mouth and Mama around the eyes.

I sat there looking at myself. I couldn't get over it. Was this the way I looked? The face in the picture was different than the face in the mirror, and I wondered if this was because you just looked different in pictures or if it was because I'd only seen myself backward till now, like the way the mirror reflected you.

My hair looked too wild. My eyes too big. My smile too wide. I could see my freckles still, even though I was all the time trying to cover them up with powder and a bit of rouge. I wasn't sure about me.

One thing I did know though: I looked happy, and I knew that came from being with my brother. I thought we actually looked a lot alike—I don't think I'd ever noticed it. I looked like Daddy around the mouth and Mama around the eyes too.

Johnny Clay said, "You look like Hedy Lamarr, Velva Jean," and before I could tell him he was crazy he grabbed the picture and fanned it to wave it dry. Then he went marching back over to Bootsy's and right up to Bootsy herself and handed her the photo. He said, "This is for your Wall of Fame." She liked Johnny Clay just like everyone did. She cackled at this like a summer hen and then she stood up on her little fat feet and whistled to the bartender. She said, "Get me a tack."

He rummaged around behind the bar and then tossed her one, which she caught one-handed. Then she stood there staring at the walls, eyes narrowed, trying to find just the place. By this time Gossie and Marvina and Harold Lee were staring at us and Gossie raised her hands, palms up, like "what's going on?"

Bootsy said, "Over here." She moved between the tables without bumping a single person. There was a spot right over the jukebox that was easy to see no matter where you sat. It was practically the first thing you saw when you walked in the door. She said, "There." And then she leaned up on her tippy-toes and tacked the picture to the wall, right in the middle of all the pictures of Eddy Arnold and Roy Acuff and Bill Monroe and Maybelle Carter, not to mention the hundreds of folks with names I'd never learn. Johnny Clay helped her tap the thumbtack in, and then we all three stood back. I felt someone over my shoulder, and Gossie was standing there, arms folded across her chest.

Bootsy said, "Right where you belong."

Gossie said, "Now there's a story, Mary Lou."

~

On September 6 I went up for my first solo flight. It was almost dusk on a warm, muggy day. The old men sat outside, fanning themselves with the playing cards and drinking lemonade. Johnny Clay lay stretched out on the ground, hands folded behind his head, eyes closed. I couldn't tell if he was awake or asleep. Duke went over the plane again and again—the safety belt, the throttle, the rudders, the engine, the wings. I thought he looked worried.

Finally he helped me up into the cockpit even though I didn't need help. He watched as I snapped on my safety belt and pulled on my goggles. He leaned forward and tugged at the belt. He said, "You've got the hours. Are you sure you're ready?"

I thought how funny this was because in his quiet way he'd always made me believe I could fly even when I didn't believe it myself.

I said, "I'm ready."

The Aeronca had stiff controls and a narrow cockpit. I thought I would feel hemmed in up there, but as I took off at forty miles an hour—a little shaky at first—the sky just opened up like it always did. I was going so fast I could hardly tell I was airborne, but then I saw the ground far below and I was part of the sky. I suddenly felt like I was flying myself, just me with my arms out, no plane, no safety belt. The first thing I noticed was how light the plane seemed without another person in it.

I circled over Duke's farm, over trees and house and barn. The evening air was quiet and there were long, blue shadows over the grass. Darkness was creeping in along the outside of the sky, just along the horizon, but the sun still burned orange and gold and pink. As I flew I imagined myself as a soldier, flying somewhere over England or France, swooping down to make a daring rescue, circling the enemy. I pretended I was off to fight the Germans and Hitler and end the war once and for all for everyone, most of all my brothers.

That night, during supper at the café, Johnny Clay told everybody how I flew that plane all by myself. I felt jumpy as a cricket and twice as excited, and later, after we went upstairs, I sat in my room and got out Mama's Bible, where I kept records of everything I'd ever done in my life, good things and bad things, and dusted off the cover. I could still feel the light of the sky high above Duke's farm and feel myself drifting over the trees and earth.

The last entry in the Bible was from August 22, 1941: "Velva Jean . . ." It was from the day I left home, and I hadn't known what to write then so I left it blank. Now, on the page where I had already written so many important life events, I wrote "September 6, 1942—Velva Jean learns to fly."

Three days later Johnny Clay left Nashville. I drove him to the train station and walked him inside, even though he told me not to. We said things as we walked, like "Tell Duke good-bye for me," and "Let me know if you run into Linc or Beach or Coyle Deal," and "Remember to keep your nose up when you're flying—you always keep it too low," and "Write me when you get there."

They were announcing his train when we got to the tracks, and Johnny Clay said, "Well, little sister . . ." And before he could finish, I threw my arms around him and hugged him tight. He just stood there like a tree, and after a minute he dropped his bag and he hugged me back and we were both crying—me a lot, him a little.

I said, "Don't you get yourself killed, Johnny Clay Hart."

And he said, "I promise."

Then he pushed me away and grabbed up his bag and ran. I watched him moving away from me fast, boarding a train to Toccoa, Georgia, where they would turn him into a paratrooper, a soldier, a fighter. He swung himself up into the boxcar and before he disappeared inside he saluted me. His face was shiny from the tears and he looked gold in the sunlight.

I wanted to run after him—to get on that train and follow him to camp, and then even follow him to Italy or Germany or France. But instead I stood still, rooted to the ground, and saluted back.

September 13, 1942

Dear V. J.,

Goddamn Georgia. I'm pretty sure hell will be like this. We call this place Camp Tombs on account of the casket factory up the way, and let me tell you it's just the right name for it. The camp is ugly as Hink Lowe. There's mud everywhere, even in the tents. We're four to a tent, and the mosquitoes are as big as Mrs. Garland Welch's behind.

We're up at dawn and every damn morning we do this run up Currahee Mountain. It's three miles up and three miles down. Sometimes we run it once in the morning and then again in the afternoon in full dress gear in this goddamn rotten Georgia heat.

"We're going to separate the men from the boys," company commander Lieutenant Peter Flick told us on our first day of training. One man dropped in the first mile. I kept going with the rest of them even though my legs stung and my lungs burned and I wanted to kill someone. Maybe that's the idea. It's each for his own here, and I ain't helping nobody that can't help himself. When we got back to camp later that night, the bags of the men who'd dropped were already packed.

When I run up the mountain, I stare at the head of the guy in front of me. I pick one who ain't going to drop. You can tell which ones will do it, just by looking at them. Already fifteen guys of the original fifty-six have gone home. Not me.

Wanna know what else I do? I tell myself, "Just one more step. One more step. One more step." I say it over and over in my head while I run. It sounds stupid, but just telling myself "one more step" makes me keep going. I say to myself, "You think you're going to die and you might, but just run one more step before you do." After all, you can't run them all at once.

Most of the fellows are fine. Some are from the South and others are from New York, California, Pennsylvania, Ohio, Missouri. This guy Mickey Gorham, from Boston, is the worst though. He was calling me "cracker" till I told him exactly what I would do to him if I ever heard the word "cracker" come out of his mouth again. We're friends now. It's usually his head I look at when I run. Part of me would still like to knock it in.

I know you're mad at me because I ain't heard from you. I know you're just freezing me out and that you still love me even though you don't want to, but someday you'll understand why I needed to go and why it's so important to me to do this. Our own daddy's always run away from everything big or hard, but you know me. I believe in taking things head-on.

Did you hear about Beach? He had to take over his plane when the pilot and copilot was killed. Shot down four enemy planes and one Jap bomber over in a place called Guadalcanal, and he ain't even carrying a weapon because he's a noncombatant.

Tomorrow we begin jump training from ground level mock airplanes, but I'm ready for a real one. I don't know when we'll be done with all this and when they'll ship us out, but I can't wait to see the faces of the enemy and the fear in their eyes—whoever they are—when they see me coming.

Love,

Private Johnny Clay Hart

P.S. The FBI arrested 158 German nationals living in the United States because they was endangering state security. And 30 of them are women. Spies!

FIFTEEN

On September 20 Duke handed me the latest issue of *Life* magazine. There was a picture on the cover of a girl, not much older than me, wearing goggles and standing in front of an airplane. He said, "I want you to take this home and read it. You're one of the best natural pilots I ever seen. You're a regular Amelia Earhart."

This was the most I'd heard Duke say all at once since the very first time I met him and he talked to me about how if I could drive a truck I could fly a plane. I stood there waiting, just in case there was more, but then he turned toward the Aeronca, and I knew that meant it was time to go up.

We flew for an hour—Duke was teaching me spins—and after we came down I ran to the truck holding the magazine close, just like it might get away from me. The old men sat outside the cracker-tin building, spitting and arguing and playing cards, and because I didn't want them to call out to me or bother me I drove fast as I could back to the Lovelorn, the magazine burning a hole in the seat next to me the whole way.

I parked just down the street and then I sat there under the streetlamp and read. The article told about two government programs started for women pilots, the Women's Auxiliary Ferrying Squadron, or WAFS, and the Women's Flying Training Detachment, or WFTD. The WAFS was started by a woman named Nancy Harkness Love. There was a picture of her in the story, and she was beautiful even in her flying gear and goggles. She learned to fly when she was sixteen, and when she was at Vassar College in New York she earned extra money by renting a plane and taking her fellow students for rides. One time she flew low over campus, and someone turned her in. She was suspended for two weeks and not allowed to fly for the rest of the semester. Nancy Love had handpicked the top twenty-five women pilots in the country to ferry military planes to training camps and airfields across the United States. They'd just flown their first mission, flying Piper Cubs from Pennsylvania to New York.

The WFTD was created by Jacqueline Cochran, who was America's most famous woman pilot and the first and only woman to fly a bomber across the Atlantic Ocean. She owned a cosmetics company, and it was her husband who suggested that she learn to fly so she could market her cosmetics around the country. She became good friends with Amelia Earhart and believed that women pilots could be trained to do more than ferrying, that maybe they could even fly in combat. The training school for the WFTD was in Houston, Texas, where the first classes of pilots were being taught to fly the army way, while living in barracks and wearing uniforms and practicing drills. I thought she looked like a more glamorous Sweet Fern.

I couldn't read the article fast enough. My eyes started traveling up and down the page, across it, back and forth. I kept thinking, This is too unbelievable. The girls in the pictures looked like me—young and happy and normal, like they'd just come from anywhere, maybe up in the mountains or a small town or a farm in the middle of nowhere. I looked at them and thought, I could be one of them.

But these girls had already been chosen. The WAFS and the WFTD already had their female pilots. I imagined them first learning to fly at fancy air bases in Washington, D.C., or New York City or Los Angeles, California. They must have had hundreds of hours of experience. They must have been flying for years.

Then I saw the last few sentences of the story, which Duke had underlined twice with a thick black pen: "The first class of twenty-eight recruits from the WFTD will be reporting to Houston on November 17, but the WFTD is looking for more girl pilots for future classes. Interested ladies should contact Jacqueline Cochran."

The *Life* article said the WFTD had originally required two hundred hours of solo flying time but that they'd just lowered the requirement to thirty-five hours. I had twenty-five hours, but I wondered if that might be enough. The article also said girls had to be at least five feet two inches tall, a high school graduate, and twenty-one years old. I was only nineteen and I hadn't gone to school past the seventh grade, but I was five feet six, almost five feet seven, and I thought those extra inches should count for something.

The next morning Harold Lee left for training camp. He was headed to North Carolina and he was as wound up as a cat. He jigged and jittered in place till I wondered if he might not dance all the way there. We stood outside the café, just me and him—he'd already said good-bye to everyone else. He had his duffel bag over his shoulder and he was on his way to the train station. He handed me a poem and he said, "Will you wait for me, Velva Jean?"

I tried to laugh, but the sight of him in his uniform, his dog tags hanging around his skinny neck, that Adam's apple bobbing up and down, made me sad. I said, "Harold Lee, you just keep yourself safe."

"You won't even try to love me, will you?"

I said, "Not like you want me to." I felt like the world's worst person. I thought how easy my life would be if I could only love Harold Lee. For one second I tried to imagine it in my mind, but I couldn't. I wondered if I would all the time love the wrong men.

He said, "I love you, Velva Jean." And then he kissed me quick on the mouth and hugged me tight and spun away at a sprint up the street, just a blur of legs and arms, disappearing into the crowd of people that always seemed to be walking down the sidewalks no matter what time of day or night.

I watched him go and then I looked down at the poem he'd handed me. It was written, as usual, on a Lovelorn Café napkin. It was called "From a Soldier," and not one word of it rhymed.

> *This boy is going to fight for his country*
> *In a war with people he's never met*

He's going to have to kill
And bleed
In a place he's never heard of
But he wants you to remember
That you knew him once
And that he loved you
And that he was here.

I folded up the napkin and slipped it into my dress pocket, and went up the stairs to my apartment and into my room and sat down at my desk in front of my typewriter.

September 21, 1942

Dear Jacqueline Cochran,

My name is Velva Jean Hart. My flight instructor sent me an article from *Life* magazine about the WFTD, and I would like to apply. I now have twenty-five hours of solo flying time. My teacher, Duke Norris, says he's never seen anyone take so natural to flying, and he's been flying for twenty years. I am five feet six inches tall, and I will be twenty on my next birthday.

Last year I taught myself to drive an old yellow truck that came to me when my brother-in-law was killed in a train wreck. It was his truck and then it was my brother's and now it's mine. No one helped me learn to drive. I did it all on my own, and then I drove that truck from Alluvial, North Carolina, to Nashville so that I could be a singer at the Grand Ole Opry. I've wanted to sing ever since I was a little girl. But now there's something I want to do more—fly.

Please consider me for the WFTD. I promise not to let you down.

Yours sincerely,

Velva Jean Hart

After that I stopped writing to Judge Hay at the Opry and started writing to Jacqueline Cochran. I wrote her at least one letter every week, even though she didn't write me back. When I wasn't writing to her and when I wasn't working, I went out to Duke's farm and earned more solo hours up in the Aeronca, just so I would be ready.

October 9, 1942

Dear Jacqueline Cochran,

I read that you came from a poor background, like me, that you were an orphan too, that you had to go to work when you were eight years old, and that you chose your name out of a telephone directory. You didn't go to high school, and you passed your flight test without even knowing how to write. I know you grew up in Florida. I may be from North Carolina, but I think we come from the same place.

I got married when I was sixteen years old. I thought I knew what was going to happen with my husband when I fell in love with him. I thought we were going to be together forever, Mr. and Mrs. Harley Bright, but sometimes things don't work out like you think. I thought there was a guarantee.

Same with the Grand Ole Opry. My whole life I've pictured myself up on that stage, wearing rhinestones and satin and playing the steel guitar. For all these years, it was never like I was dreaming it up, but like I was seeing what was going to happen in the future. Like it was predestined, and all I had to do was wait till it was time. I left my husband and went to Nashville to make that happen but I still haven't sung at the Opry. So is it predestined? I don't know anymore. Maybe it's just a dream that will never come true, and I was only fooling myself.

Now I'm in Nashville and I thought this was where I needed to be. But I don't need to be here anymore. I need to be Out There, as my mama called it—living Out There. She didn't know back then, before she died, that I would ever fly a plane. I was just ten years old. But maybe she did know somehow and maybe she meant that Out There was in the sky, high above the clouds.

All I'm asking for is a chance.

By the way, I now have thirty-two hours of solo flying time.

Sincerely,

Velva Jean Hart

―――――――

October 18, 1942

Dear V. J.,

You can tell by the address that I've moved again. That's right—no more Camp Tombs. Fort Benning may still be Georgia, but it's a high time compared to Toccoa. Here we got big brick barracks and beautiful big mess halls. The PX at Camp Toccoa only had cigarettes and chocolate bars, but the one here's got everything you could ever want on this earth.

We're in such top condition that our company got to skip the first stage of jump school—the only goddamn company in the airborne to do so. It's double time here everywhere we go. We got parachute towers like we did at Toccoa, except here we got a device that draws you up and lets you go.

The best thing about Benning, though, is the jumps. I never loved doing anything so much in my life. I mean it. I wish you would jump out of a plane and see what I'm talking about. It beats gold panning and gem mining and roping steers.

Did the army make you a pilot yet?

Love,

Your brother,
Corporal Johnny Clay Hart

―――――――

Headquarters
Army Air Forces Training Command
Fort Worth, Texas

October 25, 1942
Miss Velva Jean Hart
c/o The Lovelorn Café
Nashville, Tennessee

Dear Miss Hart:

Will interview applicants for the Women's Flying Training Program at the Nashville, Tennessee, military recruitment center on November 19 and 20, between 9:00 a.m. and 4:00 p.m.

It is suggested that you bring your logbook and student pilot's license at time of interview and be prepared to undergo a medical examination by an army flight surgeon.

If your papers are in order and you successfully pass your medical examination, you will receive official instructions as to when and where to report.

Yours very truly,

Jacqueline Cochran, Director
Women's Flying Training Detachment

SIXTEEN

On Thursday, November 19, I walked to the recruitment office. I sang the whole way there, not caring who heard me, because I hoped it would calm me down. Inside the office there were so many girls that it took me two hours to have my turn. While I was waiting, I talked to some of them and compared flying times.

One girl said, "You should pad your logbook. That's what we done." She pointed to herself and the two girls she was sitting with. "Unless you got thirty-five hours of signed time, they ain't even going to look at you."

I said, "I've got thirty-nine hours." As I said it, I sat up a little straighter.

She said, "How old are you?"

"Twenty." I didn't tell her I'd only turned twenty just two weeks before.

"Well, you got to be twenty-one at least. You been to college?"

"No."

"High school?"

"No." I wasn't sitting up so straight anymore.

She shook her head. "You better add more flying hours so they don't just send you home."

I said, "I'm not padding my book."

She said, "Now's not the time to be a good Christian girl. You need to put that aside and think of what's at stake here. Do you or do you not want to be a pilot?" I looked at her and at the other girls, who nodded. One of them handed me a pen.

I went into the bathroom and padded my logbook till it said I had fifty-five hours and then I came back and took my place in line. I felt filled up with guilt but at the same time there was nothing else to do. I was sure that Jacqueline Cochran's people would take one look at my book and know I was lying.

When it was my turn, I sat down at a desk with Miss Henrietta Novak, who was close to forty, with short brown hair and skin that was freckled from the sun. She was what Daddy Hoyt would have called a "handsome woman"—thick as a Christmas goose and wearing a crisp khaki uniform. She gave me a questionnaire to fill out and then asked me a hundred questions about flying and where I'd gone to school and why did I want to join the WFTD, and then she looked over my logbook while I held my breath and said a quick prayer that she wouldn't know I cheated.

Then a female army surgeon measured me to see how tall I was, and afterward she made me stand on a scale. She listened to my heartbeat and checked my pulse and looked into my ears and eyes and throat. She said, "Everything looks good, Miss Hart."

I'd stopped calling myself Mrs. Bright long ago. I hadn't felt like Mrs. Bright in a very long time. Part of me wondered, though, if the government would know I was married. If they did, maybe they would think I was lying on the rest of my application if I didn't put Harley's last name, since I was still his wife. I wondered if I should tell the army surgeon the truth.

After my exam, the surgeon led me back to Henrietta Novak. I sat down across from her and thought about how I wasn't Miss Hart, I was still Mrs. Bright, whether I liked it or not. Miss Novak said, "Miss Hart, you passed the physical, but I'm concerned about your lack of education and your age. Your letter from Duke Norris is one of the most glowing references I've ever read. But we have certain rules and requirements in place for a reason."

All I could think was: Miss Hart, Miss Hart.

I said, "I wanted to go to school past the seventh grade, but my mama died and my daddy ran off, leaving my sister to raise us, and she needed me at home to help with all her babies and so she made me quit even though I loved my teacher, Mrs. Dennis, very much." It made me sad to think of Mrs. Dennis being run out of town with her husband and the rest of the outlanders by Harley Bright.

I thought: Mrs. Bright, Mrs. Bright.

"But I read every book I could get my hands on, even though Sweet Fern didn't approve."

Miss Novak said, "I'm going to need to discuss this with the director of the program." She ruffled through the papers on her desk. I saw the stack of letters I'd written to Jacqueline Cochran, or copies of them. Miss Novak skimmed over these and tapped them with her finger, and then she stacked them into a neat pile and cleared her throat. She said, "It says here, Miss Hart, that you taught yourself to drive."

"Yes'm," I said. "And to take apart an engine and put it back together again. I can do the same thing with an airplane." This wasn't exactly true, but I had studied the Aeronca's engine manual and I figured I could take a plane apart if I had to.

Miss Novak sat back and looked at me, crossing her arms over her chest and her uniform. I wanted a uniform just like it. I thought it was about the smartest thing I'd ever seen.

Finally she said, "Classes are filled five months ahead. You see all these other girls here? Every one of them has hours of flying instruction. They're all good pilots, maybe as good as you, maybe better. But we don't have room for all of them."

Each word she said made my heart sink low into my chest, so far to the back of it that I couldn't even feel it anymore. I looked around me at the other girls and I thought about my padded logbook and how these other girls, some of them, probably had more hours than I did and had more right than me to earn a spot in the WFTD, and here I sat like a liar, like some sort of mountain trash, trying to cheat my way into being a pilot.

Miss Novak said, "It's a risky business, and you need to know that. You need to know that flying is dangerous, no matter how good a pilot you are, and that accidents happen all the time and there's always the chance of an accident being fatal. Every time you go up in the air, you're taking a risk."

I said, "I know that." I couldn't stand to be a liar. I didn't want that logbook on my mind five more seconds. I said, "Could I have my logbook please?"

She said, "Excuse me?"

"Just for a minute."

She handed it to me, but she was looking at me like I'd just gotten up and buck danced on her desk.

I said, "Can I borrow a pen?"

She searched her desk and found one. I took it from her and then I opened my book and crossed out the hours I'd added, the ones I never actually flew. Then I handed her the book and said, "That's the real truth. I don't want to get into this program on a lie. I'd rather not get in at all. I padded my logbook, and I'm sorry, but only because I want this more than anything I ever wanted in my life, except for my mama not to die. I'm sorry I lied to you."

"I'm sure you're not the first or the only."

I didn't say anything to this because it was true. What I did say was, "There's something else I need to tell you. My name is Velva Jean Hart Bright. I'm married, so I guess you should be calling me Mrs. Bright and not Miss Hart. I left my husband to go to Nashville and I don't feel married anymore, not for a long time. I don't feel married one bit. But you should know the truth all around, so you can call me what you want."

Henrietta Novak said, "You don't need your husband to sign for you. You don't need his approval to be here."

I said, "That's a good thing, but I thought you should know just the same."

Henrietta Novak looked at me good and hard. Then she said, "I can't promise anything, Miss Hart, but let me see what I can do."

———

**Headquarters
Army Air Forces Training Command
Fort Worth, Texas**

December 10, 1942
Miss Velva Jean Hart
c/o The Lovelorn Café
Nashville, Tennessee

Dear Miss Hart:

Congratulations on being accepted into the WFTD. Please report to the Blue Bonnet Hotel in Sweetwater, Texas, on Saturday, February 13, 1943. Further instructions will be forthcoming.

Yours very truly,

Jacqueline Cochran, Director
Women's Flying Training Detachment

SEVENTEEN

On December 19 I went to the Opry one last time, and Gossie went with me. We paid our twenty-five cents and sat in the crowd, and I breathed it all in. As Roy Acuff stood up there with his guitar, sing-ing "Red River Valley," I sang along. The people on both sides of us turned, and I knew they were watching me but I didn't care. I sang harmony, and after a minute Gossie joined in. I sang like I was stand-ing on top of the Stahlman Building, the tallest building in Nashville, or like I was up in the Aeronca. I didn't know when I would see Roy Acuff again and I didn't know when I'd see the inside of the War Memorial Auditorium. Maybe I wouldn't ever be back here, and maybe I would, but, just in case, I wanted to be able to say I'd sung at the Grand Ole Opry.

Afterward we went home to the apartment, and Gossie poured us a drink. We clinked our glasses together, and I said, "You're the best friend I ever had outside my own family, Beryl Goss. I hope I see you again."

Before she could hide it, her eyes turned to water, and she took a fast drink and pulled out a cigarette and started puffing away. She said, "Dammit, Mary Lou. The things you say." And then she took my hand and squeezed it.

Later I stood in my room and looked at my bed, my window, my desk, my chair. My first very own room. The framed Opry picture that Johnny Clay had given me was still hung up on the wall. I pulled it down and packed it into the hatbox. Someday, I thought. Maybe.

~

"It's a funny thing about a road," Daddy Hoyt used to say to me. "It's not just an incoming road, you know. It's an outgoing road too." It felt funny to be incoming again, when the last time I was on the Scenic I was heading out, the only thought in my mind go, go, go, and no idea if I'd ever be back.

On December 23 the snow was hitting the windshield, the flakes like flimsy white stars, turning to water as soon as the wipers brushed them away. Through the snow and the wet and the fog that was rolling in, I strained to see Fair Mountain. It was harder to tell the mountains apart in winter. They were a mass of smoke and snow, the dark black-green of the trees, and the raggedy sharp brown of the rock.

The Scenic was paved the whole way now, all the way to the turnoff for Hamlet's Mill. All that new black road was being covered in white. In my head I heard the song I'd sung as I first left home.

Oh, they tell me of a land far beyond the skies.
Oh, they tell me of a land far away.
Oh, they tell me of a land where no storm clouds rise.
Oh, they tell me of an unclouded day . . .

Nashville was that land beyond the skies for me. I hadn't sung at the Opry, not really, not like I'd dreamed I would. But I was going to be a pilot in the WFTD. The moment I got the letter from Jacqueline Cochran I knew I wanted to see my family before I went to Texas.

When I came to the turnoff for Hamlet's Mill, I pointed the truck down the hill and headed home. And then I saw them rising up in front of me and around me and above me—my mountains. Bone. Witch. Blood. Devil's Courthouse, where somewhere Harley Bright was preaching or eating or sleeping. And Fair Mountain, where my family was just this minute waiting without knowing they were waiting.

At the sight of Fair Mountain, I gripped the wheel tighter and leaned forward, trying to keep my eyes on the road and also on my mountain. My eyes were burning, which meant I might start crying.

And then I did start crying, but it didn't matter because there was no one to see me. Night was falling up on the Scenic—only the snow caught what was left of the sunlight and made everything seem brighter. I knew that down below, deep in the valleys, in Alluvial and Sleepy Gap and Devil's Kitchen, the sky would already be dark under the shadows of the trees and the fog.

I passed through Hamlet's Mill and then I followed the old cattle road up to Alluvial. It looked exactly the same as when I left it, except for the snow. I slowed the truck as I passed the hotel where Lucinda Sink lived, the school where I'd gone through the seventh grade, the Baptist church, Deal's General Store, Sweet Fern's house that Danny Deal built for her before he died. Everything looked the same except for the two blue stars hanging in the window of Deal's and the one blue star in the window at Sweet Fern's—one star for each boy fighting in the war.

I wound up the mountain to Sleepy Gap until I could see the roof of Mama's old house. My throat closed up tight at the sight of it. Outside the house, a girl with spindly legs and long brown hair was building a snowman while a tall boy I didn't recognize was chasing Russell with a snowball. The tall boy had brown hair and was wearing a blue cap, one that I knew from long ago. It was Danny Deal's cap, the one he'd lost in the train wreck and that someone—our daddy—had brought back. The boy must be Dan Presley, Sweet Fern's oldest, and the girl, I knew was Corrina. For a minute I studied them, thinking they were nearly the same ages Johnny Clay and me were when we were living here, just before Mama died. I thought: What if that was us? What if I was watching this and suddenly Mama came walking onto the porch, calling us in for supper? That was the thing about Fair Mountain. No matter how much the rest of the world changed, it looked so much the same that it took you a minute to remember what year it was and how old you were and who was still there and who was gone.

I drove up to the house, slow and steady, and Corrina looked up and squinted because the fading sun was behind me, and then she hollered and ran right into Mama's house and then came back out. A tall, gray-haired woman ran out behind her, and it was Aunt Zona, and she was crying and wiping her hands on her apron, and it hit me all over again how little she looked like Mama even though they were sisters. Just past Zona, looking over her shoulder, were two round girls with wide matching faces. These were the twins, Celia Faye and Clover. And pushing past all of them was Granny.

She ran right for the truck, arms flapping, white hair flying. She hollered, "Velva Jean, honey! Darlin' girl!"

I parked the truck and shut off the engine and threw open the door and ran straight for her over the snow. Then her arms were around me, wiry but strong, and she was hugging me tight and practically lifting me off the ground even though she was so small. She held me at arm's length and looked me up and down and said, "You're too thin. Don't they feed you in Tennessee?" And then her eyes went watery and she cupped my face with her hand and said, "Just as pretty as you ever were."

I said, "I'm home," because I couldn't think of anything else to say.

We ate supper that night at Granny's—Granny, Daddy Hoyt, Ruby Poole, Aunt Zona, the twins, Aunt Bird, the children, and Sweet Fern, who walked up the hill from Alluvial, carrying baby Hoyt on her hip. I met her on the front porch, out on the dogtrot that ran between the two parts of Granny's house. There were four blue stars hanging in the front window—one each for Linc, Beach, and Johnny Clay. The fourth one, I guessed, was for Coyle.

Little Hoyt had light-brown hair like his daddy, lighter than Sweet Fern's, and it curled in ringlets all over his head. Sweet Fern looked tired and older and when she saw me her face went blank. For one minute I was scared of her, just like I had been when I was little. I felt like I felt when I was twelve and I ran away from home and from her, and the panther chased me through the woods, me and Johnny Clay dressed only in our underthings. I thought of every time I'd made her mad—from almost getting arrested and thrown in jail to running away.

She walked right up onto the dogtrot and pulled me close and hugged me hard with her free arm and when she pulled away she was blinking and blinking, which was what she always did when she tried not to cry. She said, "I'm glad you're home, Velva Jean." Her lips were bare and their normal pink, and I remembered the lipstick she'd started wearing before I left for Nashville.

I said, "I'm sorry I didn't say good-bye." She frowned and brushed away an imaginary strand of hair. She bounced Hoyt on her hip and stared hard at the top of his head.

She said, "You know I went to camp with Coyle, me and the children. When it was time for him to ship out, we took the bus back. It was a hard, awful trip, one I wouldn't have wished on anyone." Her eyes got sad and mad all at once. She said, "Everyone at camp and on the bus called me a 'camp follower,' which is what they call women that follow their husbands to camp. They said it like they wanted to spit, just like they say 'Nazi' or 'Jap,' so you know it's not a nice thing. I don't see why it's bad to want to spend as much time with your husband as you can before he goes off to war where you may never see him again." She wore a little cross on a chain around her neck, and she didn't touch it but I could feel her touching it in her mind. "Coming back, I thought everything would be better, but it's all so strange here now. There are holes everywhere. But we're doing okay, the children and me."

I said, "I'm sorry I wasn't here for your wedding."

She said, "It was pretty. Simple." Then she got that old mad look that I knew so well. Her face took on a pink color, and I could almost see the top of her head start to smoke. She said, "I hope you ain't come back for Harley Bright because if so I've got a thing or two to say to you, Velva Jean." Then, before I could open my mouth, she said, "You listen to me. Mama's gone and Daddy's gone, but I'm here now, and I reckon I'm about the closest thing you have to a mama, like it or not. And strange as it sounds, I need you to go away again and get off this mountain. I was mad at you plenty when you went off last year and didn't so much as tell me good-bye, but now I need you to be free because that's what you were born to do, Velva Jean. If you don't go, why did I work so hard to raise you? Why did you fight me so much back then over every little thing? Why did we even waste our time if it didn't mean anything?"

I said, "I'm going to be a pilot in the WFTD. I'm going to train with Jacqueline Cochran, the most famous woman pilot in the world. I'm going to fly planes for the war. I go to Texas in February."

She stood there blinking at me. Then she nodded her head once, like this was exactly what she wanted to hear. She said, "You can't be rooted, Velva Jean."

In her arms, Hoyt said, "Doggy!" And pointed to Johnny Clay's old brown dog, Hunter Firth, who was lying on a corner of the porch. Hunter Firth fanned his tail back and forth without moving or looking up.

Supper was spent talking about my trip to Nashville, the Opry, meeting Gossie, the Lovelorn Café, Travelin' Jones, Darlon C. Reynolds, Johnny Clay's visit, learning to fly, and about being chosen for the WFTD. I sat there looking around the table at the faces of my family and feeling filled up in a way I hadn't felt filled up since I'd left.

After supper Daddy Hoyt and I sat on the porch while everyone else did the dishes and cleared the table and drank tea by the fire because there wasn't any coffee to be found. I pulled a blanket around me and tried not to the feel the cold, but Daddy Hoyt sat there in his shirtsleeves. He never seemed to feel the chill like the rest of us.

The snow covered everything now. It fell heavy and quiet, but if you listened, tuning out the sounds from inside the house or the creaking of the rockers, you could hear a million little ice crystals touching down. The trees were icing over and, except for the falling snow, the whole world grew still, just like we were sitting under a tent, the edges pulled down tight around us so that nothing could get in or out.

It felt strange to be rocking there on that porch just like no time had passed, just like I'd never gone away and tried to sing at the Opry and make a record, just like I'd never worked at the Lovelorn Café and met a girl named Beryl Goss and gone to juke joints and honky-tonks and learned to fly.

Daddy Hoyt cleared his throat and said, "Daryl Gordon was killed in November."

"Where?"

"A place in the Pacific called Bataan."

I said, "Have you heard from Beach?"

"He's in the Solomon Islands with the marines."

I thought about my brothers and all the boys I knew being so far away in strange places. When we were little, Daddy had told us that the reason he wandered was because he was called away to Africa and England and Egypt to visit with royalty. He would bring things back for us from his trips, little things we treasured because they came from him and also from these wild, exotic places he showed us on Beach-ard's globe. I thought how funny it was now that Daddy was some-where in North Carolina or Georgia or Tennessee while his second son was in the Pacific, going places our daddy would never see.

Daddy Hoyt sighed. His chair rocked, making the floorboards creak. He said, "I don't know how it will end, Velva Jean. There's hardly a single boy left on this mountain. They're all off fighting."

I said a quick, silent prayer that the stars hanging in the front win-dow would stay blue. If any of our boys died, I knew Granny and Aunt Zona would have to sew a gold star on top of the blue one. In school gold stars were given out when we did something good. I wondered when they'd turned into something bad that you would never want at all. Then I thought that we should sew a star for Mama.

Daddy Hoyt looked older to me, even in the dark of the porch. I could tell he was trying to sit straight and walk straight, but I'd al-ready caught him stooping, like when he first got up from the table and had to lean too hard on his cane. It was a beautiful cane, the wood twisting and turning, looking just like a serpent, and there were words carved into it from the Bible. The wood was smooth except for a part in the middle where it was darker than the rest of it.

Daddy Hoyt said, "Does Harley Bright know you're here?"

"No, sir." Rock, rock, rock. Creak, creak, creak.

"When do you plan on seeing him?"

"I don't know." The thought made me stop rocking. I hadn't thought about Harley—really thought about him—in months. I looked out at the snow, so clean and white. That's what I feel like, I thought—fresh and new.

"Do you still love him, Velva Jean?"

"No, sir." It wasn't a lie. I didn't love Harley anymore.

We rocked in silence for a while. Then he said, "The Wood Carv-er's back."

I sat straight up. "Where? Have you seen him?"

"No, but I got a message from him."

I said, "What kind of message?" I tried to picture the Wood Carver writing a note or a letter.

He leaned down and picked up the cane. "Someone left it outside my fiddle studio." He turned it this way and that. "You almost can't tell it was in a fire. He smoothed that wood down pretty good, working out the charred part, but somehow he didn't lose too much of the carving." He held the cane out so I could see it better. It shone in the moonlight. It was the cane the Wood Carver had made him, the one that almost burned in the fire that Harley started, the one that drove the Wood Carver away.

I stared out toward the trees, shining with white, up toward Devil's Courthouse, even though I couldn't see the peak of it from there. They used to say the Wood Carver took on animal form at night, that he walked on all fours and roamed the woods, snatching babies from their cribs. I wondered where he was right then and if I'd be able to see him before I left again.

We stayed up till two in the morning, turning in one by one till finally it was just Granny and Ruby Poole and me. After they went to sleep, I went over to Mama's, to my old room, and slept in one of the twin beds that used to belong to Johnny Clay and me. I lay there, feeling the ghosts. Ghosts of myself as a little girl, ghosts of Mama, Daddy, my brothers and sister. Across the hall was the room where my mama died. The air was thick with haints.

I would have to find Harley eventually. Whatever I did, I knew I had to face him head-on and see him before he heard I was back. My stomach turned over at the thought. This was one of those things that couldn't be helped but that you wished you could get out of—like scalding the hog or living with Sweet Fern or telling your mama good-bye forever.

EIGHTEEN

On December 26, Daddy Hoyt and Granny and Ruby Poole and me walked down the hill to Deal's. It was a beautiful morning, blue and bright. The tree limbs shone with ice and the snow glittered where the sun hit it. I didn't think I'd ever seen such clean snow—it made the earth seem new, like every step we made was the first. I broke an icicle from a tree and sucked it like a popsicle, just like Johnny Clay and me used to do when Sweet Fern wasn't watching.

Alluvial was quiet. The snow painted everything white so you couldn't see the gold dust that was underneath. The Alluvial Hotel sat empty, its porch covered in snow, icicles hanging from the eaves and railing. I wondered where Lucinda Sink was at this moment. Ruby Poole said she'd gotten on the train with her suitcase one day about three weeks before and no one had seen her since.

The door to Deal's was closed, but it swung open when Granny pushed it. Inside there was greenery and a giant wreath over the door and another on the opposite wall. A tree decorated with pinecones and cherries and strung popcorn and a lopsided star on top stood in one corner. The potbellied stove was lit, and a couple of old men sat around warming their hands and drinking out of mugs. They stopped talking long enough to look up. When they saw me, one of them shouted, "Look what the cat drug home!"

There were footsteps then, and Mr. Deal came down the stairs from the apartment above. He said to us, "He'll be down in a second." He called up the stairs, "Jessup Deal!"

A voice yelled back: "Coming!"

We were here to tell Jessup good-bye. He was headed to the army base at Fort Benning, Georgia, for basic training.

From a ways off, we heard the train whistle. Mr. Deal hollered, "Jessup!"

I looked at this man who was almost like a daddy to me after my own daddy went away. He was kind and strong and so much had happened to him—burying his wife, burying his middle son. And now he had two sons on their way to war.

There was a clattering of footsteps as Jessup came down too fast with his bag over his shoulder. He missed the last step and went sprawling and then sat laughing his head off. He saw me and said, "Well, holy shit. Looky here."

I thought that Jessup was even better looking than the last time I'd seen him. His black hair fell over his eyes—one green and one blue—and he looked like a man now and not a boy. He and I were the exact same age.

He jumped to his feet and picked up the bag and then gave me a hug. He said, "What do you think? I'm off to fight this war." Then he shook Daddy Hoyt's hand and hugged Granny and Ruby Poole. He said, "Where's that train?"

We could hear it rattling up outside. Mr. Deal stood by the door, with a face so straight you couldn't tell what he was thinking. He said, "Best get a move on, boy." He pushed the door open and held it, and Jessup marched out. The sun hit his hair so that it shone blue-black, and there was something so brave and young about him at that moment that I thought, *Dear Jesus, keep him safe.*

Sweet Fern and the children came out of their house just as we all walked out of Deal's. The train pulled up, the smoke from the engine climbing out in a funnel, just like a tornado cloud, winding up into the blue sky. There was the grinding of brakes—like the high-pitched cry of a panther—and the train slowed to a stop.

The conductors appeared, one lighting a cigarette, the other rubbing his hands together and blowing on them. He hopped up and down, right in place, and then hugged his arms to himself like he wasn't used to the cold. And then boys in uniform started pouring out of the train like ants on a picnic, smoking, laughing, going on into Deal's. Some of them winked at Sweet Fern and Ruby Poole and me as they walked by.

Jessup turned and grinned at us. I knew him well enough to know he was putting on a show, just like Johnny Clay would have done. He was trying to seem brave and fearless, like he wasn't going anyplace more than just over to Waynesville or Hamlet's Mill. He said, "Y'all take care." He held out his hand to his daddy, and Mr. Deal shook it hard. They both wore their best faces, the kind you couldn't see through.

Then Jessup saluted the rest of us and said, "See you when this war is done." And he swung up into the train and disappeared.

Another one gone, I thought. I heard the Carter Family in my head:

I went back home, my home was lonesome.
Missed my mother, she was gone.
All of my brothers, sisters crying.
What a home so sad and lone . . .

Sweet Fern linked her arm through Mr. Deal's, and there was something about that one little gesture that made me get a hard-swallowing homesick feeling in my throat. We stood there a minute longer, waving and watching, even though we couldn't see Jessup anymore. I wondered why he hadn't stayed out there with us till the last minute. The conductors were still smoking. The soldiers were still milling about. I figured Jessup went on in because he hated good-byes as much as any of us, and maybe if he'd hung around we would have seen just how hard it was for him to leave.

One of the conductors shouted to the other one, "It's a goddamn icebox up here in the mountains."

The other one threw his cigarette onto the ground and kicked snow over it. He said, "Next time I'm working a train down in Mexico."

The soldiers came back outside, drinking Coca-Colas, chewing gum. They started getting back on the train.

The first conductor climbed up after them, and after the last soldier went in the second conductor started to follow. Then I heard him say, "Sorry. Go on ahead, then." He backed down the stairs till he was outside on the ground, and two legs came into view. It was a tall man in a coat the color of sand and a hat to match.

He said, "Thank you," in a deep drawl of a voice that made my heart stop.

Suddenly there was Harley Bright. I stood frozen to the spot just like I was caught in a blizzard and I was a balsam fir covered in ice. My mind said: Run, Velva Jean. Run like hell, girl. But my feet weren't working. Everyone was staring at me, staring at Harley, waiting to see what would happen.

I hadn't seen Harley since I'd been back. I hadn't had the nerve yet to go up to Devil's Kitchen or the Little White Church.

Harley started toward us, away from the train, and I knew he hadn't seen me yet but it was only a matter of seconds. Before I could think anymore about what I might do or say, he looked up and saw me. He stopped walking.

There was a grinding sound of metal on metal, and the train started to pull away, gathering up speed like a giant man trying to break into a jog. Everyone waved one last time, except for me.

I thought that this was exactly what it was like when the panther cat had chased me. I felt rooted, waiting to see when it would pounce, when it would get me. Harley was rooted too. I didn't know who would move first.

Then he started toward me.

You're going to be a pilot in the WFTD, I told myself.

Harley Bright stopped in front of me with a smile so blinding I could barely see. He said, "Velva Jean."

I said, "Harley Bright."

I thought: You're going to fly planes for the war.

Harley said, "Is that any way to greet your husband?"

Sweet Fern sucked in her breath. I heard Mr. Deal say, "It sure is cold out here, folks. Why don't we go inside where it's warm."

Harley said to him, "I just spoke to Jessup, sir. I told him I'd be sure to ask Jesus to watch out for him."

Mr. Deal's face didn't move but something passed behind his eyes, and I wondered if he was remembering Harley preaching here in Alluvial against the outlanders before he rounded them up and sent them out of the valley. Mr. Deal said, "Thank you, Harley." I noticed he didn't call him "Reverend." Harley seemed to notice it too, because he gave Mr. Deal a tight smile, strained at the corners.

Sweet Fern started pushing the children toward Deal's. She said, "What a good idea to go inside. It certainly is cold out here." But she gave Harley a mean look like he was a bug she wanted to kill. Then they all shuffled inside so that Harley and I were alone.

I said "Harley Bright" again because I couldn't think of anything else to say. I wished I wasn't outside, standing in the freezing cold of December, my nose red as a turnip and my brain numb from winter.

Harley looked good but he also looked smaller somehow. Older. Under the hat there was a little gray in his hair, flecked here and there. I wondered where he'd been that he was riding the train, not as a fireman in a freight car, but as a passenger on a passenger train. Was he preaching in other towns again? Was he riding the circuit? It made me mad to think so, after how he'd made us stay, stuck and still, in Devil's Kitchen for so long after his accident, after he lost his nerve. Then I realized I was a fine one to think that, taking myself off to Tennessee.

He said, "Why didn't you write me you were coming, Velva Jean?" My heart was slowing down, starting to beat normal again. I thought about the way I must look. My hair was wet from the cold and the damp. I was wearing Mama's old winter coat, with the threads hanging off it and one button missing. Harley was still handsome. I guessed he always would be. I'd forgot how he could make me feel raggedy and threadbare sometimes, even after I'd been out in the great, big world.

He said, "That's some greeting, especially when I haven't seen or heard from you in a year." He opened his arms to me, and I could feel everyone watching from inside. I stood my ground for almost a minute, still frozen, still rooted, and his arms just sat there out in space, his smile getting tighter and tighter. At the moment he was about to lose it completely, I stepped forward and let him hug me. He said, "I'm glad you came back."

I said, "I'm only back for a few weeks. I'm not here to stay." But at the same time I said it, I was also thinking how warm he was. I was breathing him in, and he smelled new and fresh and also familiar, the exact same way I remembered him. He smelled like home.

"I'd like to take you to supper," he said. "We'll go to Hamlet's Mill. We'll go to Waynesville if you want. I'll take you back to the Balsam Mountain Springs Hotel for lime-pepper steak." This was where we stayed on our honeymoon, and the lime-pepper steak was my favorite meal. I'd eaten it every night.

My mind was racing. I didn't want to stand there talking to him or ever have supper with him. I wanted to run back up to Mama's and get in that yellow truck and head straight for Nashville or anywhere else but here.

He said, "You staying at your mama's?"

"Yes."

"I'll come up there and get you. Now, I need to go on inside and get something 'fore I go back on up to the church." He tipped his hat to me, just like we were in a movie, and then he went on into Deal's.

I stood there wondering if Harley was trying to bait me, if he was playing coy just like Hunter Firth did sometimes when he was tracking a coon, pretending to ignore it so that it got comfortable and then just when it got too comfortable, chasing it down and catching it by the throat.

Suddenly I started to run back up the hill to Mama's. As I ran I told myself: You can't be rooted, Velva Jean. You can't be rooted.

I had moved far past Harley, but I was worried that somehow he might still have a hold on me, just like he always had. I was worried he would somehow make me forget the WFTD and my flying and all I'd gone through to get here, and convince me to come back home with him, up to Devil's Kitchen, to clean his house and cook his meals and buy the sugar and look after him and his daddy.

NINETEEN

I was up and out of the house early the next day. It was a cold, bright morning, the sun hitting the snow and blinding me with all that white. My breath turned the air to mist, and I ran down the hill blowing imaginary smoke rings, just like Johnny Clay and me used to do. Not too far away, I could hear the train coming. The whistle was still the loneliest sound on earth, especially in winter when everything was so dead and silent and we were all closed off from the rest of the world. Hunter Firth started to follow me down the hill, but I shooed him back toward home. I said, "Go on, boy. Go on." I was afraid he'd start barking and give me away.

When I got to Alluvial, the train was stopped outside Deal's. There was the usual crowd of men hanging around outside to see who got off and who got on, and it struck me that this hadn't changed even with so many of our boys gone and the whole world at war.

I climbed up Devil's Courthouse, winding my way up through Devil's Kitchen. I looped around through the kudzu forest so I wouldn't have to see Harley's house. I pushed my way through the bramble and the briars and the tree limbs until I was near the top, up where the Freys and Aunt Junie, the witch-healer, used to live before the Scenic came through their land and the government made them leave.

I climbed to the highest point, up near where the giant named Tsul 'Kalu was supposed to live in the cave he shared with the devil. Here the ground flattened out and the smoke rolled across the earth and through the trees. The snow was deeper the higher I went, and I waded through it up to my shins, my knees, my thighs, until I saw a ring of fir trees, turned white, and, just past, a thicket of laurel bushes frozen in ice. In the middle of the thicket was a small wood cabin turned black in places because of fire.

I was too big and heavy now to stand in a laurel bush like I did when I was ten years old and spying on the Wood Carver. I was too old for spying. I walked right up to the cabin, past where I knew the black circle of earth was, underneath the snow, where Harley and the others had started the fire, burning all the Wood Carver's things. I walked up onto the stoop and knocked on the door. When I knocked, it swung open with a creak and there was nothing inside but some old carvings up on the shelves and snow that had blown across the floor. I said hello, even though the cabin was only one room and it was clear that no one was there, that no one had been there for a long time.

I wanted to look closer at the carvings—the dancing men and bird-houses and canes—but somehow it felt like trespassing. I stood there for another minute and then I turned away and shut the door behind me.

Instead of heading back to Fair Mountain, I decided to visit the cave at the very top of Devil's Courthouse—this was where the devil himself sat in judgment on people who were cowardly or wicked. As I walked I made a list of all the things I knew or thought I knew about the Wood Carver:

> His name was Henry Able.
> He was a carver of wood.
> He came from Spruce Pine.
> He'd worked in the mines there.
> He was married to a girl named May.
> One of the men who worked with him at the mines—a man named McAllister—tried to seduce May and she rejected him.
> McAllister tried to kill Henry Able, but Henry Able fought him off with a knife and hit an artery, which caused McAllister to bleed to death.

> May lived down near Pinhook Gap, just over the ridge
> from Devil's Kitchen.
>
> The Wood Carver knew all about which trees made the
> best carvings, about brace roots, and about nature not
> following straight lines.
>
> He was one of the wisest people I'd ever met.

There were other things too: he was so tall he nearly blacked out
the sun; he had eyes the color of midnight, a deep, dark shade of blue;
he walked with a limp; he wore a wedding ring that was all nicked up;
he had a single special carving knife he used to shape the wood.

In the end, I thought it really wasn't very much.

When I got to the giant's cave, I stood and looked at that long, paved
road that wound on top of the mountain. My daddy had been the first to
tell me about the Scenic, even though I didn't believe him: "I walked
across the tops of the mountains, with a man who's building a road. He's
building it right across the mountains, right across the tops of them.
That road is going to reach from Virginia all the way down here, right
down through these mountains we live in. It's going to be the greatest
scenic road in the world. A road of unlimited horizons."

I walked through the tunnel that cut through the heart of Devil's
Courthouse, toward the other end where I could see the sunlight, and
when I came out into the air and the sun I grabbed hold of the black-
brown rock and pulled myself up. There was an entrance to the cave
on this side that was easier to reach than the main one. Johnny Clay
had shown it to me once, back when he was thirteen and I was eleven
and we were on a wicked path. He'd dared me to climb up and go
inside the cave, but I'd been too chicken. In the end I'd watched him
as he scaled the rock like a monkey and then disappeared inside. I'd
held my breath and counted to ten and then twenty and then fifty,
praying that the giant wouldn't eat him and that the devil wouldn't
take his soul.

By the count of eighty-five, he'd come back out, face white, hair
sticking straight up, and he was running. He said, "Go, Velva Jean!"
We'd run all the way home and didn't stop till we were on Mama's

porch. When we got there, we lay about trying to catch our breath, and then I said, "What in the Sam Hill did you see?"

He said, "The bones of a dead man. At least one, maybe more. There were bones everywhere, and not animal ones. They were human. I could tell."

"How could you tell?"

"Because of the skull."

I'd never forgot this, and now as I climbed up the face of the rock, I had to will myself not to faint. I heard my brother's voice in my head: "We have to be men about this, Velva Jean," and I decided that if I could fly a plane, I could look inside a giant's cave.

As I climbed—careful where I stepped, putting one foot in front of the other just so—I held on to the rock, which was cold as ice even in the sun. When I got to the ledge, I pulled myself up and rolled to the entrance, suddenly scared to death of heights. Don't look down, I told myself. Don't look over the edge.

I stood up and brushed myself off and crept forward, quiet as a spy, as sly as Constance Kurridge, my favorite spy of all time. The front of the cave was light from the sun spilling in, but the deeper I went in, the darker it got. I stopped just a couple of feet inside because there, lying in a circle a few feet deeper into the cave, was a pile of bones.

I stood there trying to move my feet, but they might as well have been nailed to the ground. I couldn't go forward and I couldn't go back. After what seemed like three hours, I somehow made them work, and I crept closer to the bones because I couldn't help myself, even though I was telling myself to go back the way I'd come. The cave was dank and damp and smelled as stale as old cabbage, as sour as mayapple leaves. I breathed through my mouth as I tiptoed forward, trying not to smell anything, careful not to make a sound. I wished Johnny Clay were there to see me.

When I was only a few inches from the bones, I stopped. It was darker there and the air was heavier. I let my eyes adjust and then I leaned in. They weren't bones at all. They were canes and flutes and dancing men, all carved out of wood. I bent down and reached, straining with my fingertips. I picked up the thing closest to me, and it was a wooden man with his mouth open, holding a book. I turned it to the light and ran my fingers over it. The wood was smooth and cool to the touch. I inched forward, toward the opening of the cave, toward the light, and held it up. And that's when I saw that it looked like Harley Bright.

I threw the carving back into the pile and looked all around me. Was the Wood Carver here now? Was he watching me? Why was I suddenly afraid of him? He was, after all, my friend, a man who'd been nothing but wronged by the people who knew him. But there was a chill working over me and through me, growing heavier and heavier. So heavy that when I said, "Hello? Are you there?" it came out a whisper.

I stood up and tried again. "Are you there?" It was louder this time. I waited.

"Hello?"

I waited again.

Nothing.

I said, "I don't know if you're here, but I came to see you. I'm home from Nashville. I'm sure you know about the war. I been trying to find you. I can fly planes now. I'm a pilot. I'm going to be a pilot for the military. For the WFTD."

I said this louder than I needed to because I wanted the devil to hear me—to hear how brave I was—just in case he was there and wanting to pass judgment.

"If you are here, I don't know why you don't tell me so. You know I would never ever do you harm."

Nothing again.

I said, "I don't know if I'm going back to Nashville ever, but I'm still singing. And I'll go back someday. But right now I'm flying. Can you believe that? Johnny Clay helped me learn. He came out to Nashville to see me and we took lessons."

There was only the deep silence of the cave.

"Well. I'm going back down, then. I wish I could see you. I just wanted to know that you're okay, and to tell you thank you for brace roots and all the other things you taught me. Even when I'm up in the air, I guess it's good to know I have them." And then I turned and walked back to the mouth of the cave, and when I stepped outside on the ledge I forgot myself and looked down and there was the other side of the valley—the side that looked toward Pinhook Gap, where a woman named May Able lived—spread out below, so far down you couldn't see the bottom. And there were the mountains spread out in front of me, so many that you couldn't see the end of them.

This time, on my way back down the mountain, I walked by Harley's house—my old house. I was careful to stay out of sight in case he was home. I hid behind a tree, just like when Johnny Clay and me came over to get the moonshine for Mama and I first laid eyes on Harley Bright, back when I was ten years old.

From the outside the house looked just the same as it always had—a white two-story, with bright-blue trim, a slanting roof, and a wide porch that wrapped around the front and one side. The house sat in a clearing, surrounded by a barn, a chicken house, a springhouse, a cornfield, and the meadow where I'd taught myself to drive. Circling around the house was a stream, which I knew fed into a river, which fed into the ocean, which was something I made myself think about back when I was living there, all hemmed in, caged up, trapped. I thought now that Harley's house might as well be Butcher Gap Prison, surrounded by barbed wire and walls without windows and security towers with armed guards ready to shoot you if you tried to run away. Even after leaving, even just standing outside it, that house made me feel so small that I had to look down at my feet to see if I was still my normal size.

I was turning away when the front door opened. I expected to see Levi, Harley's daddy, but instead Harley himself walked out onto the porch. He was in his shirtsleeves and he was talking to someone. Then Pernilla Swan came blinking out, just like a mole, with her pale-strawberry hair and her eyes no bigger than a pig's eyes. She took Harley's hand and then dropped it and they talked a moment more. And then she set off down the stairs, stepping as gingerly as an old lady. She turned and waved at Harley and walked off toward home. He stood there watching her go, and then he looked around him, toward the meadow, toward the cornfield, and finally toward the woods where I was hiding. I held my breath, but he went inside and shut the door.

I'd never in my life seen Pernilla Swan without her mama nearby. What was she doing with Harley Bright? And more than that, what was he doing with her?

~ *1943* ~

Off we go into the wild blue yonder . . .

—"Wild Blue Yonder"
(a.k.a. "The U.S. Air Force")

January 9, 1943

Dear Mary Lou,

Nashville is boring without you. I think I might marry the next guy that asks, just for something to do.

You'd better not be falling in love with that old husband of yours. If you write to me and tell me you've run off with him again or that you're pregnant with his babies, I will come to North Carolina myself and give you hell.

The name of my lawyer friend, the one who got me my divorce, is Lucius M. Powell, but everyone calls him Lucky. His address is: 8515 Washington Street, Boston, Massachusetts. I want you to write to him as soon as you're done reading this and get that divorce. If you don't have the money for it, I'll send you some myself.

Don't you dare stay there.

Miss you like crazy.

Love,

Gossie

P.S. I know you're in the army now, but Nori and Crow say you always have a home at the Lovelorn Café.

TWENTY

On the evening of January 16, at six o'clock exactly, Harley picked me up in the DeSoto. I wore the navy dress I'd bought in Nashville, the one with the skirt that twirled. Harley wore his Barathea white suit with a red handkerchief in the breast pocket.

I said, "Where are we going?"

Harley said, "It's a surprise."

This made me think "oh no," because you never knew if surprises were going to be good or not.

We got into the car and started down the mountain, through Alluvial, down the old cattle road, and through Hamlet's Mill toward Sylva. I said again, "Where are we going?" I suddenly had a scared feeling like, what if Harley was going to kidnap me?

He said, "Just you wait and see."

The Balsam Mountain Springs Hotel looked just as I remembered it, back when I was sixteen years old and Harley and I went there for our honeymoon. It was a three-story Victorian inn built at the highest railroad depot this side of the Rockies. It sat thirty-five hundred feet above a valley, pressed against the mountain, on twenty-three acres. Harley and me stood on the wide front porch and looked out over that valley and I remembered the woman who lived down there in one of the little houses in the holler across the train tracks. When we were there before, there'd been chickens running in the yard, and she had stood out there hanging her wash on the line. There was still wash hanging outside, but I didn't see any sign of her.

It was a cold night, clean and clear, and there was a couple walking on the porch hand in hand. I looked at them and wondered if they were as happy as they seemed or if maybe one of them didn't like the other all the time and wanted to get in a truck and drive away and never look back.

Harley took my hand and for five seconds I held it, looking down and thinking how funny it was that our hands still fit but didn't fit. Then I took my hand away and tucked it in my pocket.

In the restaurant the waiters wore bow ties and aprons and had neat mustaches that made me think of Douglas Fairbanks Jr. These days there were long lines at the grocery down in Hamlet's Mill and no meat, just something called utility-grade beef, which looked like something you wouldn't feed a possum. But here at the Balsam Mountain Springs Hotel, you could still get lime-pepper steak. Harley said this was because they butchered it themselves.

We ate steak and drank sweet tea, and Harley asked me polite questions about Nashville and my singing, though you could tell maybe he didn't want to hear everything but felt he should ask.

Then he told me all about the Little White Church and his sermons. He said, "The Little White Church is mostly old folks and women now, with so many of the men gone, but I'm needed more than ever. I was mad as hell about this 4-F thing, Velva Jean. You know that. But I think I'm doing good by being here. I'm maybe even doing more. I think it's where I need to be."

I didn't tell him that I hadn't read a single one of his letters and because of that this was the first I was hearing about him being 4-F and unable to serve. I thought of all those unopened envelopes stuffed inside my suitcase. I said, "You've done a good thing with that church, Harley."

He said, "Thank you."

There was too much we weren't saying, starting with the fact that I'd left him without a word almost exactly a year ago.

I said, "How's your daddy?"

He laughed. "Up there every day working on a new still. I think he's got a couple of 'em now."

He looked younger when he laughed, with his face loosened up. I said, "I can't believe you haven't shut them down."

He said, "It keeps him happy. I want him happy. He's all I got now."

And there it was. I tried to think of something to say. Somewhere far away in my mind I was watching the two of us like I was sitting across the room or up at the bar. I saw a handsome man with a lot of charm, talking and talking, and a pretty girl sitting back and letting him, just like I was in the congregation at the Little White Church and he was preaching a sermon. I was married to this man and he was as good as a stranger. He'd seen me without my clothes on, and now here we sat like people meeting in church or at Deal's for the first time.

Finally I asked him if he knew that the top orchestras in the country were made up of women. I said, "Houston has twenty-six women players and a woman concertmaster." I was trying to learn about Texas.

He said, "Is that so?" I couldn't tell whether he was impressed or just being polite.

I hoped he couldn't remember seeing me naked. I hoped he wasn't picturing it right then. I said, "Harvard Medical School is finally letting in women." Even as I was saying these things I didn't know why I was saying them. Maybe I was testing him to see if he'd changed at all, if maybe he would actually care about something like that.

I said, "There's a research lab in Pittsburgh where this girl chemist just a year older than me helped develop a plastic glue strong enough to support the weight of a two-hundred-ton locomotive." As far as I was concerned, people didn't look their best naked. They looked better with clothes on—even Harley, who had muscles in his arms and shoulders and long, strong legs.

He said, "What are you trying to say, Velva Jean?" There was an edge to his voice for the first time.

I said, "I just think it's interesting how this world is changing." Why on earth was I thinking about Harley's legs? Now that I had the image of his arms and muscles in my mind, I couldn't seem to get it out.

"Look, Velva Jean. After you left me I had some time to think, and you know what I thought? You and me, we been through it, the good and the bad. I knew you back before your mama died and your daddy run off. I knew you when you was a girl. I knew you when you ran away from Sweet Fern and I knew you when you turned fifteen and then sixteen and I made you my wife. You saw me through my mama's death and through the train wreck, when I nearly died myself. You got me off the couch again and got me preaching and got me into believing in something other than myself. You and me, we got a history. I figure all that's got to count for something."

It did count, but he'd also left out mean Harley, wicked Harley, cold Harley, hard-to-reach Harley, holier-than-thou Harley, and the Harley that rounded up people I knew and loved and chased them off the mountain.

I said, "I can't be the person you need me to be anymore. I think you need someone who'll go to the church meetings and cook your supper and listen to your sermons and look after Levi, and who'll like doing those things and never want a single thing more." Someone like Pernilla Swan. I thought about her then, with her pale-strawberry hair and her tiny pig's eyes without lashes, but I didn't say a word or ask him what she'd been doing up at the house.

"I don't want anyone else, Velva Jean. You're my dream girl."

"That's just the thing. I'm not a dream girl. I'm a real one."

Harley laughed at this. "You're a dream girl but you don't realize it, honey. You're about the dreamiest girl there is."

I thought: You want a dream girl, but I'm not one of those. I'm real, just like I told you. I wish you'd listen. I said, "You know, I learned to fly when I was in Nashville."

He said, "Really?"

I waited, but there wasn't anything more, and then he seemed to know he was supposed to say more, so he said, "First driving and now flying. Good for you, honey."

I said, "I have my pilot's license. They're training women to fly and ferry planes for the war."

Harley laughed. He said, "What on earth for?"

I felt my hackles rising. I thought: So there you are. You've been in there all along. I said, "Because they need pilots, especially with so many men overseas. And I've taught myself everything there is to know about flying. My teacher, Duke Norris, said I was a natural. You've heard of General Hap Arnold, commander of the U.S. Army Air Forces?"

He said, "Yes." His voice was testy.

I said, "He helped create the program with a woman named Jacqueline Cochran, the most famous female pilot in history, even more famous than Amelia Earhart. It's called the WFTD. The Women's Flying Training Detachment."

He threw his napkin down and sat back. He stared off at the counter and the bar stools. A waiter came rushing up, thinking Harley was looking for him. He said, "Sir?" Harley kept on staring past him, off into space.

I said, "We're fine, thank you." The waiter looked at Harley to make sure, and that made me mad because waiters never listened to women, no matter what. Finally Harley nodded at the waiter without looking at him, and the waiter walked away.

Harley brought his eyes back to my face slow as could be. It took about a hundred years. He said, "Does this have to do with me being 4-F? The fact that they're not letting me fight? You're not trying to show me up by joining when you know I can't?"

"Of course not." I thought, I didn't even know you were 4-F till now.

He nodded, his eyes wandering off to the right of him. After a long moment, he said, "Texas? Well now, I never thought of Texas." He was charming Harley again. "I could go with you. We could get us a house there."

I said, "I'm going to Texas by myself."

Harley looked like he'd been slapped. We sat there. I thought: There is no going back, even if you wanted to. There is only going forward from here on out. Harley was still in Devil's Kitchen and I was living out there—way out there—in the great big world, a bigger world than he could even dream up. And just like that, I was finished being Harley Bright's wife, Levi's daughter-in-law, housewife, church wife, Velva Jean Bright of Devil's Kitchen. I was going back to living out there, but not because Mama told me to—because it was the only place I could live in this world.

For the rest of the meal we didn't say two words to each other, and when we got back to Mama's, Harley kissed my cheek but his lips felt dry and light as a breeze, like he barely touched me, like he was already back up in Devil's Kitchen. When I went upstairs to Mama's room, I looked out the window and he was still down there, standing by his car.

I put my hand over my heart, feeling my hand shake, feeling my heart pound. I watched till Harley finally climbed into the DeSoto and drove away and then I curled up on Mama's bed. I lay there and waited to cry. I thought about Carole Lombard, who died one year ago that very day. I thought about my own mama, who died right here in this room, right here in this bed. But instead of crying I started thinking about the old yellow truck parked down below, out there in the snow, and I breathed a little easier. Not easy, but easier. Just thinking of that old truck made me feel better. I figured that was as close to a home as I had anymore.

And then a voice in me said: No. Your home is in the sky.

TWENTY-ONE

On the morning of January 31, I found a note slipped under Mama's front door. It said:

Dear Velva Jean,

I been thinking on our visit. Coming back up to Devil's Kitchen that night after dinner and not finding you here in this house was worse almost than you leaving the first time.

Remember the Bible passage you asked me about just before you left? "For I am now ready to be offered, and the time of my departure is at hand. I have fought a good fight, I have finished my course. I have kept the faith." This passage has been playing through my head like a song.

You're still my dream girl. Maybe you always will be. No matter what you say, I can't think that's a bad thing to be. We've fought a good fight, Velva Jean. We've kept the faith. But I'm afraid we may have finished our course.

Love,

Harley Bright

I walked outside and sat on the porch steps. Hunter Firth came over and sat by me. He walked slow and favored his back leg, and it made me sad to think how old he was and that soon he might be gone too, just like everyone else.

I scratched him under the chin and behind the ears, just like he liked, and thought about the letter and something Granny had said not long after I got back home: Harley just wasn't up to it. He just hadn't been able to keep up. I wondered if he'd ever been up to it or if I just thought he was and hoped he was, way back when.

I said, "Hunter Firth, you listen to me."

He lay with his chin on the floor while I rubbed his ear, but he rolled his eyes over in my direction so he could look at me.

I said, "You got to make your own way in this world and follow your own heart. You got to not feel bad if you have to leave someone behind, if they're happy where they are and it's better for the both of you. You got to just go out there like the Bible says and wander far off. Fly away and be at rest. And don't you ever let anyone stop you."

~

Much as I wanted to take my yellow truck to Texas, I wasn't sure it would make it all the way there. On February 11 I drove it down the hill from Fair Mountain to Alluvial and left it with Sweet Fern, who promised not to let it rust. I parked it behind Deal's, next to Mr. Deal's truck, and I thought about how this was where my truck started when Danny first drove it up here from Asheville. It had sat there years ago until the train wreck, when Danny was killed trying to save a man he didn't even know. And then it went to Johnny Clay, and then it went to me.

I sat inside it for a minute, feeling the engine running through me, up through my feet and the backs of my legs and my back and my hands, just like it was my lifeblood. Then I turned the key and shut it off and kept on sitting there. Emily Post once wrote, "Is there anything more exhilarating than an automobile running smoothly along?" I knew what it was like to fly a plane, higher than a bird or a cloud, but even with that there was no better feeling on earth than driving my yellow truck, because I had done it first.

I got out and closed the door and patted the hood. I said, "Good-bye, old truck." Then I picked up my suitcase and my hatbox and walked over to join my family where they were standing outside Deal's. I'd paid for my train ticket out of the money I'd saved working at the Lovelorn Café. It would take two and a half days to get to Texas.

The usual crowd was outside Deal's, watching to see who would get off the train and who would be getting on. I remembered jumping the train with Johnny Clay when we ran away from Sweet Fern, and riding the freight train with Harley when he was preaching. I thought of Butch Dawkins and the other outlanders being rounded up on the train and made to leave. There were haints everywhere.

Everyone came to see me off, and this time I said a proper goodbye, hugging Sweet Fern twice just to make up for not saying good-bye the first time, and holding on to Daddy Hoyt so tight I almost didn't let go. Granny was crying, but not wanting anyone to see, and the children were saying, "Send us something from Texas, Aunt Velva Jean." As I looked at all their faces, I wondered who would be here and who wouldn't be here the next time I was home.

"You be safe," Granny said for the hundredth time. "You be careful."

"I will, Granny."

"Write us when you get there."

"I will."

Granny held something out to me. "Boil these leaves into a tea and drink two tablespoons twice a day."

I took the leaves from her. "Heartleaf?"

"Yes."

"What for?"

"Heart trouble. Just in case," she said. Granny's Cherokee heritage made her superstitious. It was why she made a cross in the dirt with her toe every time she left the house and why she carried a hand axe with her in case she met dark spirits or panther cats. She burned old shoes in her Dutch oven to keep the snakes away and she never swept the floor after sundown because she said it was bad luck.

The conductor came up then and said, "We're set to go, miss." I was the only passenger getting on in Alluvial, although I could see I wasn't going to be the only passenger on the train—there were plenty of soldiers hanging out the windows. Maybe I wasn't exactly a soldier, but I felt like one. First Linc and Beach and Johnny Clay, and now me, just like the five Sullivan brothers from Iowa who served together in the navy and died on November 13 when the Japanese sunk their ship, the USS *Juneau*. The brothers had asked to serve together, even though the navy wanted to keep them separate. As far as I was concerned, my brothers didn't have to be in the same company to be serving together in this war, and now I was going to be a part of it too.

Mr. Deal picked up my suitcase, and I held on to my hatbox and tried my best not to cry. I walked backward, waving at everyone. Granny turned away so that she was facing Deal's, but her shoulders—thin as a bird's—were shaking. Mr. Deal and Daddy Hoyt walked with me to the train. Mr. Deal handed me my suitcase, and then I hugged them both one last time. Before I turned away, Daddy Hoyt pressed something into my palm. He said, "This was on my front porch this morning."

I opened my hand and there was a wood carving of a girl, mouth open, arms spread wide. I turned the little statue over and over, and then I looked up toward Devil's Courthouse, up where the giant's cave was at the very top. Daddy Hoyt fixed his gaze up in the same direction. He seemed to know exactly what I was looking for.

I said, "Why didn't he say hello?"

"Because he doesn't want to be found right now, honey."

The wood figure was rough but lovely. It was like something carved from magic. The girl had long wild hair and a heart-shaped face and she looked as if she was flying.

February 21, 1943

Dear Wood Carver,

Thank you for my little wooden girl. I brought her with me all the way to Texas, where I'm training to be a pilot with the WFTD. Did you know I could fly? Did you hear me say it? I don't know if you meant for the wooden girl to be flying, but that's how I'm taking it. I think she's going to be my good-luck charm.

I wish I'd been able to see you before I left, to thank you in person. I hope I'll see you next time I'm home. I keep remembering what you said about nature dealing in curved lines, not straight paths. I think about that every time I'm up in the air. I never in my life thought I'd fly airplanes. But now that I am, I can't imagine a time when I didn't.

Your friend,

Velva Jean

TWENTY-TWO

I was an actual WFTD trainee. For the next nine months my address was going to be Barracks A-6, 318th AAFFTD (which stood for Army Air Forces Flying Training Detachment), Avenger Field, Sweetwater, Texas.

Sweetwater didn't look at all like I'd pictured it. Instead of a green place thick with trees and streams and a blue lake of water so clear that you could drink it, it looked just like a town from the Old West, like something out of the cowboy movies Johnny Clay loved.

Texas was the dustiest place I'd ever seen. The train trip across it was nothing but brown and dirt and flat, wide spaces. I thought it was ugly as sin, but I tried to remember that what was ugly to some was beautiful to others, even though I couldn't help but feel sorry for anyone who was from there. The more I saw of the world, the more I knew I was lucky to be from a place like Fair Mountain.

Downtown Sweetwater was only three or four blocks long, with dusty streets, low brick buildings, more churches than you could count, a café, and the Blue Bonnet Hotel, which stood seven stories high and was the tallest building. There was a drugstore on the first floor of the hotel, and I went in there right after I arrived and bought myself a brand new lipstick—Comet Red by Max Factor. The Blue Bonnet was where all the girls stayed the night before the cattle wagon picked us up bright and early on February 14 and drove us to Avenger Field. The cattle wagons were big, old, creaking trailerlike buses with high, tiny windows. As we started to drive away in them, one of the girls sang, "Off we go into the wild blue yonder . . ." We all raised our voices and sang along. Maybe I was singing loudest of anyone.

All around Avenger Field there was nothing but more brown, flat, dusty Texas. There wasn't a single tree to be seen and just a few patches of grass here and there. The wind never stopped blowing. Avenger Field itself had low barracks close to the flight line, a mess hall, an infirmary, offices, airplane hangars, a huge marching field, and sand. On the gate as you drove in was a sign that said "Aviation Enterprises Ltd." and above that "Avenger Field" and above that a picture of Fifinella—a little blonde cartoon gremlin with wings and flight goggles. Walt Disney had drawn her up for a movie based on a book by Roald Dahl, but Jackie Cochran asked if we could use her as our mascot, and Mr. Disney gave Fifinella to the WFTD. Pilots sometimes liked to blame gremlins for engine failure and anything at all that went wrong with their airplanes, but Fifi was supposed to protect us and bring us good luck.

Jacqueline Cochran had moved to Sweetwater from Houston and was now living on the base. We got a good look at her that first day at orientation, and I thought she looked like Sweet Fern, kind of round and pretty, only with blonde hair and a lot of makeup. When she shook my hand, I forgot my own name. I felt like I was meeting the president or the queen of England.

I was going to be paid $150 a month, and out of that we had to pay our room and board and all our expenses. Some of the girls were mad about this, but I couldn't get over the sound of $150.

Our flight gear included cloth helmets, goggles, coveralls, leather jackets, and winter flying suits lined with fleece. Our "uniforms" were GI mechanic coveralls that were old and worn out and so big that Tsul 'Kalu the giant could have worn them. They looked just like zoot suits, and we had to roll up the sleeves and the pant legs so we didn't trip on them. We wore them everywhere—to ground school, to fly, eat, drill, scrub the barracks, and to do our calisthenics. The only time we didn't wear them was when we were sleeping.

Each barrack was divided into ten bays and each bay held five or six girls. The bays were one-story rooms and each room was connected by a bathroom. This meant twelve girls shared two showers with no doors, two sinks, and two toilets. Our bay had five cots. We each had a small wardrobe and a footlocker at the end of our bed. There was a long wood table in the middle, where we did our homework and wrote our letters home. We had one trash basket between us, and that was about it.

At 6:00 a.m. we woke up to reveille, which was played by one of the cadets. We didn't know there would be boys at Avenger, especially because we'd heard from the trainees ahead of us that everyone in town called the place "Cochran's Convent." Jacqueline Cochran said the male cadet program was there a long time before the WFTD but that the cadets were shipping out in a few months and then we would have Avenger Field to ourselves. She said we were there for one reason only and we needed to "stay on task." The only time we were allowed to be together with the men was during meals.

At 6:15 we fell out of bed and pulled on our zoot suits over our pajamas and wrapped our hair in white turbans, which made us look like washerwomen. At 7:00 a.m. we fell in for mess.

At 8:00 we went to ground school. We were studying navigation and meteorology, and when we were done with those we were going on to physics and airplane mechanics. We spent an hour in each class, and then at 10:20 we went to physical education, or PE, with a funny little man named Melvin Burr, who looked almost exactly like a badger. We marched up and down and did sit-ups and push-ups on our knees and jumping jacks till I thought I was going to die.

At noon, we marched to mess, and at 12:50 we went to the flight line, where we stayed for five hours. This was our favorite part of the day.

My flight instructor was named Arnold Puckett, but we called him Puck. He had a face like a winter cabbage and walked stooped over like he was watching the ground for quarters. He was grouchy and stern as a preacher, and he didn't like girls. His wife was a housewife who had never worked outside the home and who said women belonged on the ground and not in the sky. Puck believed this was one of the smartest things a woman ever said. We hadn't done much flying yet, but they had us practicing takeoffs and landings over and over again. The day before, I'd learned how to land in a crosswind, which was a good thing to know because it was so windy all the time.

At 6:00 p.m. we changed out of our zoot suits and into our dress slacks for mess, and after we ate we had free time, except for the girls who had to go to study hall because they were doing so bad in ground school.

At 10:00 the bugler played taps, and then it was lights out. Sometimes we stayed up talking longer than we should—about boys, religion, homework, and mostly about flying. Then, after everyone drifted off to sleep, I lay there and thought about how for the first time in my life I was in a place with people like me who were dreaming about the very same things, even though all the girls were different and came from everywhere—the farm, the dress shop, the doctor's office, the circus, college, the mountains, the desert.

I had four roommates. Paula Hodges was a golf champion from Florida. She was twenty-seven and tall, with short wavy hair and a mouth that was too big for her face. She wasn't pretty, but she had a way of walking into a room that made people look at her. She swore worse than Johnny Clay and she knew more about flying than any of us because she had two hundred hours of flying time and a daddy who was a mechanic.

Mudge was a Hollywood actress. She was twenty-six and had already been divorced twice. Her real name was Eloise Mudge but Metro-Goldwyn-Mayer changed it to Barbara Fanning. She always said exactly what was on her mind, good and bad, and she was one of the most worldly girls I'd ever met. She looked just like Ann Miller.

Loma Edwards was a housewife and mother from West Virginia. She was only twenty-four, but she had a daughter who was seven and living with Loma's parents while Loma trained to be a pilot and her husband was overseas with the infantry. He was the one who taught her to fly. I couldn't even imagine that. Even so, she worried all the time that she didn't belong here. She worried on everything.

Sally Hallatassee was two years older than me. She was a secretary before the war and left her fiancé, her parents, and her five little brothers behind in Indiana so she could join the WFTD. She was as small as Ruby Poole, and always popping her gum and cracking jokes. She could talk the horns off a billy goat but she'd do anything for you. We lost her every time she put on her zoot suit because it was so big and she was so little. She wasn't shy, and she went right to Jackie Cochran to complain about her uniform, but Miss Cochran told Sally she was going to have to wait a few weeks, till another class graduated, to get one closer to her size.

And then there was me—Velva Jean Hart, twenty years old, with only thirty-nine hours of flying time under my belt, and a seventh-grade education. I liked to think that what I was doing here helped Johnny Clay and Linc and Beach and the rest of them. I had to think it was doing some good somewhere. I was trying to keep on the sunny side, but I was scared to pieces. Maybe it was good for me. Mama used to say being scared or sad or mad gave you things to write about that weren't just blue skies and spring flowers and ice cream.

TWENTY-THREE

On the morning of March 29, I sat on the flight line waiting my turn to fly. The weather had turned warm almost overnight, and I wore the legs of my zoot suit rolled up over my knees and the sleeves pushed all the way up to my shoulders so I could get some sun. I was reading a book on Morse code and trying to concentrate. Morse code was all dots and dashes, and so far I couldn't remember a single word. I tucked Granny's heartleaf into the page I was reading and closed my book. I said to the girls, "I'm going to fail ground school."

The army way of flying wasn't like what I'd learned with Duke Norris. The stalls and spins were different, and there were a hundred new maneuvers to learn. The planes at Avenger Field were tougher, harder to handle. The very first time I'd gone up with Arnold Puckett, he'd cut the throttle and pointed the nose of the primary trainer, or PT, at the sun above us and then brought the stick back, straight against my knee. The plane started spinning and the earth twirled around and around and I went jolting out of the seat, the safety belt catching me so tight around the stomach and chest that it knocked the wind out of me. Then he pointed the nose of the plane down and then up and then lifted a wing and we were flying upside down. My feet flew toward the ground and my bottom came up off the seat, and the safety belt cut off the blood in my stomach and legs. I held onto the plane, to my seat, to whatever I could, and prayed to Jesus that I wouldn't die.

Here at Avenger Field, I felt like I was starting over, like I didn't know anything. We went through spins and loops, upside down and sideways and right side up, because Jackie Cochran said learning all these moves was the only way to have total control over our planes.

Paula Hodges, the golf champion, was taking her turn in the air, so it was just me and Loma and Mudge in line. We were assigned to flight groups by height because we had to take turns with the same parachute, which meant little Sally was in a group with girls her own size.

Loma was already worrying. She said, "If anyone's going to fail ground school, it's me. I've had study hall every night this week. I'm going to wash out, I just know it, and then what will my husband say? What will my daughter think of me?"

Mudge sat next to me, eyes closed, leaning back against the building. Her goggles rested on her lap, and she'd pulled her turban off so that her dark hair hung around her shoulders. Because she was an actress, she believed in looking glamorous at all times. The wind was picking up her hair and blowing it every which-a-way. She said, "Hush up, both of you. No one's going to wash out."

A lot of the girls we knew had gone home already—at least 23 of them that we could count. I thought back to our first day and Jackie Cochran lining us up. "There are 112 of you in your class," she said. We all looked around to see if this might be true. "The odds are good that half of you won't make it to graduation day. Most of you will wash out. There are plenty of chances: ground school, link training, disobeying orders, too many demerits, dating instructors, civilian and army check rides." Those were when they sent you up with an instructor to test you on various maneuvers, but you never knew when or where they were going to happen. "All that said," she told us, "maybe you should just go home now."

Then she said, "Look at the person on either side of you, because both of those girls will wash out." And I thought, Oh poor things. It never occurred to me for one second that she was talking about me.

Now I wasn't so sure. I'd been pulling study hall myself lately, and this week Puck had yelled at me in front of everyone after I made a bad landing. I opened the book again and the heartleaf was picked up by the wind and blown away. I jumped up after it, swearing "Great holy Moses!"

Loma said, "That's a dime you owe the cuss pot." The cuss pot was a jar we'd stolen from the mess hall. It was Loma's idea that we had to drop a dime in for every *damn* or *hell* and a quarter for worse words, the ones I'd only ever heard Johnny Clay or Harley say but had almost never used myself. So far we had a dollar and twenty cents.

I caught the heartleaf just as it was flying up over my head, and that's when I saw the horizon. There was a solid black cloud, like a thundercloud but darker, and it kind of sat in the distance, covering the earth for as far as I could see, starting at the ground and reaching upward. I thought maybe it was a tornado, only the sky overhead was blue and not green. The cloud was moving, wobbling from side to side.

I said, "What in the hell?"

Loma said, "Ten more cents, Hartsie."

I looked at her over my shoulder and said, "Look."

Loma got to her feet and Mudge opened her eyes, and then she jumped up too. The three of us stood there, and soon there were other girls wandering up from the barracks, from their flight groups, from the control tower.

I said, "What is it?"

Shirley Bingham was two trainee classes ahead of us. She was a suntanned girl with freckles and bright-blue eyes and hair the color of North Carolina clay. She walked up and stood over my left shoulder and whistled long and low. She said, "Locusts."

By afternoon the black cloud covered the sun. We spent all day— trainees, cadets, instructors, officers—covering the planes with tarps, especially the open-cockpit Stearmans. In the barracks we closed the windows and locked all our belongings away in the footlockers and shut the doors to the bathroom and the hallway, stuffing paper underneath so there wasn't a single crack showing.

Then we waited.

By nightfall we could hear them—a buzzing, humming plague of locusts, hitting the base like a great, spinning meteor. Everything stopped—classes, flying, mess. The girls and I took cover in the bay, stuffing more paper under the doors. We could hear the locusts beating against the roof, the windows, the walls. The sound they made was like the beating of a million wings—like the very highest note on a fiddle being played over and over.

It was just like in the Bible: "Behold, tomorrow will I bring the locusts . . . And they shall cover the face of the earth, that one cannot be able to see the earth . . . and shall eat every tree which groweth for you out of the field."

Even though we were sealed up tighter than a drum, there was no way to keep the locusts out of the bays, the lockers, the beds, the food, our hair. They hopped and buzzed around the room while we chased them with our shoes or hid under the covers. Sally said the average swarm was made up of about fifty billion bugs and that it could be days before a swarm moved on.

The first night I didn't sleep at all because there were locusts in the bed. I pulled both the sheet and the blanket over my head, even though it was hot as blazes in the bay. Through the blanket I felt them land on me, thudding against my legs, my stomach, my arms, my face. I slapped at myself here, there, everywhere because I thought I felt them crawling on my skin, that maybe they'd got under the sheet.

I lay there fidgeting and itching and kicking the locusts off me and thinking how much I hated Texas and how much I missed the sounds and seasons of home. Why had I ever come to Texas, with its flat, ugly earth and locusts and sandstorms and tarantulas and scorpions? The locusts were hitting the windows from inside and outside and buzzing against the floor, the footlocker, the bed. I could hear one in my ear and I screamed.

"Did they get you, Hartsie?" Paula shouted from her bed. Each of us was lying just like the others, all bundled up head to toe like mummies.

"One got in my goddamned hair!" Mudge hollered.

"One tried to get in my goddamned mouth!" shouted Sally.

I slapped at my arms and legs and thought about how much money we were all going to owe the cuss pot when this was over and done.

When I finally started to drift off, after lying there for hours, I thought about Cornelia Fort. She'd grown up in Nashville but left to join the Women's Auxiliary Ferrying Squadron. On March 21 she was killed over a place called Merkel, Texas, when the plane she was ferrying was clipped by another plane in midair. She was the first woman to die on active duty for the United States. When Jackie Cochran told us the news, she said to remember that Cornelia Fort died doing what she loved most. Ever since, I couldn't stop thinking about how Cornelia Fort left Nashville only to wind up flying planes in Texas, and how strange that was because I left Nashville—where I always wanted to go my whole life—to go fly planes in Texas too.

Even though she was a stranger and I'd never known her, I couldn't get her off my mind. These were the things I knew about her: she was twenty-four years old. She was the daughter of one of Nashville's richest families. Her family gave her a debutante ball when she was nineteen and she had to be bribed before she agreed to go. She was the first female flight instructor in Nashville. She graduated from college. The week she earned her pilot's license, she flew two thousand miles to celebrate.

All of this had been in the papers along with a letter she'd written to her mother one year before she was killed. In it she talked about why she loved flying and what it meant to her: "I loved it best perhaps because it taught me utter self-sufficiency, the ability to remove myself beyond the keep of anyone at all—and in doing it taught me what was of value and what was not . . . If I die violently, who can say it was 'before my time'? . . . I was happiest in the sky—at dawn when the quietness of the air was like a caress, when the noon sun beat down, and at dusk when the sky was drenched with the fading light. Think of me there and remember me . . ."

Cornelia Fort's body had exploded on hitting the ground. Her plane came down in a pasture near Merkel, and Betty Joe Seymore, who was fourteen years old and living on a farm close by, found what was left of her—a scalp and hair. A farmer named H. H. Cargill found her insignia pin and a piece of her watch, which was smashed flat.

Merkel was just thirty miles east of Avenger Field, on the road to Abilene. I couldn't get over the closeness of it and the fact that I'd just finished my first month as a WFTD trainee when Cornelia Fort crashed and died in a field.

How horrible to die in Texas. I remembered the tarantula we'd seen outside the mess hall the other day and the scorpion that had tried to sting Sally in the shower. I thought, when it came down to it, Texas was the most god-awful place I'd ever seen. I thought about Nashville and Harley and my family up on Fair Mountain and all I'd left behind to come here. I tried to take myself home, fast away in my mind, to its streams and hillsides and trees and green and gold dust and flowers and birds. I pictured the sun—the way it fell through the leaves, making patterns of light on the ground—and remembered the way it warmed your skin without burning it right off.

And all that night; and when it was morning, the east wind brought the locusts.

I wondered if I'd brought this plague of locusts on, just like in the Bible, if maybe my leaving Harley had something to do with it. The thought of this was suddenly the saddest thing in the world, and the part of me that was like my daddy's people, that sometimes liked to dwell on sad things, stepped up and said, "You stopped loving Harley even though you promised him you always would, and now here you are being attacked by locusts. What did you think would happen?"

From her bed, Loma shouted, "Goddamned locusts!" And we all laughed over the buzzing and the humming and the high scratching of violins because it was the first time we'd ever heard her swear.

Mudge hollered, "That's twenty-five cents you owe the cuss pot!"

And Loma said, "I'll pay my month's salary! Just get these god-damn things off me!"

I was hot. I was suffocating. The locusts thumped against me like stones. Then I thought: Texas brought these locusts on itself.

The longer we stayed cooped up together, the more I got to know my bay mates in a way I hadn't on the flight line or at mess or at ground school or during the in-between times. Paula was the best listener and she was also a problem solver. She liked figuring things out, just like a puzzle. She and Mudge each kept a stash of gin outside the bay in a narrow alley between the barracks. There were hundreds of sticks in the ground, just like a little graveyard, and this was where the girls from all the classes hid their liquor.

Mudge was smart and she could be sweet. She always meant well, but she said whatever was on her mind, which could be good but was sometimes bad, like when she made Loma cry. This was easy to do because Loma was the most sensitive person I'd ever met, and she was funny without knowing she was funny or trying to be. She was always saying words wrong and getting mixed up. And Sally was smarter than she seemed for being such a chatterbox. She also talked with her gum—snapping or popping it at instructors and at us when she had something to say. Most of the time it worked better than words.

I wondered if any of us would have been friends in real life. The one thing we had in common was that we all loved flying. Whenever we heard a plane buzz the barracks, we ran outside to see what kind it was. The male pilots at nearby bases knew we were off-limits, but somehow they kept having engine trouble right over Avenger Field. They would land and holler to us while we stood there in our zoot suits or pajamas, till we were rounded up by Lieutenant Patrick Whitley or our one female instructor, Evelyn Beatty, or even Jackie Cochran and sent back inside.

Loma talked a lot about her husband, and sometimes I wished for someone—not Harley but someone who would be back home loving me, someone I couldn't wait to go back to. I was only lonely sometimes though. Mostly it felt good to be on my own and to feel like I was getting better at being on my own. It was like when you were growing, back when you were little, and suddenly you'd wake up one morning and your legs would look longer or your arms would look longer or your hands would look bigger. And before you knew it, you were growing right before your own eyes. That was the way it felt being there in Texas.

~

Two days later we spotted blue patches of sky in the direction the locusts had come from, and suddenly the plague was over and the locusts were gone. No more sealing our bays up tight, no more sleeping with the covers over our heads, no more running to mess with our helmets on and our jackets wrapped around us. No more picking locusts out of our food or our hair or shaking them out of our clothes and shoes before we got dressed. No more missing ground school or PE or, most of all, flying. No more snapping at each other and fussing at each other because we thought the plague would never end. We'd been grounded for three days.

We all came blinking out into the sun—trainees, instructors, control-tower operators, mechanics, cadets, officers, Jacqueline Cochran herself. We stood there like moles or people raised in caves who didn't recognize the sun and blue sky. The flight line was black with crushed locusts. I stood there staring out at the land around us. And I'd thought it was brown before. The ground was empty. There wasn't a blade of grass in sight. It was just sand and dust as far as you could see.

The trainees and cadets were given clean-up duty. It was the worst job I could imagine—scraping dead locust bodies off the runway, the flight line, the planes themselves. Scrubbing the planes clean from the inside out. Cleaning our bays, our latrines, the windows of the mess hall, the wishing well that sat in the courtyard between the barracks.

As I scraped the wing of a PT-13 Stearman parked outside the hangar, I said, "I'm sorry, locusts. I'm sorry you came here and scared us to death and trapped us inside. I'm sorry so many of you had to die because that sure don't seem like much of a life."

"Are you talking to the plane or the locusts?"

It was a southern voice, soft and deep, but not southern like North Carolina. It was more of a Texas voice because there wasn't music to it, and it wasn't slow and lazy like Louisiana, like Butch. It was a cowboy's voice.

I looked up from the Stearman, which I was trying to turn from black to silver. One of the cadets—the one that played reveille and taps on the bugle—was standing there grinning down at me.

I said, "Both."

He nodded like he knew this already and then he folded his arms and watched me for a minute.

"What?"

"Nothing. Want some help?"

I said, "Okay."

He grabbed an ice scraper, the kind they used on the planes in winter, and started cutting away at the black. He said, "Ned Tyler. You can call me Ty."

I said, "Velva Jean Hart."

"Pretty. Strange, but pretty."

"Hey."

He laughed. "I just never heard it before. Where you from, Velva Jean Hart?"

"Fair Mountain, North Carolina." I started to ask him where he was from, but then I thought of Butch Dawkins and how sometimes men didn't like you to ask them about themselves in a personal way.

He said, "I'm from Tulsa, Oklahoma."

I said, "My brother was in Tulsa for a while, roping steers."

He said, "That so?" He scratched away the locusts just as easy as if he was brushing sand off his shirt. He had long fingers, the kind that should have been playing piano and not scraping dead bugs off a plane.

I said, "He wasn't there long before he went on to California, but he liked it fine."

"You ever been?"

"I've only been three places: North Carolina, Tennessee, and here, not counting where the train passed through on my way down."

I thought, Don't give yourself away all at once, Velva Jean.

He said, "I never been to North Carolina or Tennessee, so that's two you got on me."

I thought that he was a kind of boy-man, rangy and tall with dark curling hair that ran wild all over his head. He had a long nose, a wide mouth, and brown eyes.

I said, "Do you have locusts up in Oklahoma?"

He laughed. He smiled fast and easy, like even if his face went serious for a minute that smile was always waiting close by. He said, "I reckon that's where they're headed now. You got 'em in North Carolina?"

"Lord no," I said. "The worst we got is mosquitoes." It made me happy and sad to think of home. "It's beautiful where I come from. The trees are so high in places you can barely see the sky, but the sun always works its way through. The ground is soft and green and covered in moss and grass and ferns and flowers, and there are streams everywhere and Three Gum River, which is where I was saved when I was ten. At night you can see the stars up above the mountains, so close that you feel they're sitting on your head. The streets of Alluvial, down in the valley, are covered in gold dust. And the mountain makes its own music—just like it's humming." I didn't know why I was telling him so much.

He wasn't scraping anymore. He was staring at me. He said, "You think of nature as a friend." I didn't know what to say to this, so I stopped working on the plane and looked at him. He said, "We think of it as fire ants and scorpions and locusts and sandstorms and things to run from and hide from and deal with all the time."

I said, "That's awful." But then I thought that Oklahoma was probably a lot like Texas and that Oklahoma was probably beautiful to him, even if nature was something to be scared of. I tried to think of something nice to say so that he didn't feel bad about where he was from. "Sometimes we got tornadoes that come through. We had a bad one when I was a little girl, and it sent some of the houses right down the mountain and even killed some people."

He said, "Oh, we got tornadoes. We had one last year that killed forty-five people, and one the year before that killed sixty."

There wasn't anything I could say to this because nothing that bad had ever happened in my mountains, unless you counted the Terrible Creek train wreck, and that had nothing to do with nature. Finally I said, "My mama always told us to keep on the sunny side, no matter what. Even in a tornado or a plague of locusts. She used to sing that song to me and my brothers and sister, 'Keep on the Sunny Side.'"

"Used to?"

"She died years ago, back when I was ten."

He said, "I'm sorry." And the way he said it sounded like he really was sorry, and not just from an outside looking in kind of way, like something people just said to you because they were supposed to, but from an inside way. He said, "I never lost a soul in this world and I can't tell you how grateful I am. I give thanks all the time because I know how lucky that makes me."

I started thinking about all the people I'd lost, but before I could count them, like I sometimes did, he began to sing: "'Keep on the sunny side of life. It will help us every day, it will brighten all the way, if we'll keep on the sunny side of life.'"

His voice wasn't beautiful, but it wasn't bad. I thought how good it felt to listen to him, out here under the sun, clearing the locusts away.

April 21, 1943

Dear V. J.,

You'll never guess where I am now: North Carolina. That's right. I'm home again, only not really. They sent us to Camp Mackall, which was named for Private John Mackall of the 82nd Airborne, who was the first American paratrooper killed in combat in this war.

It ain't long now before we join the European invasion. We know they're going to put us through it because we're just that close. One of the things they've got here is the Resistance Training Laboratory, which is a mock prisoner-of-war camp where they teach us resistance techniques in case we're captured by the enemy. I sure as hell don't ever plan on getting captured, but if I do you can know for damn sure they'll be sorry they did it.

I can't believe you're in Texas almost as soon as I'm back in N.C.

Give 'em hell, little sister.

Love,

Sergeant Johnny Clay Hart

P.S. Linc is training in Ireland with the 6615th Ranger Force.

TWENTY-FOUR

*W*ednesday, May 12, was our first solo flight. I sat on the flight line wishing for a real uniform and not a big, baggy zoot suit—something smart and stylish in a pretty color and not something that made me look like a mechanic or a service-station attendant. I was sick and tired of looking like a boy. Today I wore my hair down instead of in my turban, and Evelyn Beatty walked by and gave me two demerits.

As she walked away, Mudge said, "She's just sore because she's an old maid who's never had a boyfriend or a marriage proposal."

Loma said, "You don't know that."

Paula said, "Her whole life is flying."

I said, "Our whole life is flying."

Mudge waved her hand. "We're young. We've got other things to do. Movies. Golf. Kids. Husbands."

Mudge didn't mention singing because none of them knew I sang. Ever since leaving Nashville, I hadn't sung a note except to join in the marching songs—we marched everywhere and we sang while we marched—and I certainly wasn't writing any words or music. I felt like a phony compared to Paula, who had championships and trophies to show for her golf career, or Mudge, who had a contract with Metro-Goldwyn-Mayer. I didn't feel like a singer anymore, even though it was how I'd always seen myself. I wasn't even a real wife like Loma, with a wedding band and a husband whose picture I kissed every night. I didn't know what I was now, except a pilot and a WFTD trainee.

Suddenly Puck stalked up, stooped toward the ground, and barked at me. "Get a move on, Hart! You're up first!" Then he stalked back off.

I stood up and put on my helmet. I hoisted my parachute up behind me. I pulled on my goggles, pushing them up on top of my helmet. Then I ran after Puck to the PT, trying not to look like Granny's mule, Mad Maggie, with all that gear on me.

I climbed up on the PT and swung one leg over the open cockpit and then the next leg and then I sat down in the front seat. I snapped on my safety belt while Puck cranked the engine. Then I taxied out, swinging into position next to the runway. I pulled my goggles down, but the wind was already blowing sand into my eyes and mouth. I started coughing, and my eyes were tearing, and Puck was shouting something at me from the ground, but I couldn't hear him because the engine was so loud, rattling and roaring.

I sat there breathing in, breathing out. I breathed in. I breathed out. I was done with practicing takeoffs and landings. Now I would be expected to do spins and stalls and dives, all on my own. I thought: Get your head on straight, Velva Jean. Settle down. You can do this. You can fly this plane. The only difference is that Puck isn't going to be up here to yell at you.

I pulled on the throttle and suddenly I felt the earth rushing away and the plane starting to lift. The wind was warm, stinging my face. I wanted to yell, "Let me down! I want to get out! Let someone else go first!" But I was already climbing up into the sky, fighting the currents.

The PT was a low-winged, open cockpit, 175-horsepower Fairchild PT-19A and the largest, most powerful plane I'd ever sat in. I climbed to eight thousand feet, and I stopped blinking and tearing up long enough to look around me: there was brown and blue everywhere—the brown of the flat, endless earth and the blue of the sky—and patches of black here and there from the locusts. Even though my safety belt was on, I felt like I could fall out at any time, like nothing was holding me in my seat. The air rushed by and underneath my helmet my hair whipped around, stinging my cheeks.

I tugged on my safety belt, and it held tight, and then I rolled the plane to the left and then to the right and then I leveled the plane and pulled the throttle back and lifted the nose higher, up and up, until it went into a stall. This meant I was stock-still for a moment, which seemed like minutes strung together, and then I started diving straight toward the earth, the nose of the PT pointing down. I wanted to holler, but I couldn't because my throat was as frozen as Three Gum River in winter. Stalls always spooked me, no matter how many times I went through them. I told myself, This plane is not in charge of you.

I leveled the plane out and started to glide. I flew fast and high, the earth rushing past below me, above me, beside me, everywhere. After being left behind my whole life—by my daddy, by my mama when she died, by Johnny Clay going off to Oklahoma and then California, by Harley leaving to go preach and then leaving again when he got home by wandering away from me in his mind—now I was the one off on my own. This is why I'm here, I thought. This is why I came to Texas.

When I came down, the girls ran for me, shouting and hugging me, even with Puck standing there glaring at us because we were acting like girls and not soldiers. I was the first one to solo—me, Velva Jean Hart.

It was Loma's turn next, and I handed her the parachute. She couldn't get it fastened, so I helped her. Then she said, "Wish me luck. I'll need it," and ran after Puck.

Mudge sat down to wait her turn, and I sat down next to her. She said, "That poor girl is the worryingest girl I ever knew."

After we'd each flown solo, the girls from our class—all of them, not just my bay mates—picked me up and threw me in the wishing well. Shirley Bingham, two classes ahead of us, had told us this was tradition. Every girl to solo first was dropped in the well. I lay back, zoot suit floating up around me, and looked at the sky. The girls stood around me singing:

> *If you have a daughter, teach her how to fly.*
> *If you have a son, put the bastard in the sky.*
> *Singing zoot suits and parachutes and wings of silver too,*
> *he'll ferry planes like his mama used to do . . .*

I thought about all the times I was saved in my life—when I was ten years old and baptized in Three Gum River, when I was fifteen years old and met Harley Bright, when I was eighteen years old and drove my yellow truck to Nashville.

I closed my eyes and went under. I held my breath and stayed there. While I was under, I thought about Gossie and my brothers and Nashville, about spiders and dust storms and locusts and cadets and a little town called Sweetwater, which didn't look at all like it sounded, but which was pretty nice even so. When I came back up, the sky was even bluer than before and the sun burned bright.

That afternoon I was back in the bay, sitting at the wooden desk we all shared, studying my Morse code, when I heard someone whispering: "Girls . . . Oh, girlies."

I looked up at Sally, who sat across from me, writing in her notebook. She always said everything she was writing out loud as she was writing it, no matter how many times we told her to be quiet. Sally just loved to talk.

She stopped talking now and we stared at each other. "Did you hear that?" she said.

Paula was stretched out on her cot, reading. Without looking up, she said, "Cadets."

One week after the plague of locusts, the cadets had flown off to California. They'd come back to base this morning, engines roaring. When we ran out to watch them land, some of them sent their planes into spins and stalls and put on a show.

Sally raced to the window and I thought that there was no boy on earth, even Roy Acuff, who could get me to race anywhere right now. It was too darn hot, and, besides, I was done with boys, and not just because Jackie Cochran had forbid it. I was here to earn my wings.

Sally said, "Velva Jean, one of them's asking for you. The one that plays reveille on his bugle."

Paula looked over at me. She laid her book on her chest. She said, "I thought you were married."

"I am." I pretended to study my Morse code.

Paula yelled, "Go away! She's not interested!"

My face started burning pink, right around the temples, but I tried to act like this wasn't happening. Sally sat back down across from me and said, "The one they call Ty, that bugler, he said to tell you to listen close to taps tonight because he's going to throw a little something in there just for you."

At 9:57 that night, Sally stood by the open window and waited. Loma and Paula and Mudge lay on their beds, not reading or writing or talking, and I knew they were waiting too. I sat at the desk, writing a letter, and pretending like I didn't much care what Ned Tyler played for me, but I'd only written about five words.

At ten o'clock on the dot, we heard the bugle. Sally said, "Hartsie, get over here."

I acted like it was the last thing I wanted to do, but I sighed and set down my book and walked to the window. I could see Ty outside, standing between the barracks, just a dark shadow. There was something bright and sad about the clear, clean notes of the bugle. Sally put her arm through mine and her head on my shoulder, and we listened, and there at the end was "Keep on the Sunny Side." He played the whole thing till one of the officers shouted at him to stop.

The girls and I clapped, and the shadow bowed in our direction. I stood there a minute longer before climbing into bed.

"Too bad you're married, Hartsie," Paula said. She was smirking at me. I made a face at her and then opened Mama's Bible and wrote fast as I could before the lights went out: "May 12—Velva Jean flies solo for the first time as a pilot in the WFTD." I read the words over, and then I closed the Bible and was just putting it back into my footlocker when something fell out. The heartleaf Granny had given me for heart trouble. I picked up the leaf and held it to my nose, breathing it in. Then I pinched off just the smallest piece and slipped it under my pillow, tucking the rest back into the Bible.

June 15, 1943

Deer gurl,

Yur granddaddy and me shure does miss you. You dont no how much. We're so prowd of you. Have you flew a bommer yet?

Is Harley Bright down there? He's gone missing. You let me no if he is and if so if you need help. I can always sent Frank Lowe down there aftur him. He's about the only one left up on this mountin with good nees.

I luv you.

Granny

TWENTY-FIVE

*B*y July the air was heavy, even at night, and the wind that always blew, whether it was winter or summer, suddenly blew like a broiler. It got up to a hundred degrees in the sun, and we moved slow and talked slow. Even flying was hot because now we were in the BTs, which was what we called the planes we flew in basic training, and these had closed cockpits, which meant we melted just like we were inside a Dutch oven. At bedtime, we soaked our pajamas in the bathroom sink and then wore them to sleep in.

We started sneaking our cots outside after lights out—not just Paula, Sally, Mudge, Loma, and me, but girls from other bays too. At night the breeze blew stronger and the air wasn't cool, but at least we weren't locked up in the bay where the air was so stuffy and thick that you couldn't think to study or even talk much.

We had to watch out for rattlesnakes because they came out at night. They were trying to stay cool too. Sally said the thing to do if you saw one was to run if you were far enough away from it, but if you were close enough for it to strike, you had to stand still as a statue and then back away as slow as possible with steps so small that the rattler couldn't tell you were backing away. Then when you were far enough from it, you ran like hell. Sally said that rattlers could strike at a distance up to half the length of their bodies.

Every night after supper, Ned Tyler the bugler met me at the mess hall door and asked me to take a walk around base, and every night I said no. He was good-looking and funny and he played the trumpet just as good as anyone I'd ever heard, but that was as far as it went.

Sometimes I talked to Ty, but I wouldn't walk with him. I only talked to him about things that didn't matter, like what the weather would be like tomorrow and what to do when you saw a rattlesnake. After mess one day, I told him what Sally said, mostly just to fill up space and not let any serious conversation in.

He said, "Oh no. What you want to do with a rattler is sing to it."

"Sing to it?"

He started singing loud as could be:

You've had your day,
don't stand around and frown.
You've been a good old wagon, daddy,
but you done broke down!

I tried not to, but I laughed till I was hiccupping. I said, "Could I sing it a hymn?"

He said, "Are you kidding? Rattlesnakes only like ragtime."

He is the king of lovin',
has manners of a crown.
He's a good old wagon, daddy,
and he ain't broke down!

I watched him while he sang—right there in front of the cadets, officers, and the girls from the WFTD walking by—and I thought, *It's a shame I can't fall in love with you.* He seemed like a good man to lose your heart to.

~

On July 6 we started practicing parachute landings. We trained by running as fast as we could and throwing ourselves onto the ground. We had to learn to land on our backs instead of breaking our fall with our hands or our feet because that was the surest way to break your arm or leg. We spent all afternoon in the burning sun jumping from a platform so we could prepare for an accident. When we were done with that, we swung down on pulleys to practice our landings that way. I was black and blue, just like someone who'd been punched and prodded with a stick. Every single bone and muscle ached, sharp stabbing pains that made me lose my breath each time I moved.

I sat at the table in our bay, Sally across from me writing and reading out loud, Paula propped on her cot where she was nursing her hip with an ice pack and groaning. I stared at my book on Morse code, but the words and figures blurred so that it looked like they were being washed out—just like I'd spilled water on the pages.

Jesus, just take me now. I'm done with this. I never thought I could be so tired or so sore. Please make this heat go away and let us have a break. I'll learn Morse code, so help me. I'll practice it all day long. Just don't make me jump off any more platforms and don't let them swing me from any more pulleys.

I wondered if Johnny Clay was throwing himself on the ground and jumping from platforms right now, somewhere in North Carolina, if he was even still there. The thought of him was like another bruise, another ache. I closed my book and said, "Sally, can I borrow some paper?" She didn't even look up, just pushed her notebook over to me and kept talking to herself. I picked up a pen and started writing my brother a letter.

"Dear Johnny Clay," I wrote. "Where on earth are you? Are you still in North Carolina or have you gone to Europe? Please answer me as soon as you get this because I want to know you're okay."

~

On July 8, just after bed check, we were lying on our cots, each of us tossing and turning. We could hear the sounds of airplanes outside, which meant the trainees in the class ahead of us were night flying.

Mudge said, "I'm too hot to drag my cot outside tonight."

Sally said, "I've never been so hot in my life. Our Indiana summer ain't this bad." She cracked her gum three times in a row.

Paula sat up and said, "Blast it. I can't sleep. Let's go watch the show."

Loma said, "What do you mean? Where?"

"The control tower."

Loma said, "We're not allowed up there."

"Well, we'll just have to be quiet about it." Paula got out of bed and reached for her boots and her zoot suit.

Mudge and Sally started getting dressed, Sally chattering away. "There's the cutest boy that works the control tower. Rodney Bloom. Red hair, blue eyes, built just like a football player." She whistled. "I've had my eye on him for weeks now and the most he's done is smile at me."

Loma said, "I'm not going."

I felt a thrill deep down as I stood up, the cot creaking, and pulled on my zoot suit over my nightgown, which was still wet in places.

Mudge said, "All for one and one for all, Lolo. If you don't go, we don't go."

Loma was quiet. We all stood there waiting for her, and then she sighed and swung her feet onto the floor.

It was a dark, moonless night, but we didn't dare use flashlights. We tiptoed in a line, Paula leading the way, Loma falling last, and climbed the steep steps of the control tower. The boys in the tower nodded at us, but otherwise didn't pay us much attention. We huddled together by one of the windows. Paula whispered, "They think we're here to wait our turn in the flight line."

Sally leaned into me and said, "He's over there."

I looked past her at a red-haired boy sitting behind a panel of switches. We watched him for a minute until he glanced up and saw us and smiled at Sally. She pinched my arm and put her hand over her mouth to keep from laughing. Then we watched the lights on the wings and tails of the planes as they took off and climbed into blackness. The lights traced a pattern around the field, just like floating, gliding stars, before coming back to land. We watched the traffic controllers direct the planes, waving different colored lights—red, green, amber. White was for emergencies. Shirley Bingham had told us about more than one girl that had an electrical failure, which meant the plane would plunge into darkness and the gear had to be pumped by hand. It also meant the radio would die, so the girl would have to land in silence.

Just the thought was scary enough to keep me up nights long after the others had gone to sleep. I thought about Mudge saying Loma was the worryingest girl she knew. But she had no idea how much I worried each time before I flew and after. I could imagine every single thing that might go wrong. The only time I didn't seem to worry was when I was actually flying.

Tonight I didn't worry though. I just stood there with my friends and watched the bright-white lights of the planes taking off and landing and soaring high above us.

~

On Saturday nights the girls and me went to the Avengerette Club in town and danced with the cadets. Every week Ty asked me to go with him as his date and every week I said no. This didn't mean I didn't dance with him now and then, but I never danced more than three or four dances with him a night. On Saturday, July 10, I danced six.

On Monday, July 12, I was sitting on the runway in my BT, waiting to take off, and suddenly Ty appeared, pulling himself up into the plane. He sat in the seat behind me and slouched way down, looking out the window at the ground below. He said, "Go, go, go—before they see me!"

I said, "You're not supposed to be in here."

He said, "Go!"

"You're going to get me in trouble!"

"Go, Velva Jean!"

I pulled the throttle and I went. I took off faster than I should have because he'd surprised me and shook me up a little. It was one thing to try to dance with me but another to get into my plane when I was supposed to be flying solo. I lived for these moments up in the air all by myself. I thought, Ned Tyler, you're going to be sorry you got in my plane today. I thought I might take him into a dive or a spin, or maybe one spin after another, over and over.

The clouds were rolled into huge, billowy masses. They looked like mountains made of snow. I took us in and out between the clouds, up and down. When we climbed above them, Ty leaned forward and said, "I like it best up here. Up above the overcast. Look around you—nothing but blue."

I didn't say anything to him, and he leaned forward then and said in my ear, "You ever been fence hopping?"

"What's that?"

"We have to find a farm first." The way he said it was funny because all there was out here was farms. "You just put her down, low to the ground as you can, and when you come to a fence you have to hop it. Just watch out for bushes and cows."

We flew for a bit and I thought: I'm not going fence hopping just because you tell me to. I'm not doing anything I don't want to do myself. There was a white fence down below, and there were horses grazing behind it.

"Now!" he said.

I dropped us down sharp and fast, soaring over the ground as close as I dared. I hoped I'd scared him. The fence was right in front of us, and I thought: This is so stupid. Do you want to get yourself killed? But I didn't feel scared because suddenly I felt his hands on my shoulders and this made me feel like I could hop a hundred fences all in a row.

I pulled up just as we got to the fence and then I dropped back down and found another one. We did that over and over, both of us laughing, till Ty started singing "Don't Fence Me In." Then I flew us high up into the air so we could head on back to Avenger Field. I looked down at the ground and everything looked the same and I didn't see any sign of the base.

I said, "Which way is it?" I was trying to remember what Puck said about knowing your compass because sometimes you found yourself without any landmarks to go from. He had been making us practice this again and again—naming each town we passed over, not by the water tower, but by direction. He always said: "You have to figure it out on the basis of what you know, not what you see."

Ty said, "I think we need to go east."

I had a doubtful feeling in the back of my mind, but I turned the nose of the plane eastward, and we circled over more farms, more fences, more cows. I said, "I don't think that's right."

He was checking his compass. He said, "Try south."

I pointed us south, and we flew for a while over more farms and cows and fences. Then we flew west and then north till we were right back where we started but not anywhere close to Avenger Field. I waited to feel the panic that I usually felt when I got lost and didn't know where I was going. This was one of the worst things about flying—trusting your judgment, knowing where you were, where you'd been, where you were headed. But I didn't panic because Ty was sitting right behind me, and all I could think was that I was finally having adventures and wasn't that what I'd been missing all along?

We landed at Bruce Field in Ballinger, where they trained Army Air Corps flying cadets. I knew that the base was southeast of Sweetwater by about forty miles. Ty helped me down from the plane as some of the cadets came to meet us. He said, "They won't believe their eyes when they see you."

I radioed back to Avenger to tell them where we were, and then we were invited to stay for dinner. We ate country fried steak with gravy and mashed potatoes, and I could barely eat because it was so hot and my stomach was jumping around from the excitement of it all. The cadets wanted to know everything about the WFTD, and sometimes I talked and sometimes Ty did. I liked sitting back and listening to him talk about my flying and how brave I was and how brave all us girls were because we weren't just doing the same jobs as men but were having to prove ourselves on top of it.

And then the cadets talked about their flying and about why they did it. When it was Ty's turn, he said, "The reason I fly is simple—because no matter how much shit life deals you, the sun is shining up above any overcast if you just climb high enough. I call it 'ceiling and visibility unlimited.'"

I turned this phrase over in my mind and gave it a good think. I decided ceiling and visibility unlimited sounded like something I believed in too.

Afterward we walked to the BT and flew back to Avenger Field, where I was given two demerits for losing my way, and Ty was given six for stowing aboard without clearing it first. He walked me to my bay and said, "Sorry for getting you in trouble, Velva Jean."

I said, "It was worth it," which it was.

He said, "I'm thinking Bruce Field was a pretty nice base." As he said it he moved in closer and my heart went thud-thud-thud. "Maybe I could put in a request so that when we're transferred they'll send me there instead of to California." He was standing over me, and I had to tip my head back to look at him. The moonlight was catching the side of his face, and I decided I liked his long nose and his broad mouth and the way his hair was standing up here and there. He was bright and alive. There was nothing black and white about him.

I said, "I like your hair."

He sighed. "Ah, that's it, then. You only want me for my hair."

I laughed. "It's just about the best hair I ever saw."

He said, "And would you love me just as much if I was bald?"

I'd never teased like this with a man before and I realized I liked it. I wondered if I was flirting, and if so if I was good at it. I said, "I don't think so."

"Well." He rubbed his jaw. "I don't blame you, although I'm pretty sure I'd love you if you were bald as a bullfrog." For one moment, I thought he was going to kiss me, but then he said, "Velva Jean, I want to take you on a proper date. We don't have to go walking or dancing if that's too much for you. We don't even have to go fence hopping. But maybe something safe and harmless like drinking tea or sitting. We could even eat a meal of some sort, but I don't want to push it."

I laughed even though I didn't want to, because the thought of going on a date with someone—anyone—right now was enough to make my head go light. I told myself: It's only tea or sitting. It's only a meal. You don't have to marry him. You don't have to fall in love.

Good, I told myself. Because I can't.

And then I thought, He may not like you anymore anyway after you tell him about Harley.

"Okay," I said to him. "I'll go."

July 16, 1943

Dear family,

I wish I could send you a picture of what I look like. I know newspapers and magazines are telling us to "Cheer the way to Victory by looking your loveliest." But up at 6:00 a.m., sharing a bathroom with ten other girls, mess at 7:00, followed by PE, Morse code, flight simulation on the Link trainer, and flight training, leaves no time for primping. Also, we donated our lipstick tubes, all but one each— did you know they're being turned into bullet casings? Between the four of us, we gave up eleven lipsticks, though most of those belonged to Mudge. We're sunburned and freckled, windblown and covered in dust, tripping around in coveralls that are five sizes too big.

We started cross-country this week. Mudge and me flew to Big Spring, Lubbock, and Spur, and today Sally and me buzzed over the lake at Abilene doing lazy eights and chandelles, which is a climbing turn that starts with a dive to gain speed and uses the momentum of the plane. When we're not flying, we're marching in parades, doing infantry drills, cleaning our barracks to get ready for inspection (trying like everything to get rid of the sand), and studying, studying, studying. My back aches so much at the end of each day that I can hardly stand up. I'm afraid I could walk in the door and you wouldn't know who or what I was.

But I'm happy. I think that even with all the fighting in Europe and the Pacific and worrying about my brothers and missing you all, I'm maybe happier than I ever been in my life because I know I'm being useful and that I'm playing a small part in this great big war.

I love you, each and every one—

your Velva Jean

TWENTY-SIX

For our proper date, Ty and me packed a picnic and drove to Lake Sweetwater. On the way there, I thought about all the things he didn't know about me and wondered how long it would take to fill him in on everything, all these things Harley already knew. How could he get to know me without seeing Daddy Hoyt and Granny and all the people I loved, in the place where Mama was buried and where my songs came from? He wouldn't know about Indian message trees. He'd never heard the way Fair Mountain hummed like it was making its own music. He'd never been to Deal's or ridden up on the Scenic, that road on top of the mountains. He didn't know about the giant that lived in Devil's Courthouse or the Nunnehi that helped you find your way if you were lost in the woods. I sat there thinking all these things and I got myself so worked up that I thought, You should just get out right now and start walking back to Avenger Field.

Lake Sweetwater was built by the Civilian Conservation Corps, just like the Scenic. Besides the lake, there was an open amphitheater, a baseball field, two fish hatcheries, a stone clubhouse, a boat pier, a fishing pier, a nine-hole golf course, and a suspension footbridge over the lake. There were picnic benches, camping areas, rock bridges, lookout houses, gravel walkways, and a paved road that ran around the outside of the lake.

Ty carried the food in a brown paper sack, and we walked over the suspension bridge and the rock bridges until we got to the picnic area. We didn't hold hands because I was careful to keep mine in my pockets, but we walked side by side. It was a beautiful day—a little hazy, the sky white instead of blue. I could see people playing golf and swimming, but we had the picnic tables to ourselves.

Ty set everything up, and I helped him, and then we sat down. I looked around me for a long time before I started eating, and thought what a lovely place this was and how I wouldn't want to be anywhere else at just this moment, not even the Opry.

Ty said, "I hope you don't eat like a girl."

I said, "I love to eat."

"Thank God."

We ate watermelon and ham sandwiches and potato salad. I thought the food tasted better sitting outside in the sun at Lake Sweetwater than it ever would have if we'd been sitting inside the mess hall.

Ty said, "I'd like to thank you for coming on a proper date with me, honey, even though I'd a lot rather show you an improper one." He clinked his bottle of Coca-Cola against mine and drank it down. "One thing at a time though."

Then he set his Coca-Cola on the table and said, "Tell me about you."

"About me?"

"Yes." He leaned back on his arms and smiled at me. "Don't leave anything out, because I'll know if you do. And don't just tell me the good stuff."

I thought, There's more bad stuff than good stuff. And I wondered how that had happened to me. I was charmed. I was lucky. Everyone from my own mama to Aunt Junie, the witch-healer, had told me so. I didn't feel like one of those people that other people felt sorry for because they had too much sadness and heartbreak. But when I sat down and added everything up I realized I could have been.

I told him about Mama and Daddy and Sweet Fern and my brothers, especially Johnny Clay. I told him about being saved and going to fetch the moonshine when Mama was sick and how I prayed to Jesus to save her. I told him about the note that Daddy left and how Mama took to her bed afterward and never got up again. I told him about my daddy leaving us with Sweet Fern and how Johnny Clay and me ran away and then how we came back and the panther almost got us. I told him about the road that was built across the mountains and how my brother and my daddy went to work on it. I told him about the Wood Carver and how I would go visit him and the train wreck that killed Danny Deal. I told him about Lucinda Sink and Johnny Clay and about how he gave Danny's yellow truck to me and how I taught myself to drive it. I told him about making my record and saving up money for Nashville. I told him about the outlanders and how the Wood Carver was chased away along with so many of my friends, and I told him how I knew then that I had to leave no matter what and that my daddy had left me money and Johnny Clay gave me a map and he also gave me the note my daddy wrote Mama, back before she took to her bed, and how all it said was that he loved her and was trying to earn some money to help her feel better.

And then I told him about Harley. I didn't want to tell him everything, no matter what he said. (I thought: But you did just tell him everything, girl—you told him things that no one else knows the whole of, not even Harley, not even Johnny Clay.) So I just said that I was young once and fell in love and got married and then I left him.

Ty said, "Do you still love him?"

"No. I haven't for a long time."

"No regrets?"

"No."

Ty was quiet for a moment and then he said, "Thank you for telling me about that. I imagine it wasn't easy to do. Thank you for telling me about everything, honey."

I said, "You're welcome." And suddenly I felt lighter, like I'd just set down one of the burdens I always carried around with me.

That night we watched a baseball game—Champion versus Divide—and after Champion won there was a pop and then a crack and then a burst of color, just like a star exploding in red, green, and blue. Ty and I sat side by side and watched the fireworks, and I thought about how fireworks were a good idea because they made a person happy to see and to hear. Then I remembered the fireworks at the Tulane Hotel and the way Charlie Jones had kissed me.

Ty took my hand then and he was warm and strong, and I could feel his pulse beating into mine. There was an explosion of purple and gold, and I said, "Oh!" Then that was it—after just a minute they were over. I sat waiting for more.

Ty said, "They have to skimp on the fireworks because of the gunpowder used to make them. Too valuable to waste these days."

I said, "They were pretty while they lasted." I was still watching, just in case.

He said, "Well, look. There's another one."

I said, "Where?" The only light in the sky was the moon.

He said, "And another. That was a good one—red, white, and blue." The sky was quiet and dark.

I thought, He's making them up just for me. It was the sweetest thing I could imagine. I said, "There goes another. Purple and green. Like a starburst."

He said, "Red this time. Then blue. Then red again."

I said, "I like the gold ones best."

He said, "Well looky there, honey! A gold one. And another." He was pointing. "And another. There and there and there."

In my mind I could see them clear as day. I said, "They're beautiful."

Ty brought my hand to his lips and kissed it, never taking his eyes off the sky.

Back at base I started wishing time would slow down. I wanted to go back to the beginning of the day and start over again so I had everything to look forward to. I moved slow as could be getting out of the jeep because I didn't want the date to be over.

Ty stood there holding my door. He said, "Please take your time, honey. The longer you take, the longer the date lasts." I laughed because he had read my mind.

When I was out and standing there, he shut the door behind me and we stood looking at each other. I felt like I should say something but I didn't know what to say. Thank you for the most wonderful day? Thank you for listening to me and wanting to know so much? Thank you for sitting there while I talked on and on about the deepest things in my heart and for never looking twitchy or bored or bothered and for not thinking bad of me for having a daddy that left and for having a marriage that didn't work out?

He said, "You should see your face."

I put my hand to my cheek in case my thoughts were showing through—things like, Thank you for hearing all the bad things that ever happened to me and still making me feel loved.

And then I thought: Oh my God. I feel loved.

He said, "Hell." And then he kissed me. For a minute I let myself be kissed. And it was warm and electric and sweet, and my stomach dropped right into my feet. I thought I might melt right into him, right into his skin, and then he pulled away and he said, "I hope that was okay." He had his hands on my shoulders, those long fingers playing with the ends of my hair. "I mean, I know it was okay because I'm a damn good kisser, but I hope it was okay to do that."

I looked up at him and for a split second, there in the moonlight, he looked like Harley—tall and dark and handsome—but different. I felt a chill, even though it was hotter than hot out. I said, "It was."

He said, "I thought it was a bit . . ." He frowned, thinking. "A bit *blam!* Like in comic books. Pow! Blam! Magic!"

I laughed even though I was shaking like I was standing in a snow bank. I said, "Blam!"

He said, "You make me feel fifteen again, honey. But only in the very best way." He leaned in, and this time I put my hand on his chest. I said, "I want you to do it again, but you shouldn't." There was so much else to say: I'm married, but not married, and until I'm not actually married I can't fall in love with someone new. I'm here to be a member of the WFTD and earn my wings and that's what I'm going to do. I've traveled a long way to get here and I won't let anything come in the way of that now.

He looked sad, somewhere behind his eyes. But he smiled when he said, "Too much magic?"

I said, "Yes."

And then I turned around and walked to the barracks and didn't look back once. That night he played taps in the normal way, without anything added. Three days later the cadets were transferred out of Avenger Field and sent to Ontario, California.

~

On the afternoon of July 20, just before mess, I was in the latrine washing my face and hands, trying to get the dust off me, when I heard a crash from our bay and, right after that, another. I dried my hands and walked into the room to find Loma lying like a dead person, facedown on her cot, her books and shoes scattered on the floor. Mudge was standing in front of her wardrobe mirror, brushing her hair.

I said, "What happened?"

Mudge said, "I don't know. She just came in here throwing stuff."

"Loma?" I sat down beside her on the cot. Her shoulders were shaking and she was making little sounds into the pillow.

Suddenly Sally and Paula came running in. "We just heard," said Paula.

"Heard what?" Mudge shut the door to her wardrobe.

Loma said something into the pillow.

Mudge said, "What did you say, Lolo?" She looked at us. "What did she say?"

Sally sat down on the other side of Loma and started rubbing her back in little circles. "She washed out." She cracked her gum like an exclamation point.

"What?" More and more girls were washing out—31 from our class of 112 already. But those were other girls in other bays. Loma was one of us.

She rolled over, her face red, her hair sticking to her cheeks. I brushed her hair away and handed her a handkerchief. She wiped her eyes and then cried harder and then wiped her eyes again, and then she sat up and said, "I knew it. Didn't I tell you all along? I knew I was going to wash out."

Paula sat right down on the floor beside Loma's cot and said, "Tell us what happened, Lo."

"I was up for a check ride today, but no one told me ahead of time, and they gave me three, one after another. Three! The first one was okay, but the second was bad, and I blew the third one by coming down bumpy and overshooting the runway."

"There's got to be something we can do," Mudge said. She was looking at us. "Talk to Puck? Go to Miss Cochran?"

Loma said, "You think no one else has tried that? You know as well as I do that once you wash out, you're out."

We sat there, all of us, not talking. And then Sally cracked her gum—one, two, three times—and started to cry. Suddenly Mudge was crying and I was crying and even Paula was crying a little. We wrapped our arms around Loma in a big group hug and just rocked back and forth, back and forth.

When we pulled away, all of us sniffling and snuffling, Loma said, "I can't go back to making supper and cleaning the house. My little girl and my husband are so proud of me. Now I'm nothing but their stupid old wife and mother again."

This made me think: Why wasn't it enough for Loma to be a wife and mother? Would it be enough for me? For any of us? Could we go back to regular life after being here, after we'd lived up in the sky? I thought that after the war was over the ones that could put away their silver wings and go back home and have babies and not feel like they were missing out on anything would be the lucky ones. I thought about Sweet Fern and her tidy house and her tidy hair and her quilts and the curtains she'd sewn herself. And I remembered her telling me to go because she couldn't. That she needed me to.

"How can I ever tell you fools good-bye?" Loma said. "I'll never in my life have friends like you again." Then she swore for the third time in her life, and put a whole dollar in the cuss pot.

Loma left the next morning. The rest of us flew to one of the aux-iliary fields they'd set up to help with air traffic, and we rode home in the cattle wagon. While the other girls talked and laughed, Paula, Mudge, Sally, and me sat in the back in silence. I stared out the win-dow at the flat, brown landscape, and it suddenly hit me how beautiful it was in its own ugly way. What if I had to leave it? Where would I go? What would I do? Go back to work as a waitress? Go home to

Fair Mountain and sit up in Mama's old house, up in my old bedroom, when a big, terrible war was changing the world?

As far from home as I was in that flat and dusty place, I felt home again. I guessed that was who I was now, this person meant to struggle on my own, out in the great wide world, doing things for myself. One thing I loved about flying was that no one could keep you grounded or rooted like a bush or a tree when you were in the sky.

———————

July 31, 1943

Dear Velva Jean,

I hope you don't mind my writing, but I couldn't help myself. I'm here in Ontario, California, at the Ontario Army Airfield. You'll have to come to California sometime because I think you'd like it. The sun shines all the time, but it's not hot as Hades like it is in Texas. It's a desert, but there are also palm trees and mountains, even if they're brown and scrubby and not the kind you like. I haven't seen the ocean yet, but we'll start maneuvers soon, and I plan to fly over it even if I have to steal a plane to do it.

In case you couldn't guess, I sure did like meeting you and I hope it's okay if I write you now and then. I'd love to hear from you in return because, as you know, the best time of the day is mail call. You're about the loveliest thing I ever did see, Velva Jean, inside and out, and I want you to know that even if I never see you again, I'm happy to know you.

The main reason I'm writing, though, is because I was just in the rec room, where they were playing the radio. What do you think was on? "Keep on the Sunny Side." So of course I thought of you.

Hope you're keeping the dust out of your eyes and your feet off the ground.

Your friend,

Ty

August 3, 1943

Dear Ty,

Thank you for your letter. I'm sorry I didn't get to say good-bye, but I want you to know that you can't count on me to write you letters and be your friend. I'm not in any place to be romantic with anyone. I left my husband a long time ago, but he's still my husband, and I don't want to drag anyone into my life when I'm not free. I wish we'd gotten to dance more and that we could have gone on another picnic, but it's better that we didn't. I hope you see that.

Thank you again for the letter. But I don't think you should send any more.

Your friend,

Velva Jean

August 6, 1943

Well now, dammit, Velva Jean. I don't give a hang if you're still married, as long as you're not married in your heart. Now you'll say I don't know you all that well, and I guess I don't, but it don't take much to recognize that you're a rare girl. Maybe you don't see me in quite that same light, but sometime, someday, you'll lose your heart to some stupid man and I think it might as well be me.

Your husband's not the problem. The worst rival any man will have with you is your love for flying and driving and the fact that you just ain't cut out for living a normal, boring life. In other words, don't stick Velva Jean back up on that mountain. But you know what? I don't want a housewife and I don't want a girl who can't fly. I want you.

I'll tell you this—if I hear about you giving your heart to the first guy who comes along after me, I'm coming back to Avenger and giving you both what for. All I want is a chance.

I hope you know I wouldn't give you hell if you hadn't stole your way into my heart. And I know, I know you didn't mean to. Another thing—don't worry about hurting me. I've been hanging around for a long time on this earth (twenty-five years to be exact) and my heart is tough enough on the surface that it would take a pretty hard blow to break it. (Although I've got a feeling that a blow from you would pack a pretty punch.)

Take care, little one.

Your friend,

Ty

_____

August 9, 1943

Dear Ty,

Mercy, how you talk. I'm so afraid of doing something that will lead you on that I'm scared to open my mouth or, in this case, my typewriter. At the same time, I want to lead you on. In spite of everything you say about how tough your heart is, I know it's a good and sweet heart and it would kill me if I ever was to break it. But if I don't write you and I tell you not to write me anymore, I just might break my own.

What to do?

Your cautious friend,

Velva Jean

_____

August 13, 1942

Dear Velva Jean,

For God's sake, woman, you're sweet to be so worried, but listen to me good here. You asked me what to do, and I'm going to tell you: go ahead and lead me on. That's right— break my heart if you can (and I'm sure you can), because you already gave me fair warning. If I choose to ignore it, it's my own foolish fault.

Love,

Ty

_____

August 16, 1943

Dear Ty,

You're going to wear me down, aren't you?

Love,

Velva Jean

_____

August 19, 1943

Dear Velva Jean,

Yes.

Love,

Ty

TWENTY-SEVEN

On August 20 newspapers reported that First Sergeant Beachard Samuel Hart, twenty-five, a medic from North Carolina, led a marine platoon to capture a hilltop on New Georgia, in the central Solomon Islands, overlooking the Munda Point airstrip. Reporters said the New Georgia jungle was "the worst terrain of the Pacific campaign." The marine invasion forces had to cling to hillsides while nine thousand Japanese soldiers hid below in dugouts.

It took the marines weeks to reach the airstrip, which was seven miles from the shoreline. On August 3, Beachard and his platoon found themselves in front of a hilltop overlooking the airstrip. While the Japanese fired machine guns and threw grenades at them, they pushed right on through to a point midway across the hilltop.

When his soldiers ran away and Beach was left by himself, he crouched behind a tree stump and continued fighting, even though he wasn't carrying a rifle and was shot in the hand and also in the ear. He hurled thirty grenades at the Japanese dugouts, forcing the enemy to run. Twenty-eight Japanese soldiers were killed in the attack.

When asked how he found the courage to do it, Beach replied, "Have you ever prayed?" When told he might be a candidate for the Medal of Honor, he said, "I'd rather they didn't. I did what anyone should have done, even if not everyone would have."

I clipped the story out of the newspaper and folded it into my hatbox along with other stories printed about my brother, Beachard S. Hart, who never did believe in wars between men or fighting or killing but who believed in peace and forgiveness and who was happiest when he was on his own, wandering the woods and the mountains.

~

We started night flying the week of August 23, and while the other girls were finishing mess or taking turns in the showers I reported to the flight line early and sat down on one of the low wooden benches that were lined up by the runway. It was dusk, and the sky was turning all shades of pink and gold and orange. I watched the lights of the airplanes circling the field: white, red, white, red.

And then I got out my notepaper and wrote a letter to Ty. We were writing every week, back and forth, and I was trying to be reasonable and not like him too much.

I wrote to him about learning cross-country flying, instrument flying, and how to fly in formation. I wrote to him about learning to fly the beam, which was what they called it when you hit just the right spot on the radio signals that were beamed out from airports. If you were exactly on the beam, there was a hum that went out, but if you were to the right of the beam you heard what they called an *A* sound, which was like a dot-dash, and if you were to the left of the beam you heard an *N* sound, which was a dash-dot. The two sounds blending together made the solid hum of the beam. It was like a perfect note in music.

I wrote to him about Puck—about how he said, "When you're sitting in that cockpit, I want you to picture the flying you're doing in that particular airplane. It's just you and that one plane. You've got to know just what that plane can do for you." I wrote to him about how, on August 5, the WFTD had merged with Nancy Harkness Love's WAFS, and we were now officially the WASP, which stood for Women Airforce Service Pilots.

And before I could write about anything else—like how I missed him and how I thought about him and how I got sad sometimes because he wasn't there, even though I was glad he wasn't there because I would want to spend time with him and not be working and studying like I was supposed to—Paula and Mudge and Sally and the other girls came out of the bays one by one. They sat down beside me, and Sally put her head on my shoulder and went right to sleep.

That night we were flying the Cessna C-78, which was a twin-engine wood-and-fabric advanced trainer that had a range of 750 miles. The best thing about this was that we got to fly with each other, three to a plane—two WASP trainees and an instructor. One of us girls would fly out and the other one would fly back. We drew straws to see who would go first.

I folded up my letter and put it in my pocket. We sat there waiting our turn—Mudge and me were flying together, going up with Lieutenant Whitley, who Mudge had her eye on. Shirley Bingham walked up to tell us that *Life* magazine was coming to Avenger Field to do a story on the WASP and take photographs of us.

Mudge said, "How do you know?"

Shirley said, "I work in the office. Jackie Cochran told me."

Mudge started fixing her hair, just like a photographer was there right now.

Shirley said, "She gave them a list of the most photogenic girls and you two"—she looked at Mudge and me—"are on it."

I thought about the most famous magazine in the world coming here, to Avenger Field, and taking pictures of us and how funny it was that somewhere—wherever *Life* magazine's office was—someone had a list with my name on it. I thought maybe I would tell Ty about it in my letter.

"It's a lovely night for flying."

We looked up and there was Jacqueline Cochran standing next to us, so close we could touch her, looking at the sky, watching the planes already in flight, her hands shoved in her trouser pockets. It was surprising to see her because she didn't spend a lot of time on base. We heard she was spending more and more of her time in Washington, D.C., trying to get the status of the WASP changed from civilian to military.

Her lipstick was faded, like she'd just had a cup of coffee, but she looked as handsome as ever. Shirley Bingham had told us that Miss

Cochran also ran her own cosmetics firm and had created something called Wonda-matic mascara.

We sat blinking at this woman, the most famous female pilot in the world, and finally Paula, who was the bravest of us all, said, "Yes, ma'am."

Jackie Cochran walked over to the wooden bench where we were sitting and sat down right beside me. She said, "You're Velva Jean Hart."

I said, "Yes, ma'am." The other girls gawked at me.

She said, "You sent me a number of letters."

I said, "Yes, ma'am." I thought about the last one I'd written her, all about how I knew she was an orphan who didn't go to school and who had to choose her name out of a telephone book and how her and me were alike because we came from the same place. I suddenly wished it was my turn to go up in the Bobcat because I thought these might not be things a person would want to hear about herself, especially from a stranger, even if they were true.

She crossed her legs and smoothed her pants and pulled a cigarette case out of her pocket. It was beautiful—made of gold, with rubies and diamonds and emeralds on the face—and it shone in the light. She opened it and pulled out a cigarette. She offered me one, and I shook my head. Everything she did seemed elegant.

I couldn't help myself. I said, "How pretty." More than anything, I wanted to hold it and run my hands over the stones. I thought about the emerald my daddy had given me years ago, back when he used to come around before he left us for good, and the gems he tried to mine for a while.

She handed it to me and said, "Do you see the pattern on this case?" She reached over and tilted it in my hands so I could see it in the lights of the control tower and the planes overhead, and the moon high above. I could see that the jewels made some sort of pattern, but I couldn't tell what it was.

I said, "It looks like a route, like a course that's been plotted." Paula, Mudge, and Sally were leaning around me, trying to look over my shoulder. Shirley Bingham and some of the other girls waiting nearby were doing the same.

She said, "It's the route of the Bendix Trophy Race." The Bendix Trophy Race was a transcontinental, point-to-point air race that was supposed to interest engineers in building faster, more reliable planes. The pilots that entered the race flew from Burbank, California, to Cleveland, Ohio. Miss Cochran had won it in 1938, and by doing so opened the race up to women. "My husband gave it to me as a memento."

I said, "It's beautiful." I wanted to own it. I felt jealous of the case and jealous of Miss Cochran for having something so pretty that meant so much to her. I wanted something like that myself and a husband who was so excited about me being a pilot that he would take the time to think it up.

I handed the case back to her because I was afraid if I didn't I might put it in my pocket. She said, "My husband's confined to a wheelchair." This was something we'd heard about her husband, Floyd Odlum, a rich lawyer who had sponsored her in one of her earliest races. He stayed at home in New York while she traveled the world and flew.

She held the case, turning it this way and that in the light. She said, "We write to each other every day."

I tried to picture this man in his wheelchair, writing his wife letters while she called herself "Miss" Cochran and broke the sound barrier and won air races and created a program for women pilots, the first of its kind. I thought he must be about the best man in the world to give her a beautiful cigarette case like that, to help her remember a race she'd won.

Jackie Cochran said, "In real life, I'm Mrs. Floyd Odlum, but up in the air and on the flight line I'm Jacqueline Cochran. I like being both."

I thought, He gets to fly through you and he helps keep you on the ground, but not in a rooted way like a tree.

She lit her cigarette and inhaled. Her fingernails were painted a dark, shiny red. Her hair was curled, resting just above her shoulders. She inhaled again and stood, slipping the cigarette case back into her pocket. "Safe flights, ladies." Then she walked away toward the control tower.

"Well," said Mudge.

"Well," said Paula. "What do you think that was about?" Before I could think about it or answer her, it was my turn to go up, and Mudge and I walked to our plane.

The runways were lit by flares, and as I took off with my quadrant— the four of us rising into the sky one by one—all I could see were the flares on the ground, which looked more like flames. They seemed closer than they were and for a minute they were blinding and I couldn't see anything but the burning red-orange of the fire and the blur of taillights. For one awful moment I thought I was out of formation and that I'd lost everyone.

I remembered something Puck had said about using your artificial horizon if you lost track of where you were. I thought I never would get used to something called an artificial horizon, and then I wondered if that might make a good song or at least the name of one. Something about learning to fly without looking at the sky, just trusting your judgment and letting it guide you even though you didn't know where on earth it was taking you.

I'd plotted my course that afternoon, drawing a line on a chart, listing the checkpoints—Roscoe, Loraine, Westbrook, Big Spring, Stanton, Midland—and the miles between each one. The weather said we'd have a tailwind heading out.

I was flying the takeoff and Mudge would do the landing. This suited me fine because I liked takeoffs better. I loved the thrill of pouring the coal into it, as we called it, and holding the throttle and pointing the plane up into the sky.

Night gathered around us like a blanket. The sun was gone and there wasn't a moon. We were at three thousand feet and the cockpit was dark. Only the instrument panel was lit, the dials looking like little points of starlight.

I said to Mudge, "How long does a divorce take?"

She didn't ask me why I wanted to know. She said, "A year. Sometimes longer." Our voices sounded strange, like they were hovering above us.

I thought about being Mrs. Harley Bright for another year. I suddenly felt like I couldn't be Mrs. Harley Bright for five more minutes.

Mudge said, "But not if you go to Mexico."

I thought about what flying meant to me, how it was so much bigger than anything. Being up in the sky with the ground below, spread out this way and that way, made a person realize how some things in this world are big and some things are small. I loved flying because it taught me to stand on my own and be on my own when I was most scared of doing both. In an AT-6 or Cessna or Stearman or AT-17 Bobcat, I was beyond the keep, which was something we always said to each other. "Beyond the keep" meant that no one had a hold on you, no one could keep you, because you couldn't be pinned down. Flying made me feel free, like I could go anywhere.

August 30, 1943

Dear girls,

Well, I'm back in Monongah, and I still can't believe I'm here. Peggy is happy to see her mama, and it's amazing how much she's grown. She's as tall as Sally, but of course that's not too tall, is it?

I hope you all will write me the news, because even though I'm not there I want to know what you're doing and what's going on. How are things developing with Lieutenant Whitley, Mudge? Is he paying any attention yet? How much money have you added to the cuss pot since I've been gone, Paula? Have you heard from your bugler, Hartsie? Has Sally stopped talking and chewing gum in her sleep? Has she got a date yet with her redhead?

Tomorrow Peggy and I are going to the picture show to see *Song of Bernadette* starring Jennifer Jones, who's almost as pretty as Hartsie. I can't wait for the day when I can go see Barbara Fanning, alias Eloise Mudge, in pictures. Then we're going to eat supper at the diner and maybe do some shopping. I'm going to have to figure out how to fill my days now that I'm not up at six and going from the mess to the classroom to the flight line. You should see me trying to walk like a normal person! I'm still marching wherever I go.

I miss you all. You're the best group of girls I've ever known.

Love,

Loma

September 1, 1943

Dear Velva Jean,

I hope you're happy. I don't sleep. I don't eat. I'm almost bald from the stress of being away from you. The guys all say I'm worthless on the flight line. Just about the only thing I can do these days is play the damn bugle, but instead of reveille or taps I start playing "Keep on the Sunny Side."

Is it strange to say I miss you? Probably. I know we didn't get much time together in the scheme of things. So forget I said it.

But I do.

Love,

Ty

———

September 3, 1943

Dear Ty,

We have a cross-country trip coming up, to Blythe, California. I'll let you know as soon as it's on the books, but I thought maybe, just maybe, I could see you. How far is that from Ontario? Will you come?

Please?

Love,

Velva Jean

———

September 6, 1943

Dear Velva Jean,

Hell yes, I'll come to Blythe, wherever the Sam Hill that is.
Are you kidding? I'd go to the goddamn moon, girl.

Love,

Ty

TWENTY-EIGHT

Juárez, Mexico, was the divorce capital of the world. Mudge said this was where everyone went, even movie actors like Hoot Gibson, the rodeo champion, and his wife, Sally Eilers.

On September 7, Paula and me were scheduled for a cross-country to the Army Air Forces base in Alamogordo, New Mexico. We were flying together in the AT-17, or Bobcat, but this time we weren't taking an instructor along. Alamogordo was about one hundred miles northeast of Juárez, which was just over the border from New Mexico and Texas. We figured we could make our trip, and on the way back we could stop in Juárez and get me a divorce. I knew it might be a serious matter, flying a military plane out of the country during wartime, but I didn't care what they did to me. I needed to be beyond the keep, and I figured I would rather be locked in an army prison than stay married to Harley Bright.

Paula was flying when we ran into an electrical storm just after we passed over the New Mexico border. We were above the rain and above the clouds, but there was lightning on all sides of us. I stared out the window and saw what looked like flames. I sat straight up and thought: The wing is on fire. The engine's on fire. We're going down. I was going to have to die Mrs. Harley Bright.

Paula shouted, "Do you see it? Saint Elmo's Fire?"

I said, "What?"

"Saint Elmo's Fire! The flames outside. It looks like ball lightning, but it's not. It's an electric discharge that happens during thunderstorms, usually over the ocean. Sailors use it to travel by."

I stared out the window and watched the flames dancing. They were spindly and delicate, like miniature lightning strikes. They looked like tree limbs covered in bright-white ice. I thought, They're helping me find my way.

We lost our bearings and overshot Alamogordo, landing at the first airfield we saw. As far as we could tell, we were somewhere north of Albuquerque. As we came in, we could see that the airfield was really some sort of huge, sprawling compound built on a sandstone mesa in the middle of what looked like a desert of other mesas. The land went on for miles—flat scrubby desert ringed by mountains—and as we got nearer to the ground we could see that barbed wire ran around it, sometimes just two or three feet high, like it was made to keep in cows or horses, and sometimes as high as nine or ten feet. There were armed guards stationed in a tower and along the fence, and as Paula took us in I said, "They're aiming their guns at us."

She said, "Who is?"

"The guards."

"Which ones?"

"All of them."

"Jesus, Hartsie, where are we?"

"I don't know. Some sort of military base?"

As soon as we landed, bumping down onto the flat of the desert, the guards ran for us, guns out and pointed in our direction, and yanked us out of the plane. Two young men in beige pants and white shirts—one of them with a shock of dark hair that stood straight up, the other skinny and balding with big, round glasses—stood frowning at us. They were the only ones that weren't in uniforms.

The dark-haired one said, "Where are you coming from?" He made it sound like we were out for a joy ride, like maybe we'd stolen this plane and were just flying it around for fun.

The rain was pouring and thunder boomed in the distance. There was a lightning strike over one of the mesas, and then another. Even though it was hot as an oven, I started shivering. Paula said, "Texas." But it was hard to hear her over the thunder.

The guards surrounded us then, and we took off our helmets. One of them said, "It's just a couple of girls." I didn't like the way he said it, like this meant we couldn't be dangerous or important.

Paula said, "We're WASP trainees from Avenger Field in Texas. We were headed to Alamogordo."

The balding man with glasses said to the dark-haired man, "Jackie Cochran's girls." He had a strange accent.

The dark-haired man said, "A little off-base, aren't you?"

"Yes, sir."

"Let me see some ID."

We pulled out our ID badges and handed them to him. I was good and mad by now because I was wet as a sponge, standing there in the pouring rain, thunder booming all around us, guns pointing at us from every angle.

He said, "Do you know where you've landed?"

Paula said, "No, sir."

"You're in Los Alamos." Los Alamos was at least 250 miles north of Alamogordo. I was trying to think of an airfield in Los Alamos. Just like he read my mind, the man said, "You've just landed at the Los Alamos National Laboratory."

The balding man said, "Feynman." It sounded like a warning.

That was all they said, but by not saying anything, by the guards and the guns and the barbed wire, I knew there was more to it than that.

Even with the storm crashing around us, we were told we couldn't overnight at the lab. The officer in charge, Colonel Martin Hascall, offered to send someone back to Avenger with us, or at least down to Alamogordo. We sat in a private office in one of the low, ugly buildings that was built into the desert. It was Paula, Colonel Hascall, and me. One of the other guards had come in and brought us food.

I said, "We're not heading back to Sweetwater yet. We're on our way to Juárez, Mexico."

He said, "Mexico? No. Never land in Mexico, because they'll put you in jail and not let you out."

I said, "I have to go to Mexico."

Paula said, "She's getting a divorce."

I said, "Paula."

She said, "Maybe he can help us."

We both looked at Colonel Hascall. He said, "You can't get this divorce any other place?"

I said, "It takes too long."

Paula said, "Juárez is the divorce capital of the world."

He said, "Among other things. It's also the prostitution capital, the drug capital, the murder capital."

I said, "We just need to go for one day, just long enough to get me divorced. You don't understand, sir. I need to be beyond the keep."

When the storm died down, Colonel Hascall sent us to Alamogordo with two of his men, Gene Gilbert and Roger Keil. We called Avenger Field to check in, to let them know where we were and that we'd be home the next day. Then, after spending the night at the Alamogordo base, we set off for Juárez with the sergeants.

We landed at noon, just over the Texas border, near El Paso, at Fort Bliss, and from there the four of us drove to Juárez. Sergeant Gene Gilbert was in his late twenties, tall and blond and pale as a ghost, with bright blue eyes and red-framed glasses. Sergeant Roger Keil was a head shorter, dark as a gypsy, and built like a freight train. He was my age.

We were stopped at the border where we showed our IDs and the guards let us through after Sergeant Gilbert told them we were only there for a day and that we'd be leaving by nightfall. The guard said, "Welcome to Mexico. Watch out for those two girls. Don't let them out of your sight. And be back before dark."

I felt a thrill go through me. I'd never in my life been outside the United States, and here I was in Mexico. I suddenly felt as far away as the moon from my family up on Fair Mountain and Gossie in Nashville.

Gene Gilbert was driving and Roger Kiel sat next to him. Up in the front seat, Sergeant Gilbert was talking about what we should do and how we should act when we got out of the car. He said, "I want you girls to hold our hands and stick close to us."

I felt another thrill as I imagined a place so dangerous that girls couldn't be out alone. I couldn't help it—the thrill was the same kind I felt when I thought about prisons or crazy people or walking through the woods at night, watching out for haints.

Sergeant Gilbert said, "The divorce should take a couple of hours at most. We've got a buddy that came down here last month, and it only took him an hour."

I looked at my door and tugged on the lock just to make sure it was in place. I looked across at Paula's, and it seemed to be pushed in. I wanted to see Juárez, to see the whore ladies and bad men and murderers walking the street, but I also didn't want them in the car with me.

We drove through downtown, and Paula and I stared out the windows at the old crumbling buildings and donkeys and painted ladies. I counted at least twelve murderers as we headed for City Hall. I grabbed Paula's hand and squeezed it. She said, "Shit, Velva Jean." Then to the boys: "I'm glad you fellas are with us." I thought she had her eye on Sergeant Keil even though he didn't say two words.

"Much obliged," said Sergeant Gilbert.

To keep my mind off the sagging store awnings and the trash in the street, the chickens running wild, and the balconies crowded with men drinking tequila, I thought about all the things I would write to Johnny Clay in my next letter. He would be sick with envy when he knew I'd come here.

Then I looked around me—really looked—and the closer we got to City Hall, the sadder I felt because Juárez was a sad, dirty place, and this was where my marriage was ending. I thought about how it began—about the pretty little church up on Fair Mountain that Daddy Hoyt founded, and Reverend Nix asking me if I took Harley Bright as my husband while my family watched. I thought about my white dress, the one that had belonged to Aunt Bird, and the Balsam Mountain Springs Hotel, where we danced under the stars and ate lime-pepper steak.

I started to think about Harley and got a creeping feeling in my heart. Right now he was probably sitting up in Devil's Kitchen at his house or at the Little White Church. He might be at Deal's buying more sugar for his daddy's moonshine or preaching a revival down by Three Gum River. He might be sitting in his mudroom writing a new sermon or rocking on the porch with Pernilla Swan. And here I was in a car with two strangers and a girl he didn't even know, in another country—a dirty, dangerous place that smelled like whiskey and farm animals—about to end our marriage.

We pulled up in front of City Hall, which looked like a grand old Spanish castle. Sergeant Gilbert opened my door and Sergeant Keil opened Paula's, and we took their hands and walked up the steps. My heart was thudding in my chest, and I suddenly felt like I might faint right there. Sergeant Gilbert stopped and said, "You okay, Velva Jean?"

"I'm okay, sir."

He laughed, looking down at his hand holding mine. He said, "Gene."

He helped me on up the steps and to the front door and inside, Paula and Roger Keil leading the way. Roger asked one of the armed guards who was stationed just inside where we should go. The guard pointed down the hall, and I let myself be dragged along, not feeling my feet or my legs anymore. The only thing I could feel was Gene's hand around mine, pulling me forward.

We walked down the hall and turned a corner and then another corner and suddenly we were in a big room, and there was marble everywhere and cracks in the floor and in the walls. I looked up at the ceiling and there were cracks there too, and I wondered what had caused them. There was a line of people and we stood in this and waited.

Paula said, "If the girls could see this."

Avenger Field felt as far away as Fair Mountain. I wondered what Mudge and Sally were doing right now, and I thought of Loma and wondered how it felt to her, being a wife and mother again. Soon I wouldn't be a wife anymore. I would be an ex-wife, and I thought this was a horrible word, like *boogeyman* or *rickets*. Now, and forever after, I would be Harley Bright's ex-wife. I would be divorced. Just like I was half an orphan. All bad words that meant I was scarred and used up, just like an old pair of shoes or a coat no one wanted anymore.

I could hear one of Harley's sermons in my head: "A wife is bound to her husband as long as he lives."

When it was my turn in line, I stood at the counter and before I could even say why I was there the man handed me a stack of paperwork. He said, "Fill this out and pay five dollars." His accent was thick. He had coal-black hair and a bushy mustache. He said, "Bring back here when done."

I'd brought fifty dollars with me because I wasn't sure how much it cost to get a divorce and I didn't want to go all the way to Mexico and not have enough money. I counted out five dollars, and thought I would have paid all fifty if that was what it took. Then we sat down on a bench where there were other men and women filling out forms. Roger handed me a pen, and I started to read.

The form asked for everything from my name to Harley's to when we were born to where we were from to when we got married and where. There were four pages, and I filled them out as best I could. When it asked what Harley did for a living, I wrote "preacher." It didn't ask what I did, but I wrote in "wife's job: pilot." The last question said, "What is the reason for your divorce?" And instead of giving you space to write, it gave you five things to choose from: "abuse, infidelity, mental instability, criminal behavior, abandonment."

I thought about all the reasons I was here in Juárez filling out these forms when I'd thought, six years ago, that I would be married forever. There wasn't room for all the reasons, and none of the five choices fit. I finally checked "abandonment" because that was how I'd felt for a long time, even if Harley hadn't ever gone off and left me like my daddy did.

The words played in my head over and over, like a record: *What therefore God has joined together, let no man separate.*

Let no man separate.

Let no man separate.

I signed the papers and then I stood in line again, and when it was my turn I gave the forms to the same man, who said, "Come back in three hours."

And that was that. I looked at Paula and Gene and Roger and suddenly felt ashamed that these three people who I barely knew had to see me like this, here in the Juárez, Mexico, City Hall, asking for a divorce from my husband.

I said, "Thank you all for being here."

Paula threw her arm around me. She said, "What say we go get a drink?"

We spent the afternoon at a place called La Fiesta Supper Club. It was still early, but we walked inside and they sat us at a little table near the dance floor. The Supper Club was swanky and bright—a million different colors, palm trees in the corners, lanterns in blue and pink and orange hanging from the ceiling. The waiters wore red and there was a large dance floor with a stage.

Gene said, "You wouldn't believe the folks that play here."

We ordered champagne and flautas, which were little corn flatbreads rolled up like cigars and filled with chicken and cheese, and the waiter brought chips and something green and thick that Roger said was "guacamole." I thought it tasted like fresh-cut grass, or what fresh-cut grass would taste like if you were to eat it. We ate every last bite, and then the waiter brought us more and we ate that too. I decided getting divorced made me hungry.

I'd only tasted champagne once before, at the Tulane Hotel, and I wasn't sure I liked it. The taste of it made me feel mean and happy all at once, but I liked the way the bubbles went up my nose.

We asked the boys questions about the Los Alamos National Laboratory, but the only thing they said was that it sat on the site of the old Los Alamos Ranch School, which was a private school for teenage boys, and that the work being done there was going to win the war and change the world forever.

Then the music started, and it was Count Basie and his orchestra. I'd never seen Count Basie before, but I knew his songs because he was one of the most famous bandleaders in America. He was a short colored man with a wide-open face and a great big smile. He wore a checkered suit and black tie and sat down at a white grand piano, facing his band.

I said to Paula, "Let's get ourselves up to the front so we can see him better." I wanted to get a closer look. We danced through the men and women who were suddenly filling the floor, looking young and colorful, just like pictures out of a magazine. They called out to us as we pushed through—Paula, me, Gene Gilbert, Roger Kiel. When we got to the front, Count Basie started to play "One o'Clock Jump," and we spun each other around. For the first time in a long time I felt the worry melt away. I forgot why I was there, in this other country, in this particular town. I thought, I can't go back to being Mrs. Harley Bright any more than I can go back to the seventh grade.

In between songs, Count Basie said, "This goes out to all the girls and boys who are fighting right now." He nodded straight at me. He said, "Git up here, honey."

I said, "Me?" Paula pushed me toward him.

He said, "You there, in that uniform. What are you? A WAVE? A WAC? Come sit up here and help me with this."

Paula shouted, "We're WASP!"

He said, "Pilots! Even better."

He opened up sheet music and set it in front of him. He said to me, so no one else could hear, "Can you read music?"

I said, "Yes, sir."

He laughed. "Good." Then he signaled his orchestra and started singing a song called "Beyond the Blue Horizon," which was all about saying good-bye to the things that bored you and saying hello to a new horizon filled with joy and sunshine.

When it came time for the last chorus, I sang with him. He looked at me like he was surprised and then he nodded. He let me sing the very last verse all on my own. They went right into "Jumpin' at the Woodside" after that, but he winked at me as I walked away. People started clapping, and I took a little bow.

Paula said, "Holy shit, Hartsie. Where'd you get those lungs?"

We danced after that, the four of us, and as we danced the words to "Beyond the Blue Horizon" raced through my head over and over. It felt good to sing again. It had been much too long. I thought that when I got back to Avenger Field I might write Darlon C. Reynolds a letter just to remind him I was out there.

On our way back to City Hall, we stopped at a market where Gene Gilbert bought a bottle of tequila, and we all bought straw hats, and I bought a six-stringed mariachi guitar the color of sand. It was made of rosewood and had a starburst painted in the center, and it was the prettiest guitar I'd ever seen. As we climbed the steps to City Hall and walked down the hallway, turning and then turning again until we were in the same room with the same cracked marble, I thought of all the songs I'd write on my Mexican guitar. I could hear Count Basie in my head and me singing along with him. I thought that I was walking beyond my blue horizon right then, right that minute.

We waited in line at the same counter, and then the same man with the same mustache handed me a single piece of paper that said I, Velva Jean Hart, was now a divorced woman.

I wondered at what moment it had happened and why I hadn't felt it. How could I not have felt it? Was I drinking champagne? Eating guacamole? Singing with Count Basie? Dancing with Paula and Gene and Roger? I stood there suddenly feeling like a soldier missing an arm or a leg. My phantom limb—the Mrs. Harley Bright that was cut off and gone.

"Congratulations," the man said, but he was already waving the next customer up to the desk. I wondered how many divorces he oversaw each day and if he himself was divorced or if he was happily married. Maybe he had a wife he went home to each night. Maybe he climbed in bed next to her and held her close and told her how lucky he was, how lucky they both were to have each other.

On the drive back to Fort Bliss, Gene Gilbert passed the bottle of tequila back to me. He said, "Congratulations, Velva Jean. To being beyond the keep."

~

The day after we got back from Mexico, I went up by myself in the AT-6 and I sang as loud as could be. It was a day of blue sky and white clouds, which hung low and didn't get in the way of the sun. The sunlight caught the plane and turned it from silver to white, shining it from nose to tail, wing to wing.

As I flew I sang marching songs and songs from the radio and one or two of my very own songs too. I sang "Beyond the Blue Horizon" three times in a row, making up words when I couldn't remember the real ones, and then I sang "The Unclouded Day." How long had it been since I'd sung like this? Not since Nashville. Not since flying in the Aeronca. I sang into the airplane radio and thought about Judge Hay and Darlon C. Reynolds and wished somehow they could hear me.

After landing, I climbed down from the plane and walked across the runway and suddenly I heard the sound of whistling and clapping. Paula, Mudge, Sally, and the other girls were standing around in their zoot suits and turbans or baseball caps. They were all cheering. "You been holding out on us, Hartsie," Sally shouted.

I stopped right there and said, "What are you talking about?"

Paula said, "That radio goes straight to the control tower, honey. As soon as you started song number two, they put you through the loud speakers."

It wasn't the Grand Ole Opry, but without knowing it I'd just given my first concert since singing with Travelin' Jones and his band two years ago. I pulled off my helmet and pulled off my turban. Just then a man walked up and he was carrying an enormous camera, so big it looked more like an accordion. He had gray hair and wore sunglasses, and a black string with a badge hung around his neck. He said to me, "You there. I'd like to take your picture up on that plane."

I thought about how I must look. No makeup, lipstick faded, my hair in a ponytail because this kept it out of my face when I was flying, dressed in my zoot suit, sleeves and pants rolled up. I said, "My picture?" The other girls were staring at him, staring at me. Mudge was rummaging around in her pockets, and she pulled out a lipstick and held it out to me.

He said, "No no—like you are. I want to catch you just like that. Up on that plane you just flew."

I handed my helmet to Sally and then I climbed up on the plane, up on the wing, and sat there, my legs swinging off the side. I didn't know what to do with my hands. I didn't know whether to smile or look serious. No one had ever taken my picture before, except the photo booth next to Bootsy's in Nashville. I hoped I wouldn't look silly.

The man said, "I want you to act natural. Sit there, just like you are, and let me worry about the photograph."

I swung my legs and tried not to fidget, and then all of a sudden there was a roar overhead and a Beechcraft AT-11 went zooming past. I forgot about the camera and the man with the gray hair and raised my chin to watch it go. I would never get enough of flying—the power of the planes, each one so different, the rush of feeling, the race of your heart as you started climbing and went faster, faster, faster, higher, higher, higher. I closed my eyes and felt the sun on my face and listened to the engine roar as it headed away, beyond the keep, beyond the blue horizon.

"Perfect," the man said.

I opened my eyes and remembered where I was, and there was the man with his accordion camera and my friends standing around behind him.

He said, "Thank you, little lady." And then he set off toward the mess hall.

I called after him, "Wait a minute. What's this for?"

He stopped and called back, "*Life* magazine." Then he turned around and kept walking.

═══════

September 9, 1943

Dear Harley,

I need to write this right now because if I don't I will keep carrying you around inside me where I don't want you. I truly loved you or felt I did. I loved you the best I could. When I married you, I did it with my whole heart. I loved being Mrs. Velva Jean Hart Bright, Harley Bright's wife.

Then something changed, though it's hard to say when. It's like we were on this happy ride together, side by side, enjoying it all, and then the next minute I was looking over my shoulder to see where you'd gone.

I'm sending you a copy of the divorce paper along with this letter. I wish you only the best in this life.

Love,

Velva Jean

Telegram

SEPTEMBER 11, 1943

TY,

MY CROSS-COUNTRY TO BLYTHE, CALIFOR-
NIA, IS SCHEDULED FOR WEDNESDAY, SEP-
TEMBER 15. DO YOU THINK YOU MIGHT BE
ABLE TO MEET ME THERE?

VELVA JEAN

Telegram

SEPTEMBER 12, 1943

VJ,

WOULDN'T MISS IT OR YOU.

TY

TWENTY-NINE

On September 15, the girls and me took off as a group from Avenger Field. We flew over El Paso and Lordsburg, New Mexico, and the mountains just north of there, and then instead of stopping for fuel in Phoenix, where a bad storm was brewing, we landed at the Camp Navajo military base near Flagstaff. From there, we took off together again, but this time, one by one, I lost sight of Paula and Mudge and the others till it was just Sally and me, and then finally just me. It was always hard to keep other planes in sight when you were up in the air.

I was on my own, flying over the San Francisco Peaks, a group of ancient volcanoes, some as high as twelve thousand feet, which was twice as high as my mountains back home. They were the highest mountains I'd ever seen.

I'd never flown so high before or so far and the AT-6 bumped and jumped like a little toy plane. It suddenly felt so small and flimsy, more like a paper airplane than a real one. They hadn't given us much training in mountain flying and suddenly I realized how scary this was. I'd been so excited leaving Avenger Field, because leaving this time meant nothing but Ty, Ty, Ty. Some of the girls had been sick to their stomachs over the idea of long-distance mountain flying. Before we left, Sally said, "Aren't you worried, Velva Jean? Aren't you scared shitless?" She dropped a quarter in the cuss pot.

"No," I said. "I know the mountains. I'm not scared of mountains."

But these mountains weren't like my mountains—these were taller, bigger, larger, wider. They were sharp and jaggedy and bare, like they'd been whittled and all the hard edges were left, none of them smoothed down or polished. These mountains didn't slope and curve like the ones I was used to. They were all cold, hard surface and no trees, and they pointed up toward the sky, toward my plane, like a knife, the white of too-early-in-the-season snow mixing with the brown of the rock. This left me chilled inside because I thought about what the air must be like at the peaks—windy and cold as the North Pole.

One thing I knew was that I would never want to get lost there. I'd plotted my course as careful as I could before I left Texas, and I knew I was closing in on Blythe. I could see desert down below, scrubby and sandy. The mountains dropped down some and smoothed out, but they were still high and rough and rugged.

The closer I got to Blythe, the more my stomach jumped. I felt twitchy and nervous at the idea of seeing Ty. I thought how nice it would be if Ned Tyler was the man I was supposed to be with forever and ever, and then I wouldn't have to meet lots of men and go on dates with them and hope that they fell in love with me or that I fell in love with them.

But what if he didn't like me? What if I didn't like him? What if I liked him too much? What if he liked me and then changed his mind about me? What if I changed my mind about him? I'd only just got myself free of Harley. Was I ready to fall in love with someone again? And could I help falling in love anyway? What if it was too late and I already had?

Ty was at the base when I got there. I climbed out of the cockpit and he was the first thing I saw before Paula or Sally or Mudge or any of the others who were climbing down from their planes, peeling off their flight jackets, goggles, helmets. We lined up and filled out our paperwork, and just like that we were on leave for the night. I looked up and there was Ty with his big smile and all that dark hair. He picked me up and swung me around and for a minute I thought he was going to kiss me, but then he threw me over his shoulder and carried me off.

Paula shouted, "Hey, Tyler! Bring her back!"

And Mudge yelled, "Let him keep her. At least till tomorrow when we fly home!"

He dropped me down into a jeep and then ran around to the driver's seat. He said, "Time's a wastin', honey. Let's go see what this town is all about."

Ty and I ate dinner at Valentino's, a little restaurant in Blythe where the waiters spoke Italian and wore red shirts. I ate chicken Parmesan, and he ate lasagna, and we drank red wine out of blue glasses. The wine made my head feel light and a little bumpy, like the AT-6 going over the mountains, but it also made me feel warm inside in a way that kept growing and growing, like I'd swallowed a hundred lightning bugs.

We talked about Oklahoma and North Carolina and his family and my family and music and the war and us. He said, "Honey, I think you're the most wonderful girl. I'm sitting here listening to you, but I keep getting distracted because you're not a damn sheet of paper." Then he said, "Blam!"

I said, "Magic!" Then I said, "I'm sorry we didn't get to say goodbye before you left for Ontario."

He took my hand then. "That's the thing about looking back."

When he didn't say anything else, I said, "What's the thing?"

"When you're looking back, you can't look forward. And sometimes you run smack into something and hit your head."

I laughed. "So looking forward is much better."

"Unless you like head injuries." He raised his blue glass. "Forward."

"Forward."

We clinked glasses and drank and I thought, I am sitting here falling in love with you. And instead of making me want to run away, the thought made me feel calm and happy. I sat there feeling loved, way deep down. I thought that maybe I'd had to leave Harley to meet Ty, that maybe it all came down to that. I thought that meeting Ty was just like *The Wizard of Oz*, and that after I'd been living in black and white for years and years he suddenly came through and turned everything into color.

Afterward we walked through downtown Blythe holding hands. Blythe was just a few blocks of flat, square buildings right in the middle of the desert. The landscape was all sand and cactus. There wasn't anything pretty or romantic about it, but it felt pretty and romantic because I was there with Ty.

While we walked, he told me about his favorite explorer, a man named William Clark. He was an American soldier, territorial governor, and Indian agent, and with Meriwether Lewis he'd led an expedition across the upper Midwest to the Pacific Ocean. Ty said it was because of William Clark, not the Wright brothers or Charles Lindbergh, that he learned to fly. He said he always wanted to be an explorer, that it was his life's dream since he was a boy.

We talked about the Opry and rhinestones and Hawaiian steel guitars and expeditions and making maps and making discoveries. All of a sudden a giant bird swooped overhead, with a wingspan as long as an AT-6, black body, red head. I jumped ten feet and Ty laughed. He said, "It's a turkey vulture, Velva Jean. It's a big, ugly thing, but it won't get you."

I said, "I'm not sure I like the desert."

The turkey vulture landed nearby and didn't give us a single look. He was going after something on the ground, but I didn't want to see what it was. Ty grabbed my hand and ran me to the other side of the street.

The door to a café stood open. It was called Lulu's. There was music coming out into the night from the inside. There was a family in the window—a mother, father, and son. The son was spinning a pinwheel round and round, and I watched as the mother took it away from him. The father grabbed it then and stuck it in his coat pocket and blew on it till it twirled. The mother and son laughed, and I wondered where they found a pinwheel. It seemed like such a happy thing in the middle of a war.

Ty pulled me close and we started to dance, right there in the street. This wasn't something I ever would have done in my old life, and I thought: Look at me. Velva Jean Hart. Divorced woman. WASP. Dancing in the streets with a strange man who isn't Harley Bright.

I said, "You know, I just got divorced." I was suddenly feeling worried.

Ty said, "I'm glad you're divorced. It means you're not still married."

I said, "I don't know where I'm going after Avenger Field or what I'm going to do when the war is over." It was important right now to say these things. I wondered if I'd like Tulsa or if maybe we could live somewhere else, like Nashville. I tried to picture Ty in Nashville and decided he would fit there just fine.

He said, "We can figure that out. There's time."

I said, "I want to go back to Nashville some day to try to record my songs." I thought: You're going to scare him off, girl. He might think you mean that you're going there no matter what, with or without him. Or he might think you're asking him along.

Ty said, "Then you should go back to Nashville. I want you to do all the things you want to do in this world. I've never been to Nashville, but I'm sure I could find something to do."

He kissed me then, and this time I let myself kiss him back. His lips were soft and firm and full and warm. His arms were around me. They felt strong and sure. I closed my eyes tight and made a memory so that I would always be able to conjure this moment. I breathed him in and felt the memory click just like a camera, and I knew that he was in there forever.

The girls and I left early in the morning, just after first light. Ty was leaving right after. He said he wanted to watch me take off first. He said, "I'm working on a song for you. I already got part of it in my head. I'll play it for you when I see you next, honey. I'll come down to Avenger."

I said, "When do you get shipped out?"

He said, "About a month."

The sadness started creeping in. I could feel it coming over me like a fog. He said, "Hey now. Look forward. And remember what Puck is always telling you: have faith in your compass. And if that doesn't work, just be thankful I'm not bald."

I laughed at this.

He said, "That's better." Then he put his hand in his jacket pocket and fished around and pulled out his compass. He said, "I want you to have this. My dad gave it to me before I left home for the army. He said it would help me find my way."

I took the compass from him and turned it over in my hand. It was the most beautiful shiny gold with a little cover that popped open and something etched into the back: "NET."

Ty said, "I reckon I already found my way, so I want you to have it."

I said, "What's NET?"

He said, "Ned Edmund Tyler."

I said, "I can't take this." It was smooth and cool in my hand. It was a part of him and I held it tight. I thought it was worth fifty of Jackie Cochran's cigarette cases.

He said, "You already did. Just remember—ceiling and visibility unlimited."

Then he kissed me again and told me he'd write me, and I climbed into my AT-6. Ty was flying a P-38, and as I taxied down the runway I saw him lean against it. He waved and through the glass I waved back, although I didn't think he could see me.

Flying back over the San Francisco Peaks I got as high as I could over the pass, the route I'd charted through the mountains. The wind was stronger flying east, and the plane slugged through, every now and then hitting a rough current and bouncing or dropping. It felt like driving my old truck over the cattle road down to Hamlet's Mill—all bumps and thumps. When I was just clearing the pass, the engine sputtered and coughed and then shut off.

My hands started shaking and for one second I went clammy all over, thinking, *You just lost an engine over these ancient volcanoes, these San Francisco Peaks, the highest mountains you ever saw, maybe* even the highest mountains in the world for all you know. In my mind I saw the newspaper pictures of Carole Lombard's plane on a Nevada mountainside, smashed into a thousand pieces. I thought about every single person and thing I had to live for in this world, from Ty and Johnny Clay and my yellow truck even down to Hunter Firth, that old brown dog.

Then I tried to remember everything I'd learned about flying— how to restart an engine, how to trust my judgment. I nosed the plane downward till I was flying at a lower altitude. I undid my safety belt and double-checked my parachute and rolled back the canopy that covered the cockpit so I could jump if I had to. I counted to ten, getting ready to pull myself out and through. Where would I fall? Where would I hit? The side of a mountain? The forest below? Suddenly the engine caught again, and I thanked Jesus right then and there. I shouted it loud as I could.

I snapped myself back into my safety belt. If I was going to clear the mountains, I'd have to climb back to my original altitude, so I pointed the plane back and up, bouncing and bumping on the current, until I was as high as before. Two minutes later, the engine quit again. This time my heart skipped a beat in my chest so that my breathing was off and I had to think to catch my breath. I wanted to cry but didn't let myself. I said, "Dammit, Velva Jean."

I dipped down again and the engine caught. Went back up and the engine died. I figured it was carburetor ice because the carburetor heaters never did work in these old planes and the engines would sometimes quit now and then. But I'd never had one die over the San Francisco Peaks.

Puck took me up once in a PT, back when I first started flying with him. He cut the engine and said, "You need to learn what to do when you lose power." The plane had hovered for a moment and then started to fall. For some reason, all I could think of then was Harley. As we fell toward the earth, Puck said to me, "You can't always restart an engine once you've cut it. You can't go back once you've gone."

And then he told me to picture practicing letdowns and landings at a pretend airport in the sky. He said, "You can correct any mistake if you just go high enough. If your engine dies on you, just stay high as you can."

Now I pictured Puck's pretend airport. I dropped down and waited for the engine to catch—holding my breath until it did. And when it did, I climbed back up just a little, but not as high as before, and then I imagined myself reporting my positions to an imaginary control tower, slowing the plane to make a downward entry into the traffic pattern, dropping the gear, rocking the wings back and forth to make sure the gear was down and locked. In my mind I dropped two inches of flaps at 150 miles per hour, propped to 2,350, made my final approach, dropped full flaps, and then glided at 135 miles per hour to a perfect landing.

I was flying so low over the white-brown peaks that I felt I could reach my hand out of the window and feel the cold of the snow on my fingertips. I hugged the mountains so tight, I could see the valleys and the dips and the lines in the rock face. Compared to the mountains, my AT-6—the *Sweet Six*, as we called it—was small as a toy. I would just trust my compass—Ty's compass—and trust myself. I would follow the outline of the mountains until I was over them safely.

I stopped for gas at the army airfield in Deming, New Mexico, and climbed out of the plane—legs shaking, knees buckling—because I wanted to feel the earth underneath my feet. It wasn't enough to stand there and so I sat down, right on the hard, warm pavement of the runway, and when that wasn't enough I lay back so that every part of me was touching the ground. I lay there for thirty minutes, staring at the sky, thinking how high and far away it was and how crazy I was to ever want to go back up there. All I wanted was some food and to sleep in my own safe bed, but first I had to get on home to Texas.

An hour later I took off for Sweetwater. Just south of Dallas, a dust storm swept up and for the next sixty miles I had to fly blind. I flew into Avenger Field blind as a bat, and then I suddenly saw the flares lit along the runway.

I touched down thankful, weary, and hungry. I wanted food and my bed and never to fly over mountains again. The first person I saw was Paula. She was staring up at the sky with a mad look on her face. Then there was Mudge with her eyes all pinched in a way she hated because she said it gave her wrinkles. And Sally just beside her, crying. I climbed out of the cockpit and my feet hit the ground like lead. Sally liked to talk, but she wasn't one to cry. I tried to think what might have happened.

As I started walking toward them, they looked at me—all at once—and I stood still, yards away from them, because I didn't want to get any closer. I thought if I stayed there, rooted to that spot, I wouldn't ever have to know what it was.

Ty's engine caught fire on the outskirts of Blythe, just above the mountains. The plane crashed into the side of Eagle Mountain, near the Kaiser Steel mine. The miners followed the smoke and flames to a flat spot at the base of the mountain, a place covered in snow, and that was where they found Ty. He had tried to jump before landing, but his parachute slammed him against a cliff. The miners took him to the nearest hospital, where he died an hour later.

Paula said Ty lost consciousness and never came to again. He just drifted off, and suddenly his heart—the one he had written about in songs to me—stopped beating.

THIRTY

During the week of September 27, three weeks before graduation, we took our final exams and had our final flight checks. As the four of us fell asleep at night, one of us would say something like, "Is the rule, 'Never have high manifold pressure with low RPM,' or is it the other way around?" Meanwhile, another one of us would be mumbling "GUMP" in her sleep, which stood for "gas, undercarriage, mixture, and prop," which was the way we had to execute the routine cockpit check before landing. Eventually, one by one, the other girls would drift off to sleep, and I would lie awake till morning. I hadn't slept more than an hour each night since getting back from Blythe.

On September 29 a letter came for me from Blythe, California. I stood in the PX and stared at the envelope. It was from Lieutenant Ned Tyler and it had been mailed before he left Blythe in his P-38 to go back to Ontario.

I walked outside into the fall air, which was turning cooler now, and sat right down on the steps and opened the letter. My hands were shaking so that the words on the page looked like they were moving.

He wrote:

> I think the hardest thing I ever did was watch you take
> off this morning. I stood there till I couldn't see you any-
> more and then I sat right down on the flight line and
> finished this song. I know it won't beat you home, but I
> wanted it to get there not long after you do. I hope you

like it, honey. You deserve a million of them, better than
I can write.

See you at Avenger fast as I can.

You Make Me Happy

You make me happy.
Whenever you're around I'm safe inside your sunshine smile.
You make me handsome
whenever I feel my nose just seems a bit too round.
You make me special, and God knows I've longed to be that kind of guy
to have around.
You make me lovely, and it's so lovely to be lovely to the one I love.

Remember how we flew to Blythe
without a locust in our sight
and Valentino's cozy corner felt like heaven for a moment,
while the waiters brought us wine and drink
and I led you dancing down the street?
And though it's simple, it still means the best day that I've lately seen.

And don't forget the funny bird, and pinwheel that seemed so absurd,
    but must
have meant a lot to them.
And in two weeks we'll fly again, perhaps a Chinese dinner then.
You make me happy; you make me smile.
You make me love you,
and that could be the greatest thing my heart was ever fit to do.

I laid my hand on the paper and felt the lines of the pen, the way the
words pressed harder here, lighter there. I ran my fingers across every
letter, thinking about Ty's own fingers—the ones that played the bugle
and held my hand and brushed the hair out of my eyes—writing each
one. And then I thought about what he said to me in Blythe—telling me
to look forward, to fly above the clouds so I was higher than the overcast.
"Ceiling and visibility unlimited." I knew enough in my life to know

that people died and went away and you could look backward and stay looking backward or you could pick yourself up and go on.

I saw him sitting across from me, raising his blue glass. I heard him say, "Forward."

"Forward," I said, just like he was there to hear me.

~

For my last flight check with Puck, I sat in the AT-6, which was, of all of the ones I'd flown, my very favorite airplane. Duke Norris once told me to get to know the cockpit of any new plane so well that I could sit there wearing a blindfold and touch and name every single instrument. He said, "It may save your life one day."

On the afternoon of my last flight check, I sat beside Puck and closed my eyes and thought: I'll never be able to do this. After all these months of training and all these planes I've flown, I'm going to wash out right now, just three days before graduation.

Puck said, "You know this." His voice was firm and gruff, but there was something in it that I'd never heard before—kindness.

I reached out my hand and went through all the instruments, naming each one. I told him the takeoff and landing speeds, the stalling speed, the throttle setting for cruising, and afterward I repeated the cockpit procedure.

Then I went up for my very last training flight. As I took off, the wind was gustier than normal and I got caught in a swell. The plane rocked from side to side and I tried to steady her. It leveled out as soon as we were over the clouds.

You make me happy . . .

I followed the railroad for a bit, which we sometimes did to keep our bearings, and then I started naming the towns as we flew over them, trying not to name them by their water towers. Each tower had a sextant on top that helped you know what direction you were flying, but I didn't use them now. I headed east toward Abilene, then south toward San Antonio, then west again to Avenger Field.

As I brought the plane in for landing, I thought about the time

Johnny Clay and I went flying and crash-landed in a cow pasture. It seemed long ago and far away, and I thought what a lucky girl I was to have so many people I loved in this world, even if they were, most of them, far away, and even if some of them were as far away as heaven. I was lucky to be a WASP and lucky to be a girl who could fly planes and lucky not to be a housewife back in the woods up on a mountain.

You make me smile . . .

When I climbed down from the AT-6, I rested my hand against its side, and it was so bright in the sun that it nearly burned my hand. I left it there another second, and then I followed Puck off the flight line.

And just like that, my WASP training was over. My class had fifty-five hours of primary training in the PT-19, sixty-five hours of basic training in the BT-13, and sixty hours of advanced training in the AT-6 and twin-engine AT-17. We had thirty-eight hours of instrument flying, and that included time in the Link trainer, which was a box shaped like a ladybug that simulated flying. We'd finished PE and ground school, and our tests in navigation, aircraft engines, mathematics, meteorology, and Morse code were done too.

On October 14, the Thursday before graduation, Puck gave me my evaluation, and I passed. On it, next to all the numbers and percentage points I'd earned, he wrote: "Tendency to take things too hard and doubt herself, but listens well. One of the most natural pilots I've ever seen."

The next day Jackie Cochran passed out copies of *Life* magazine to each trainee. *Life* didn't just write a short article on the WASP—it gave over twelve pages of photographs and story. The headline called us the "Lipstick Squadron," and the reporter, a man named Herbert Langley, described us as "sun-bronzed and trim as the streamlined planes." He also quoted field supervisor Major Donald Mackey, who said that "gentler treatment" was the only change required for the instruction of women trainees. Then Miss Cochran was quoted saying, "I worry that combat might harden and brutalize our girls, who still need to be wives and mothers after the war. But when it comes down to it, these women are perfectly capable of flying combat missions. After all, when aroused, women make the nastiest fighters." We knew she meant it but that she was also campaigning, trying to get the military to recognize us officially once and for all.

The pictures were taken by Oliver Sheehy, who I guessed was the man with gray hair. There were photos of girls on the flight line, girls at the wishing well, girls sunbathing between the barracks, girls in the classroom, girls in PE, girls at mess. There was one of Mudge sound asleep on a cot after a day of flying, lying on her stomach, her face turned to the camera, eyes closed, hands brushing the floor. There was one of Sally and Paula lying on the floor in navigation class, charts spread in front of them, plotting their courses. And on the cover was a girl with a ponytail and no makeup, wearing a zoot suit, sitting on the wing of a plane. The caption said: "Velva Jean Hart, pilot."

~

On Saturday, October 16, we pulled on white shirts and tan pants—we called these our "general's pants" because the only time we wore them was when generals and other high-ranking military officers were visiting the base—and marched across the field two by two behind an honor guard carrying the American flag. The Big Spring Bombardier School Band played while we marched. And we sang one last marching song.

It was a warm, clear day with the brightest, bluest Texas sky I'd ever seen. I knew my family wouldn't be able to come to graduation, but I still wished for them, just like I wished for Ty. I wondered if I would always wish for Ty, even after I'd met someone else someday and gotten married again. I thought of the locusts and the first time I'd met him and I felt the same swift stab of pain sweep through me.

Most of the other girls had at least one person there to see them. I wasn't going to feel sorry for myself, though, because there were so many girls who weren't there—Loma Edwards and other girls we'd known who'd washed out or gone home. I remembered my very first day at Avenger Field, back on February 14, when Jackie Cochran had told us to look at the girls on either side of us because they wouldn't be here at the end. Only 59 out of the original 112 were graduating.

Sitting up on the reviewing stand were Jackie Cochran; Brigadier General Isaiah Davies, who was commanding general of the air force's 34th Training Wing and one of the guest speakers; and General Hap Arnold, commanding general of the U.S. Army Air Forces, and the man who had given Jackie Cochran the approval to create the WASP program. General Arnold had been taught to fly by the Wright brothers, was the first United States pilot to carry the mail, and then went on to be one of the first military pilots in the world.

We stood in the blazing sun during the speeches, our white shirts sticking to our skin. General Arnold said: "We will not again look upon a women's flying organization as experimental. We will know that they can handle our fastest fighters . . . ; we will know that they are capable of flying anything put in front of them. This is valuable knowledge for the air age into which we are now entering . . . We of the Army Air Forces are proud of you."

I couldn't help it—standing in the blazing sun, shoulder to shoulder with other WASP like me, I started to cry. It wasn't the gulping, sobbing kind of crying, but the tears rolling one by one down my face kind. I thought of where I'd been and where I was, and where I was going, which I didn't actually know yet because we hadn't got our assignments. We'd each be going to a military base somewhere, to do the work we'd been trained to do. The only place I knew I would never go—not even if they tried to send me there—was Tulsa.

After General Arnold finished talking, we passed over the stage one by one, and Miss Cochran pinned our silver wings to our uniforms. And just like that, we weren't trainees anymore. We were Women Airforce Service Pilots.

Before the ceremony was over, we stood in front of Jackie Cochran and General Hap Arnold and Brigadier General Isaiah Davies and sang one last song. This wasn't a marching song. It was a hymn to Avenger Field.

In the land of crimson sunsets,
skies are wide and blue,
stands a school of many virtues,
loved by old and new . . .

Long before our duty's ended,
a mem'ry you shall be,
in our hearts we pledge devotion,
Avenger Field to thee!

I'd been working on a song myself—not on paper, but in my head. It was a song about a girl who trades in her old yellow truck for an airplane and goes to a tiny little place in the middle of Texas, where the earth is brown and the sky is blue, and where there are other girls just like her, wanting to live out there, and she learns to fly. She buys a Mexican guitar and meets a boy who loves to fly like she does and then he dies doing what he loves, but she keeps on flying anyway.

After we finished singing, we marched back down the field, away from Jackie Cochran, away from the crowd. As I marched I looked at the faces of all the parents and children and sisters and brothers and husbands who were gathered in the stands and on the ground to watch us. The sun was behind them, so that they were just a sea of dark figures, outlined in shadow, the colors of their shirts or dresses breaking through here and there. At the very back, standing behind the very last row, was a man in a cowboy hat. He was wiry, with long legs and long arms, but I couldn't see his face. There was something about the way he moved, even though he wasn't moving. Even standing still he seemed to be in motion, with legs that looked like they were dancing.

When I broke free from the marching line, I circled back around to look for him. "Where are you going, Hartsie?" Sally hollered.

I didn't answer her because I started running. My heart was in a clinch. Even as I ran, I told myself: Stop running, Velva Jean. What are you running for? Just because you saw some old Texas cowboy who's probably somebody's husband or father or maybe just some farmer from Sweetwater.

The crowd was breaking up now, everyone chattering and talking, shading their eyes from the sun, fanning themselves with their paper programs. I wove through it all, trying not to crash into anyone, dodging elbows and waving arms, and people who weren't looking where they were going. I went up into the stands and back down to the ground.

I called out, "Daddy? . . . Lincoln Hart? . . . Daddy?"

But the man in the cowboy hat was gone.

~

The day after graduation, Sally and I were called to Jackie Cochran's office. She said, "I'm sending you to Camp Davis, North Carolina. This is a secret mission, and the reason I've chosen the two of you is that you're my most skilled pilots."

At the words "secret mission" I felt my skin prickle. Just like Constance Kurridge. Just like Flyin' Jenny.

"You'll be flying almost everything—all big ships, like the B-34, the P-37, and maybe even the B-17." The B-17 Flying Fortress was thought to be the most powerful weapon in the war. The people who flew it said it was so powerful that it could unleash great destruction and even defend itself all on its own without a man steering it. She said, "I can't tell you anything more, but this is an important experiment you're taking part in. I hope this assignment will serve as a stepping-stone to bigger responsibilities, perhaps even overseas. What you do at Camp Davis will affect not only the WASP program but the future standing of women pilots."

It didn't matter that Fair Mountain was four hundred miles away from Camp Davis. I was going home again, maybe not right up to Fair Mountain but to North Carolina, with its streams and waterfalls and tall, tall trees and green and mountains that curved and sloped—that were big but welcoming and not all sharp edges and rock.

Jackie Cochran said, "I won't lie to you, girls—Camp Davis has its challenges. But I want you to remember that nothing can be more important to the future of the women pilots program than what you'll be doing. As you know, we're still civilians. We aren't military. This is our chance to prove that women can handle anything they throw at us. It all depends on your success. I expect you to do your best."

The next morning Sally and I packed our things while Mudge and Paula watched. When we were done, we all sat on our cots, facing each other, knees tucked up under our chins, and talked. Mudge was going back to Hollywood to fly stunt planes for Metro-Goldwyn-Mayer, and Paula was being sent to Aloe Army Airfield in Victoria, Texas. When she found out Sally and me were going on a secret mission for Jackie Cochran, she said three of the most colorful swear words I'd ever heard and then added seventy-five cents to the cuss pot.

I told Paula, "I'll never forget what you did for me, going with me to Mexico."

She blinked at me, and I could see her eyes watering. She said, "Shit, Velva Jean." Then she wiped her eyes and added another twenty-five cents to the jar before we poured the money onto Sally's bed and divvied it up between the four of us—there was $45.85.

One hour later Sally and I were flying over Avenger Field in an AT-17 Bobcat. Lieutenant Patrick Whitley was in the pilot's seat, which meant Sally and me could look out the windows. We pressed our faces to the glass, watching Avenger Field and the brown of Texas fade away under the clouds. A lump grew up in my throat, and I suddenly couldn't swallow. I thought of all the friends I was leaving behind, of Paula and Mudge and even Arnold Puckett, and I wondered if I would ever see this place again.

October 18, 1943

Hey, little sister,

I know I ain't written you in a while, but we landed in England two weeks ago and as soon as we got here we started jump and tactical training. Something big is getting ready to happen, but I can't say what. Just know that I'll be in the action and that Hitler don't stand a chance in hell.

Now on to bigger things. Not only are you a graduate of the WASP, you're on the cover of *Life* magazine. You could have knocked me over when one of the fellas all the way over here in England said, "Look at my latest pinup." He'd ripped off the cover and tacked it up by his cot. I told him I was sorry and he said what for and I said for what I'm about to do, and then I punched him hard in the jaw. When he asked why, I told him because you're my little sister and no one's going to pin you up on their wall.

Congratulations on earning your wings, Velva Jean. I'm right proud.

Don't worry if you don't hear from me for a good long while. But know I'm not going to let anything happen to me. I know you'll worry because you just will, and I know Granny and Sweet Fern are worried too. Daddy Hoyt wrote me and told me he was proud of me, and maybe he's worried some, but you know him—he'd never show it.

Just remember: I promised you a long time ago, right after Mama died, that I'd never leave you and I aim to follow through.

Love,

Sergeant First Class Johnny Clay Hart,
brother of a famous WASP

P.S. What's this I hear about you getting divorced?

———————

October 20, 1943

Mary Lou,

Honey, I've been thinking about you. How is your heart?

I tried like hell to come to graduation, but at the last minute I had to go home because my little brother signed up for the navy, and Mother was fit to be tied. She asked me to come back and talk some sense into him, but of course he's a Goss and he's going to do whatever he damn well pleases. By the time I got home, he'd already climbed out his window in the middle of the night and run away. We just got a letter from him and he's somewhere in South Carolina.

But, good grief, I wanted to be there to see you get your wings. How was it? Do you wear them everywhere? I sure would if I was you. Are you getting recognized on the street now that you're famous? I bought three copies of *Life* and I'm sending one to you with this letter because I want you to sign it for me, just like a movie star.

I'm so proud of you, and not just for becoming a full-fledged WASP. I'm proud of you for going down to Juárez and getting yourself a divorce.

I'm going back to Nashville in two days, but I don't know how long I'll stay. I'm bored as hell without you and I'm tired of working at Gorman's.

Sending you a big fat hug,

Gossie

————

October 21, 1943

Dear Velva Jean Hart,

I read with terrific interest the *Life* magazine article on the WASP, and of course I celebrate the wonderful cover photo. Congratulations on being accepted into such a prestigious program. I wondered where you had gone.

Are you writing songs? I'd imagine you don't have a lot of time to write but that you're getting plenty of material to write about. I'd love to see or hear anything you've been working on when you feel like sharing.

Let me know when you're back in Nashville.

All my best,

Darlon C. Reynolds

THIRTY-ONE

The commanding officer of Camp Davis was a man named Colonel Randolph Wells, who looked like Errol Flynn without the smile. The first thing he told us was that the planes were expendable and so were we, which meant he didn't care what happened to either the planes or us.

The second thing he told us was not to expect a warm welcome. He said, "I can't speak for all fifty thousand men on this base, but the army air force pilots don't want you here, and I don't want you here. Remember that you're civilians, not military, and as such you're guests on this base. While you're here, you'll follow our orders and follow our rules."

The last thing he told us was that we were there to replace two girls who had been killed in training exercises. When he saw our faces, he said, "Jacqueline Cochran didn't mention that to you?"

Sally cracked her gum so it sounded like a rifle shot. "No," I said. "She didn't."

Camp Davis sat on the edge of the Atlantic Ocean near the town of Holly Ridge. It was built on forty-six thousand acres of pine barren and swampland. There were hardly any trees, but there were more than three thousand ugly wood buildings and tents crowded together in tight little rows like they were trying to stay far away from the swamp. Colonel Wells said we should watch out for snakes and bobcats and Nazis—a half-dozen German U-boats patrolled deep below the water just a mile or two offshore.

He said, "The planes you'll be flying at first are, for the most part, scrap. They've been retired from combat, but that doesn't mean we can't use them for training. Once you've cut your teeth on those, you'll be ferrying newer planes to other bases, planes that will be put into service overseas."

Just like Colonel Wells said, there were fifty thousand men on the base, including five hundred army air force pilots, three hundred German prisoners of war, a squad of Lumbee and Navajo Indians, one British unit that had already seen actual combat fire, and Lieutenant Bruce Arnold, General Arnold's son. Not counting the women who worked in the hospital or in the offices, there were only twenty-five girls, including Sally and me, all of us WASP.

The last thing the colonel said to us before we left his office was, "I'm giving you a chance right now, ladies. You can go home or you can stay. I advise you to go home and knit socks for the troops."

Neither of us said a word to that, just stood there and faced him. I was a Women's Airforce Service Pilot. Jackie Cochran had pinned on my silver wings. General Hap Arnold himself had said we were capable of flying anything put in front of us. I tried to stare down Colonel Wells like I'd seen Johnny Clay stare people down. I didn't blink or flinch. But inside I wanted to run away from him and this place as fast as I could go.

~

We were assigned to the bay that once belonged to the dead girls. The only thing left to show that they'd been there were some white curtains with black polka dots and maps pinned up across one wall. But I could feel their ghosts all around us. Colonel Wells didn't tell us how they'd died, and we didn't ask.

That night Sally and me lay in our beds, and I wondered if it was too late to go back to Avenger Field and ask for another assignment. The barracks were right next to the runway, which meant the lights from circling planes and the control tower flashed in our window.

Sally said, "I hate this place. It's the ugliest place I ever saw. Tomorrow I'm going to plant a garden right outside our window so we have something pretty to look at."

We heard shouting and then running down the hall. There was a banging at our door and the door across from us. Someone tried the handle, but it was locked. I sat straight up and so did Sally.

A male voice said, "Come out, Waspies!" Then laughter. Then running.

I wondered about the girl who used to sleep here before me. What was her name? Where was she from? How old was she? Was she married? Engaged? A mother? A sister? Did she lie here in this same cot and think about how much she hated Camp Davis? Where did she hope to go next? What did she do before she learned to fly?

~

For the first month, Colonel Wells kept us grounded. We worked in the dispatcher's office with an old woman named Louella Corbett, who was simple and polite, and who gave us letters to type and papers to file. Sally said, "I can't believe I earned my wings just so I could go back to being a secretary."

When we weren't working, we went to ground school. This included classes on some things we already knew from Avenger Field and some things we didn't know—military courtesy and customs, how to pack a parachute, navigation and weather, automatic pilot, flight regulations, aircraft maintenance, flight logs, fuel systems and carburetion, radio compasses, Ferry Command rules, and military law.

We went to classes with the men and we ate with the men, and when we weren't going to class or the mess hall we were marching everywhere with the men. We found right off that Colonel Wells wasn't lying—they didn't want us here. They called the barracks telephone all night long asking for dates, but not the kind of dates a decent girl went on. They might as well have been calling the Alluvial Hotel and asking to speak to Lucinda Sink. They slipped notes under our doors and knocked into us in the mess line so our food spilled everywhere and laughed louder than they needed to if we missed a question in class. I thought I might as well be in the sixth grade again, up at the little one-room schoolhouse in Alluvial. These were grown-up men but they were acting worse than Hink Lowe or the Gordon boys ever did back when we were kids.

On November 29, Colonel Wells let us out from behind our desks and put us on the flight line. Each day after mess, we checked the flight board to get our assignments. The men had what was called a "ready room," which was more like a lounge, where they waited for flight assignments, but we got ours in the dispatcher's office, where we sat on hard benches and weren't supposed to talk too loud.

Major Albert Blackburn started us off in the L-5, which was a small Cub-type airplane. He was a stout man who stood stiff as a poker and never looked us in the eye when he gave orders—like he couldn't bear the sight of us. We had to fly low and slow, following a tree-top-level pattern over the camp, going round and round for hours, testing artillery tracking. I thought it was shameful. We'd been trained on bigger, faster planes than this L-5, and now here we were, puttering around like old men. As I flew circle after circle, I looked down over the base—at the runway where A-24s and B-34s were lined up, waiting for the male pilots to take off in them, at the B-17s, which loomed over all of them like silver giants, the daylight catching them and holding them so that they seemed brighter than the sun itself.

After the second day of shuffling about in the L-5, Sally sent a telegram to Jackie Cochran, telling her what was going on. The next day Miss Cochran flew into Camp Davis in her militarized Beechcraft and called a meeting with Colonel Wells.

The day after she returned to Washington, D.C., we were ordered to go up solo in the A-24, which was a two-seater single-engine dive bomber, to test radar tracking by the gunner trainees. One of the other girls told us that these A-24s were returned from the South Pacific because they weren't fit for combat anymore. Their tires were rotten, the instruments weren't working right, and parts of the plane would fall off in the air. But it was better than putting around in the L-5, and we knew Jackie Cochran had gone to bat for us, which made us feel looked after and important.

The week of December 13, Sally and I checked the assignment board in the dispatcher's office and this time our mission was tow targeting. We stood around the board with the other WASP, the ones who had been there longer, and I said, "What's tow targeting?"

Janie Bowen said, "Just what it sounds like—you're going to be pulling a target behind you while gunners shoot at it." Janie was from Greenville, South Carolina, and she'd been here for three months already. She was one of the tallest girls, gawky as a bird, with curly blonde-brown hair. She didn't wear a stitch of makeup.

I said, "Shoot at it?" I was getting a bad feeling, the same kind of sinking, nerves-on-edge bad feeling I had when I was running through the Terrible Creek train wreck looking for Harley, not knowing if he was alive or dead.

Janie said, "Fifty-caliber machine guns and twenty- and forty-millimeter automatic cannons. Did Jackie Cochran tell you she was sending you here on a secret mission?"

Sally said, "She sure did."

Janie said, "Well, this is part of it. You're not allowed to talk to the newspapers or tell the folks back home what you're doing."

Suddenly I wished for my yellow truck. I thought if I had that truck I would climb into it and drive back home right now. I'd drive up Fair Mountain, right up to Mama's, and get on out and go lie up under the porch, which was where I always used to take myself when the world got to be too much.

On December 18, I sat in the cockpit of the Lockheed B-34, high above the Atlantic Ocean. There weren't any uniforms for the WASP at Camp Davis, but for flight training we wore giant coveralls that looked a lot like our zoot suits. I was wearing my coveralls now and towing a raggedy cloth target behind my plane. One of the enlisted men, a fellow from Ohio named Gus Mitchell, was riding in the backseat, operating the target and cable. He had brown hair thick as a boot brush, and ears that stuck out like trophy handles.

As soon as we were over the beach, I radioed the artillery officer who was in charge on the ground, and at the same time Gus turned the winch handle and let out the cable that the target was attached to. I wondered if the cables were made of nylons, just like the ones Gossie and I donated back in Nashville—maybe a pair of my own nylons was being used on this very plane. After we'd flown up and down the beach, just over the water, I was supposed to swoop down, and Gus would release the target, dropping it to the ground so the gunners could see the number of hits they'd made.

To the rear of the plane I could see little black puffs of smoke, which meant the gunners down below and in near-flying planes were aiming at the target. Then there was a puff to the left of me, just by the cockpit. Then two more puffs even closer. Every fourth or fifth bullet was a tracer that sparkled just like a firecracker. These were to show the gunners where their bullets were going.

The B-34 was a twin-engine bomber a lot like Amelia Earhart's Electra. I tried to think of this and think about what she might have done if they'd made her tow targets while cadets and officers shot at her. All I could really think about, though, was that I didn't want to die up there, because there was so much I wanted to do in this world: sing at the Opry, make more records, see my family again, meet a man and fall in love and have it last forever. Three more black puffs exploded to the left of the cockpit.

Over the intercom, Gus said, "What the hell are they doing?"

"Trying to hit us?"

He said, "They're trying to hit you, not me." He said it like this was something I'd asked for.

I thought, I hope they do hit you. I hope they blow your ears right off. Then I swore into my radio, hoping Sally would hear me in her B-34. I said, "The gunners have chicken feed for brains. They're trying to kill me."

There was a blast of static and then I heard a faraway voice say, "I want to turn this plane around and head back, but I'm afraid they'll shoot me out of the sky." It sounded like Sally.

When I finally came down, the target was torn to shreds and the tail was shot full of bullet holes. There were three holes on the left wing and two in the cockpit door. I climbed out and ran my fingers over them. The holes were as small as quarters. I thought about the bullets that made them and how any one of them could have killed me.

Sally was still in the air, flying over the sand dunes. The gunners shot twenty or thirty rounds at her and finally the target she was towing fell blazing into the water before it could even be released. The officers and enlisted men standing on the ground started clapping and shouting "Good work!" I knew they were talking about the gunners and not us.

Sally swung her plane toward the runway. Major Blackburn stood nearby watching, arms folded across his large barrel chest. An officer standing next to him looked around at no one and everyone. "Hell," he said, "they missed the girl." Everybody laughed.

"*Life* magazine."

I turned to see an officer who was just my height, maybe a little taller, with stooped shoulders, a round waist, and hair the color of mustard. He had one of those fat-boy comedy faces, like Fatty Arbuckle's or Oliver Hardy's, the kind that always looked like it was smiling whether he was or not. I knew by his stripes that he was a first lieutenant.

I said, "Excuse me?"

He said, "I thought that was you. You're better looking in person." He sounded like he was from Alabama or maybe Georgia.

"Thanks." I was too shook up right now to think about anything other than the holes in my plane.

Like he read my mind, he said, "Look, the gunners are assholes."

I said, "What's going to happen to them?"

"Nothing."

"They tried to kill us."

"Colonel Wells will say there's no way to prove they ain't just bad marksmen."

I said, "If they're bad marksmen my name is Fifinella."

The officer laughed at this. He said, "Good to meet you, Fifinella. Lieutenant Bob Keene, at your service." He shook my hand. "They're just scared—all the men here are. You girls have got 'em all stirred up, afraid you all are going to show them up and show everyone that you're better than they are."

I said, "And what about you?"

"Me?"

"Are you afraid we're going to show you up?"

He laughed again. "It never crossed my mind." He walked away, whistling.

I thought to myself, Well, maybe it should.

That night Sally and I sat with Janie Bowen at supper. The mess hall was drafty and sprawling—long picnic table after picnic table seating a thousand men at a time and us, just twenty-five girls sitting side by side at one table in the middle of the room. Dinner was fried oysters. The night before it had been oyster stew. I pushed my food around and wished for Sunday, when we could go to the Post-Service Club Restaurant and buy eggs and bacon for thirty cents.

I turned to Janie and said, "Tell us about the girls we replaced. I want to know how they died."

Sally sucked in her breath. She said, "Don't tell me. I don't want to hear it. If I hear it, I'll picture it. Don't tell me." She covered her ears and looked down at her plate, like she was trying to figure out how to keep eating without her hands. She sighed and took her hands off her ears. She picked up her fork and said, "Well, I'm not listening."

Janie said, "A girl named Laurine Thompson was flying just over the runway when the engine caught fire. She couldn't get out fast enough, and she crash-landed. The plane exploded on impact."

I stopped eating. Sally's fork sat in midair, on its way to her mouth but now completely forgotten.

Janie said, "The second girl, Sandy Chapman, lost an engine over the ocean and her plane went into a spin that she couldn't get out of. She plunged nose-first into the water and drowned."

She took a bite of her food. When she did, a girl with glasses and her hair pushed up under a baseball cap leaned forward across the table. Her name was Ruth Needham. She said, "There was another one. The very first one. This was about six months ago. They never talk much about her."

Janie said, "Dora Atwood. She lost her landing gear just south of the camp, on a routine ferrying mission down to Florida. She jumped from the plane and the parachute didn't open."

Another girl, Helen Stillbert, who was slim and pretty and had the air of a proper lady, said, "We think it was sabotage."

Sally let her fork fall with a clank. "Sabotage?"

Ruth said, "They check out all the planes that crash, and one of the mechanics said it looked like each of them was tampered with. The head mechanic is a guy named Harry Lawson. It pays to get to know him and his crew, make friends and all that."

Janie held up her hand and started counting on her fingers. "Harry Lawson said they found an old oil rag in the engine of Laurine's plane, sugar in Sandy's fuel tank, and a razor blade tucked inside Dora's parachute. When she tried to open it, the razor tore a hole in it."

Sally said, "Did they do anything? Colonel Wells?"

I said, "What about Miss Cochran? Does she know?" I thought about Fifinella, our mascot, flying over the gate at Avenger Field, and how she was supposed to keep us safe from gremlins and engine failure.

Janie took a drink of water. She set down her glass—a tall tin cup—and it made a ringing sound on the table. She said, "She knows. She came down here after Sandy's accident to investigate, I guess because enough WASP started protesting. A couple of girls quit. But she never did anything about it. She told us she'd take care of it, but we're still waiting."

Sally said, "I didn't come all this way to die. If I'm going to die, it's going to be in my sleep when I'm ninety-eight years old, lying next to Cary Grant or Robert Taylor, not being shot out of the sky like a goose."

Janie said, "Best thing you can do is make friends. Favorite girl pilots get to fly with the top men pilots, and the men pilots kind of look after the girls they like most. They call them 'pilot's girls.'"

"How do you get to be a pilot's girl?" I asked, but I wasn't sure I wanted to know.

"You go on dates with them."

Sally said, "I'm not dating a pilot just so he won't shoot at me." She snapped her gum.

Janie said, "You don't have to sleep with them. Just date them, make friends with them."

Ruth said, "But run the names by us first. We have yes and no lists." She looked around. Gus Mitchell was sitting at a table with a short, dark man with a face as flat as a bulldog's. She said, "Yes to Gus, no to Leonard Grossman." She pointed at an officer across the way. She said, "Vince Gillies. No." Vince Gillies had thick red hair and looked like something that lived in the ground. I remembered him from our first day of tow targeting. He was the one who'd said, "Hell, they missed the girl."

I sat there not eating and wondering exactly what kind of mission we were on, here in the middle of swampland, surrounded by men who were making it clear they didn't care about silver wings or Jackie Cochran or *Life* magazine or whether we knew Morse code or night flying or instrument flying or flying the beam. I felt a sharp stab of homesickness—for Avenger Field, for the Lovelorn Café, for Mama's house up on Fair Mountain, for under the porch.

Across the room Lieutenant Bob Keene sat on the corner of a table, talking to some of the other men. He glanced up and saw me looking at him and nodded. I thought it was good to see a friendly face when I was surrounded by a thousand strangers, men who hated me and wanted to shoot me out of the sky without even knowing me.

—————

December 20, 1943

Dear family,

Camp Davis is swell. The food is great and the other girls are nice. We can't believe we're actually here on assignment, that we're official WASP now and just as good as doing active duty for the military, even if we are still civilians.

The men are handsome and there are so many of them! You wouldn't think there were any boys fighting this war right now in Europe or the Pacific with how many officers and cadets are stationed here.

We march everywhere, just like at Avenger. We fly six days a week, and if we're weathered out for a day or two, we fly the weekend to make up for it. We wait at the flight board for our assignments, and if we don't have a flight that day, we go to the Link trainer for practice or we work on Morse code or study the latest airplane information so that we're up to date.

Sally says hi. She's one of the best friends I ever had, next to you all. Do you have any news from Johnny Clay, Linc, Beach, Coyle, or Jessup? Every now and then I read about something brave and dangerous Beachard has done and it gets me thinking about when he was little and they didn't think he'd live and how he would go out in the woods for hours and just walk, all the time getting stronger and stronger. I think maybe he was preparing for this all along.

That's all the news that's fit to write. I just wanted you to know I'm safe and happy. I hope the winter isn't too bad up on the mountain. I love you all.

Velva Jean

THIRTY-TWO

On December 20, at two o'clock in the morning, I was thrown out of my bed. The floor was shaking, the walls were shaking, the glass in the windows rattled, and all the books and notebooks and pens flew off the desk and onto the floor. There was a great boom, like thunder, from somewhere in the distance, but it was the kind of thunder you felt deep in your chest, like something exploded in your heart.

Sally hung on to her bed like she was riding a bull. She said, "Hartsie, what is it?"

"I don't know!" A plane crash? A bomb? The Germans?

Just then the room settled. The night got quiet. I was able to make out the details of shapes—polka dots on the curtains, the shoes under my bed, the red of a book cover. I could almost see Sally's face.

The two of us met at the window and looked out into the night. From the direction of the ocean we could see a great orange fireball, like the sun had fallen into the water. Smoke covered the stars, making it the blackest of nights.

We pulled on our coats and ran outside and stood there with the other girls, the pilots, the officers. We watched the fireball burn, but instead of shrinking down it seemed to get larger and brighter. Everyone was buzzing and humming: "Is it one of ours?" "A bomber?" "A ship?"

Major Blackburn walked out onto the runway, still in uniform. He said, "Looks like a German U-boat torpedoed one of our freighters. Too soon to know the damage."

I knew the Germans were out there but I couldn't believe they were so close to us—under the water just like giant sharks or sea monsters, way down deep where you couldn't see them in an A-24 or a bomber, not even in the B-17, which was supposed to be magic, or the B-29, which was the biggest bomber of all.

All of us, men and women, stood in the winter cold, watching the fireball burn and burn. I was shivering so hard—from the damp coming off the water, from the thought of the Germans just miles away—that one of the officers gave me his jacket and helped me pull it on over my own. For those minutes that we stood there, we were on the same side, looking out at this enemy we had in common. I thought that if you didn't know what it was and what had caused it, that glowing sun would be almost pretty.

Two hours later there was another explosion, louder than the first. It didn't wake me up because I was still awake, lying in my bed, trying not to picture German soldiers climbing out of the ocean and walking up the beach, guns in hand, breaking into the barracks, knocking down our door. I thought I might never sleep again.

In the morning we learned that forty-seven of the forty-nine men aboard the freighter *City of St. Mary's* were killed. Two hours later all fifty-one of the men aboard the supply ship *Jacksonville* died when the same German U-boat opened fire. The *Jacksonville* had been carrying oil, gasoline, and fresh fruit and vegetables to our allies in Europe. For the next week, crates of cabbages, apples, carrots, and oranges washed up on shore, and oil covered the beach.

Now that I was stationed on the coast, the war seemed suddenly closer, and not just because of the U-boats. Planes came and went and pilots came and went, leaving for England or Scotland. We heard about battles from the soldiers who returned to the base hospital, missing a leg or an arm or a hand. We read in the news about the U.S. Marines landing on the Solomon Islands, and U.S. soldiers fighting the Japanese on Makin and Tarawa in the Gilbert Islands, where forty-six hundred Japanese and eleven hundred Americans lost their lives.

In Iran, President Roosevelt and Winston Churchill, prime minister of the United Kingdom, met with Joseph Stalin, who was the leader of Russia, to talk about the invasion of France. American troops landed on the island of New Britain, in a place called the Bismark Archipelago. General Eisenhower was appointed supreme commander of the Allied Expeditionary Force to lead the European invasion, starting in France. And the United States sent fifteen atomic scientists to Los Alamos National Laboratory in New Mexico, where Paula and I landed when we lost our way.

On December 21, the day after the *City of St. Mary's* and the *Jacksonville* sank to the bottom of the ocean, a navy patrol torpedo boat, commanded by marine lieutenant and medic Beachard S. Hart, sank after being cut in two by a Japanese destroyer off the Solomon Islands. The newspaper story said, "Lieutenant Hart swam to a small island in the Solomons, where he freed thirty-five American prisoners of war and captured five Japanese soldiers."

I showed the story to every single one of the girls. I said, "That's my older brother." I thought about the way Beach didn't like attention or a fuss being made over him. He was happiest when he was by himself and on his own, writing "Jesus loves, Jesus heals, Jesus weeps" on trees and rocks. I thought this was just another way of carving his messages.

~

On December 24 we woke to rain. A fog rolled in off the ocean, covering the black of the swamp and the dirt-brown of the buildings and the ugly green of the planes so that Camp Davis looked almost pretty.

At seven o'clock that evening, I spun my hair into a victory roll, painted my lips with my Max Factor Comet Red lipstick, and pulled on my dark-blue dress with the skirt that twirled. Sally and I met the rest of the girls outside the barracks, and together we walked to the service club for the Camp Davis Christmas dance. As we walked, I looked out over the water and thought about the U-boats that were hiding there, way in the deep. The thought chilled me all over. It felt strange to be done up in my prettiest dress and going to a party when the war was being fought right there, just miles away.

The ballroom of the service club was a handsome room, large as the Fiesta Supper Club in Juárez. It was decorated with red and green streamers and twinkly lights and the biggest Christmas tree you ever saw. Round tables with white cloths were set up all across the room, and there was a stage in the middle, with music stands and instruments but no orchestra.

After we ate a turkey dinner, the orchestra came out and started to play. I thought of Charlie Jones and wondered where he was, if he was entertaining troops overseas with his band or if maybe he was in the trenches somewhere.

Sally and the girls and I walked over to the table where drinks were set up, and we poured ourselves punch and stood comparing stories about how mean the men at Camp Davis were. A few days before some of the pilots had gathered up a bunch of stray dogs and painted "WASP" on their sides and then turned them loose on the base. This was supposed to mean we were either dogs or bitches, or maybe both, and we had to spend all afternoon chasing them down and cleaning up after them while Major Blackburn shouted at us.

A girl named Francine, with a sweet, freckled face, said, "They treat the Injuns just as bad."

I knew there were Indians on the base, but I'd never once seen any of them.

Sally said, "I don't see a single Indian in this room."

Janie said, "They keep them hid away, just like they wish they could do with us."

I said, "Aren't they training with the other men?"

Ruth said, "We think they're rounding them up to be code talkers, which means they'll be shipped out to the marine base in San Diego or the army base at Fort Benning."

I had no idea what a code talker was, but I decided it sounded wonderful, like being a spy.

The band left for intermission. Most of the men were standing around drinking and talking to each other. There were groups of girls off to the sides, keeping to themselves. I thought it was just like school, with the boys on one side and the girls on the other.

Ruth said, "Do any of you play or sing?"

Sally said, "Velva Jean sings. You should hear her."

Ruth grabbed my hand. "Come on." She dragged me along till we were up on the stage. She sat down at the piano, and Janie sat behind the drums. Ruth pushed her glasses up on her nose and started playing "Over the Rainbow."

Sally said, "I want to play something," even though I knew full well she couldn't play anything. She picked up a pair of maracas.

I didn't want to sing "Over the Rainbow," even with all those nice words about bluebirds and blue skies and trouble melting like lemon drops and dreams that you dared to dream really coming true. I wanted to sing one of my songs or one of the songs I grew up on. I wanted to hear some mountain music with guitars and banjos and fiddles.

I said, "Do you all know 'I'll Fly Away'?"

They sat staring at me and then Ruth began picking out the tune on the piano.

I thought: Great holy Moses. It's been so long since I sang anything. What if I forgot how? What if I can't remember the words?

And then I sang. The men kept talking and drinking. I heard Vince Gillies—the one that looked like he lived in the ground—laugh louder than he needed to at something one of his friends was saying. A few men glanced over and then some of them stood there looking. Little by little, they fell quiet. Behind me I heard Janie say, "Good grief, Velva Jean. Sally wasn't lying."

When the shadows of this life have gone,
I'll fly away . . .

In all, we sang three songs, and the orchestra played with us on the last one, which was "Don't Fence Me In." I loved that song. I loved it because it made me think of Ty, and the memory of him singing it was both sad and sweet. And I loved it because it was exactly how I'd felt in my life—until I came to Camp Davis—ever since I left Harley, ever since I learned to fly. When we were done, there were whistles and clapping and I tried to slip away without anyone noticing, but then Bob Keene asked me to dance with him.

He said, "There's more to you than meets the eye, Fifinella."

Sally danced by us with Gus Mitchell, who was two heads taller than she was. She waved and I waved back.

Bob Keene said, "You sure can sing. Tell me, is there nothing you can't do?"

There was plenty I couldn't do, but I didn't say so. Instead I said, "I've always sung, ever since I was little. My whole family plays music."

He asked me more questions then, all about my singing, and I thought it was nice that he wanted to know but I felt like I was telling him something about me from the outside in, instead of showing him from the inside out. I thought about Butch Dawkins, how he had known my music and my songs and how I didn't have to tell him about them because he knew that part of me from the inside. I didn't think music was something you could talk about like this, dancing at an Army Air Forces service club while an orchestra played "Little Brown Jug" and while there was a war going on not only across the ocean but underneath it.

He said, "I played guitar for a while. Never was much good at it. I wanted to be outdoors too much, not cooped up inside. I played baseball, I wrestled, I boxed. I wanted to be heavyweight champion like Max Schmeling or Max Baer." He talked on about boxing—Jack Dempsey, Henry Armstrong, Joe Louis—and then he said, "But all that stopped when I learned to fly. I was eleven when Charles Lindbergh made his flight to Paris in the *Spirit of St. Louis*." He talked for a while about Lindbergh, about his races, about the kidnapping and murder of the Lindbergh baby and what a goddamn rotten shame that was, and then he told me about his own flying and how he joined up with the Army Air Forces long before Pearl Harbor.

He said he was from Social Circle, Georgia, born and raised, though he always itched to get out and do something more, especially once he started flying. He said he knew he was meant for other places, and I said, "You're living out there, just like I am. You're going after your destiny instead of waiting for it to come to you."

He said, "That's right."

The song ended then and one of the pilots cut in. Bob Keene thanked me for the dance and walked away. The pilot said, "Zeke Bodine, good to meet you." He had bright-yellow hair and front teeth that crossed in the middle. He seemed like a nice boy, but I thought he looked like a duck.

I said, "Velva Jean Hart, good to meet you too."

We danced, and while we danced we talked about all the polite things you talk about when dancing with someone you didn't know—how did we get here, what did we do before the war. I thought: Here we go again. How many more conversations like this do I have to have tonight?

When he asked me where I was from I said, "North Carolina."

He said, "Charlotte?" Zeke Bodine was from lower Alabama, so I knew he wouldn't know Fair Mountain.

I said, "Alluvial. It's near a town called Hamlet's Mill."

He said, "Alluvial . . ."

I said, "It's in the mountains."

Zeke Bodine said, "We got a guy here from Alluvial. No, not from there, but he spent some time working up there."

I said to Zeke, "You're making that up." I thought maybe he was trying to charm me by pretending we had something in common.

Zeke said, "Why would I make that up? This guy spent some time working up there in a CCC camp, up on that road they built."

I said, "The Scenic?"

He said, "No. Some parkway. The Blue-something Parkway."

I stopped dancing. There were a lot of boys that worked up on that road, hundreds of them. But somehow I knew without asking. I said, "Do you know his name?" Vince Gillies was on his way over to me. I could see him coming.

Zeke Bodine said, "I don't know. Indian fella, at least part Indian, part something else."

I told myself: Don't get ahead of yourself, girl. It could be anyone.

He said, "Doesn't talk much. Keeps to himself. And plays the guitar like one mean and angry son of a bitch."

December 25, 1943

Dear Hartsie and Sally-Hally,

So here I am, still in Texas, only without my best pals. Texas ain't the same without you girls, and I'm hoping to transfer soon as I can. This is going to sound dull as dirt to you, but I'm flying cargo and ferrying new planes from factories. So far I've been to Salina, Kansas; Detroit, Michigan; and Long Beach, California. Do me a favor and don't tell me too much about the important work you're doing in North Carolina. I don't think my ego can handle it, and you know how fragile my ego is.

Guess what? Some of the officers built a golf course nearby, so that's the one good thing. I'm practicing every day when I'm not flying and studying. (I thought we were done with ground school—what gives?) It's scary how rusty I am, but by the time I leave here, I aim to be better than I ever was. When this war's over, I'm getting right back on the circuit.

Seriously, I miss you like hell. I'm not much of a letter writer, but I wanted you to have my address so you know where to send care packages.

Love,

Paula

P.S. Did you hear about Mudge? She got a part as a female pilot in a movie called *Thirty Seconds Over Tokyo*, starring Spencer Tracy and Van Johnson!

December 25, 1943

Merry Christmas, Mary Lou!

What do you know? I'm engaged. Not to a gardener or a married man this time or anyone my father would ever approve of—this one's a soldier. A sailor, actually. He came through Nashville on his way to New York, and we spent one week together, mooning around the town. His name is Clinton Farnham, and he's not dashing at all, which is one thing I love about him. He's just the nicest guy I ever met and he loves me exactly for me. We'll get hitched after the war, although I wanted to do it before he went. He wants one of those fancy weddings with a hundred guests and a champagne fountain, so I guess we'll have to wait. He's been gone two days now, and I'm a wreck. I've given up all plans of going to China and hunting snow leopards. Instead I'm thinking of joining the WAVES just to be near him.

You take care of yourself. Don't fly those rotten ol' planes for rotten ol' Jackie Cochran if you don't want to.

Your old pal,

Gossie

THIRTY-THREE

*C*hristmas fell on a Saturday, and Sally and me spent our morning in Holly Ridge, since it was the closest town to Camp Davis, lying just outside the swamp. We called it "Boom Town" because it was so small that boom, you were in it; boom, you were out.

We wore the only everyday uniform we had, not counting coveralls, which was men's dress pinks and greens—a light-drab shirt with an olive-drab tie and dark-olive trousers. The Army Air Forces General Headquarter's patch was sewn on the upper left sleeve of the shirt, and we wore our silver WASP wings above the left breast pocket.

Over all this we were bundled up in wool coats and scarves so that you couldn't tell we were girls at all. I thought we looked like penguins. We walked up and down the three short blocks, and everything was closed up tight except for a music store that sold records.

We went inside and I rubbed my hands together. They were freezing even in my gloves. Up on the wall over the cash register was a banjo, the only instrument in the place. It shone bright and silver, and Sally stood there staring at it, her hands on her hips.

There were records in bins and crates, and some were stacked up in corners and against the wall. I started looking through them, and I heard Sally ask the man at the counter how much that banjo was. I said to her, "I didn't know you played banjo."

She said, "I don't yet."

I picked out an album of Xavier Cugat playing congas and one of Martha Tilton, who had the sweetest voice I'd ever heard. As I walked to the counter, I passed a stack of records and there on top was Roy Acuff. I almost picked it up and then I didn't because I decided that was my old life—a life spent worrying about the Opry and singing for Darlon C. Reynolds—and Roy Acuff had no business here in my new one. When I went up to the counter to pay for the records, Sally was counting out just enough money for the banjo.

She said, "Once I learn to play, I'll be able to serenade Gus Mitchell." She winked at me.

I said to the man behind the cash register, "Why are you open on Christmas?"

He said, "I'm not. I just came in to fetch something for the wife." He held up a record—George Gershwin's *Piano Rolls*. He said, "I had to hide it here otherwise she would have found it before today and ruined the surprise."

I said, "Thank you for letting us buy these things."

He said, "Merry Christmas, girls."

Sally picked up her banjo and held it like a baby. She said, "What do you know, Hartsie? It was meant to be."

Back at the barracks, a group of us gathered in Janie's bay, the one she shared with Ruth. The two of them had an old Victrola that Ruth had brought from home. We put on Xavier Cugat, and I brought out my Mexican guitar and Sally sat down with the banjo, plucking away at it even though she didn't know what she was doing. Janie played the drums on her footlocker, using pencils as drumsticks, and we all sang Christmas carols. It sounded awful, but none of us cared. Even with a war going on everywhere you looked, and my brothers off to God knows where, and me worrying about them and missing them and missing everybody up on my mountain, even with all that, it was one of the happiest Christmases I'd ever had.

~

On December 26 we were back in the air. Even though it was a Sunday, we had to make up the time we lost during the holiday. An A-24 had just been delivered to Camp Davis from Wyoming, and Ruth and I were scheduled to fly it down to a base near Fort Myers, Florida. A captain named Leonard Grossman—the man with the bulldog face from Janie and Ruth's "no" list—flew with us, and we knew that we were carrying something important that he would be dropping off, but we didn't know what it was. Head mechanic Harry Lawson wasn't even allowed near the plane when the officers were loading it.

I was first pilot on the trip down. I pretended the A-24 was the B-17 Flying Fortress. I liked ferrying work not just because it got me out of the swamp but because it made me feel like I was really doing something—taking planes to men who would be using them in combat. But I still wanted to do more. I wanted to fly farther and in a powerful ship like the B-17. I wondered if that feeling would ever go away, if I'd ever feel like I finally got far enough and high enough.

Just over the Okefenokee Swamp, the plane started to pull and suddenly I couldn't get hold of it. The engine shook so hard that my teeth rattled and I knew we were running out of oil.

Ruth said, "Should we land at one of the auxiliary fields?"

Captain Grossman said, "I think we should limp home, get back to base."

I couldn't see anything but green and black down below for miles around us. I said, "I think we can make it to Jacksonville."

We double-checked our safety belts. I didn't say anything to Ruth or Captain Grossman, but I could barely keep control of the plane. It was trying to go in a circle, and I was fighting it. I retracted my flaps to restore normal flight altitude, but the speed was too low. Then I saw a town down below, and a field. I knew it wasn't Jacksonville—it was too soon—but I could land in a field. The A-24 wasn't an Aeronca, but I figured I'd done it once and I could do it again.

I aimed the nose in the direction of the field and said a quick prayer to Jesus. Somehow I brought it down, the plane jerking to the right and bumping along. When we came to a stop, Ruth burst into tears and Captain Grossman slapped me on the back. "Good work, Waspie," he said.

I sat there trying to breathe. Slow and steady. Slow and steady. I closed my eyes and then I undid my belt and climbed down.

When we checked the engine, the oil was gone. There wasn't a single drop left. Captain Grossman stayed with the ship while Ruth and I hiked to the nearest farmhouse. We came back with the farmer and enough oil to fill our tank. We flew on down to Fort Myers, and the next day we filled up the oil tank for our trip back to Camp Davis.

When we landed, there were cadets, men and WASP, gathered around, and when the three of us appeared they started clapping. Major Blackburn stalked up to me and I thought "oh no." But he said, "Good work, Hart. Congratulations on bringing it home." And then he stalked off.

Chief mechanic Harry Lawson inspected the plane and said that the oil had been drained—maybe because of a leak—even though the check-out sheet said oil was added before we took off. Harry Lawson was a balding man, formal and stiff as a drawing room, with the slightest hint of an accent, but not a southern one—it was a faraway, over-the-seas one that made me think of the young man at Los Alamos, the one with the round glasses. Harry Lawson seemed more like someone who should be reading books than someone who worked on airplanes. I went to bed that night thanking Jesus for keeping us all safe and for helping me land that plane in a field instead of in a swamp.

The next day Mr. Lawson wrote up his report, which held me responsible because I hadn't double-checked to make sure the oil was in the plane before we left. Colonel Wells gave me an official reprimand because he said I burned up an engine, which was going to cost the government money. He said, "What's the matter with you? Are you flying for the Nazis?" Everyone was, all the time, worried about spies. "That's no scrap plane, Miss Hart. That airplane cost sixty thousand dollars!"

I walked out of his office, trying not to cry or hit something or kick something or yell. An hour before takeoff, I'd gone over the engine and double-checked the oil. I'd been doing this on every plane I flew since my flight back from Blythe, the time my engine went out over the San Francisco Peaks. The thing I'd forgotten to do was sign the check-out sheet saying I'd looked everything over and that all was okay.

I walked onto the flight line even though it was dusk and time for mess and the girls would be expecting me. I stood there thinking about rainbows and bluebirds and blue skies, and they all seemed too far away. All I could see was swamp everywhere. I thought: That's it. I'm going to be court-martialed. I might as well just pack my things and go on home. And maybe it's a good thing. This place is the worst place I ever did see. It's worse than Devil's Kitchen.

I heard someone walk up behind me but I didn't budge or look. I didn't care. It would probably just be one more person getting ready to write me up for something I didn't do or lecture me or shoot at me.

"Nice landing." It was a lazy-sounding voice, gravelly and rough, like the person speaking had just woke up. I froze. The hairs on the back of my neck and on my arms prickled like I'd seen a spook.

I turned around and saw the wide, high cheekbones and sleepy dark eyes, the brown-black hair, still long, not cut short like a soldier's. In addition to his medicine beads, he wore dog tags, and he had the same crooked, gap-toothed smile. His uniform was the olive green-brown of an army man.

As I stood looking at him, the first thing I thought was, There you are. Then I heard his song in my head, the very first one I'd ever heard him play that long-ago July night down at Deal's.

I said, "Butch Dawkins."

He said, "Velva Jean Bright."

I said, "It's Velva Jean Hart now."

He nodded like he'd been expecting it.

I tried to say I was sorry then for Harley and for everything, but he said, "It's good to see you." And that was it. I knew somehow we were square.

We walked to the mess hall but didn't go in. Instead we sat down on the wooden benches just outside. I told him about Johnny Clay, who I hadn't heard from in weeks, and how I learned to fly, and even a little about Nashville, and he sat there and listened, not saying a word. I didn't mention Harley or Juárez, but I told him I'd gone home again and that I didn't know when I'd ever be going back.

Then he said, "You'd best eat something, girl, before they put it up." And he got up and walked me to the mess-hall door and said he had to go, and suddenly he was gone—back to join the other Indians? Where did they keep them? What was he doing here at Camp Davis? I stood there wondering if I was going to see him again or if maybe I'd made him up, just like a haint.

~ *1944* ~

I'm flying high above the clouds.
I'm flying swift and free . . .

—"Beyond the Keep"

THIRTY-FOUR

On January 1, Ruth Needham picked up an A-24 in New York, stopped at Camp Davis to refuel and check in, and was flying the plane down to South Carolina when she lost all the controls except the throttle and had to jump. An antiaircraft lieutenant was flying with her and when he jumped out of the plane he hit the propeller.

The lieutenant died instantly, but Ruth was still alive. Sally, Janie, and I went to see her at the base hospital, and she looked small and bruised lying in her bed. She broke her leg in the fall and cracked three ribs, but otherwise she was okay.

I took Ruth's hand when she held it out, and Janie said, "What happened up there?"

Ruth said, "I don't know. One minute all systems were go, the next the fuel pressure warning light started flickering. Then the prop control went out, then the trim tabs, the wobble pump, the fuel selector, and the radio. The only thing that didn't fritz out was the throttle."

We asked her questions, and she answered them for as long as she could, and then her head started nodding and her eyes drooped closed and she drifted off to sleep. We slipped outside, and in the hallway Sally said, "I'm sorry—all the controls go fritzy at once? I don't buy it."

Janie shook her head. "Me neither."

They looked at me and I said, "Me neither." And as I said it a chill ran up my spine, uncoiling just like a snake. I thought of Laurine Thompson and Sandy Chapman and Dora Atwood, girls just like me, just like Ruth, who came to Camp Davis to fly and then died when something went wrong. I heard Colonel Wells's words in my head: The planes are retired. The planes aren't fit for combat anymore. And then I heard Helen Stillbert saying, "We think it was sabotage."

The day after Ruth got out of the hospital, they sent her to base court to face charges for damaging government property and for putting her passenger in harm's way.

Three days later, she was cleared. She kept to herself after that, sitting silent at mess while the rest of us talked around her, her nose in a book while waiting on the flight line, turning in early at night, long before bed check.

Through it all, I wondered just where Jackie Cochran was and if there was anyone on this base that we could trust. Some of the men were nice enough. They didn't seem to mind that we were here as much as the other army air force pilots did. I wondered about the other 49,500 men on base—would they have been nicer if we were assigned to work with them? Or would they have been just as unhappy to see us as the pilots were?

The night Ruth was cleared, I was scheduled to fly my first searchlight mission. This was a kind of racetrack pattern at different altitudes, so I would be going up and down and up again while the artillery men tried to spot me and follow me with their searchlights. Before I took off, I told Harry Lawson that I wanted to look over the engine myself.

He said, "It already checked out. I have the paperwork here."

I said, "If you don't mind, I'd like to go over it again."

While he watched me, I went over the gas tank, the carburetor, the oil, the engine, the landing gear, the propeller—every control and dial and lever. When I was done, I made sure to sign my name to the papers to say everything was okay.

I still felt nervous as I took off. What if the engine caught fire? What if I lost a wheel? What if the controls went out? I looked outside the windows and all I could see was the blinding yellow-white of the searchlights. I couldn't read the instruments or see where I was headed, and so I tried to remember everything I'd learned at Avenger Field about flying blind. I remembered what Puck had taught me: "When you're sitting in that cockpit, I want you to picture the flying you're doing in that particular airplane. It's just you and that one plane. You've got to know just what that plane can do for you."

By now I knew the A-24 better than any other plane I'd ever flown. I closed my eyes and pictured the control panel. At first it was blurry, but little by little all the levers and dials and buttons filled themselves in until I could see them in my mind. I reached forward and adjusted the prop control, the trim tabs, the throttle. I saw the sky above Camp Davis just like I was looking at it. I pictured it like a road I was driving in my yellow truck.

An hour later, after I was sitting on the ground again, I thought that searchlight missions were a bit like life. Sometimes you could lose your way and not know where in the world you were going, but you just had to keep your head and remember your instruments. I thought maybe I was knowing my compass more and more.

Jackie Cochran arrived the next morning in her Beechcraft. She called all twenty-five WASP together in the office she sometimes used, which was a small room next to the dispatcher's office. We crowded around the table, lining the walls, sitting in the chairs and on the floor. Ruth sat front and center, her leg in a cast, her face still bruised.

Miss Cochran looked like she'd been awake all night. There were little lines around her eyes underneath the makeup. She sat on the edge of the table, hands on either side of her, legs stretched out in front, ankles crossed.

A couple of the girls raised their hands. Miss Cochran nodded at them. "You'll have a chance to talk. First, I want to address this latest accident." She looked at Ruth, who was staring at her through her glasses, blank as a stone wall. "The plane's log showed that there had been a complaint about the engine, Miss Needham, prior to your flying it. The complaint was written up but for some reason the plane was never repaired. I imagine this was just an oversight, but I assure you I'm going to look into it."

Sally snapped her gum in Jackie Cochran's direction in a way I knew meant "I just bet you will." Miss Cochran glanced at her and frowned.

Ruth said, "Why even bother?" Her voice was flat and far away.

Miss Cochran looked at her long and hard and then she looked at the rest of us. "Anyone else? I want to hear what you have to say."

Sally cracked her gum again, and then we all started talking at once, telling her just how scared we were, how angry we were. We told her about the crude comments, the teasing, the target shooting. We told her the A-24s were faulty and not fit for training, especially at night.

She held up her hands and said, "All right, all right. This is what I can do. I'll talk to the mechanics. I'll test-fly some of the planes tomorrow. I'll see if we can't get to the bottom of this, but you have to be quiet. If I hear or read so much as a cough in the press about things not running well here, about anything less than perfect harmony between the WASP and the male pilots at Camp Davis, I'm going to make some personnel changes."

The next day Jackie Cochran test-flew several of the planes, including the A-24s. Afterward she met with Harry Lawson and went over the squawk sheet, which was where pilots reported all aircraft technical problems and the mechanics responded with how they'd taken care of them and when.

The twenty-five of us waited on the edge of the flight line, and when Miss Cochran was finished she walked over, hair blowing in the wind, smiling. She said, "Yes, the planes have some problems. They're old. They've been through it. But I don't see anything life threatening."

When some of the girls started to talk, she held up her hand. "Look. They have problems, but what plane being flown these days doesn't?"

Sally said, "I'd like to be relieved of my target-towing duties."

Helen Stillbert said, "Me too."

Janie said, "And me."

I said, "And me."

A half dozen other girls spoke up, but by now Miss Cochran was frowning and shaking her head. "No," she said. "No one's resigning and no one's being relieved of any duty. You're here to perform a mission. The future of this program is at stake."

Sally said, "We could go to the FERD." FERD was the Ferry Division of the Army Air Forces, and even though we were nonmilitary, we could go there to complain or even resign.

Jackie Cochran said, "If you do, I can still override them." She was smiling but her tone was cold. It was a look I'd seen before on Sweet Fern, on Harley.

By nightfall she was gone, and the next day we were back on the line, taking our turns towing targets in the A-24s. When I came down, I counted eleven bullet holes in the tail of my plane, five in the wing, five in the cockpit, and one in the nose. I thought to myself, If you can fly here at Camp Davis, you can fly anywhere.

~

On January 14, I got two letters at mail call, one from Janette Lowe, Hink's sister, who wrote me all the way from England to tell me how she was a nurse for the Red Cross and to thank me for all I did to help her, back on Fair Mountain, when she was attacked by the German from the CCC camp. The other letter was from Butch Dawkins. All it said was, "Girl—you free tomorrow night around seven? I got someplace for us to go. Butch."

I sat down on the flight line and waited my turn, and while I waited I thought about Butch and then I thought about Ty. I reached into my pocket for his compass and ran my fingers over each letter: N-E-T.

The thing I'd never said to anyone, much less to myself, was that Ty would be alive if it wasn't for me asking him to meet me in Blythe. I should have just been happy to write him letters and let him write me songs and see him the next time he came to Avenger Field. This was something I went over in my mind again and again—my telegram telling him I would be there, his telegram saying he would come—like going over it would change it somehow. Like maybe if I thought enough about it and pictured it different in my mind he would never have been in Blythe in the first place, which meant he would never have crashed into that mountain.

Sometimes I made myself think about what our lives would be like if he was still here. I went beyond the good and the happy and wondered if I ever would have stopped loving him like I stopped loving Harley. Would we have fought about little things or big ones? Would he have got tired of me? Would I have stopped talking to him about my songs? Would he have stayed away from home more and more? Would I have woken up one day and find out I didn't love him anymore?

When I got back to my bay, I opened my hatbox and set Ty's compass inside it, on top of all my other treasures. "I'm sorry," I said, and it was silly to say it to something so small that was only made out of metal, but as I closed the lid to the hatbox and locked it up in my footlocker I felt like I was leaving a part of me behind.

At seven o'clock the next evening, I met Butch Dawkins outside my barracks. I was wearing my blue dress and my Comet Red lipstick and some of Sally's best perfume. Outside it was already night, the last traces of the sun fading right into the ocean. Butch was dressed in his uniform. His skin was dark against the green. Some of the army air force pilots walked past and stared at us. They called out to Butch—"You lost, Injun? You need some help finding your way back to your teepee?" They all laughed at this like it was the funniest thing and then they walked off, blowing kisses at me.

He said to me, "I guess I should've met you someplace."

I said, "It's just as bad for you to be seen with me."

He said, "Well, then. We're going to have us an adventure."

He didn't say a word about how I looked, didn't tell me I was pretty or that he liked my dress. He didn't tell me I had the prettiest face on Fair Mountain—Fair Mountain or anywhere.

He said, "Ready?"

I wondered why it should matter to me if Butch thought I was pretty. Maybe because there were other girls in this world he probably did think were pretty and I at least wanted to be one of them. But maybe he didn't like girls with hair that waved too much in the heat or had eyes that weren't one color but a lot of them. He might not like girls with heart-shaped faces who weren't tiny like Sally or big-bosomed like Sweet Fern. He probably liked Indian girls or Cajun girls, exotic-looking ones with dark hair and almond-shaped eyes and skin the color of caramel.

There was a juke joint out in the country, just past Holly Ridge, called Leona's. I talked and talked on the drive there, thinking how silly I sounded going on about everything from *Life* magazine to Dan Presley's airplane spotting to the Los Alamos National Laboratory. Yet I kept on talking. Butch stared straight ahead, one hand on the wheel, the other arm crooked out the window. The cold air blew in through the window flaps, but I was warm from the heater. I liked the feeling of hot and cold, hot and cold. Just when I got too hot, there would be a rush of cool air. Just when I got a chill, I could feel the heat.

I kept thinking: I am here with Butch Dawkins. The world sure is a small place. I couldn't get over it.

Every now and then Butch said, "You up to somethin', girl. Sho 'nough."

I chattered on and on and then I made myself stop talking so that he could talk. I said, "Where did you go after you left Alluvial?"

He said, "Here and there."

"Did you make it to Chicago, home of the blues?"

"Not even close."

"Did you make it to New York?"

"No."

I said, "Where did you go?"

He said, "Around and about."

I sat there for a while and remembered driving him in my yellow truck, back when he would come visit me up in Devil's Kitchen and we were writing songs. I thought about us driving and singing, him playing his steel guitar. I said, "You still writing songs?"

He said, "I been trying to. What about you?"

"Not as much anymore."

He said, "There's a lot I been brewing on since I joined up. I've got words all around me, ones I want to put down, but so far they don't want to come together. I got tunes, though, all through my head."

I thought it was nice to hear him talk, even if it was the one thing I'd ever heard him talk about—his music. Then I thought with a pang how long it'd been since I had anyone to talk to like this about writing and how I'd missed it. I was starting to get tired of singing other people's songs.

I said, "I'm going to write a song about flying a plane while men are shooting at you, trying to blast you out of the sky just because they're afraid you're better than them."

Butch laughed at this. I sneaked a look at him, trying to see his smile. His teeth shone white in the dark. He said, "Some fellas have a hard time with the fact that women can do the same thing they can, and better even. I know it, Velva Jean. They feel the same way about Indians."

I soaked in the feeling of the way he said my name, which sounded both old and new. It was a long time since I'd heard someone say it who knew me so well, and I thought about what a difference it made, how it sounded good to my ears. I liked having someone who knew me, not just from Camp Davis or Avenger Field, but from back home, from years ago. Butch Dawkins stirred up music that I didn't think was in me, or that I'd only heard far, far off in my mind, like it was coming from miles away.

I wanted to ask him about the work he was doing in the army, but instead I said, "We should write a song about it."

He said, "You onto something there, girl. Fo' sure, fo' sure."

Leona's was a clapboard shack with a tin roof, sitting in the middle of a field at the end of a dirt road. I could feel the music as we drove up. It traveled out the door and down the steps and into the ground surrounding the shack, snaking along the dirt road, reaching up through the tires of the jeep Butch had borrowed from base, into the seats of the car, and into me.

Inside, Leona's was no bigger than the bay I shared with Sally. Just like the juke joint in Nashville, the one I'd gone to with Johnny Clay and Gossie, there were so many people—every single one of them colored but us. Two men stood in a corner playing guitar and drums. Butch grabbed my hand and led me through the crowd till we were standing right by the band. The air was smoky, the lights dim. I leaned in to Butch's ear and said, "How can two men make that big sound?" The sound was bigger than anything I'd ever heard. It made me want to cry and dance at the same time. I wanted to climb inside of it and live there.

He said, "Music at its purest." From his pocket he pulled out a brown square of paper and some tobacco and started rolling a cigarette on his leg. I watched him for a moment. The grace of his hands, which were wide and strong. The loose, smooth way he moved. He stuck the cigarette in his mouth and lit it. The music was pulsing through me so that I wondered where it stopped and where my own pulse started. I stared at the cigarette and for some reason I had the urge to take it from Butch and smoke it myself.

Then Butch took my hand and pulled me to him, cigarette between his teeth. I was so close that I could feel his dog tags against my chest, could feel his breath in my ear. My head went spinny from the smoke and the music and the nearness of Butch. He was both easy and electric. Sexy. I forgot about Camp Davis and target towing and Colonel Wells and reprimands. I even forgot all the Indian and Cajun girls in the world while I just let the music run through me.

On the way home, we pulled back the window flaps and let the cold, raw air beat in. My hair whipped around and I could feel it curling but I didn't care. Butch's cigarette glowed red in the dark.

He talked all the way back. He talked about the blues. He told me about all the different types. He said, "There's St. Louis blues—that sort mixes blues with ragtime and jazz. There's country blues, like

Jimmie Rodgers and Blind Lemon Jefferson. That's usually played on banjo and guitar, and then Sylvester Weaver brought in the steel slide guitar, which he fretted with a knife blade, and that led to Delta blues, which is just plain old steel guitar and singing. Blues stripped down to the basics. I call it naked blues."

I thought, That's the kind of blues you play.

He talked about Piedmont blues and Memphis blues, boogie-woogie and big band blues, and jump blues like the kind Count Basie played. I told him about singing with Count Basie in Mexico, and he whistled long and low. He held the cigarette in his left hand, the one hanging out the window. He said, "Damn, girl." His voice was scratchy, like he'd yelled it raw.

He talked about Robert Johnson, about how all he wanted was to be a great blues musician. How, in the 1920s, he was just a young colored boy living on a plantation in Mississippi when one night at midnight he stood at a crossroads and sold his soul to the devil, who took his guitar from him and tuned it so that he could play the guitar like no one else before or since. Years later, when Robert Johnson was twenty-seven, just a few years older than me, he was killed after drinking whiskey poisoned with strychnine, like what they drank up at the snake-handling church on Bone Mountain.

I sat there listening to Butch. I thought how much I loved to hear him talk and that this was the most I'd ever heard him say. I said, "All this time, I thought there was just one kind of blues." Then I told him about all the names Daddy Hoyt gave the blues—not the blues you played but the blues you felt. The Gentle and Wholesome Blues, the Sadistic Blues, the Mean Devil Blues . . .

Butch said, "*J'ai le blues*. 'Have the blues.' *J'ai le blues de toi*. 'I have the blues for you.' There's a song in there somewhere."

I looked at his profile, and I suddenly thought of the first time I ever saw him, driving up to Harley's house with Johnny Clay in Danny Deal's old yellow truck—my truck now. I wondered where my brother was and wished he was there with us, riding in that jeep. I wished we could go back to that moment when he and Butch pulled up in front of the house and I stood on the running board feeling the rumble of the truck for the first time. When Johnny Clay asked me to go for a ride, I wished I'd got in that truck right then, between my brother and Butch Dawkins, and just driven away.

Butch started humming, like he was searching for the song.

I said, "We should write it."

I sneaked into the bay around 4:00 a.m., taking off my shoes just outside the door so I didn't wake up Sally. For such a little girl, she could snore louder than a steam engine, but she was quiet now. I heard her stirring around in bed. She said, "Hartsie?" Her voice was blurry. "How was it?"

I said, "Go back to sleep. I'll tell you tomorrow." I wanted to keep the night to myself just a little longer. I wanted to get in bed and give Butch Dawkins and Leona's juke joint and Robert Johnson and all the different types of blues a good think.

Sally said, "Gus Mitchell kissed me tonight . . ."

I said, "Was it wonderful?" She didn't say anything. "Sally?" I could hear her breathing slow and even, in and out, in and out, and then she started to snore.

After I washed my face and brushed my teeth, I climbed under the blanket and rolled onto my side. I pulled the covers up over my shoulder but poked my left foot out, just a little, because I liked having one leg free, even in winter. Then I set about to thinking:

Butch Dawkins is a different sort of man than Harley. He's a different sort of man than these army air force pilots. He isn't one to chase a girl or fall in love with her right off without even knowing her. He isn't one to sweep a girl away to the Balsam Mountain Springs Hotel or take her away on a train here and there and everywhere and be wild and bold and loud.

I thought of all the ways he was different from Ty and this should have made me like Butch less, but it didn't. I just wished I knew more about him. The only thing I'd ever really heard him talk about was music. I remembered Bob Keene telling me all about himself at the Christmas dance. I realized, as I lay there, that Butch hadn't answered a single question—not really, not truly—all night.

I got up and dug my hatbox out from my footlocker, careful not to wake up Sally. I pulled open the lid and searched with my fingers till I found Ty's compass. There were the initials: N-E-T. I shut the hatbox and closed the locker and got back into bed. I slid the compass under my pillow and rolled onto my side. I wrapped the fingers of one hand around the cool, hard metal and after a good, long while I went to sleep.

THIRTY-FIVE

The Norden bombsight looked just like a lopsided camera and was one of the most closely guarded secrets of the U.S. military. It was an analog computer that calculated the path of a bomb based on the crosswinds, altitude, and airspeed. The bombardier told the computer the airspeed, wind speed and direction, altitude, and angle of drift, and then the bombsight calculated the route of the bomb. As the airplane got closer to the target, the pilot turned the plane over to autopilot, which took the plane to the exact location and dropped the bomb over the target. The bombsite was accurate enough to hit a hundred-foot circle from an altitude of twenty-one thousand feet. Basically, it could shoot a tick off a dog.

The bombsight was loaded onto the aircraft under armed guard and covered until it was in the air. Bombardiers were required to take an oath promising to defend it with their lives. If the plane had to make an emergency landing on enemy territory, the bombardier or pilot was responsible for shooting the bombsight with a thermite gun, which was able to melt the Norden into a lump of metal. When you were ferrying a Norden bombsight, you had to fly with the gun strapped to your hip.

On January 18, we—a select group of WASP and army air force officers—were told we'd be ferrying a Norden bombsight, and then we were taken to the Cemetery, which was what we called the scrap yard where crashed planes were stored, looking for things to melt with our thermite guns. Lieutenant Bob Keene and Captain Theodore

Dailey and head mechanic Harry Lawson led us through—Sally and Helen and the rest of the girls and some of the male pilots too. There were guards with guns pacing back and forth around the borders of the scrap yard, and one of the guards was Zeke Bodine. We made our way through the wreckage and past wings, propellers, a cockpit all by itself, engines, tires, control panels, cables, a pilot's seat.

Suddenly Bob Keene stopped and said, "Here." We lined up around him. To the left and the right, stacked up and scattered around and sitting on the ground were twenty or thirty little black boxes no bigger than my mandolin.

Sally said, "What are those?"

Bob Keene said, "Flight recorders. Not all ships have them yet, but they record aircraft performance parameters and conversations in the cockpit, radio transmissions, background sounds." He pointed the thermite gun at one. "In case of a crash you can open them up and try to figure out what caused it."

I said, "They look all closed up. Shouldn't they be opened?" I wondered if Ruth's plane had a black box, if it was one of these. I thought, Maybe we need to see what's inside.

Bob Keene said, "These are old ones—ones they don't need anymore." I wondered if this was true. He shot at the nearest black box and it melted right into the ground. Captain Dailey, who was so skinny he looked eight feet tall, started lining everyone up so we could all take a turn.

I stood at the back of formation, just behind Helen. The breeze blew my hair around my face and up in the air. The ends of it kept getting stuck in my lipstick, the part that hadn't come off. I was tired and run-down because I'd stayed up too late the night before, trying to write a song. The words were coming, but I couldn't hear the music like I wanted to because every time I got near it I started thinking about the parts of an AT-17 or A-25 engine or things I'd learned in physics class, like that water wasn't compressible but air was until an aircraft passing through it reached the speed of sound.

As I moved up the line, closer to the black boxes, I thought that they were like the heart of a plane—the place where all its secrets were locked up—and that it felt wrong to be shooting at them.

When it was my turn, I wrapped my hand around the thermite gun, just like they'd showed us. Bob Keene stepped in and said, "Let me help you, Fifinella." He tried to correct my grip, but Captain Dailey said, "What are you doing, Lieutenant? She's got it perfect."

Bob Keene frowned and stood back, while I raised my gun and aimed at one of the black boxes. I thought they looked like broken hearts, all sealed up and shattered and melted into nothing.

~

The following week we started survival training and gas-mask drills. Captain Dailey said this was something we needed to learn because even if we were just ferrying planes around our own country we still had to be prepared for the enemy. We could be hijacked. We could be shot down out of the sky. Some of the planes we were flying were new and used advanced technology. Captain Dailey said this made them as good as actual weapons, which meant the Germans and the Japanese wanted to get hold of them and find out their secrets.

We had to wear our masks and run through tents filled with poison gas. Then Captain Dailey made us run through with our masks off, over and over again until we could recognize the odor of each kind of gas: mustard, phosgene, lewisite, chloropicrin. The one I hated most was tear gas, which burned my face and neck and left me blind for hours.

By bedtime, my eyes were still tearing. I stood in the bathroom of our barracks, staring at myself in the mirror—red eyes, puffy circles underneath, tears forming at the corners, nose like a clown, cheeks stained with little lines of water creeping down my face. I looked like a dirty little urchin, like a down-and-out. I looked like one of the Lowe boys, always hanging around on their daddy's porch, faces brown, hair sticking up, chewing tobacco. I looked like a girl doing man's work, but for once I didn't care. I wasn't here to be crowned Gold Queen or get my picture taken for *Life* magazine.

I leaned in close to the mirror and said, "Just look at you, Velva Jean Hart. You don't even look like yourself." I felt my phantom limb again. Now that the "Bright" was officially gone, I thought my name was like a soldier missing a leg or an arm, like how they knew it was gone but they could still feel it there, in the hole where it used to be.

January 30, 1944

Dear Velva Jean,

We had a letter from Linc yesterday morning. He's on one of 240 ships that set sail from the Bay of Naples on January 21. He said there were thirty-five thousand men, American and British, sailors and infantry, and that Coyle is there too. They're headed to a beach someplace between Naples and Rome, though he can't say where.

I never really knew Butch Dawkins, but any friend of Johnny Clay's is a friend of ours. What he's doing is good and important work. Daddy Hoyt says to tell you that after the Civil War, the Navajo were punished if they were caught speaking their own language. And now the government's asking for their help! He says he wonders where Butch learned it because if you don't learn Navajo or Comanche as a child, you usually can't learn it at all.

Daddy Hoyt also says to tell you this story: There's an Indian legend about hero twins that fought off monsters that were threatening their world. The twins went to the sun to ask for a weapon that could kill the monsters, and the sun gave them a thunderbolt. The twins came back down to earth and used the thunderbolt to kill the monsters and save the world. One of the things that saved them was that the monsters couldn't understand them because the twins used a language that only they knew.

Remember we love you.

Ruby Poole

THIRTY-SIX

On February 1, Ruth resigned from the WASP and went home to Illinois. I wondered what would happen if we all dropped out, and I liked thinking of Jackie Cochran coming to Camp Davis on her next visit and finding us all gone. But where would we go? What would we do? I couldn't go back to Fair Mountain now for anything. Just like how, once I taught myself to drive, I couldn't very well teach myself *not* to drive, now that I knew how to fly, I couldn't very well stop flying.

Two days later three female reporters came to Camp Davis to interview the WASP. The day before they came, Colonel Wells gave orders to clear out a storeroom in the administration building and brought in a table and chairs. A sign was hung on the door—gold and shiny just like the one outside his office. It said "WASP Nest."

In groups of five or six, we were rounded up and brought to the WASP Nest to talk to the reporters. They were nice but businesslike. They said, "Oh what a nice office the Army Air Forces has given you." We didn't tell them that up until yesterday our office was a storeroom.

The reporters said they'd been hearing rumors about men sabotaging the WASP, about women being harassed and even shot at. One of the reporters said, "Before we came here, we were up at Camp Lejeune, talking to the women marines. Some of them say they fear for their lives."

We answered politely and carefully, not saying a word about ferrying Norden bombsights or being shot at by male pilots, all except Sally, who said, "There's truth to everything those girls told you. We've been going through it since we got here."

The reporters started asking a hundred questions then, and Sally answered all of them.

On our walk back to the bay, I said, "You shouldn't have said those things."

Sally said, "Aren't you tired, Hartsie? This isn't what I signed up for. This isn't why I learned to fly. I'm sure I'll tick some people off when the articles come out, but how's that any different than the way they're feeling about me now? At least this way I know I'm being honest."

She was right, and I knew she was right. I wished then that I hadn't just sat there like a stump. I wished I'd been as brave as Sally. "Or as reckless," I heard a voice say.

The next morning Sally and I walked over to the WASP Nest to get our assignments, but the sign was gone. We went up and down the hallway, searching for the office, trying to see if we'd remembered it wrong. Then we walked back to the first door we'd stopped at and opened it. Instead of the table and chairs, the room was filled with boxes and brooms and equipment. Our WASP Nest was back to being a storeroom.

~

I didn't see Butch again till Thursday. I came out of the mess hall just after supper, with Sally and Janie and Gus Mitchell and Vince Gillies, and he was standing outside smoking a cigarette. He shook the hair out of his eyes and said, "Hey." His eyes flicked over at Gus and Vince. "Hey," he said again, but they just stood there.

I said, "Hey." I thought: Where have you been? Where did you go? What are you doing here? How can I find you?

Sally started talking to Gus and Vince, pulling them away.

Butch said to me, "It ain't going to do you any good to be seen with me. They hate us more than they hate you."

I said, "I don't care." And I didn't.

He said, "I been working on a song."

He didn't ask what I'd been doing or how I was. He didn't ask me if I'd been shot at lately. He didn't know anything about Ruth's accident or Jackie Cochran or the Norden bombsight.

I said, "I been working on one too, but it's stuck. I can't get it out no matter how I try. When I moved to Nashville, I just wrote and wrote, but ever since the war, ever since learning to fly, I wonder if I'll ever be able to write again. All I can think about is airplanes."

He said, "Maybe you're still learning to fly."

I thought this was about the craziest thing I ever heard. I was a WASP. The most famous female pilot in the world had pinned my silver wings on my uniform. I was ferrying planes for the military.

He said, "What time's bed check?"

"Ten o'clock."

He nodded. He took my hand. He said, "Come on." I turned back to wave at Sally and the others, and Gus and Vince were still staring at Butch, only now they were staring at our hands.

The Indians lived on the far side of the base, nearest the swamp, over by Highway 18, which ran right past Camp Davis on the other side of the marsh, and an old runway that was now covered in moss. They slept in large brown wood-frame tents, and the ground around them was muddy from the rain that seemed to come in off the ocean every day till you were surprised you didn't find moss and mildew growing all over yourself.

I said, "Why do they keep you over here?"

He led me past the tents to a small square building with lights in the windows. He pushed the door open and said, "Go on in."

Inside there was just one room and it was warm and bright. Half a dozen men sat in front of a fireplace, playing cards, smoking cigarettes. One of them was playing the guitar and another was singing. They didn't look like Cherokee, and I guessed these were the Lumbee— light skin, brown-black hair, dark eyes—and maybe some of the Navajo and Comanche too. The Lumbee were supposed to come from the Croatan Indians and the white men of the Lost Colony, which was a group of the first English settlers that came to America and vanished one winter. No one ever knew what happened to them.

The Indians hollered to Butch as we came in, and nodded at me. The air was friendly and easy. I wanted to sit down and talk to these men. They reminded me of home, of Granny, who was part Cherokee, and Beachard, who looked the most Cherokee of any of Mama's children.

Butch's steel guitar was propped in a corner. He picked it up, and then we sat down away from the fireplace and the card players and the man playing guitar. There were three chairs, and Butch set his steel guitar on one of them. He pulled off his jacket and rolled his shirt-sleeves up over his elbows. I thought about the tattoo on his arm—a guitar with writing on the neck and flames shooting out of the pegbox and the words "The Bluesman," written across it.

I said, "Are those the other code talkers?" I liked the way "code talkers" sounded. It made me think of the Indian message trees on Fair Mountain, of how the Cherokee used to bend the trees to mark their way and leave messages to each other in the ones that were hollowed out.

He said, "How did you hear about code talkers?"

I said, "Some of the girls here. They said you all might be rounded up to do code talking."

"I guess *classified* don't always mean 'classified.'"

I said, "Oh, is it top secret? Like spies?"

He smiled, "Something like that."

"What kind of code do you talk in?"

"Navajo. Comanche. Choctaw." He ran his hands through his hair and pushed a piece of it behind his ear so it wouldn't fall in his face. He looked at me. It was the kind of look that was hard to read. He looked like he was thinking things over.

I started getting nervous a little, the way I sometimes got around him. I felt the need to fill all the spaces when I was with him.

I said, "Code talking sounds important."

He said, "It is."

I said, "I heard each code talker's assigned an officer and that officer has to protect them." Sally told me that the officer had orders to shoot his code talker if the enemy tried to capture them.

Butch said, "You know a lot." He rubbed at the back of his neck. He leaned forward in his chair, arms resting on his legs. "The important thing's protecting the code, not the man talking it."

I looked around at the other Indians. "They look young."

"Most of them never been off their reservation till now." He picked up his guitar again and started tuning it. I thought he always wanted to be doing something with his hands—rolling a cigarette, playing guitar. "Navajo's the rarest language on earth. It's never been written down. All these years, they have to memorize it and then pass it down and around. Like a song. Like the way you know it first, before you write it. And the way it's hard to write down sometimes because it's just in you."

"I thought you were Choctaw."

"Half-Choctaw. Half-Creole. But I learned the Indian languages a long time ago. I speak Cajun, Creole, French, Patois, Gullah, Geechee. I figure the more words you know the better." He strummed the guitar. "At the start of the world there were words. The first word was *light*. The second word was *earth*. Then *water*. Then *air*." He said the word for each one in Navajo, and it sounded strange to me, like he was making it up. "The Navajo believe the universe was created by words."

I believed this because, when it got down to it, words were just about my favorite thing and you didn't have much if you didn't have words. I thought that maybe they were the most powerful thing on earth. Sometimes they could lift you up like you'd just been saved, and sometimes they cut through you till you couldn't breathe. I loved the feeling when you found just the right one after you'd been looking for it for a while. I hated the feeling when you couldn't catch them like you wanted to or when someone used them against you.

Butch said, "Navajo's one of the hidden languages of the world. In Navajo there's no such thing as choosing the wrong word. You have to say it right or you end up saying something else."

Then he started to sing, low and growling. It was a bluesy song, but not deep-down-in-the-gutter bluesy like the ones I'd heard him play back up in Alluvial. This one was yearning and lonely and raw right down to the bone. His voice was deeper, scratchier, more whiskey-and-cigarettes than the last time I'd heard him sing. It seemed older and had more shades of something in it—a kind of aching, a kind of heartbreak.

I thought, Something's happened to you, Butch Dawkins, since I seen you last.

I wanted to know what it was—if it was a person or maybe some sort of misfortune or tragedy—that had changed him. I wanted to climb inside that song right now and try to heal the heartbreak.

After he was done singing, I tried to think of something to say. He might wonder why he was sharing this song with me when all I did was sit there and stare at him and not have anything smart to mention about it.

I thought about talking to him about burdens and scars and the things we carry around with us in this life. The more things that happened to me, the more I thought it was like carrying a suitcase—you kept adding things to it, like your mama dying and your daddy going away, heartbreak over your husband, heartbreak over a boy that died. You just started adding these things to your suitcase until the case got heavier. You still had to carry it around wherever you went, and even if you set it down for a while you still had to pick it up again because it belonged to you and so did everything inside it.

I thought of saying all this, and then I just said, "What's that song called?"

He smiled, a slow and lazy grin. I liked what it did to his face, shifting the angles, making them softer. Butch said, "It don't have a name yet. I'm thinking of calling it 'The Bluesman.'"

"Like your tattoo?"

He laughed and then nodded. "Yes, ma'am. I know I want to write a song called 'The Bluesman' someday, but I'm still waiting for the right one. Nothing I ever wrote's been good enough."

I said, "You never told me how you got your tattoo."

He sat back in his chair, strumming the guitar a little more so that I knew he was about to start another song. He said, "I know."

~

I went to bed that night hearing his song in my head. Just the memory of it made me sink a little deeper into the bed, my heart weighing down my body till I thought I might break through the mattress and fall onto the floor. I thought about a language that couldn't be written. I thought about all the words on this earth that I didn't know. I wondered if learning them would mean being able to write more songs, better songs.

Then I tried to remember the words that began the world. I said "light," "earth," "water," "air" to myself one by one, first in English, then in Navajo, until I fell asleep.

Not All the Risk Is in the Sky

By Lydia Lowe for the *Wilmington Morning Star*

February 19—Cold nerve, steady hands, keen mind, and a willingness to do a job that takes patience and more patience. No glamour and no cheering crowds, just hard sober work and the kind of courage that can carry on when the probing search-lights blind you and you have to fly by your instruments to keep the course.

That's the sort of women pilots Jacqueline Cochran has trained, and is training, to help the army. The girls have made the transition from 450-horsepower ships to 1,250 horsepower in a single jump, a move to "hot" ships that land at 110 mph. They are flying everything these days. Most had little more than thirty-five hours of flight time when they started their course at Sweetwater, Texas. They had everything to learn. They dug their toes in and did learn, but they aren't through yet.

They may not be overseas, but these girls are turning in extraordinary contributions. Several of them have even given their lives for their country, when the planes they were flying crashed. But they don't just fear for their lives in the air. They live in fear on the ground too, specifically at Camp Davis, the Army Air Forces base to which they've been assigned, on a swamp along the coast. They live in fear of harassment by male officers, fear of so-called friendly fire by gunners that shoot recklessly at the planes they fly while target towing, fear of sabotage on the planes themselves. There is enough risk involved in flying powerful warplanes without adding in these factors. Perhaps Jackie Cochran should spend less time in Washington, D.C., and more time looking after her pilots. Who says there isn't a war being fought right here at home?

February 21, 1944

Hey, girl,

Been working on something here. See what you think. I ain't sure if what I got is a verse or the chorus. Maybe you can tell me.

(Sorry I ain't one for letter writing. Got to save all the words up for songs.)

You made somethin' out of nothin'—
made me look around and see.
You made always out of never—
you made a man out of me.

Your smilin' eyes saw somethin'
no one else could see.
(Somethin' somethin' somethin')
You made a man out of me.

I don't know. I think there's something there, but the words just drift on off before I can catch them. I'm stumped.

Butch

———————

February 22, 1944

Butch,

I think what you've got here is the verse *and* the chorus. I did some work on it after I got off the flight line yesterday and again today. See what you think.

Do you have the melody yet? Because I started singing one today when I was up in the A-24.

You made somethin' out of nothin'—
made me open my eyes and see.
You made always out of never—
you made a man out of me.

Your smilin' eyes saw somethin'
no one else could see.
Makin' somethin' out of nothin'—
you made a man out of me.

Your listenin' ears heard somethin'
yearnin' to be free.
Makin' somethin' out of nothin'—
You made a man out of me.

That first one's your chorus. That's the part I been singing all day, ever since I went up and then ever since I landed. It needs more verses of course, but what do you think?

Velva Jean

February 23, 1944

Velva Jean,

I think you know how to throw it down, girl.
Can't wait to hear the tune. Lay it on me.

Butch

THIRTY-SEVEN

On February 25 a man named Rolf Stigler was arrested in New York City where he'd been working as a cook on the SS *Argentine*. The newspaper said he'd come to the United States in 1935 and was made a naturalized citizen two years later. From the SS *Argentine*, he'd been transporting microphotographs and other materials from the United States to South America, where the information was then sent on to Germany.

Two days later Fritz Kramer was arrested in a section of New York called Yorkville where he was running an Italian restaurant named Little Dominic's. The restaurant was a sort of undercover clubhouse for other German spies, and most of his customers worked in national defense production. He learned information from them without them knowing it, and then he reported it to the German gestapo. When the FBI arrested him, he was carrying twenty letters addressed to people in Europe. They also found books about magnesium, aluminum alloys, uranium, and plutonium.

Colonel Wells sent out a warning that spies could be anywhere. Suddenly we were on lockdown, having to sign in and out every time we came and went from the base, even if it was just to go into town. I started looking at everyone, wondering if they were spies: Gus Mitchell, Harry Lawson, Major Blackburn, Vince Gillies, Bob Keene. Sally and I stayed up late at night and talked about who we thought might be spies. We decided that if anyone was a spy it would be someone like Zeke Bodine, who was so nice and normal that he was almost certainly hiding something, or Colonel Wells, who looked almost exactly like a spy in a movie.

~

After the newspaper article appeared in the *Wilmington Morning Star*, Sally was pulled off the flight line and given desk duty. At eight o'clock each morning, she reported to Louella Corbett in the dispatcher's office, and at five o'clock at night she was released. She received an official reprimand from Jackie Cochran and was told she would be returned to the flight line only when she could be trusted to hold her tongue and "maintain discretion regarding the mission to which you've been assigned."

On February 28, Miss Cochran herself showed up at Camp Davis. I was on the flight line, just climbing out of my A-25, when I saw her plane on the runway. Louella Corbett met up with me and said, "You're wanted in the office."

I said, "What's going on?"

She didn't answer. She trudged on ahead, her skirt rising up in folds over her enormous bottom.

Inside the dispatcher's office, Helen Stillbert was sitting on a chair, legs crossed neatly. She said, "What do you think, Hartsie? Miss Cochran wants to see us, just you and me."

I waved at Sally, who sat behind a desk answering phones. She rolled her eyes at me and snapped her gum good and loud. Louella Corbett jumped like she'd heard a gunshot. I sat down next to Helen. I tried to think of anything I might have done wrong.

Helen said, "Maybe we're being transferred."

As much as I didn't like Camp Davis—as much as I hated the tow targeting and the rude comments and the attitudes of the men and the swamp that surrounded us—I wasn't ready to go. Not yet. Not till I helped Butch finish his song.

Jackie Cochran sat in the office she sometimes used when she was on base, and Helen and I stood in front of her because she hadn't offered either of us a chair. She brushed a hair out of her face and said, "The male pilots are refusing to fly the B-29."

Helen said, "The Superfortress?"

Jackie Cochran ignored this because she didn't like people to interrupt. She said, "It's the largest long-range bomber ever built, but it's complicated and it has a habit of catching fire. The men are afraid of it. They say it's too big to manage and it's unsafe."

I said, "Is it?" Although I'd never seen one close-up, I knew that the B-29 Superfortress could fly higher and faster than any other bomber on earth. It was the biggest, fastest, and most advanced airplane ever built. It was twenty-five feet longer and twice as heavy as the B-17 Flying Fortress, and its wingspan was forty feet wider. In 1942 the Boeing Airplane Company's chief test pilot, Eddie Allen, took up a B-29 on its second flight ever and an engine caught fire and burned through the wing. Eddie Allen and his ten crew members died, along with eighteen workers on the ground, when they crashed into a meat-packing plant.

Miss Cochran said, "General Arnold has ordered me to select two pilots to train on the B-29. He wants you to travel from base to base to prove to the male pilots that the bomber is safe to fly. Obviously it's a big ship and you can't fly it alone. You'll go as pilot and copilot, but we'll assign you a crew."

"That will make us even more popular with the men," Helen said, but Miss Cochran ignored this.

I remembered what Colonel Wells had said about us being expendable, and thought: If they want the male pilots to fly that plane, then make them fly it. Why should we have to? We'd be in a fine mess if all the brave boys fighting in this war were suddenly too scared to fly or fight.

Miss Cochran said, "I won't lie to you. It's a hot plane, difficult to handle. The engine's temperamental. There have been some accidents, some deaths. But it's a well-engineered plane and it's easier to fly than some of the twin-engine ships."

She looked at us like she was waiting. We didn't say anything. "It's vital that we do this. Not only to demonstrate once and for all how valuable this program is, but you'll be transporting some important cargo to a base in New Mexico."

I said, "Los Alamos?"

She looked surprised. I knew I caught her off guard because she answered me. "Yes."

Helen said, "Why us?"

"In wartime we need the best we can get up in the air, and you two are the best pilots I have. This is a highly classified mission, ladies. The B-29 hasn't been used in combat yet. The government considers it one of our secret weapons. That means this doesn't leave the base, which means no talking to reporters."

I thought about Sally sitting outside answering phones. "Yes, ma'am," we said.

Then she handed us each a book. As she did, she said, "Whatever you do, don't make any mistakes or it will go against the whole organization." The book was the *Airplane Commander Training Manual for the Superfortress*. I flipped it open to the table of contents: "Operating Instructions"; "Flight Operating Data"; "Emergency Operating Instructions"; "Operational Equipment"; "Flight Operating Charts, Tables, Curves, and Diagrams." I wanted to stop right then and read the book from cover to cover.

The B-29 manual reminded me of *Man and the Motor Car* and *How to Drive*, the books I'd borrowed from the library when I was teaching myself to drive. That night after mess I sat on my cot and studied diagrams of the manual controls, the pilot's control stand and switch panel, the engineer's control stand and switch panel, and the aisle stand. I'd made a brown-paper cover for the book so no one could see the title.

Sally walked into the room from the bathroom, her hair wrapped in a towel. She said, "What are you reading, Hartsie?" She picked up her banjo and played the first few notes of a song and then she set it back down. She was getting better.

I hated to lie to her, but this was classified, and even though she would find out after I started training, I thought about the way she'd told the newspaper reporter too much, and so I said, "Just studying up on the A-25."

She said, "I miss flying."

"You won't have to sit behind that desk forever."

She made a face. "I know." Then she picked up the watering can she used for her garden and went back to the bathroom to fill it up. When she carried the can outside, I lay down and read a little more until my eyes grew as heavy as the summer air on Fair Mountain. When I couldn't keep them open any longer, I put my finger in the page to mark it and thought: I'll just close my eyes for a minute. Then I'll read some more.

Before I knew it, it was morning, and I woke up with my finger still marking the page. I went back over some of the things I'd read the night before, trying to memorize the manual controls location diagram, and then I dragged myself out of the bed, body aching, and got myself ready for another day.

The B-29 arrived sometime in the night. My cot rattled me awake and for a moment I thought the U-boats had attacked us again, that maybe they'd pulled right up on the beach and opened fire. From her bed, Sally was shouting but I couldn't make out what she was saying. There was the sound of thunder, as loud and terrible as the explosion of the Terrible Creek train wreck. I jumped out of bed and threw the window open wide and stuck my head out.

The sky was lit up and bright and something silvery-white was dropping toward the airstrip. At first I thought it was the moon. Sally was beside me standing on her tiptoes. "A plane," she said. But not just any plane. The biggest plane I'd ever seen. The B-29.

Sally said, "Is that a Superfortress?"

I said, "I'm not sure," because she wasn't supposed to know anything and I didn't want to give myself away. But all I could think of was Miss Cochran and what she'd said to us: "This is a highly classified mission, ladies. The B-29 hasn't been used in combat yet. The government considers it one of our secret weapons."

I lay awake the rest of the night, and the next morning Sally and me rushed out to mess with the other girls, all of them chattering about the explosion that woke them up and what it might have been—a rigid airship, a fleet of bombers. The airstrip was empty except for the usual A-25s and B-24s and C-47s, and there was no sight of the B-29. Helen sat next to me, setting her tray down with a smack. She leaned in close and said, "Did you see it?"

"I heard it before I ever saw it."

She said, "They brought it here for us, Hartsie. Just you and me." The thought of it made my skin go prickly.

That afternoon, after ground school, an officer, one of the ones that worked under Colonel Wells, found first Helen and then me and told us we were wanted at Hangar 12, which sat behind the other hangars, near a small grove of pine trees and jungle trees and the ooze of the swampland. Instead of the green-and-gray camouflage of the other planes, the bomber was silver and the sun beat down on it, catching the shine of the metal so it looked like the bomber was on fire. There were other bombers being used in this war—the B-17, the B-24, the B-26. But the B-29 was the biggest one of all and I, Velva Jean Hart, was learning to fly it.

Major Blackburn and Bob Keene were in charge of our actual flight training. On the first day, Bob said to Helen and me, "Nothing personal, but I should be flying that bomber, not you. I'm trained on it. I got experience on it. I'm supposed to be the one flying it. The other fellas may be chicken livered, but not me. The only reason they gave it to you girls is publicity." His face didn't look so friendly anymore.

After he walked away, I said to Helen, "How are we supposed to not take that personal?"

Helen and I took turns sitting in the pilot's seat and studying the controls. I'd been reading about these very same gears and levers and pedals and wires for days now, but I had never in my life seen so many up close and not in a diagram. Some of them were labeled and some of them weren't. I remembered sitting in my truck for the first time and looking at the dashboard. "Clutch, brake, gas," I heard myself say back then, over and over till I got used to it.

Even if someone could figure out all these knobs and levers, I wondered how on earth you could actually get the B-29 into the air. It weighed seventy thousand pounds unloaded and had a wingspan of

141 feet and a length of 99 feet. It sat 27 feet off the ground and had a maximum speed of 375 miles per hour. It could hold 9,501 gallons of gasoline.

The B-29 held the first onboard computer of any airplane. This was called the Central Fire Control system and it guided the turret guns—each turret was controlled by its own computer. Altitude, speed, air temperature—they all made a difference in how well and how hard the bullets hit their target.

I was getting to know the Superfortress from every angle. I figured I could take apart that bomber and put it back together again if I had to. I thought, when you got down to it, that the B-29 was just like an enormous yellow truck.

Harry Lawson said the cowlings around the four 200-horsepower engines were too tight and this was why the engines overheated so often and even caught fire on the ground before takeoff.

Bob Keene said to Major Blackburn, "We could only be so lucky."

I said, "What did you say?"

Bob smiled. He said, "Relax, Fifinella. I was only joking."

I just wondered about that.

On March 14, Helen and I pulled on fleece-lined leather pressure suits and boots and spent time in a pressure chamber in one of the base labs. In the pressure chamber, test crewmen had to deal with the stratospheric temperatures and pressure conditions we could expect while flying a B-29 at heights of up to thirty-three thousand feet.

I didn't like the pressure chamber because it made me feel penned in like an animal. The heat turned me dizzy and the pressure changes made me sick to my stomach. I felt like I was being thrown around in the back of my truck or buried alive.

By March 16 I'd grown what Major Blackburn called my "sky legs." He was waiting for me outside the pressure chamber, making notes on a clipboard. As I wobbled out, he said, "How was it, Hart?"

I said, "Fine, sir."

"Easier?"

"Yes."

He turned to the officer working the controls. He said, "Hear that? What do you think?"

The officer said, "I think she's ready to fly."

~

Sally turned twenty-four on March 18. Sally, Janie, Helen, and me dolled ourselves up and went to the service club. We heard the service club before we got to it, and that was because the music coming out of it was as blistering as a hot day in Texas when the heat rose off the ground and hovered there—so hot you could see it. It made me think of a thunderstorm and lightning and the way I felt after a good cry.

Butch.

Inside the club the army air force pilots were talking and laughing. I saw Leonard Grossman and Zeke Bodine across the way, talking to two girls I didn't know, but they didn't seem to see me. Some members of the British unit were there and some of the officers, including Bob Keene and Theo Dailey and Vince Gillies.

The band was set up on the same stage I'd sung on at the Christmas dance. I recognized the drummer and bass player as two of the Lumbee Indians. Butch Dawkins was playing guitar. He was wearing a white undershirt, just like the one I'd seen him wearing that night at Deal's. And he was bent over his guitar, hair hanging down, working the fingerboard with the broken bottle neck. The tattoo on his arm changed as his muscles shifted, tightening, relaxing. "The Bluesman." I thought how he was just like a haint, showing up here and there, going away, coming back. I never knew when I was going to see him.

He started to sing and he sounded wild and mad, like an animal caged up in a trap, trying to lash its way out. His voice was a growl, then a howl—just like at Deal's—but there was something else in there that unsettled me. Sorrow. Lonesomeness. Loss. I wondered what was in the suitcase he was carrying around with him.

One by one, cadets and officers came up to ask Sally and Janie and the other girls to dance, till soon it was just Helen and me standing there. Some of the men would walk by and look right at us only to keep on walking, asking another girl to dance.

Helen said, "Brrr. I should have brought a wrap."

I stood there telling myself that it was okay, that it didn't matter, that I didn't want to talk over this music or dance to it anyway. The music was too deep, too raw. It was Butch Dawkins up there, naked from the inside out, for everyone to see.

Butch was singing with his eyes closed. Something about El Paso and Las Cruces, New Mexico—about being on the road, about trying to go home. Sally went dancing by with Gus Mitchell. He was looking down at her like she was the only girl in the room, and she was looking up at him like he was the only boy.

Helen was saying something about leaving, about getting out of there, but I didn't say anything because I was thinking about El Paso and Las Cruces, New Mexico, and the B-29: "The B-29 is equipped with five power-operated gun turrets, remotely controlled, with each turret housing two .50-caliber machine guns . . ."

Helen said, "I mean it, Hartsie. I won't stand here like Hester Prynne. We might as well have a scarlet B-29 stitched on our dresses."

Suddenly, just like he was waiting for that moment, Butch said, "I want to thank you all for listening to us tonight. If you don't mind, we're getting ready to throw it down." Only the way he said it was like: "we're getting ready to throw. It. Down."

Then he started in on a wild, thumping song that reached so fast and far inside me that I couldn't breathe. That music thudded and stomped and wailed and howled till I thought I would go crazy if he didn't stop it, because it was too much to hear and feel.

Vince Gillies danced by with one of the other WASP, and said, "What's the matter, Fifi? Injun got your tongue?" He laughed at this, and even though it was a big, friendly laugh it didn't sound friendly at all.

Helen grabbed my hand and said, "That does it," and started pulling me toward the door.

Butch looked up then. He sang the next line, which was something about hitching to a truck stop and being a long way from home. He was staring right at me, and suddenly I was surrounded by haints—

Mama, Daddy, Ty. I didn't have to conjure anything because it was being conjured around me, spirits stirring up and reaching for me, trying to pull at me. It was like the fire up at the Wood Carver's, when they threw all his carvings in to burn and the flames and the smoke climbed up into the night, reaching for more, burning, burning.

March 19, 1944

Velva Jean,

I couldn't sleep tonight for writing. Too many words traveling in my head. I wrote some down. See what you think.

Butch

The Barefoot Blues

I got me some blues,
got the blue-sky blues
got the low-down blues
got the high-flyin' blues
got the blues from my head
down to my shoes,
if I had any shoes.
Got the barefoot blues.

Got the piano blues
and the guitar blues
and the singin' blues
and the silent blues
and the hard-time blues
down to my shoes,
if I had any shoes.
Got the barefoot blues.

Got the lovin' blues
and the leavin' blues
and the lyin' blues
and the cheatin' blues
and the makin'-up blues
down to my shoes,
if I had any shoes.
Got the barefoot blues.

Got the crazy blues
and the hurtin' blues
and the lovin'-somebody-
don't-love-me-back blues
and the lonesome blues
down to my shoes,
if I had any shoes.
Got the barefoot blues.

Oh, I got me some blues,
got the blue-sky blues
got the low-down blues
got the high-flyin' blues
got the blues from my head
down to my shoes,
if I had any shoes.
Got the barefoot blues.

March 20, 1944

Butch,

I love your song, especially because it makes me think of
driving back from Leona's juke joint and talking about all
the different kinds of blues in the world. I think my favorite line is: "And the lovin'-somebody-don't-love-me-back
blues." Now I want to hear you sing it.

I wish I had something to send to you.

Velva Jean

THIRTY-EIGHT

Major Blackburn and Bob Keene flew to New Mexico, to the Los Alamos National Laboratory, on March 23, which meant we had a four-day break from training on the B-29. After ground-school classes in safeguarding military secrets and defense against chemical attacks, I thought I might go see Butch Dawkins.

It started raining as I walked down the rows of barracks and tents, heading in what I thought was the direction of the Indian camp. The rain came down harder and heavier, puddling at my feet. The air smelled like salt water. I passed a group of enlisted men—more boys than men, all Adam's apples and gangly wrists and big feet. One of them said, "Where you going, sister?"

One of his friends pushed him and said, "Can't you see? She wants me."

I started to get a bad feeling. There were four of them and one of me. I walked faster, and suddenly one of them came running up beside me. He said, "Hey, where you going? Not real friendly, are you? Where you off to in such a hurry?"

Another one ran up and now he was on the other side of me. He said, "Don't play coy, Waspie. We know the real reason you're in the military." He reached out for me.

I started to run, splashing through water till I had soaked myself up to my knees, my hips, my stomach. I must have run over that whole base till I finally saw a grove of trees that looked familiar. It was hard to tell in the rain, but I ran toward them, and there was the old runway, washed out by the water, and there were the tents, and, just past them, the small box building that the code talkers used. I thought: What if Butch leaves for the war and doesn't even tell me? What if he's already gone? How will I find him again? I pushed the door open and hurried in from the rain, my pants and shirt sticking to me, my shoes squishing on the carpet. I shook myself off, just like a dog, and pushed my hair out of my face.

I heard a voice say, "Look what the cat brought." And there sat Butch, by the fireplace, guitar on his knee, papers spread out in front of him. He was wearing an undershirt, his dog tags and medicine beads shining against the material. He stood up and handed me a blanket. I wrapped it around myself, shivering, even though it wasn't really cold outside.

He said, "You okay?"

"What?"

"You look spooked."

"I'm fine."

"You sure?" He was looking into my eyes like he was trying to see if this was true.

"Yes." And I was fine now that I'd seen him, now that I knew he was still here.

"Come on over, then, and dry out." I followed him to the fireplace. I was careful not to drip on his papers as I sat down in one of the chairs. He moved the papers around, tidying them up. He said, "I don't usually like writing these things down. I like carrying them in my head."

I said, "Why are you writing them, then?"

He said, "Because I wanted you to look at them, and it's easier on paper. I was going to mail them to you. I didn't know when I'd see you next." He pushed one of the papers forward. "That's the one I been working on most. It's sort of following me around and not letting me alone."

"You put down music?"

"Some. Chorus mostly."

I said, "Ever since I left Nashville—I don't know." I pushed the paper back to him. "Maybe you better do it on your own."

He said, "Do you remember that song we wrote up at Devil's Courthouse?"

I pulled the blanket tight around me. I thought of days spent with Butch on my porch when Harley was away and afternoons up at the Devil's Tramping Ground, playing and singing, and—one time—dancing. I saw Butch sitting outside of Deal's and me standing there and us singing the song we wrote together while Harley stood off and watched.

Butch said, "I never wrote with anyone else, girl. I never showed my songs to anybody. You're the only one I ever done that with, and that one we wrote together is still one of my best songs." He said it matter-of-fact and not at all romantic, just like he was talking about the weather or what he ate for breakfast.

He handed me the paper. I saw the words and the music and they started blurring on the page, right before my eyes, like they were jumping, fighting, spinning. He didn't ask if I had my heart set on anyone or why the officers and cadets hadn't asked me to dance at the service club the week before, and I sat there thinking that maybe the only reason Butch talked to me was because I liked to write songs. What happened if he stopped writing music one day? Would he still want to talk to me then?

He said, "Why you think you're stumped?"

"I don't know."

He sat there studying me. He rested his elbow on his knee and his chin in his hand and just looked right into me. Finally he sat back and said, "Girl, we got to get you out of here." He tapped me on the head. "And get you back into here." He tapped me on my heart, just over my left bosom. This was enough to make me go short of breath. I started breathing raggedy and quick, just like I'd run up a mountain. I tried to be quiet about it so he couldn't tell, and the quieter I tried to be, the more out of breath I got. "Now, tell me what you want to write about. Don't think about it. Just say it. First thing that comes to mind."

I said, "Being beyond the keep." I waited for him to ask me to explain what that meant, but instead he picked up his guitar.

He said, "Okay. Good. That's where we start." He thumped the guitar a little and twirled the broken bottle neck. He said, "Indian army soldiers get themselves ready for battle the same way their ancestors got ready. There's a belief in keeping balance in yourself and with everything around you. They make an offering to the universe to ask for whatever they're asking for—keep me safe, keep me healthy, make me rich, make me happy. They all carry something to protect themselves, a talisman." When I looked at him funny, he said, "Like a lucky charm." He switched his cigarette to his left hand and held the broken bottle top with his right.

I said, "That's yours."

He said, "Since I was ten."

"Where'd you get it?"

"My daddy." The way he said it made me know there was a story but that I wasn't going to hear it right now. He rubbed his thumb back and forth over the sharp edges. I held my breath a little, waiting to see him draw blood. He said, "What's your lucky charm, Velva Jean?"

I thought about this. All my treasures were locked away in my hatbox. The framed Opry picture, Mama's old hair combs, the clover jewelry we'd made when I was little, Mama's wedding ring, the emerald Daddy gave me before he went away for good. I thought about the two little carvings I had from the Wood Carver—one of a girl with her mouth open in song, the other of a girl with her arms open in flight. I thought about the compass Ty had given me the last time I ever saw him. One of these was probably my talisman, but I wasn't sure which one.

He said, "Take your time. You got to choose wisely. More than likely, it'll probably choose you."

As he said it, I thought that talismans might be like brace roots and that you could probably have more than one.

For the next three days, in my off-duty time, I met Butch at the code talkers' building, where we sat by the fire and worked. I brought my Mexican guitar and also my songs, the ones I'd written in Nashville and after. There wasn't much I was proud of, but we talked about them and ideas I had for songs, and mostly he played me things he was writing.

When we weren't doing that, he taught me some French, Geechee, Patois, and Cajun, and even some Navajo and Comanche and Choctaw, so that I could learn more words than just the ones I knew already. Once we sang the song we'd written up on Devil's Courthouse, the one I'd helped him with, about a girl that was as lovely and loving as she was loved. Something went through me as I sang with him. He bent his head over the guitar while he played, and I watched his face. I thought how he was the kind of handsome that sneaked up on you, that you didn't see right away, but how it was also the kind that grew and grew until you couldn't stop looking at him.

Butch glanced up at me with the last line of the song, and we sang it together, eyes locked. I tried to make myself look away but I couldn't. Looking at him direct like that was, I thought, like staring at the sun—I felt blinded.

═══

March 28, 1944

Butch,

Here's a song I wrote just now. It's isn't much, but it's the first one I've finished in a long while. I wrote the music for guitar and banjo. My roommate, Sally Hallatassee, is learning the banjo part right now and sometimes we play it together, her on the banjo and me on my Mexican guitar.

Thank you for getting me out of my head and back into my heart.

Velva Jean

Music in the Stars

*I'm mountain bred
and Opry bound
and free as a lark in spring—*

*I'm gettin' me some wings
to spread in the sky
and some brand-new songs to sing—*

*There's music in the stars,
there's songs in the clouds,
like some heavenly jubilee.*

*Can you hear it, can you feel it,
can you bear it, can you share it?
Can you fly away with me?*

THIRTY-NINE

At quarter past two on Friday, March 30, General Hap Arnold arrived at Camp Davis with Jackie Cochran and a group of men who stepped onto the airfield looking very important. One hour later, Helen and I were in the B-29 hangar with Harry Lawson, Bob Keene, and Major Blackburn when General Arnold and Miss Cochran came bustling in, followed by the five men. Everyone shook hands all around while Miss Cochran made the introductions: World War I fighter pilot Eddie Rickenbacker; two army air force officers from Washington, D.C.; radio news reporter H. V. Kaltenborn; Lieutenant Bruce Arnold; and his daddy, General Hap Arnold, commander of the Army Air Forces.

Eddie Rickenbacker was tall with white hair and the blackest eyebrows you ever saw. He carried a cane, but he didn't seem to need it. He said, "I want to see inside this thing. Let's see how different it is from the planes I flew in the first war."

Harry Lawson said, "By all means."

The men crowded into the fuselage. Harry pointed out the pilot's control stand, the copilot's control stand, the aisle stand between them, the engineer's switch panel and instrument board, the radio operator's table, and the hydraulic-panel access door.

General Arnold was studying the engineer's switch panel. He was wearing a uniform with lots of medals. He said to Harry Lawson, "What do you do with this tugboat in case of an emergency takeoff?"

Eddie Rickenbacker said, "Tugboat is right. This is a different ship from the ones we took up in '18."

Before Harry Lawson could say anything, Bob Keene started talking about wing flaps and cowl flaps and crew inspection and then he explained how to make an emergency landing—only most everything he said was wrong.

Miss Cochran, General Arnold, the officers, the radio reporter, and Eddie Rickenbacker all stared at Bob Keene. Harry Lawson stood watching him like he was a skunk that had just wandered into his house.

General Arnold barked out, "Dammit, son. I'm not asking about the landing. I want to know about emergency takeoff. How in God's name do we expect these little girls to get this monster off the ground if conditions aren't favorable?"

Eddie Rickenbacker said, "The thing must weigh a hundred thousand pounds."

Bob Keene said, "Seventy thousand pounds, empty." But I don't think anyone heard him because by this point they were grumbling.

I cleared my throat and said, "I'm sorry." The men turned to look at me. I smiled my sweetest smile at Bob Keene and said, "The officers are always wanting us to prove how much we know. I think Lieutenant Keene might rather one of us explain it."

Bob Keene was giving me a look so cold I nearly shivered. I said, "If an emergency takeoff is necessary before the engines are warmed up, you need to dilute the oil to lower its viscosity to a point where there's no danger of the hose connections being blown loose. Then you check all flight controls, check that the fuel boost pumps are on, and the mixture controls are set to Auto-Rich. You set the turbocharger to 8 and the propellers at 2,600 miles per hour."

The men were staring at me like I'd started speaking in tongues. Miss Cochran beamed. Just days ago, Senators Joseph Hill of Alabama and Harold Burton of Ohio made a proposal to the United States Senate that female pilots be officially recognized as part of the Army Air Forces. If Senate Resolution 1810 went through, it would mean her dream of turning the WASP from a civilian group into a military group would finally come true.

General Arnold said, "What if the engine fails during takeoff?"

I put my hand in my pocket and felt Ty's compass. Every day I picked a different talisman to carry around with me. I said, "Then you need to feather the propeller right away and shut off the fuel valve and mixture control. You retract the landing gear as soon as possible and use the trim tabs to make up for unbalanced conditions."

General Arnold crossed his arms and said, "What if the engine fails during flight?" His mouth was serious but his eyes were smiling.

I thought: Go ahead and challenge me, old man. I will answer any question you have. I said, "In that case, you turn the AFCE master switch off, close the throttle and cowl flaps, and shut the booster pump controls for the engine that failed. You need to feather the propeller and trim ship to correct any unbalance, and then you can turn the AFCE switch back on."

General Arnold opened and closed his mouth without saying anything.

I said, "You just have to make sure you don't attempt to feather more than one propeller at a time because it uses too much current."

General Arnold leaned over and shook Jackie Cochran's hand. The radio reporter said, "What's your name, soldier?"

"Velva Jean Hart, sir."

The reporter said, "You girls are WAVES?"

"WASP," Helen said.

"WASP. Right." The reporter made a note. He said, "Impressive program, General, Mrs. Cochran. Good work. Too bad your male pilots aren't as knowledgeable. But then maybe that's why you need women to fly this plane."

Eddie Rickenbacker said, "We're only as strong as our weakest link," and smacked the floor with his cane. "Maybe somebody needs a demotion."

General Arnold frowned at Bob Keene, and then turned to the reporter. "This just goes to prove what Mrs. Cochran and I believe about the WASP: our best pilots are pilots first, without regard to gender. The aircraft doesn't know whether there's a man or a woman at the helm. Women can fly our big planes with the same skill and savvy

as men, if they have the talent, the training, and the will—and Miss
Hart is one of our best pilots."

I felt my face go red. Everyone was looking right at me, and Jackie
Cochran was smiling at me so wide and bright that it was just like the
sun. I thought: It's hard to believe there was ever a time in my life
when I went to the sewing circle and canned jars of preserves and
made care baskets for the heathens with Berletta Snow and Sister
Gladdy Harriday and cleaned Harley Bright's house while I waited for
him to come home from church and notice me.

I didn't always let myself stop to think how far I'd traveled, but
when I did stop to think about it I figured I was about as far away from
Devil's Kitchen as a person could get.

An hour later I left the hangar. Helen stopped to talk to Harry
Lawson, and I walked out into the sunlight and straight into Bob
Keene.

I said, "Lieutenant."

He said, "Fifinella."

I looked around, but we were alone. I kind of nodded at him and
then started walking toward the bay, hoping he wouldn't follow me.

He caught up quickly, falling into step beside me. He said, "You
know, there's a mine in the mountains west of the Salton Sea in California that contains the only available source of this calcite crystal
needed to make the Norden bombsight." His hands were shoved into
his pockets just like he was out for a stroll in the sunshine. I thought
again that he looked like Oliver Hardy or Fatty Arbuckle, but not as
friendly because the smile he wore was a baiting kind of smile, the
kind that always set me on edge.

I could see Janie up ahead with some of the other girls, heading to
the mess hall. I waved but she didn't notice me.

Bob Keene said, "It's called Iceland spar because the first place they
ever found it was in the cavities of solidified lava, which is what Iceland is made of. It's one of the rarest materials on earth."

I wasn't sure what he wanted me to say, so I said, "How interesting." I shivered. There was something about the ocean damp and the

wind always blowing in from the water that chilled me deep in my bones, even with the sun beating down.

He said, "You think you're like that, don't you? Like Iceland spar."

A voice behind us said, "Lieutenant Keene."

General Arnold was heading for us, his face as red as a tomato. He was followed by Eddie Rickenbacker, the army air force officers from Washington, D.C., and his son.

Bob Keene's eyes went dark and he wasn't smiling. He leaned in close to me and said, "Don't ever try to show me up again." And then he said, "Coming, sir," and walked away.

That night I had a dream I was up flying in the AT-6, just like the ones I used to fly at Avenger Field. It was a black, moonless midnight, and I was out over the ocean, so far over it that I couldn't see land anywhere. I thought I was alone in the cockpit, alone in the sky, and then I looked at the seat next to me, and Harley was there. I said, "Harley? Where did you come from?" But he didn't say anything. I said, "Harley?" He just sat there, staring out the window, out into the dark nothingness of the night and the water. "Harley? Harley? Harley?"

Suddenly I knew what I had to do. I undid my safety belt and checked my parachute and kicked open the cockpit door and jumped. I fell fast and hard and started counting, "One . . . two . . . three . . ." I pulled my rip cord and for one minute I didn't think my parachute would open. I was free-falling toward the water. Above me the plane disappeared. I pulled my cord again and this time the chute opened. I started floating then, just like a cloud, just like a leaf spinning its way down from a tree in fall. I was a foot above the ocean when I closed my eyes and sucked in my breath, ready to go under. I hit the water and went down, down, down.

I woke up kicking off the sheets like they were a parachute. For some reason, I couldn't breathe. I started coughing. From her bed, Sally said, "Hartsie? What is that?" She was coughing too. I pulled myself out of bed, lungs heavy, eyes heavy, and flipped on the light.

There was smoke sneaking under our door, curling up into the room and spreading out around us. At first I thought it was fire, but then my eyes started tearing and my stomach started lurching and I knew by the smell that it was tear gas. I said, "Grab your gas mask."

I threw open my footlocker and pulled mine out. Sally opened the windows and I opened the door, and there was a brown metal canister right outside, gas pouring out of it. Sally threw me my gloves, and I picked up the can and ran outside with it. I was sick and dizzy, and tears were streaming down my cheeks. I ran with it right over to the edge of the runway, to the swamp, and threw it into the muck. I watched it sink, my eyes stinging, my stomach cramping into a ball.

I thanked Jesus that it wasn't mustard gas or nerve gas. Mustard gas blistered the skin and sometimes caused pneumonia, and nerve gas attacked the body's nervous system. There were different types of nerve gas but the worst was soman. After you inhaled it, you only had a couple of seconds before you went into convulsions. According to our army manual, a victim of soman would die within two minutes.

~

Colonel Wells was in New York for the week, which meant that Sally and I met with Major Blackburn in his office the next morning to report the tear gas incident. My eyes were still watering so much that I looked like I was crying. Sally kept dabbing at her nose and eyes with a handkerchief. The major sat behind his desk, frowning, looking more like a bad-tempered bear than an officer in the Army Air Forces. He listened to every word we had to say and then he asked us to fill out a report.

He said, "You did the right thing to come to me. I'll pass your report through the proper channels. And I'll post a guard outside your barracks to see it doesn't happen again." He stood up then and marched to the door.

I felt my heart sink like a stone to the very bottom of my chest. Major Blackburn laid his hand on the doorknob and frowned at us. He pushed open the door and waited till we walked out before closing it.

~

After lunch Sally and I fell into marching formation with the other pilots and officers outside. It was her first day back on the flight line after being grounded by Jackie Cochran. Bob Keene was on one side of me and Zeke Bodine was on the other. We marched from the mess hall to the runway. The only sound was Captain Grossman counting us off, until Bob Keene said, "How'd you sleep last night, Fifi?"

I turned my head to look at him, just enough so Captain Grossman yelled at me. Bob Keene stared straight ahead like he'd never said anything at all.

That night a young cadet was stationed outside our door, gun at his hip. He was big and broad and looked as serious as Mrs. Garland Welch trying to save her soul at camp meeting. He nodded to us as we walked up, and after we showed him our IDs he let us into our room, where we climbed into our beds without brushing our teeth. Sally didn't even take off her shoes. In minutes, she was asleep. I lay there listening to her snore and thought that maybe one day I'd write a song about two girls, one from North Carolina and the other from Indiana, who wanted to fly even though everyone tried to stop them.

FORTY

Two nights later Sally and Janie were scheduled for a routine check on the A-24. I remembered when I liked flying the A-24, but now it seemed dull and ordinary after the B-29, although I didn't say this to Sally because she was excited to be flying again. Besides, ever since she'd found out about Helen and me and the B-29 mission, she said she was "jealous as a hen," even though I knew she was proud of me.

Janie was scheduled to go up with Gus Mitchell just as the sun was setting, but she hadn't eaten since breakfast and she was so hungry we could hear her stomach growling. Sally said, "I'll go, Janie. You get yourself a good meal." When Sally cleared it with Gus, he said he didn't care who went first as long as they got back in time for him to buy her a drink at the service club.

Inside the mess hall, I sat with Janie and Helen and the other girls. I could see Vince Gillies and Bob Keene across the room. First Vince and then Bob turned in my direction, but they looked right through me, like I wasn't even there. Then Bob said something to Vince, and they laughed loud and long.

I stared at my plate—fried chicken and rice. There was too much gravy on everything, and I tried to dig the rice out from underneath. I made myself think about the B-29: Hydraulic pressure gauge. Lamp controls. Throttle levers. Elevator tabs. Control wheel. Turn indicator. Flight indicator. Tachometer. Suction gauge. Radio compass. Blind landing indicator.

Suddenly the emergency siren blasted, cutting the night in two. I dropped my fork and pressed my hands over my ears. I hated the way the siren went through you. My first thought was that the German U-boats had torpedoed another one of our ships. The next thought I had was: Sally.

Everyone ran outside, tripping over each other, pushing each other, falling into each other. The smoke filled my lungs. Four hundred yards or so from the end of the runway I could see the flames. All of us, men and women, officers and enlisted, ran for the plane. It was surrounded by a deep ditch on one side and the swamp on the other.

Gus Mitchell lay on the ground, jacket and shirt burned off. His skin was raw and pink, and I thought of Harley after the train wreck. Gus wasn't moving. The emergency crew rushed in to pick him up and take him to the hospital. I ran after them. "Gus! Did Sally get out? Where's Sally?"

Gus didn't blink or move. I couldn't tell if he was alive or dead. I started running for the plane. The flames were climbing into the trees, spreading up and out and over so that it looked like everything was on fire—the swamp, the ditch, the ground, the sky. I was choking on the ash and the smoke, which was black and thick and covering everything. My eyes were watering just like I was running through tear gas. I hollered, "Sally!"

I could hear something. I told myself: It's the siren. Just the siren. The sound was high and loud and horrible. I stopped running and looked at the faces of everyone else standing there—Janie, Helen, Bob Keene, Major Blackburn, Harry Lawson, Vince Gillies, Colonel Wells, the cadets, and, off to themselves, the Indians. They were listening too. But it wasn't the siren. The siren was quiet. There was the rush of water from the fire trucks and the shouts of men as they tried to fight the fire and the rumblings of everyone standing there watching. And there was the sound of screaming coming from the plane. I ran toward the wreck again and suddenly Butch was there, grabbing me out of the way. He said, "They're trying to get to her, but the fire's too strong. Stay back." He had to shout to be heard over the flames.

"Sally!" I was crying now and coughing because the smoke was everywhere, filling every space inside me. "Sally!" My throat felt raw from the smoke and the shouting, but I kept at it until I felt a hand on my shoulder. I turned and there was Jackie Cochran, tears running down her face. She said, "Hush, child." I couldn't tell if she was talking to me or to Sally.

Five minutes later the screaming stopped. The silence that followed was worse than the screams. The firemen could only get within three or four feet of the plane. The flames fought them off, keeping them away. Thirty minutes later the firemen weren't any closer. An hour later the flames were still climbing into the sky.

I knew then that Sally was gone, really and truly, and even if the fire died down and the firemen could reach the plane, it would be too late.

Gus Mitchell woke up in the ambulance as they were driving him to the base hospital. He said that the takeoff and flight were normal until just before landing. Toward the end of the check flight, the control tower called Sally and told her to shoot a landing on runway two. She entered the pattern at eleven hundred feet and let the wheels down. Gus said he could feel the throttle moving back and forth and realized the engine was dead. At seven hundred feet and just over the runway, he took over flying from the backseat and hollered at Sally to jump. He finished the ninety-degree turn, flew a shortened downwind and base leg, and was trying to round out a turn into the final approach when the landing gear of the A-24 hit the tops of the tall sea pines that surrounded the field. The plane nosed down, hit the ground, and split in two. Gus felt the airplane shudder and then he blacked out.

Janie and me sat on the steps of the barracks, right by Sally's garden, and watched the fire burn itself out. Janie had smuggled two bottles of beer from somewhere—I didn't ask where—and we drank them while the ash fell on us like rain. I didn't want to go back to my room that night or ever. I couldn't stand the thought of being in there by myself. Instead of two dead girls haunting that room, there would be three.

Janie said, "It should have been me."

I said, "You didn't know, Janie. No one could know."

She looked at me and said, "How am I supposed to forgive myself?"

I put my arm around her. We sat there watching the flames, and then I started singing "I'll Fly Away," and Janie joined me. Halfway through, we started crying so hard that we couldn't sing anymore. We didn't stop crying until the fire finally went out.

Back in my bay, I sat on my cot and looked at Sally's bed across from mine. Her things were everywhere—her shoes, her dresses, her books, her packs of gum, her banjo. I picked up the banjo and held it in my hands without playing it. I felt the cold of the metal against my skin and thought, I wonder where Ty's bugle is. Did he have it with him when he crashed? Did it go back to his parents? Did they throw it away or is someone somewhere playing it?

I looked down at the banjo and started playing the song I'd written, the one Sally and I were learning together. I sang the words and played it through and then I lay the banjo on her bed, peghead and tuning keys resting on the pillow, just like it was a person.

March 18, 1944

Dear Mother,

I thought I'd sit down on my twenty-fourth birthday and write you a letter to thank you for each and every thing you and Dad have done for me. If it wasn't for the two of you, I wouldn't be a pilot or a WASP—I'd still be typing letters at old Doc Cady's office.

Thanks for helping me get here and for understanding why I had to break it off with Joe. Maybe I'll be a wife and mother one day. That's what everyone expects and what I guess I expect too. I'll probably be good at it. But so far I never met a boy I liked so much as flying.

You asked what I love most about it and here it is: I love watching the earth change below me from brown to green, from flat to hilly, depending on where and how far I go. Being high up is a good place to see what the world is made of.

I love my friends, maybe best of all, and I love red wine and dancing at the service club with handsome men who don't expect me to settle down and knit them socks anytime soon.

I love the deep bone-weariness after six hours of flying and the soreness in my hands that means I've wrangled a plane that was built for a man and not a "little girl."

I love my flight jacket and my helmet and I even love my coveralls because wearing them means I'm getting ready to do what I love most in this world.

Most of all, I love being happy. Know that if anything ever happens, I don't want you and Daddy to be sad for too long because I went out flying.

All my love,

Sally

FORTY-ONE

*A*s WASP, we were still civilians and not military, which meant Sally's funeral wasn't paid for. The other girls and me pooled our money and paid for her casket to be sent back to Indiana, where it would be buried in the little church cemetery, next to Sally's grandparents and a baby brother that died in 1928.

Janie and Helen and I flew to Indiana with Miss Cochran in her Beechcraft. Gus Mitchell wanted to go, but he was still in the hospital. Sally's mama was smaller than Sally, but her daddy was a great big man, almost as big as the Wood Carver. Sally's brothers were all too young to go to war—the oldest was just fourteen—and all her sisters were there: me, Janie, Helen, Paula, Mudge, and Loma.

At the sight of my old friends, the tears started spilling out. I hated crying. I thought of all the times in my life I'd had to cry over people I'd lost and I was sick of it. I decided that after I got through this, I wasn't ever crying again, no matter what.

Paula looked tan and fit. She'd been transferred from her base in Texas to Dodge City, Kansas, to train on the B-26. Mudge was painted up and fancy, wearing a smart suit she said was made by one of the MGM studio designers. She brought her new boyfriend with her— Van Johnson, the movie star, who was tall and blond and looked just like a regular man, only nicer. He wore a dark suit and stood by Mudge's elbow like he was waiting to see if she needed anything.

Loma hugged each of us so hard I thought she'd squeeze the life out of us. She was crying and crying as she said, "I've missed you fools more than you know."

I'd never seen so many flowers. Mudge said, "There are too many here for the living." Somehow I knew what she meant, and the thought made my heart ache. There were letters and telegrams that talked about Sally in the past tense, and I couldn't make sense of this because to me Sally was still there. I kept waiting for her to show up, barreling in the door, cracking her gum, playing her banjo, chattering like a squirrel.

At the funeral I looked at Jackie Cochran and thought, This is all your fault. I wondered what she was going to do about Sally's death, if she was going to look into it or just pretend it was an accident like she'd done with Ruth and with the other girls, the ones that died before we got to Camp Davis. I stared at this woman, the greatest female pilot on earth, and I thought, Maybe you're a great pilot, but you're not a very good person. She looked at me, and I held her gaze for one long moment before I looked away.

Sally's casket wasn't draped in the United States flag and there wasn't a twenty-one-gun hero's salute. She was laid in a plain wood casket and put deep in the ground, in her small hometown, where, after a while, no one would remember how brave she was.

After the funeral I found Sally's daddy and gave him her banjo. I told him about how we went to town on Christmas Day and how the music store was open even though it wasn't supposed to be, and how Sally saw that banjo and decided right then and there that she was going to learn it. He held it for a moment, picking at the strings. He said, "Sally always did the things she set her mind to." Then he handed me the banjo and said, "Why don't you keep it to remember her? Sally wrote me about your music. She said you're as good as Martha Tilton or Anita O'Day. That banjo needs to be played, and it'll only sit here collecting dust."

I hugged him and then he turned away, wiping his eyes with the backs of his hands. I walked out to the front porch, where the girls were sitting. I sat next to Mudge, in the porch swing, the banjo on my lap. Janie, Helen, Loma, and Paula sat on the steps and on the railing. Van Johnson stood in the yard, smoking a cigarette and talking to Sally's brothers.

Paula said, "FUBAR." I knew exactly what this meant, from Johnny Clay.

Loma said, "Twenty-five cents please."

We laughed, but it didn't last, winding down fast and fading away till there was nothing left. Mudge and I rocked back and forth slowly, pushing the swing together. She fished something out of her purse, and it was a silver flask, sleek and shiny. She took a drink and passed it to Paula. I watched as Paula drank and then Loma, and I thought I wouldn't mind getting good and drunk for the very first time in my life. When it was my turn, I took a long gulp and nearly coughed it all back up.

Mudge slapped me on the back till I stopped coughing.

"Easy, Hartsie," Paula said.

I held up the flask. "To Sally." I took another drink and passed it to Janie.

"To Sally."

One by one we toasted Sally Hallatassee and emptied that flask of whiskey till you could have held it upside down and not a single drop would have come out.

Sally's mama had been cleaning all morning and buzzing around just like a hummingbird. I'd never seen anyone so busy. Sally's daddy stood watching her and he had that helpless look that I'd seen men wear before—Danny Deal and Coyle, Linc, my own daddy. He said to us, "I don't know what she'll do when this funeral is over. It's the only thing keeping her going right now."

I thought, I don't know what any of us will do. Sally was one of my best friends. That wasn't anything you could replace, just like you couldn't replace Ned Tyler or my mama. I would go back to base and expect Sally to be there, but instead there would be no one. I would fly the B-29 with Helen, if they still wanted me to, and I would go around to all the military bases and show the men how things were done.

I felt the place where Ty used to be, and where Sally used to be. The phantom limbs were multiplying.

~

When we landed at Camp Davis, Janie, Helen, and I climbed out of the plane and stood on the runway, waiting for Jackie Cochran. I held the banjo in my arms like a baby. Finally she came down from the cockpit, pulling off her helmet, running her hands through her hair, squinting in the sun. She said, "Ladies," and started past us.

I said, "We need to know what's being done about Sally."

She stopped and looked at me. She said, "What do you mean?"

Janie said, "About the investigation into what happened."

Miss Cochran said, "I promise you I'm doing everything I can to make sure we get to the bottom of this. We don't know that it's sabotage, but if it is, I plan to find out and something will be done about it." Her face was hard to read—I thought she seemed tired and sad but that she was also on her guard with us.

I said, "Sally wanted to fly more than anything else in this world, just like we all do. She came to Texas to fly for you, to be a WASP. She came here to take part in your program. She did all she could to be a good pilot and make you proud."

She didn't say anything for a good long moment and then she said, "I'll do my very best."

Jackie Cochran left for Washington, D.C., the next day. She didn't say a word to any of us about her investigation into the crash or what she might have found out. She didn't even tell us good-bye.

I watched her plane take off and then I walked over to the Cemetery. I looked for Zeke Bodine and at first I didn't see him. One of the other guards said, "What are you doing here?"

I started to tell him: I'm trying to find out the reason why one of the nicest girls you could ever meet, one of the best friends I ever had, is dead. But then I saw Zeke Bodine and waved at him, and he came over and said, "What's going on?"

I said, "I need to see Sally's plane."

Zeke said, "Sorry, Velva Jean, we can't let you in here."

I said, "Just so you know, Zeke, I plan to get in there one way or the other."

The other guard started to say something, but Zeke said, "I've got this." He waited till the guard walked away, looking over his shoulder, watching us, before he said, "I'm awful sorry about Sally."

"I need to see her plane. I know they've already picked through it." Or maybe they hadn't. Maybe no one was even paying attention. "But I'll feel better if I see it. I need to know what happened." And when I do find out, someone will be sorry. I don't care if I have to become Bonnie Parker again, just like when Johnny Clay and me were on a wayward path and following Harley Bright around Alluvial with his bad Barrow gang. I don't care if I get locked away in Butcher Gap Prison just like Junior Loveday, who killed all those men just because there was a meanness in him that he couldn't help. Maybe his meanness comes from being a Loveday—my mama said they were all of them mean as dirt for as far back as anyone could remember—but my meanness comes from one terrible thing happening after another, and I'll be damned if I'm going to put up with much more of it.

Zeke stared at me, and I stared right back, not blinking, not flinching. I knew I looked mad as a wild boar. Finally he said, "Go on." He glanced around him to see if anyone was watching. "But if you get caught, you're on your own."

I thought: I already am.

I didn't know where to look, but I figured her plane—what was left of it—might be near the front since the accident had only just happened. I made my way through the maze of olive drab and silver and looked for the black of fire damage. Walking through the crushed metal and parts of airplanes made me think about the fact that every day I was going up in these ships that were made out of bolts and steel and glass, and that it didn't matter if the cockpit was armor plated because all these things could be broken, which meant you could be broken too.

Five minutes later, toward the middle and not the front, I found an A-24 cracked in two. The engine and cockpit were thick with black. I pushed through parts from other planes, sending some rolling to the ground. I laid my hands on the cockpit and the metal felt thin and cold. The glass of the windshield and canopy was cracked and foggy. The glass over the backseat was shattered. That must have been how Gus was thrown out. I wondered if Sally had kicked the glass from inside or if the cracks were made by the fire. They said she was still strapped in when they got to her.

I climbed up on the wing and then stepped on top of the cockpit. I wanted to get a good look at the safety latch, to see why it was she couldn't get out of there in time. I ran my hands over the hatch, the place where it should open. I thought about where this plane had been before it came here. Maybe it flew in the Pacific. Maybe over Guadalcanal. Maybe Beachard had flown in it while he was there or it might have flown over Italy. Linc and Coyle Deal might have looked up from the beach somewhere near Naples and seen it. I wished I could find the little black box. What would it tell me?

Rumors were spreading around the base that Sally's plane was brought down by friendly fire. Some of the pilots said they were there when Lieutenant Bruce Arnold, son of General Hap Arnold, snatched a gunner's hand from the trigger after he saw a .50 millimeter round fired at Sally's A-24.

The inside of the cockpit was charred as black as the outside. I could suddenly hear her screams and I tried quick to think of something else—anything else: marching songs, Ty's songs, Butch's songs, Sally's banjo, the cracking sound of her gum.

I crawled through the hole in the side of the plane—the one the firemen made when they were trying to get Sally out—and sat down in the pilot's seat. I reached up for the canopy safety latch, wrenching it back and forth, up and down, but it wouldn't move. I stood on the seat and ran my fingers over the hinges, over the joint of it. The latch was bent like a pretzel, right at the tip. There were marks on the side that shouldn't have been there, like someone had tried to twist the latch out of shape, and I couldn't tell if this was from fire or something else.

Someone wanted this to happen.

I tried to push the thought out of my head, but it kept coming back. The hairs on the back of my neck stood straight up, which meant that it was probably true. But who would do something like that?

"You there." I turned at the voice. Harry Lawson was walking up. He said, "Get down from there. What are you doing? Do you have permission to be in here?" His accent was shorter, more clipped than usual.

I said, "My friend was in that plane. She died in there." I thought maybe if I told the sad truth of it he'd feel sorry for me and let me keep looking. I said, "I need to know what happened."

He said, "You can't be in here. It's regulations." I took a last look at the cockpit—at the safety latch—before climbing down. He reached out a hand to help me make the jump from the wing.

I said, "What about the black box?"

"The black box?"

"Was there a flight recorder on her plane? One that could tell us something?"

I thought about all the people I knew who had little black boxes—my daddy, the Wood Carver, Harley Bright. Butch had a little black box all locked up tight, full of secrets that I would never get to open no matter how much I wanted to see inside it.

He said, "No."

I said, "Are you going to report me for being here?"

He took his time answering and finally he said, "No."

~

On the morning of April 3, I typed a letter to Major Blackburn and a letter to Colonel Wells, asking them to investigate the rumors about Sally's plane. Each of the girls—there were twenty-three of us now— signed it. We delivered copies to their offices, and then I went back to my bay and wrote another letter, this one to Jackie Cochran. In it I thanked her for the experience of being a WASP and told her I needed to resign. As much as I loved being a WASP, I couldn't be part of a program that didn't look after its people. This was not the way I wanted to serve my country. Flying for Jackie Cochran was starting to feel a little like flying without a parachute or a safety belt. I listed every awful thing that had happened since I'd been there—the oil draining out of my engine, Ruth, the tear gas, Sally—even though she already knew it all too well. I wrote: "Flying is dangerous enough without feeling like a target. I might as well join our boys overseas and drop bombs on Germany because I wouldn't be near as scared as I am here."

Janie and three of the other girls wrote letters too, all telling Miss Cochran that they were leaving the program and why.

That afternoon I went up in the sky for the first time since Sally's accident. I was in an A-24, but I was by myself. The air was so rough that it shot me up from nine hundred feet to twelve hundred feet and then back down to eight hundred. I thought: I could die just like Sally. I could be gunned down or I could lose an engine or the engine could catch fire. Each time I go up, there's no guarantee I'll come down in one piece. Every single time I fly from now on, I am on my own.

I was taking chances, but they were small chances compared to the ones taken every day right now all over the world. Beach in the Pacific. Linc in Italy. Johnny Clay who knows where. I could be at home on Fair Mountain and be caught in a storm or slip down the hill. I could fall in the bathtub or be run over by a car going out of control. I could lose my way in the woods and be attacked by a panther cat. I could drown in Three Gum River. I could choke on an apple or trip over a tree root and hit my head or be bit by a mad dog. I figured there were a lot of ways to take chances in this world, that every single day was a chance. It wasn't up to us to say where or when.

My landing was bumpy. As I taxied in I looked over my head at the safety latch. I flipped the latch with just two fingers of one hand. It opened quick and easy.

Five days later I got a telegram from Miss Cochran saying, "Resignation denied." That night, I sat at the desk in my empty room and typed out a will. I wasn't sure how a will was supposed to read, but I thought it was a smart thing to do.

I, Velva Jean Hart, being sound of mind and body, do make this my last will and testament.

I don't have a lawyer and haven't ever made a will before, so I hope that this will be good enough and that all my wishes will be carried out.

I don't have much in this world, but what I do have I want to leave to my family: my mandolin, my Mexican guitar, my hatbox of treasures, my clothes, my record. I leave Sally's banjo to her mama and daddy. Maybe they can learn it someday so that it doesn't go dusty.

I leave all my songs to Butch Dawkins. Of all the people on this earth, he'll know what to do with them.

I don't have much money, but I leave what I have to Sweet Fern to help with the children.

I don't want anyone to wear black for me. I want to be buried beside Mama. I want "The Unclouded Day" played at my funeral. Get Johnny Clay to sing it, if you can find him. And tell him he's worth more than Lucinda Sink. Tell him he's worth the whole world.

Know how much I love all of you, each and every one, and how much I'll miss you. And know that I died doing what I loved most.

Sincerely,
Velva Jean Hart

~

Butch and I sat side by side on the steps of the control tower. It was Sunday and the airfield was quiet. He'd shown up after breakfast, just like a haint, to tell me how sorry he was about Sally. The sight of him—the brown-black hair, the sleepy dark eyes, the unshaved face, the crooked smile, sadder today—made me start to cry even though I'd promised myself I'd never cry again. He said, "I know." And then he pulled me in and gave me a hug—right in front of everyone—and I breathed in the smell of woods and tobacco. He was the closest thing I had to home right now, and I held on to him.

I could hear his heartbeat, could feel him breathing. When we broke apart, he said, "You know what I like about you? You are one down-home girl, Velva Jean." He said it soft and lazy, his voice scratchy as sandpaper. The way he said it sounded sweet and sexy.

I was still breathing him in. I said, "What's that mean?" I wondered if it was a good thing or a bad thing.

He said, "You got the strongest spirit I ever did see. I think I'm gonna write a song about that and dedicate it to you."

I didn't feel strong. I felt small and sad and weak. I felt just like I was inside one of Butch's songs—one of the angry, mean, deep-down-in-the-gutter songs that made me want to run and shout and cry and take his guitar from him and smash it. But I also felt like I was lost in one of the heartbreak songs—the downhearted, bluesy ones that made my hair stand on end and filled me with a deep, way-down sadness I couldn't shake for days.

Now we sat with our knees almost touching, working on a song. His guitar rested against his leg as he played. I was trying to put my mind into the music, but it kept spinning away from the words and the tune. Every time I got back to focusing, there would go my mind, flying away like a butterfly.

Butch strummed the guitar. He was humming. I said, "I don't know anything about you."

He said, "Yes you do." He kept humming. He sang a couple of lines.

I said, "I don't. You know everything about me but you won't tell me anything about yourself." I pictured a black box inside Butch, locked up tight, where his heart was. I wondered if anyone had ever seen inside it.

He plucked at the guitar and then was quiet for a second and then he grinned, but it wasn't a real kind of grin, the kind that lit up his face. It was the kind someone gives you when they don't know what else to do. He said, "You can add me to your list of conquests, girl. Is that what you want?"

My heart was racing. I was suddenly mad. I said, "Don't be like that."

"What? Isn't that enough?"

"Don't be one of them. Some normal boy. Don't do that when it ain't you."

He said, "Why don't we just work on a song? That might be the best thing to do, sho 'nough."

I didn't feel like talking or writing a song. I wanted him to do the talking for once. I said, "I need you to tell me something." I pictured aiming a thermite gun right at his black box.

He said, "What?" He didn't sigh or roll his eyes or sound impatient. He sat there waiting to hear what I had to say.

I said, "Something. Anything. I'm tired of doing all the talking." I thought: I'm tired of talking through music. I was as stirred up as a hornet. I told myself, Calm down. This isn't about him. This is about Sally and Harley and Ty and your daddy. Don't do this to Butch. Remember who you're talking to. He never did anything to you. Be quiet, Velva Jean. Stop it right now. I said, "I need you to tell me something about you or I'm going to get up right now and go back to the barracks."

Butch got quiet and part of me thought, Oh no. Now I've made him mad. But the other part thought, He's got to learn to speak up sooner or later.

We sat there a long time, and then he said, "I grew up in Louisiana. Little place called La Coupe in Lafourche Parish, down on the bayou, down by the Mississippi, but we call it Cut Off. About two thousand people. My mama was Choctaw. My daddy was French Creole. I don't have brothers or sisters, none that I know of, but with my daddy you can't be too sure. I grew up with music—Indian chants. Hymns. My mama was religious. She said God was in nature. I left home when I was thirteen and earned my way as a ranch hand. I went up through Louisiana and over to Texas, one dusty small town after another. Then Oklahoma, then New Mexico, where I lived with the Comanche and then the Navajo, one of them my great-granddaddy. I learned guitar in the Mississippi Delta from a famous old bluesman."

I looked down at his arm where his tattoo was. I said, "What was his name?"

He smiled and there went his whole face, lighting up. He said, "I can't tell you that. I promised him not to. But he was magic. I never heard anything like him."

He started to roll a cigarette, then put the paper back away. He rubbed his hands together and stared out toward the horizon. Little drops of rain started falling, but I kept sitting there, not wanting to break the spell.

He said, "I played the rodeo circuit, riding bulls, roping cattle, sleeping in the back of my truck, and when that broke down, hitch-hiking between border towns. I hitchhiked all the way to Knox-ville . . ." He kind of drifted off here and it seemed like he was remembering something he would rather not remember. I thought about his black box again and wondered if somewhere in Knoxville there was a girl who'd seen inside it. Maybe she was the reason it was shut up so tight.

He closed one eye and then the other and said, "I was there for a while, and then I came down through Virginia, thinking I would go to Nashville, and that's where I heard about that road being built in the mountains. The Scenic. I was out of money by then and needed a job pretty bad, so I went to the CCC and applied." He stopped talking.

I waited for more, but when he didn't say anything, I said, "And that's how you got to North Carolina."

"That's how I got to North Carolina." He seemed restless, like talking so much was making him itchy. I wanted to ask him where he went after North Carolina, after Harley drove him out, but I didn't.

I said, "How old are you?" I didn't know why this seemed impor-tant, why I thought it would tell me anything much about him.

He seemed to be counting. "Twenty-five, I guess."

"What about your talisman? The bottle neck?"

"Let's just say it's a reminder to me of the kind of life I used to lead. And the kind I don't want for myself anymore." He seemed to be done talking.

Then, because I could—because he was there and alive and real—I reached out my hand and laid it on top of his. I let it sit there, light as could be. I looked out at the horizon. I thought, If I never learn another thing about Butch Dawkins, he told me these things for me. Because he knew I needed to hear them. Like a gift.

Sitting there with him made me feel peaceful and good, down in my whole self. It was a different kind of feeling than sitting with Harley or even Ty. I felt like Butch and me were sitting here side by side, each going halfway, on the same level, believing in the same things, loving music, understanding music, understanding and knowing sorrow and loss but also knowing how to pick yourself up out of that loss and keep going. I could look at Butch and know that he saw me—not just my hair and face and figure—but the inside me that not everyone could see.

I thought about the Navajo hero twins, how they fought the monsters and saved the world by speaking their own special language that only they could speak. We had a language like that, Butch and me. I didn't know what it meant or what we were to each other, but sitting there side by side, looking forward, felt good.

April 5, 1944

Dear family,

Thank you for all your notes and thoughts. Camp Davis isn't the same without Sally. We've been together since Sweetwater, and I don't know what it's like to be a WASP without her.

You asked how it feels to get back in the air after something like that happens. I think you just have to keep going. It's really only when I stop and only when I'm on the ground that I think of all the things that could go wrong. When I'm in the air, I only think of flying.

I wanted you to know that I'm going to be flying over you soon. Look for me on April 11. I can't tell you what I'll be flying, but it's big and loud and you can't miss it. Tell Dan Presley to get out his aircraft spotter's manual so he can give you all the details after. General Hap Arnold himself asked me to fly this plane for the Army Air Forces. I'm going to all the bases in the country to show the men pilots it's safe to fly.

I love you so much.

Watch for me.

Velva Jean

———————

April 9, 1944

Velva Jean,

I finally finished the song. Don't know why this one was giving me so much trouble, but I'm feeling right about it now. Thanks for being part of it.

Butch

Somethin' Out of Nothin'

You made somethin' out of nothin'—
made me open my eyes and see.
You made always out of never—
you made a man out of me.

You took a half-count, no-good man
with nothing left to give—
and with your smile and with your touch
you made him want to live.

Your smilin' eyes saw somethin'
no one else could see.
Makin' somethin' out of nothin'—
you made a man out of me.

Your listenin' ears heard somethin'
yearnin' to be free.
Makin' somethin' out of nothin'—
you made a man out of me.

You made somethin' out of nothin'—
made me open my eyes and see.
You made always out of never—
you made a man out of me.

FORTY-TWO

On April 11, the day I was scheduled to fly the B-29, three things happened that nearly kept me grounded. The first was that Helmut Stein was arrested at the Wilmington shipyard, where he was working as a painter. Mr. Stein was a German spy who had worked at the shipyard for two years, gathering information about ships—materials, equipment—sailing for England. He had also gotten his hands on a classified booklet put out by the FBI, which contained information about national defense materials, and he had stolen detailed charts of the United States coastline. He was linked to Rolf Stigler, the man arrested in New York City, where he'd been working as a cook on the SS *Argentine*, and Fritz Kramer, who was running the restaurant Little Dominic's. The three of them were part of a spy ring, but there was no way of knowing yet how many more were involved.

Wilmington was just thirty or forty miles from Camp Davis, and Major Blackburn and Jackie Cochran told me that they didn't want me flying the B-29 until we were sure Camp Davis was secure. They came to me two hours later and said I was cleared to go.

The second thing that happened was that Harry Lawson uncovered misfiled papers stating that traces of sugar were found in the gas tank of Sally's A-24. He found Janie and me on the flight line and said there was something we needed to know. Harry Lawson hadn't paid us much mind since we'd been at Camp Davis, so we couldn't believe he was talking to us now. He told us about the sugar in the tank. As he said, "Enough to stop an engine in no time at all."

I couldn't understand what he was saying, why he was telling us. "Do you think the papers were misfiled on purpose?" I asked him.

"Yes," he said.

"Who could have done that?"

"Anyone with access. Anyone wanting to cover this up."

Finally I said, "Why are you telling us this?"

He didn't say, "I'm so sorry about your friend." He said, "Because a time long ago I knew a girl who flew."

I decided to go back to my bay and write another letter of resignation to Jackie Cochran. But on my way to the barracks I saw, under my window, Sally's garden. All of us girls had been taking turns watering it, and now every flower was blooming and it was only April 11. It was just a little patch of sunshine in the swampy dirt that surrounded the building. I thought about Sally and how proud she was of me for flying the B-29, how much she wished she'd been chosen to fly it herself. And I turned around and walked back toward the runway.

The third thing that happened was that Butch Dawkins showed up to tell me he'd got his orders and that he was being shipped out to Fort Benning, Georgia. He was officially a code talker now. We stood on the flight line, me in my coveralls and turban, Butch in his uniform, and said good-bye. There were only a few other WASP around, but not a single army air force man, and I was grateful.

I thought: I'm not ready to say good-bye to you.

Everything was happening too fast and too much at once—Sally, the accident that might not be an accident after all, Butch leaving, flying the B-29.

The sun was beating through the clouds. The morning had been rainy and wet, but the sky was turning blue.

I thought: Don't go. Not yet. We've got too many songs to write.

He said, "I want you to remember something." And then I thought: This is it—the moment he tells me how he feels about me. Maybe he's in love with me. Maybe he's loved me ever since the last time I saw him, ever since he left Alluvial. Maybe he's getting ready to open that little black box.

He said, "Words have power. Words and language have blessing and protection. The Navajo pray by asking the sun and the earth to spare them from any bad thing."

What was he saying to me? He didn't say, "I'll miss you. I can't wait to see you again. I hope I don't get my stupid self killed so that I can come back to you."

He said, "My granddaddy was one of the original eight code talkers in World War I. They placed corn pollen on their tongues as a blessing so they could speak more clear."

"Corn pollen?" What was he trying to tell me?

"You don't know how many times I wish for corn pollen, girl. Like right now."

The sun suddenly broke its way through the clouds, blinding me. For a moment I couldn't see him.

He said, "I finished a new song."

I thought how I must look, standing here in the bright, white sunlight, every tired line on my face showing, every freckle. My eyes were puffy from crying over Sally—it hit me at strange times, when I least expected it. For some reason her death was bringing up Ty's all over again. My heart ached so much that I knew you could see it in my face. I thought about how heavy my suitcase was right now.

He leaned in and touched my cheek. I held my breath. I thought that one touch was more than anything I'd ever felt before. Our faces were inches apart. I could smell the tobacco on his breath. I tried not to stare at his mouth. He kissed me then, on the forehead, and I wanted to laugh out loud with relief and shame and disappointment and heartache. I was such a fool over Butch Dawkins. Right then I thought: I will run away with you. Just ask me.

Then he pulled away and the moment was over. It was gone. It had only been sunlight and clouds and a silly hope, melting like a black box under a thermite gun in the harsh light of day.

"Good-bye, Velva Jean," he said.

I was suddenly back in Alluvial, watching Butch get on that train that would take him out of the valley, rounded up with every other outlander who Harley said didn't belong.

Don't go, I thought.

"Good-bye," I said.

One hour later the B-29 rolled out under the sun. Officers, cadets, WASP, reporters, Jackie Cochran, and even General Hap Arnold were scattered across the runway, huddled in groups, hands over their eyes to see past the glare. It hit me that everyone was fighting this war. Each of us standing there was a part of it.

Then, for the very first time, another thought hit me, and this one was horrible: This plane I was getting ready to fly was a bomber. In addition to the bombs it carried, there were ten machine guns and one cannon on board. I didn't want to picture what those bombs or guns or cannon might do someday to someone I didn't know, in a country I'd never seen.

I climbed into the bomb bay and watched as a fire truck pulled up on the landing strip. I was traveling with two engineers and two flight technicians—all men, and not a one of them happy about being there. I wasn't sure if this was because they were afraid of the bomber or afraid of me, the girl pilot. Helen and I would fly around the country together in the B-29, but today my copilot was Captain Leonard Grossman. He was there in case anything went wrong.

Inside the cockpit, I strapped myself in, wearing my parachute, my life jacket, my electrically heated flying clothing, my oxygen mask, a knife, and a quart of water. A steel helmet, flak vest, and oxygen bottle were right beside my chair. Just before I started the engine, the door to the plane opened and Captain Theo Dailey appeared in the cockpit. He said, "There's been a switch, Grossman. You're out. Keene's in."

"What the hell?" Captain Grossman was already strapped in and ready.

"Sorry, Grossman. Orders."

"Who from? Blackburn? Wells? Don't tell me Jackie Cochran."

"Sorry. I'm just the messenger." Captain Dailey was already climbing out.

Captain Grossman muttered to himself as he unstrapped his safety belt and unhitched his oxygen tank. He pulled off his helmet and said, "Goddammit." He left without one word to me.

Jackie Cochran's voice scratched over the radio from where she sat up in the control tower. Her voice came through in a blur of static. She said, "Remember we need you, and not Lieutenant Keene, to fly this ship to prove the point that a woman can do this. He's just there in case of emergency because he's trained on this plane longer than you have."

"Yes, ma'am."

Bob Keene sat next to me. He hadn't said a single thing since he strapped himself in. Just got up into the plane and didn't even look at me. I thought he was pale, like maybe he'd caught the flu. His face looked clammy and his hands shook on the controls. I thought: We'll see who's Iceland spar. He may have been trained on this plane but when it comes down to it, he's just another man that's too afraid to fly the B-29.

After all the hatches were closed, I fastened my seat belt and adjusted my seat and I put on my throat microphone and earphones. I told the engineer to start the putt-putt, and when he didn't do it, Bob Keene gave him the order again. This time the engineer listened, and so I turned on the emergency ignition switch. I tested the lights and the alarm bell. I depressed the brake pedals and set the brakes. I tested the throttles while Bob Keene tested the flaps.

The B-29 had to be handled carefully. To start the engines you had to see that the automatic pilot master switch was off. Then you checked over the four surface control adjustment knobs making sure all their pointers were up. You set the manifold pressure selector to the zero position and pressed all four propeller switches to increase their rpm, holding them till the lights on the copilot's panel flashed.

I told the engineer to start number one engine, and then Bob Keene had to repeat the order because the engineer still wasn't listening to me. I pushed the throttle to 1,200 rpm and signaled for number two. I did this over and over till all four engines were running.

I signaled the ground crew, released the brakes, and after I was cleared for takeoff I turned the plane around and pointed it down the runway. Bob Keene lowered the wing flaps. I pushed hard on the brakes and opened the throttle slowly. Then I let up on the brakes and accelerated down the runway till we were at ninety-five miles per hour.

You sometimes needed to juggle the throttle, the pedals, and the superchargers before you got it just right, but that was the only way to get a B-29 into the air. As Jackie Cochran told us again and again, "It's a big, heavy, powerful airplane. Handle it kindly, handle it precisely."

This plane was called *Flyin' Jenny*, after my favorite comic-book pilot, Jenny Dare. Walt Disney's Fifinella—the official WASP mascot—was painted on the side. The bomber was heavy taking off, and I thought for one minute that we wouldn't make it. The engines roared like a tornado, and I wondered if I'd be able to hear again for a week.

I thought: I must be crazy to take this big contraption up into the sky. It's like flying a battleship.

I couldn't breathe and almost reached for my oxygen mask. Above ten thousand feet, an oxygen mask had to be worn by one man—or woman—in each compartment. But I knew the reason I couldn't breathe wasn't because of the pressure. It was because going up, up, up in this bomber was the most thrilling thing I'd ever done—even more thrilling than singing for people or learning to drive. I thought: This plane will make its way to Germany or Italy or France or the Pacific. This could be the very plane that wins the war. I wish I could be the one that flies it then.

As I flew up higher and higher, a song started somewhere in my head. It was a song I'd never heard before and was writing right then in that moment. It went something like:

Shadows fall but I'm above them.
I'm flying free,
changed my ground legs for my sky legs,
and now I'm flying free . . .

Over my headset, Miss Cochran said, "How are you doing, pilot?" The radio crackled.

I said, "Great, ma'am."
She said, "Jackie."
I said, "Jackie!"
She said, "We're all the same up there."

We're all the same up there, she said.
I'm flying free.

I flew up above the mountains, which were enormous and dark and smoking. My route was to fly to the Tennessee border before turning back. This meant that I would fly directly over Fair Mountain and Alluvial and the rest.

I hoped my family was watching. I wanted them to look and say, "There goes Velva Jean, our own Velva Jean. Look at her way up there." I forgot all about Bob Keene sitting in the copilot's seat, drops of sweat running down his face. Instead I thought about Harley. I hadn't heard a word from him since I told him about our divorce. He had stopped writing me long ago. I hoped he might be watching from Devil's Kitchen or the Little White Church, and I hoped Pernilla Swan was watching too. I could hear every last thing he'd say about women knowing their place and if the good Lord had meant for women to fly he would have given them some sense. I hoped wherever he was he'd forgiven me.

My yellow truck was something, and the Scenic—built on top of the mountains—was something, but the sky was a different kind of highway. We were flying high enough that we could soar smooth over the mountains but low enough so I could at least get a good look at them. The mountains were climbing higher and growing darker. They were black and brown and green. This was the land of Tsul 'Kalu, the giant; and the fairy people and Spearfinger, the witch of the woods; and the devil himself, whose courthouse and tramping ground were up near Devil's Kitchen.

I could see the smoke and then the mountains that I knew were mine. They looked so small from up in the sky. I saw a dark ribbon winding its way from the top of one mountain to another—the Scenic. I wanted to go lower, lower, lower till I could land on the peak of Fair Mountain and run down the hill and see Daddy Hoyt and Granny and even Sweet Fern in Alluvial. I thought of all the people I loved, right there below me, and I almost started to cry.

In my headset, I heard Jackie Cochran say, "Everything all right up there?"

I said, "Everything's fine. It's just so good to be home."

I circled over Cherokee, right at the Tennessee border, and then headed east again, back toward the coast. I was making one more pass over my mountains when one of the engines caught fire. Down below I could see the peaks—Blood and Bone and Witch and Devil's Courthouse and Fair Mountain, which belonged to me and my family. I was losing altitude fast. I shoved the throttle all the way forward to blast out the flames. I held the stick all the way back and slammed on the toe brakes. The fire grew brighter, bigger, spreading toward the cockpit where I sat, and then the flames reached out across the wings, where the gas tanks were. I could hear the engineers in my intercom, but I couldn't understand what they were saying.

Next to me, Bob Keene had gone white as a haint. He was gripping the gears and talking fast and furious. I wondered if he was praying.

I thought of aiming for the Scenic, of using it as a runway, but the road curved and twisted too much. I would never be able to land there without going over the side. The mountains were too high, too wild, too rough. I tried to think of a place I could bring the plane down. Alluvial was too small, too protected. I didn't want to risk the lives of the people who lived there—Sweet Fern, Mr. Deal, Elderly Jones, Lucinda Sink.

I wouldn't let myself think about Carole Lombard crashing into a Nevada mountain or Ty crashing into the mountains around Blythe. I thought: Use these mountains as a compass. You know them better than any place on earth. Let them guide you. Down below I saw thick green trees and the blue-black of water—Three Gum River. I remembered the game I used to play back when I was trapped up in Devil's

Kitchen: I pictured Three Gum River emptying into the Pigeon River, which flowed into the French Broad River, which merged with the Green River and then with the Broad River, which eventually flowed into the ocean. I knew every twist and turn, and I followed that river now, downward, eastward, knowing it would take me out of there.

The B-29 was dropping. I steered it as best I could away from Fair Mountain, and then away from the bordering mountains of Franklin, Highlands, and Cashiers. I prayed, *Lord, if I crash this plane, please let me crash it far away from anyone.* I wanted to get as far off from everything and everybody as I could. I followed Three Gum River and then the Pigeon River and the Scenic and the mountains that rolled one after the other. I looked for a wide-open place to take the plane down.

Then the mountains thinned and dropped and suddenly I could see a blue wall of hills—just hills, not mountains—and more blue-black of water. Know your compass, I told myself. I thought we were in South Carolina now, just below the North Carolina line, and over the Jocassee Gorges. They were a series of steep-sided gorges, but down below them was a flat forest floor with rivers surging through.

I suddenly heard my daddy's voice, back when we would sit on our porch and he would teach me about the mountains, about where we lived: "Streams named Saluda, Toxaway, Eastatoe, Laurel Fork, Thompson, Whitewater, Horespasture, Devils Fork, Bearcamp, and Chattooga carved the gorges and made waterfalls." I knew it rained here more than any place on earth and because of this it was green in a way that only Ireland or emeralds were green. I knew the Indians had named it Jocassee and that it meant "place of the lost one."

Suddenly the B-29 dropped, and we hit the surface of the water. As soon as we did, engines one and three were torn completely off the airplane. The fire was in number four engine. I could hear one of the engineers now. He was saying that part of the skin on the underside of the left wing was torn off and that the left horizontal stabilizer was twisted. I closed all engine shut-off valves and also the throttles, then I tried to feather engines two and four.

I heard Bob Keene say something in my headset. It sounded like "I'm sorry."

I said, "What? Why? What are you saying?" The bomber skipped and left the water, gaining three hundred feet. The plane was shaking so hard that I could barely hold it.

He said something but I could only hear parts of it. "I'm sorry," he said again. He was struggling with his safety belt, struggling with his parachute.

I said, "Don't you leave this plane! Not yet!"

Bob Keene's speedometer showed an airspeed of 45 miles per hour but mine showed 150 miles per hour. He sank back down in his seat, his safety belt still unlatched, and together we fought to hold the plane, to keep the nose in the air. I thought about Jackie Cochran saying I had to fly this plane by myself, no matter what, and wondered where in the hell she was at a time like this.

We were still flying at 150 miles per hour when the airplane hit the water again. In my earpiece, I could hear the technicians at the back of the plane. There was the sound of raised voices, of yelling. Something in those voices—a kind of wild panic—went right through me and made my knuckles go white more than the fire in the engine or the way we kept dropping into the water. I thought I would rather land on earth than water, because I knew if we landed in water we'd only have a few minutes before the plane sank, and that might not be enough time to get out.

I pulled as hard as I could on the throttle, and the bomber shook like an earthquake. I felt something cold and wet on my hand and knew that I'd pulled so hard that I was bleeding. The plane rose to three hundred feet and then five hundred. I heard Bob Keene in my ear: "They bailed. The bastards jumped."

I looked out my side window and saw two figures falling. Where were their parachutes? I had to look away, back through the windshield, and when I looked back again they were gone. They were too close to the ground. There were too many trees.

"Did they have chutes?"

There was a blast of static and Bob said, "I don't know."

In a split second, I remembered everything I'd learned about flying—how to land in a crosswind. Flying the beam. Flying blind.

Restarting the engine once it was cut. Night flying. Flying cross-country. Knowing my compass. Trusting my judgment.

And then I remembered flying in the Aeronca with Johnny Clay, coming down fast over a field while I thought about everything that had happened to me so far in my life—Mama, Daddy, panther cat, Harley Bright, Wood Carver, Butch Dawkins, learning to drive, recording my songs, leaving home, Nashville. My whole life going by like a newsreel.

I remembered my prayer: *Dear Jesus, please don't let us die. I don't want to die. Not like this . . . I've got too much to do in this world. Please help me land this plane safe and, so help me, I will earn my leaving home.*

I knew enough about flying not to crash. I knew before going up in the B-29 that it might catch fire and that the propellers might fail. It was part of the risk. There was always a risk when you flew, really flew. Like Carole Lombard, serving her country and flying home to see her husband. Like Ty, going back to his base after flying to see me. Like Sally, taking Janie's place so she could eat her supper, and flying the mission she was given to fly.

Bob Keene shouted, "Jump!"

I shouted, "You jump!" I was going to stay with the plane as long as I could.

We were coming down fast over rocks, water, and trees. The B-29 was in an inverted spin, which meant I was upside down. I fought with my safety belt before cutting it loose, and then I flipped the latch and scrambled out. My leg was hit hard by the rudder, and for a minute I saw stars. The ground was hurtling toward me, and I jumped. I felt myself falling and it felt slow and fast all at once. I remembered what Johnny Clay said about the seconds it took to die.

I counted to two and pulled the rip cord on my parachute. I knew I'd stayed with the plane too long, and my chute still wasn't open when I saw that the ground was already too close. It was sandy and marshy. There were so many trees. I looked for Bob Keene, to see if he'd got out, but I was falling too fast to see anything but a blur of blue and green and black.

My chute opened and the wind caught it and flew me just like a kite. I slammed into the ground and popped the release on my left leg and chest buckles. I was working on the right leg when a gust of wind lifted me into the air. I pulled the cords on one side, trying to collapse the chute, but the wind was too strong. It slammed me against the ground again and then carried me up into the air over and over.

My heels were dragging and I could feel holes burning through the soles of my boots. I started praying hard to Jesus. *Please let me live. Please let Bob Keene live and the engineers and the technicians too, even though they jumped. Please don't let me die. I've got too much to do in this world and in this life. I have songs to write and songs to sing and planes to fly and I want to see my old yellow truck again.*

And then I started singing, because Mama always said that singing was like praying twice.

Oh, they tell me of a home where my friends have gone.
Oh, they tell me of that land far away,
where the tree of life in eternal bloom
sheds its fragrance through the unclouded day . . .

And then I heard another song, the last one Ty had written me, with its funny tune that I'd made up myself. Even though he'd never sung it to me, I could hear him singing it now.

You make me love you,
and that could be the greatest thing my heart was ever fit to do.

I thought I was underwater. I drifted in and out and I could see pieces of things—all blurred and at a strange angle. Trees. Earth. Dirt. Water. Rock. Sky. Flames. I could see my arms thrown out in front of me, only they seemed to stretch on and on, my hands lying yards away. I tried to move, but then I would drift off again. When I drifted back, I was lying just like before, arms stretched on and on, hands out of reach. My eyelids felt fuzzy, my head heavy. I told myself to move, to at least turn to the left so I was lying on my back. I felt like

I was at the bottom of a river, feet trapped in the sand, trying to pull myself to the surface through oceans of water pushing down on me, filling my lungs, my throat, my head, all the empty spaces inside my body. Everything was foggy, like the fog was settling around me, pressing me down. Water. Fog. Water. Fog. I thought I was moving, but I wasn't. I was drowning.

I woke up sometime later and things were less blurry. I blinked at the sky. All around me was the green of emeralds, of Ireland, or the way I'd always pictured it to be. The first thing I thought was: Heaven's above me. I'm not dead. I felt the ground underneath my body. I thanked Jesus and prayed I wasn't broken anywhere. I moved my limbs one by one, and my right ankle burned like it was on fire. I had to raise my head to look at it, just to be sure it wasn't, and when I raised my head the fire moved to my brain. I saw stars and lightning and closed my eyes fast, hoping they would go away. My breathing was raggedy. My ribs felt tight like someone was sitting on them, like they were being strangled. I opened my eyes to make sure I wasn't wrapped up in my parachute. And then the stars came back. I lay there with my eyes closed, wondering how many things were broken.

When I could, I opened my eyes again and slowly, carefully, pulled myself up to my elbows. I lay in the middle of a clearing edged by trees. The B-29 was smoking in the distance, shattered in pieces, burning as bright as twelve bonfires. The blue sky was black and gray with smoke. I didn't know how long I'd been knocked out, but I could tell by the slant of the sun that night would be coming soon.

I pulled myself up all the way, to my hands, to my knees. Each move brought new shots of pain, like gunfire hitting me here and here and here. I leaned over my parachute and yanked the rip cord off.

I got to my feet and it took about a hundred years, and then I started walking toward the plane. The B-29 was broken into three pieces, scattered across the ground, in the clearing, in the trees. Each section of the bomber blazed with fire, the smoke rising in three fat columns that joined together in the sky in a giant, billowing cloud. The flames were crackling and snapping and climbing up tree trunks and limbs, and underneath the crackling and snapping I heard a great, echoing roar. I shouted for Bob Keene. I shouted for the engineers. I went from section to section, held back by the flames, and I strained to see them. I shouted till I was hoarse and my throat was raw from the hollering and the smoke. I started coughing then and couldn't stop. I doubled over and held my stomach and felt a stab of pain in my ribs as they cinched around me like someone was squeezing the breath out of me. I almost blacked out again.

I backed away from the plane, my throat burning from the smoke, my face burning from the heat of the fire. I tripped over a rise in the earth and kept backing away on my bottom, scooting myself backward as fast as possible.

When I got to my feet, yards away, I looked in every direction, expecting help. Where were the emergency trucks? The crowds? How could no one have seen or heard such an explosion? How could no one see the smoke and the flames? I started walking away from the crash, following my compass. I waded through field and grass and dirt and mud, through thickets of trees and open land. I came to an old split-wood fence, flecked with white like it had been painted once, long ago. Without thinking, I stepped on the rail with my bad ankle, and the pain was a sting that made me holler, so I climbed through instead of over. My head felt tight, like it was closing in on itself, and every now and then I turned so dizzy that I had to stop and close my eyes.

There was a road on the other side of the fence—just overgrown dirt tracks covered up with weeds and tall grass. I held on to the fence to keep myself up and pulled out my compass. It was the compass Ty gave me with his initials on the back. I felt them now in the metal: N-E-T. "Okay," I said to myself for no reason except that I needed to hear a voice, even if it was my own.

My hand was shaking as I held the compass, and I put my left hand under my right one to try to steady it. I needed to head west, which meant, more or less to the right. I set off down the road that wasn't much of a road—it called to mind the old cattle road that came down from Alluvial to Hamlet's Mill. I was dragging my ankle and trying not to worry. And then I reached into my pocket and felt for the wooden flying girl. Today I'd brought the compass with me as something I might need for my flight and not as a good-luck charm, but I'd brought the wooden girl as my talisman. I pulled her out and she was in two pieces, broken in half where her heart would be.

I walked for an hour, maybe more, judging by the way the sun was dropping in the sky. I started singing to keep my mind off the pain of my ankle and the pain of my ribs and the pain of my head. I was making up words now like I used to up in Devil's Kitchen—just a jumble of words with no real tune, to help me keep going. "One foot forward, next foot forward, one foot in front of the other, one step closer to home. You don't have to walk all the steps at once. Just one step and then another." What was it Johnny Clay had said? "One more step. One more step . . . After all, you can't run them all at once."

And then I heard Ty saying, "When you're looking back, you can't look forward."

I started singing Ty's song then, running through it again and again. His words were good company. They made me feel like he was close by.

Every now and then I stopped to catch my breath because my ribs were tightening up, just like they were closing in on themselves, and my ankle was throbbing so bad I almost felt I could hear it. The sun was settling in the sky and I was still in the middle of nothing but fields and trees and an overgrown dirt road. I hadn't passed a single house.

An hour later the sky was a hazy mix of gold and orange and pink and blue. The moon was shining where the sun used to be, and I felt night coming down around me. I had turned off the dirt road and was now heading west on a road that was paved in some places and gravel in others. I was hoping for a car or a truck, but that road was just as empty as the sky. I was beginning to wonder if maybe I'd died in the crash and maybe this was heaven after all and I was just wandering around and around. The thought spooked me. I thought, What if I'm really dead? I started walking faster, through the pain of my ankle and my ribs and my head. Would a compass work in heaven? Could it help you find your way? Or did all roads lead to the same place up there?

And then I thought: Oh my God. What if I'm not in heaven at all? What if I've gone straight to hell, even if I did get myself saved when I was ten?

There were two figures coming toward me, and for a minute my heart stopped. Mama? Ty? Danny Deal? Sally? Suddenly I saw the faces of all the people I'd lost in my life, even the Gordon boys and Reverend Nix.

The figures were on horseback, and one of them wore a cowboy hat and the other one didn't. It hit me that if I was in hell, I'd be down there with bad people, and that these men coming toward me could be wicked and depraved.

But maybe I wasn't dead at all. Maybe I was alive and here were just some regular, alive people who could help me. I wanted to run, but my ankle wouldn't work and my head went dizzy, so I just kept on toward them, slow as could be, running in my mind.

When they got to me, the one with the hat said, "Where'd you come from, boy?" He whistled. "You look like you been through it."

The other one, the younger one, jumped down from his horse and said, "Jesus. What happened to you?"

The older one, the one with the hat, climbed down, and they were both standing there, and I thought that they were probably father and son. They had the same sandy hair, the same sandy skin, the same kind brown eyes and wide noses. Suddenly I couldn't speak. I held up my rip cord to show it to them.

The son said to his daddy, "He must have been in an accident." To me he said, "Did you crash your plane?"

The only thing I could do was nod. My ribs had closed up and my throat had closed up and my head had closed up and my heart. I nodded till my head felt like it was going to spin off my body. Then I pulled off my helmet and the father said, "Why it's just a little girl," and that did it. Down-home girl or not, I started to cry.

The next thing I remembered was lying in a hospital bed. I woke up once and saw a doctor standing over me, checking my pulse, checking my eyes. I said, "Am I dead, then?"

He said, "You're very much alive, young lady."

I said, "Really?" My voice sounded shadowy and far away.

He said, "Yes."

"Good." I thought of Mama and Ty and Sally and all the people I wanted to see. And then I thought of all the people on this earth, still alive, that I wanted to see even more.

I said, "There were men with me. Lieutenant Keene . . . engineers . . . technicians . . ." My eyes were heavy. My head was heavy.

The doctor said, "I'm sorry."

He was sorry. So sorry. Bob Keene was sorry. "I'm sorry." This meant my crew was gone. They were dead. They weren't very much alive anymore. They weren't alive at all. Bob Keene, who should have been Leonard Grossman, who should have been Sally—and Sally was dead too. I tried to remember the names of the other men. I didn't even know them. One was Wallace . . . or Warren . . . I thought one was Richard . . . or Raymond?

I closed my eyes again and slept.

I had a dream that I was holding on to my rip cord, the one I'd taken off my parachute, and Butch was there, standing over my bed, dark eyes worried, hair falling in his face. I could see his dog tags hanging over me, swinging back and forth, back and forth in the air. I tried to touch them, but my arms were heavy and my eyes were heavy and I couldn't move. He was saying something, or maybe singing something, but I couldn't understand it. "Your heart is in the music . . . your soul is in the song . . ."

I dreamed that my daddy was there, his face lined from the sun and the wind. He looked older but the same. His hand was rough around mine. I could feel the calluses from the work he did with his blacksmithing tools. I said, "Where have you been? I thought I saw you at graduation." But my mouth wouldn't move and the words slurred and stayed inside when they should have been outside. I told myself: Wake up, Velva Jean. Wake up so you can look at him and make a memory because you don't know when you'll see him again.

I said, "Don't go away this time. I need you to stay." But I couldn't tell if the words got out or not.

The rough hand tightened. A voice said, "There now. There now." It was a voice as rough as the hand holding mine. "There now," it said over and over. "There now."

I dreamed that I woke up and saw Daddy Hoyt and Granny, one on either side of my bed. Granny sat with her eyes closed, rocking back and forth, muttering something low. Daddy Hoyt stood watching me. The doctor was frowning in the doorway. I could feel the weight of something on my head, on my heart, on my ankle, and I knew Daddy Hoyt had made a poultice for me and that he was healing me with his herbs just like Granny was healing me with a witch spell. The doctor won't like that much, I thought.

I woke up again and Daddy Hoyt and Granny were still there. I blinked my eyes and suddenly I could feel the pain spreading through my body, starting in my ankle and moving up into my ribs, my chest, my head. I cried out and the sound of it surprised me. I tried to pull myself upright, through the haze. Granny laid a hand on my arm and said, "Hush now, honey. We've come to take care of you."

Terror in the Sky, Terror on the Ground

By Humphrey R. Moore for the *Charlotte Observer*

On April 11 one of Boeing's top-secret B-29 Superfortress bombers caught fire an hour and twenty minutes after takeoff from the Army Air Forces' base at Camp Davis and crashed into the Jocassee Gorges, on the border of North and South Carolina, just east of the Great Smoky Mountains. Lead pilot Velva Jean Hart, twenty-one, survived, while five crewmen perished in the crash. Although the event could not be concealed, the purpose of the mission remains classified.

A fire erupted and two engines were lost after the aircraft hit the water. Two army technicians bailed out of the plane, but their chutes could not deploy in time. The giant bomber slammed into the earth just short of Lake Jocassee, killing two engineers aboard as well as the copilot.

The Jocassee Gorges lie mostly in Transylvania County, North Carolina, an area that encompasses the Toxaway, Horsepasture, Thompson, and Whitewater Rivers as they flow into Lake Jocassee in North and South Carolina. Lake Jocassee splashes against the base of the Blue Ridge Escarpment, the "Blue Wall" of hills that delineates the sharp transition between the Carolina mountains and the plains and hills of the western Piedmont.

At 4:30 p.m., residents of Box Creek, just three miles away, heard an unusually loud aircraft pass overhead. Seconds later the sound of the engines ceased abruptly as the bomber impacted the earth and was consumed in a huge fireball.

Without hesitation, the people of Box Creek responded to the crash. Ronald Butterfield, Andrew Pitts, and Phil Woodbine arrived at the scene of the wreck within an hour of the crash and were soon followed by others who tried to assist in the search. The would-be rescuers found a large area of wet, burned ground littered with molten metal and debris. Pockets of aviation fuel lit up the scene as they ignited with a dull roar. The gallant efforts of the townspeople were for naught; there were no survivors. Or so they thought.

Brave Velva Jean Hart, in spite of a sprained ankle, four

broken ribs, and a partially fractured skull, walked five miles, looking for help, until she was discovered by Hugh Ray Sr. and Hugh Ray Jr., who found her on Old Highway 64. She was heading west, she said, before she collapsed. They assumed she was an enlisted man before she took off her helmet. "Why it's just a little girl," Hugh Ray Sr. recalls remarking.

The brave little pilot is fighting for her life at the base hospital at Camp Davis, where she is serving her country as a pilot with the Women Airforce Service Pilots, or WASP. Jacqueline Cochran, director of the WASP, said she was proud of Miss Hart and of all her girls. She said, "When the men of the Army Air Forces refused to fly the B-29 because of safety concerns, Ms. Hart stepped forward to volunteer herself as pilot. This accident had nothing to do with her skills as a flier, and everything to do with simple engine malfunction. I guarantee she will be back in the sky again as soon as she recovers."

April 12, 1944

Dear Velva Jean,

I ain't writing to lecture. I'm writing to say I'm glad you're alive. And I'm writing to tell you to stay safe. I'll always worry on you because that's my job, but that don't mean I want to keep you here where you don't belong. Even after the crash, I know you belong where you are, up there in the air.

I wanted to come look in on you with Granny and Daddy Hoyt, but I got to stay here with the children. They promised to bring you these letters from all of us back home.

Do you know I started watching for you? Dan Presley and me goes out at night and climbs up on the roof of the house and looks for airplanes. We don't see many, but every time we do we say, "I wonder if that's Velva Jean." Yesterday we saw that bomber going overhead and Dan Presley said, "That's a B-29, the biggest bomber in the world." And I just knew it was you flying it. I still got chill bumps on my arms.

So you get better. No more crashes. And don't you give up. You've come too far.

Your sister,

Sweet Fern

FORTY-THREE

When they heard news of the crash, Granny and Daddy Hoyt packed one bag between them—full of medicines and herbs and letters from my family—and climbed into my yellow truck. Daddy Hoyt didn't know how to drive too well, but he said it was amazing how fast you could learn something when you needed to. He said by the time they got to Cedar Rock, just west of the mountains, he knew what he was doing.

Just like the newspaper said, I had a sprained ankle, four broken ribs, and a partially fractured skull brought on by a hard knock on the head, which almost scalped me. Now that I'd sent plenty of prayers to Jesus, thanking him for saving me, I wondered if it was vain to thank him for saving my hair too.

I said, "You didn't have to come." Even though I was glad they did. I'd never been so happy in my life to see anyone.

Granny said, "Yes we did." Then she got up and left the room because I could tell she was about to cry.

Daddy Hoyt sat beside me, holding my hand. His old face was sad and worried. His white hair was thinning a little in front and on the sides. I felt so bad for worrying him, for making him leave the mountain and drive all this way.

He said, "You're going to be okay. You just need to stay in here for another day or two."

I said, "The others? The men that were with me?"

He shook his head. "I'm sorry."

I'm sorry. What was it Bob Keene said to me before we crashed? "I'm sorry."

We sat there, both of us thinking about five men we didn't really know, who were dead now. I said, "Did they find out why this happened?"

"If they did, we haven't heard anything."

I thought: If they did, they probably wouldn't tell us anyway.

I'm sorry.

I'm sorry . . .

I said, "Before I was awake, did anyone else come visit me?" I thought of Butch, of my daddy.

Daddy Hoyt said, "A lot of those girls, the WASP. They said they were friends of yours. Nice girls."

I said, "Anyone else?"

"Jacqueline Cochran and some sort of colonel or major."

I said, "Didn't anyone else come? Did you see anyone else?"

He seemed to give this a good think. He said, "No, honey. I don't remember it if I did."

I tried not to let this pull me back down into the deep of the water, into the fog. My mind went blurry for a minute, and then I made my-self concentrate and focus and not think about dreams and haints, which was all they were.

I said, "Tell me the news from home."

Daddy Hoyt was sitting quietly already but now his face got still.

I said, "Something's happened."

He squeezed my hand and then he let it go, sitting back in his chair. He rubbed his hands on his pants—the same old work pants he always wore, except when he was wearing his herb-gathering overalls. He said, "We haven't heard from Johnny Clay."

I said, "Isn't that normal? I mean, he's never one to write much. He's probably off fighting . . ." There had to be some reason he was bringing this up, and it made me uneasy in my mind.

He said, "We're sure he's fine." He didn't sound sure though.

I felt that same underwater, sinking feeling that I felt when I woke up from the crash. "What do you think's happened?"

He shut his eyes, just like he was trying to sense Johnny Clay in this world. He opened them again and looked at me, and his eyes—blue and gold like my mama's—looked two hundred years old and full of burdens. He said, "I don't know."

I was released from the hospital a week later, and Granny and Daddy Hoyt left a few days after that. I stood, leaning on Janie, waving good-bye as they pulled away from the base in my yellow truck. I hadn't cried since the day the Hugh Rays found me, but seeing my grandparents drive away—taking home and the mountains with them—sent me to bawling. Janie put her arm around my shoulder. She said, "That sure is one hell of a truck, Hartsie."

I wanted to run after them, but instead I laughed. I said, "It is one hell of a truck." Then I wiped my eyes and told myself I was a down-home girl and that this meant I would just keep on going no matter how loaded up and weighted down my suitcase was.

Back in the barracks, I pulled my parachute rip cord out of my pocket and laid it under my pillow, where I kept it when I slept. Maybe it was my talisman now, or one of them. Then I got out Mama's Bible and sat on the bed, careful with my ribs, my ankle, my head. I opened the book and wrote: "April 11—Velva Jean flies a B-29 and survives."

I stared at the page, and it didn't seem like enough to write. There was so much more to it than that. I sat there for a long time, thinking of all the things I hadn't written down and all the things that could be written: from Avenger Field to Ty's crash to Sally's funeral to the songs I hadn't written, the songs I was trying to write, learning the B-29, Butch leaving, waking up from the accident, meeting the Hugh Rays, the dreams I had in the hospital about Butch and my daddy—I also dreamed Granny and Daddy Hoyt, or thought I did, but they were really there. Were Butch and my daddy there too?

But I didn't write any of it. Instead I put the book away again, and then I lay back on my bed and closed my eyes and waited till the room centered itself. Lately when I shut my eyes, the room spun around me. The spinning got slower and slower until finally the room stood still. I conjured my dreams till I could see Butch's dog tags swinging over me and feel my daddy's rough hand in mine.

~

On Friday, April 21, I dressed in my pink and greens and stood in front of Colonel Wells and Major Blackburn and Jackie Cochran and General Hap Arnold, inside one of the Camp Davis courtrooms. Vince Gillies, just promoted to first lieutenant, was there, staring blankly at me from his chair. He shifted around during the meeting, cracking his knuckles, scratching his cheek, looking up at the ceiling.

I tried not to show my nerves, which were cluttering my stomach and jittering my mind. I stood still as could be and answered all their questions, like how low did I fly over the mountains and when did I first notice the fire and why did the technicians jump when the rest of us stayed and why did I leave the plane. I answered every question, calm as could be, trying to keep my voice from shaking.

When I was finished and they were finished, I said, "I'd like to say something." General Arnold nodded at me. I said, "When I was little all I wanted to do was grow up to sing at the Grand Ole Opry. I saved my money for years and years, ever since I was seven years old, just so I could get there one day. In 1941 I left everything and everyone to go to Nashville to make that dream come true. And then the war happened and I learned to fly, and suddenly the Opry didn't matter quite so much because I had a new dream." I looked at Miss Cochran. "I wanted to be like Jacqueline Cochran and I wanted to serve the country I love."

Miss Cochran started to say something, but I said, "I left everything and everyone to come here, just like Sally Hallatassee left everything to be here. We all did, each and every one of us, but ever since we came to Camp Davis it's been nothing but close calls and accidents and tear gas under our doors at night and now this. Sally is dead. No matter how many times I ask Jesus to bring her back, he can't. I can't. But I need to know that you're going to figure out why these things are happening, and why I almost died too."

General Arnold said, "Are you finished?"

I said, "Yes, sir." My heart was beating so fast I was afraid it might fly right out of my chest. My stomach was jumping like I'd swallowed a hundred crickets. There was more to say, but none of it was fit to say to a general, a colonel, a major, and the woman in charge of the Women Airforce Service Pilots. I thought, If I only wasn't a lady, the things I could say. Which was a funny thing to think because all these years of Sweet Fern telling me I would be a lady one day, and all these years of me telling her not to say it, to take it back, I guessed I finally was one.

I remembered what the Wood Carver said to me after Harley and the others burned his carvings and turned him out of his house: "They've violated the sanctuary of my home. They've violated the spirit of who I am. There's no going back, Velva Jean. This place will never be the same." I thought that, next to Sally's death, this was maybe the worst thing of all—they had violated the sanctuary of my home and the spirit of who I was. For me, the WASP would never be the same.

General Arnold said, "I give you my word that military intelligence is looking into this matter, Miss Hart." He seemed like a kind man and a fair man. There was something in him that made me think of Daddy Hoyt.

I said, "Thank you, sir."

He dismissed me then, but as everyone was standing up to go, Lieutenant Vince Gillies said, "I have a question."

General Arnold said, "Go ahead." He didn't sit down again. He looked impatient to get away.

Vince Gillies said to me, "How did you manage to get out of the plane in an inverted spin?"

I thought of something Beachard had said when they asked how he managed to single-handedly fight off the Japanese to capture a hilltop overlooking the Munda Point airstrip in the central Solomon Islands. I looked right back at Vince Gillies and said, "Have you ever prayed, Lieutenant?"

My answer hung out there in the air. No one said anything. Vince Gillies rubbed his face and cracked his knuckles and tipped his chair back so only two legs were on the floor. I wished I knew a Cherokee spell to make him fall over.

General Arnold said, "You have my word, Miss Hart." And then he turned on his heel and clipped out of the room, the others following. I walked right after them, right past Lieutenant Vince Gillies. I walked right out the door and into the sunlight and didn't stop walking till I got to my bay.

~

Jackie Cochran grounded all bombers for a week. It turned out that the rudder cables in my B-29 had been tampered with, and even she couldn't pretend it was just the mechanics overlooking something by accident. When reporters stopped by the base asking for me, I was given orders not to talk to them.

I waited to see what Miss Cochran would do about it this time, but she left Camp Davis without a word to any of us, even me, who had almost died, and went back to Washington, D.C. Janie and I stood by the barracks, by Sally's garden in full bloom, and watched her take off.

I thought: There goes the most famous woman pilot in the world, the woman that gave me my chance and gave me my wings. And after all that, I'm nothing but a guinea pig—just like Sally used to say. Jacqueline Cochran might as well be sabotaging the planes herself for all she's doing about it.

I couldn't believe we'd come from the same place, her and me— both orphans with no real education, who believed in following our dreams. I thought back on the last letter I'd written her, back when the only thing I wanted was to be a WASP. Right now I felt like the queen of Egypt compared to her, for all we had in common.

Janie spat on the ground and said, "That's what I think of Jackie Cochran and her experimental program." She turned toward the barracks where Sally's flowers were blooming, the only bright spot on the base. "You coming, Hartsie?"

"No," I said. "In a while."

What I wanted right now was to fly, but I was still grounded because of my ankle, my ribs, and my head. I found Gus Mitchell and asked if I could borrow his jeep. He was out of the hospital and on crutches, but he couldn't drive yet.

I said, "How are you doing?"

He said, "One day at a time. I miss her like hell. How are you doing?"

I said, "The same. I miss her too."

The jeep was louder than my truck and it rattled so much I was afraid it would fall apart. I drove fast as I dared through the base and past the base and onto the dunes and the sand. I looked out toward the ocean, where the U-boats were probably hiding, and then I parked the jeep and sat there and this time I didn't think about Jackie Cochran. Instead I thought about Johnny Clay and where he might be. I didn't need to know where he was. All I needed to know was that he was somewhere and that he was safe.

And then I thought about Butch. I hadn't heard a word from him since my accident. Would it have hurt him to write to me to say something like "I'm so happy you didn't die"? The thought of almost dying made me impatient with everyone—Jackie Cochran, Colonel Wells, Butch. I thought about all the times it felt like I was trying to get his attention, just like I tried to get Harley's attention and my daddy's attention, trying to get them to see me.

I remembered everything Butch had told me about himself—Cut Off, Louisiana; Indian mama, Creole daddy; Navajo great-granddaddy; leaving home at thirteen; riding the rodeo; hitchhiking; learning the blues in Mississippi; Knoxville; the broken bottle neck talisman; his age. I'd been so happy when he'd told me things, but now I realized it wasn't much at all when you got down to it.

Life was too short to spend it trying to get a man to tell me how he felt about me. I wanted to feel like the most special girl in the world—a girl who was as loving and lovely as she was loved, just like Butch once wrote in a song that may or may not have been about me.

~

On the morning of May 1, twenty-five new WASP arrived on base. I watched as they jumped down from General Arnold's personal airplane and stood in the sunshine, hands on hips, looking over Camp Davis, faces mixed with excitement and nerves. I watched as they took in the swamp; then as they turned their eyes up to the sky to gaze at a B-17 roaring past. I thought with a pang that this was what Sally and I must have looked like when we got here, months ago.

This was only the start. One of the girls who worked in the dispatcher's office said Louella Corbett told her more women were coming. She said the army was sending members of the Women's Army Auxiliary Corps, or WAAC—now officially the Women's Army Corps, or WAC—to work in the office and as radio operators and mechanics and air-traffic controllers.

Later I saw one of the new WASP talking to Zeke Bodine outside the rec building, and when I ran into her in the hallway of the barracks after that I said hi and told her my name, and she said her name was Trudy, which was short for Gertrude, which was her mother's name and her grandmother's name and her grandmother's name before that.

She was telling me about Maryland, where she was from, when I said, "Whatever you do, look over your own airplane and don't trust anyone here, not even Jackie Cochran." Her mouth popped open into the widest *O*—big as a doughnut—before I walked away.

Two hours later Harry Lawson was arrested. The afternoon had gone cloudy. A storm hovered over the ocean. I was walking to the flight line, ready for my first flight since my accident, when I saw him being taken away by men in dark suits. Gus Mitchell was standing nearby, leaning on his crutches. I thought, Here we are, both of us survivors.

Gus said, "It's the goddamned FBI."

Harry Lawson was led past, staring ahead like he didn't see any of us.

Now everybody had stories to tell about Harry Lawson, and everybody said they saw it coming. The truth, we learned piece by piece, was that his real name was Felix Lewison, and he was from the Rhine Province in Germany. Thirty-one German agents had formed a spy ring in the United States. Helmut Klein, Fritz Kramer, Rolf Stigler, and now Harry Lawson, were all a part of it. They'd been placed in key jobs around the country to get information that could be used to carry out acts of sabotage. One person worked on an airline so he could report allied ships that were crossing the Atlantic Ocean; some worked as delivery people so they could deliver secret messages alongside normal messages; some worked in shipyards and air bases.

Harry Lawson grew up in Germany and was hired out to a draftsman when he was eleven. He fought for Germany in the First World War, when he was seventeen. He was a machine gunner on the Western Front before he went to sea. According to the newspaper report, he lived a "lonely, rootless life," until he went to California when he was twenty-five and became a U.S. citizen under the name Frank Lewis. He worked as a mechanic for Consolidated Aircraft and got married to a local girl, a pilot named Rose.

When Harry was twenty-eight, Rose was killed in an airplane crash, and he went back to Germany because, after her death, there was nothing for him here and his life in the United States was over. He got a job in a turbine factory, where he worked until he was recruited to be a spy. They never found out the cause of Rose's accident.

After learning codes, photography, microphotography, radio transmission, and other spy techniques, Harry Lawson was sent back to the United States to meet Inspector Herman Lang, who had secured a position with the makers of the Norden bombsight. Weighted down with instructions, five messages in microfilm hidden in his watch, a thousand dollars, and a new name—"Harry Lawson"—he took a job as a mechanic at Camp Davis, North Carolina, where the Norden bombsight was being tested and the B-29 was going to be ferrying top-secret parts to a laboratory in Los Alamos.

Colonel Wells released an official statement in the afternoon, which said that Harry Lawson had been arrested on suspicion of being a German spy engaged in sabotage. He said that a complete investigation was under way by the highest authorities.

At mess that night, the entire room was buzzing with the news, everybody offering up pieces of information they'd overheard from Major Blackburn or Colonel Wells or from one of the radio operators or the reporters that were lurking around. Everyone seemed happy that there was finally someone to blame for the accidents, for Sally's death.

I couldn't believe Harry Lawson had been a spy all this time and I hadn't caught him. I prided myself on being able to recognize spies and murderers and other crazy types of people. Johnny Clay and me had practiced being spies since we were little, and then practiced seeing spies when we were in Nashville. And there was Harry Lawson, all that time, right under my nose. They were blaming the sabotage on him, but he had told me about Sally—about the latch that was tampered with—and the misfiled papers. Why would he tell me about them if he'd done these things himself?

As Janie and Helen and I walked by a table of officers on our way out the door, I heard one of them say to another, "What will the girls do with one less mechanic to blame for their accidents?" They all laughed at this like it was the funniest thing they'd ever heard.

I thought about taking my tray and knocking him over the head with it, but instead I said, "What makes you think we blame the mechanics?"

Maybe it was Harry Lawson that was responsible for the sabotage, but I thought that was too easy. He might have been to blame for some of it. Or it could have been Bob Keene who did most of it or some of it or all of it. I might never know for sure. Only a handful of people were allowed near the B-29, but that didn't mean an officer couldn't break some rules and step over hurdles. It happened all the time.

The officers got quiet, and I turned around then and left, Janie and the other girls right behind me. My ankle still hurt, but I walked out of there just as tall and majestic as I could, like an Indian princess.

~

By morning the storm had blown over and the sun was burning bright over the water. I met Major Blackburn at Hangar 4, which was where they were keeping what was left of the *Flyin' Jenny* under guard. Ever since Harry Lawson was arrested, there were guards on patrol everywhere—along the beach, along the highway, along the runways, around the hangars.

Major Blackburn didn't say anything, just nodded at me and at the guards. We showed our IDs and one of them opened the hangar and let us in. Even in pieces, the B-29 looked giant as a monster. If I didn't know it was an airplane, I might not have been able to guess what it was from the crushed and twisted metal, all of it burned black, even on the inside.

Major Blackburn said, "Five minutes, Miss Hart."

After seeing what was left, I couldn't believe I'd survived at all. I climbed through the wreckage, going over every inch of that plane. I knew it would have been picked clean by now by whoever might have made this happen—if someone made this happen—just like a dead squirrel in the woods. Unless, of course, the person that made it happen wasn't here anymore. I remembered Bob Keene's white knuckles, his pale face, the sweat on his brow.

I'm sorry.

He didn't know he'd be flying on the B-29. He thought it would be someone else.

I looked for anything that might be a clue as to what happened, why it happened: an oil rag, sugar in the fuel tank, sand in the carburetor. I checked the propeller, the landing gear, and the rudder cables. They'd been nicked, like Jackie Cochran said, just enough—as neat as the split of the Wood Carver's axe against a tree limb. I heard his voice in my head, telling me you had to know just where to make the cut.

I dug through the ruins looking for the flight recorder, but it wasn't there. Then I thought about my real black box, the one where I kept all my hurt and sorrow, all my scars.

Major Blackburn walked up then and said, "Did you find what you were looking for?" There was something in his voice that was almost kind.

I said, "No, sir. Not here. Not yet."

May 2, 1944

Dear Velva Jean,

Thank you for your long-ago note. I'm glad you like the wooden figure. Yes, she's meant to be flying. She's meant to be you. I'm glad she's one of your talismans and that you are healing from your crash, but I'm sorry she got broken. I don't know that she had anything to do with you surviving. I think that was up to you.

I am sending another flying girl to you. I made her from my Jesus tree, or dogwood, the one that sits in front of my old cabin. You'll remember that tree has been through a lot but always stayed standing, even in the most terrible storms. I've never made a carving from it because, as I told you once, its brace roots are too strong. This means it needs to become a tree and stay a tree, which is what it was meant to do. But I thought it was time to make an exception. As you see, she's a very small girl but a sturdy one. I doubt the tree will even miss the wood it took to make her. I thought if you were going to be taking this little girl up in the air with you, we had to make sure nothing can break her.

Don't worry about your old friend. I am making my peace.

I'm glad to know your light is shining bright, just like it was meant to do.

I will see you again.

Your friend,

Henry Able

FORTY-FOUR

On May 5, I sat alone in my bay, at my desk, at my typewriter, all my notes and papers spread out in front of me. There were papers with just a word or two and papers with stanzas. There were scratch marks where I'd crossed things out and napkins because I couldn't find anything else to write on. There were sheets of notebook paper with lines I'd drawn across them, just like Butch had taught me to do back in Devil's Kitchen, when I was trying to write the tunes.

I took all those words and lines and papers and for the first time in a long time I was able to pick just the ones I needed and put them together. I thought maybe it came from being grounded, from having nothing else to do.

After I had typed all the words and had the music in my head, I sang the song to myself, sitting there at my desk. I played Sally's banjo as I sang it. The windows were open and the day came in, the sun hitting the floor like the shadows of dancing men, the wooden ones made by the Wood Carver. The white curtains with black dots floated up like a haint, then back down, then up again.

It was funny about writing. It was like flying or driving or playing an instrument. When you were doing it like you were supposed to be doing it, you knew it right inside you. You could feel that this was the way it should be. But when you wrote a word that you didn't believe in, that didn't fit, it stuck out just like a bumpy landing or a bad turn or a false note.

The other funny thing about it was that you couldn't hide from the bad things. If you were going to write anything good or deep or true, you had to let in the sadness and the sorrow and the loss. These were all the things I tried to keep at a distance, but sometimes you needed to let them in, just like the blues—you needed to feel them to write them.

I pulled the paper out of the typewriter as careful as I could. I carried it just like a baby over to my cot, where I laid it on the pillow. I pulled my hatbox out from under the bed and opened it up. It was full of treasures that wouldn't look like treasures to anyone else. The clover jewelry that Mama and I had made years ago was brown and dry. The pictures of Carole Lombard and Charles "Buddy" Rogers I'd cut from movie magazines were fading yellow. Even Daddy's emerald—the one he brought me from the Black Mountains—was dusty. I pulled it out and rubbed it green.

The breeze from the window lifted my song up like an airplane and sent it sailing. I caught it and laid it on top of everything in the hatbox, and then I shut it away. I wasn't sure if I would ever fly again, which was why I needed music and songs and writing. I needed to remember my real life's dream, the one I had before I ever wanted to learn to drive or to fly.

It wasn't a smart song or a fancy song, but I thought it might be the best song I'd ever written.

~

On May 7, General Hap Arnold's plane arrived at base, only he wasn't on it, because he was somewhere in England. The plane was delivering forty-five members of the Women's Army Corps. The WAC were going to be living on the other side of base, separated from the men by the highway. Janie said they were going to have their own PX and mess hall.

The WAC uniforms were neat and smart. They didn't have to wear coveralls and turbans or pink and greens when they went to town. The jackets they wore were short and snug, the color of sand. On one collar was a brass disk with the initials "U.S." On the other collar was a brass disk that showed the head of Athena, the ancient Greek goddess of war. They wore smart little hats that looked just like the ones the male officers wore, and straight skirts that hit right at the knee.

We stood in our caps and coveralls, rolled up to the knees and elbows, watching as the girls—who looked like girls and not boys dressed up in clothes they stole out of their daddy's wardrobe—marched smartly out of the plane and across the runway in two orderly lines. I knew I should be glad they were here because they were girls like us and they'd had to deal with some of the same things we'd had to deal with on military bases—men being rude and crude and making mean comments. But I wasn't one bit happy to see them.

I thought, Where have you been while we've been here in the swamp, being eaten up by mosquitoes and shot at every day, risking our lives going up in old, worn-out planes that men are too afraid to fly? These girls looked like girls that would sit behind desks and type things and file paperwork. I wanted to wear a pin of Athena on my collar, but I didn't even have a collar. I didn't think they'd done a thing to earn those uniforms.

~

On the morning of May 10, the base doctor gave me a letter that said I was ready to fly again. As I walked to the dispatcher's office to get my flight assignment, I looked at the letter and thought: How does he know I'm ready? How can he look at my ankle and look at my ribs and look at the outside of my head and tell me I'm ready to fly? He's probably never even been up in a plane, and if he has he's never flown it himself. He doesn't know what it's like to crash and nearly die. He doesn't know if I'm ready to do it again. How dare he say I'm ready to fly.

I almost ripped up that letter right then, but instead I walked into the dispatcher's office to get my flight orders. A half dozen of the WACs typed and filed away in their neat little uniforms.

Louella Corbett looked up from her desk and said, "How's the recovery? Ready to go up again?"

It was easy for her to ask me that from behind her desk where the biggest thing she had to worry about was a paper cut.

No, I'm not ready to go up again. I don't know if I'll ever be ready to go up again.

"Dr. Geary says I am." I handed her the paper.

She glanced at it, and while she did I looked at the WACs. Their fingernails were painted red or pink to match their lipstick. Their makeup was fresh and their hair was curled. They looked like they'd had a long night's sleep on a bed made of clouds.

Louella Corbett said, "Colonel Wells has your assignment for you." A telephone rang at a nearby desk. One of the WACs answered it.

I said, "Colonel Wells?"

The WAC held the phone out to Louella and said, "Mrs. Corbett, it's General Thomas."

Louella said, "Thank you, Mona." She smiled at me as she stood up to take the phone. She said, "Good luck, Miss Hart."

Colonel Wells sat behind his desk, frowning over his mustache. Helen Stillbert and I stood across from him at attention. There were files stacked on his desk, and I could see upside down that they said "WAC." I wondered how he must feel having his base overrun with more girls.

He said, "Normally these orders would come from Jackie Cochran or General Arnold, but she's in Texas right now and the general has flown to England. You've been ordered by Ms. Cochran and Brigadier General Ralph Dodson to ferry a plane to the U.S. Air Transport Command base at Prestwick Airport in Scotland. It's a classified delivery mission. You will be the first women during this war to fly overseas for the military, and only the second . . ." he looked at me, "and third," he looked at Helen, "in history." He frowned deeper as if to say this was the last mission on earth he'd ever have come up with on his own.

In spite of my ankle and my ribs and my head—and even in spite of my heart—I felt myself leaning forward but not actually leaning forward. It was a leaning forward in my mind, wanting to hear every word he was about to say to me.

"You'll do a checkout ride on the B-17 next week and depart for Scotland soon after. This is a top-secret mission. We don't want any press attention until the flight has been completed."

I could feel chill bumps rise on my arms even though it was warm in the office and warm outside. I had been wanting to fly the B-17 ever since I got to Camp Davis and saw them gleaming silver in the sun. The B-17 Flying Fortress was a four-engine bomber that newspapers and newsreels called one of the greatest weapons of the war. This was mostly because it was being used for daylight precision strategic bombing against the Germans. It was a high-flying, long-range ship that was as mythical as Tsul 'Kalu or the Nunnehi because the people who flew it said it could unleash great destruction, that it could actually defend itself, just like a soldier, even without a man at the throttle, and that it had the ability to return home despite serious battle damage. So far it had dropped more bombs than any other U.S. aircraft in the war.

I said, "Sir?"

He said, "Yes?"

"I thought we were supposed to fly from base to base demonstrating the safety of the B-29." I let the question hang out there, hoping he wouldn't think I was mocking him or Jackie Cochran or the entire Army Air Forces.

He seemed to sigh into his desk without actually sighing. He said, "We've shelved that mission for now. This is more urgent."

I thought: I just bet. You mean Jackie Cochran got wind of another chance to show us off to the world. The B-29 didn't work? Fine—let's send some girls across the ocean in a B-17.

Before we left, Colonel Wells said, "Miss Hart, the flight recorder from your B-29 is under review. Investigations like this take time, but I did want you to know we are doing everything we can." I looked at this man and remembered how he told me on my very first day that I wasn't wanted. Now he seemed like just another man sitting behind his desk, trying to do his job. I wondered who he was before the war.

I said, "Thank you, sir."

Outside the office, Helen said, "How do you feel about getting back up there, Hartsie? Are you ready for that?" There was a cloud hanging over her face, and I wondered if she was nervous about the idea of flying with me.

I said, "I'll be fine." I had to be. Jackie Cochran was the only woman in the world who had ferried a bomber to Britain. I was going to make history.

~

At the end of the week Helen and me started our training on the B-17 with a bomber pilot just back from England where he'd been flying for the 8th Air Force. His name was Tommy Collins and he was big and rambling and blond and blue eyed and had a grin like a little boy up to no good.

The B-17 was smaller than the B-29, but it was still seventy-five-feet long and had a wingspan of over a hundred feet. Helen and me followed Tommy Collins around and through the plane. He said, "When I trained on this ship, we needed 130 hours in the air, which means you'll be on the flight line 5 hours a day—maybe more—seven days a week. You need to learn to synchronize all four engines, basic flight maneuvers, how to handle stalls, and how to fly and land this thing when one or two or three engines go out."

Helen looked at me and I thought: He doesn't know about the accident. He doesn't know that I've already landed a four-engine plane when two of its engines were out and one of the other ones was on fire. He doesn't know I've flown the biggest bomber on earth and that this one could almost fit inside it.

I listened to him talk about the hours of cross-country experience we would need, day and night, so that we could get enough navigation and radio experience to fly across the Atlantic Ocean. He told us this was a $300,000 weapon of war that weighed fifty thousand pounds and carried ten hours worth of fuel. We went over the cockpit procedures and the pilot's checklist. And through it all, I wasn't worried. I felt far away from myself, like I was floating up above, looking down on Tommy Collins and Helen and me. I could see myself standing in the cockpit, sitting at the throttle, but it was just like I was watching someone else.

At 7:30 the next morning and the next morning and every morning after that for the next two weeks, we met Tommy at the B-17, walking past the army air force officers who said, "What's this war coming to that they're giving girls the same training that we're getting?" I took my turn in the pilot's seat and went through the checklist.

I liked going about my business without anyone worrying over me. I was glad Tommy Collins didn't know about my accident. It let me keep to myself and concentrate on what I needed to do. But on Tuesday, May 23, I arrived at the flight line just before Helen and saw that Tommy Collins was wearing a worried look. He said, "Velva Jean, I heard about your accident."

Something in me sank. I didn't want him to know. I didn't want anyone to know. I wanted to go on like nothing had happened, without having people looking at me like I needed to be fussed over and watched and treated like a glass figurine.

He said, "I don't know why they're sending you back up so soon, and in this monster of all things."

I said, "It's okay." My voice had an edge to it, though I knew he was being nice.

He said, "You poor poppet." And something about those three words was sincere and sweet and made me mad. "You don't have to fly this if you don't want to."

I said, "I'm a WASP. I have to fly it. It's why I'm here."

And then, without waiting for Helen, I climbed up into the plane, my hands shaking, and sank into the pilot's seat. I sat there seeing red. I was sick to death of people telling me I couldn't do this or that or that I was a girl who had no business being there. All I wanted was to do my work, the work I was chosen to do, and have everyone leave me alone.

In a moment Tommy came through the door and up behind me, and then Helen poked her head in and said, "Sorry I'm late."

I waited till everyone was strapped in, and then I flipped on the electrical switch that activated a hydraulic pump that gave oil pressure to start number one engine. I pushed the button that read "start engines," and the eleven-foot-seven-inch propeller shook itself awake and started to spin. In less than two minutes, all four engines were thundering and I couldn't help it—I felt a thrill deep down.

I put my hand on the engine throttles and steered my way down the runway, edging the four throttles forward so that the bomber began to roll. At 110 miles per hour, I pulled back on the control wheel and the Flying Fortress lifted off the runway. When we reached the end of it, I pushed the control wheel forward, bringing down the nose so that the B-17 could gain speed. The plane hummed as the main landing gear and tail wheel came up into the belly of the plane. The airspeed rose to 135 miles per hour, and we started to climb.

Beside me, Helen pulled her earphones off one ear. This was something we usually did because even though the headphones were supposed to help protect our ears, the noise of the engines was so loud that it could leave you deaf for days. But this time I left my earphones on. I wanted to hear the roar of the engines. I wanted to feel the power of the plane go through me. My skin hummed and my teeth jittered. The B-17 was rough and strong, like flying a mountain.

I could crash at any moment. One of the engines could catch fire or one or two or three of them could die. The ship could go into a dive or a spin that I couldn't get out of. There might be an oil rag on the engine or sugar in the gas tank or sand in the carburetor. Another plane might clip one of our wings, or we might go crashing into the side of a mountain just because the fog rolled in and we didn't see it. My parachute might not open in time, and even if it did I might land too hard.

I thought of all the things that could happen to me. This was something I never used to do till Sally was killed, but now I made myself run through every single kind of crash, every single kind of accident. Then I settled back behind the throttle and looked out at the blue sky—the bluest I'd ever seen. There wasn't a single cloud. Only sunshine and sky stretching for miles and miles so that the whole world seemed to be made up only of blue. I heard the song I'd written—my new song—start up in my head.

> *I'm flying high above the clouds.*
> *I'm flying swift and free.*
> *I'm flying with my own true heart*
> *toward my destiny . . .*

The B-17 was lighter and sleeker than the B-29 and seemed to fly even faster. I climbed to three thousand, four thousand, ten thousand feet. When I got to twelve thousand, I put the B-17 Flying Fortress through a slow roll. It was like dancing, like music. It was the most beautiful plane I'd ever flown. In my earphones I heard Tommy Collins say, "Christ, Velva Jean. That was mad." But it was an admiring sort of comment.

As I came out of the roll, I thought that when you got down to it every plane was the same. Some were bigger, some were harder to handle. But they were all just wings and power and speed and height and glorious, joysome flight.

When I got back to the barracks, I ran into Janie in the bathroom. I stood in front of the sink brushing my teeth while she rubbed cream over her face. She said, "This is the third pot of this stuff I've run through since I've been here. That swamp air just sucks it out of you."

I wiped my mouth and said something like yes, isn't it awful, but my mind was actually on the B-17.

Janie said, "Oh hey. A girl was here looking for you. A WAC."

"Who was she?"

"Beats me. She didn't want to leave her name or anything. Said she'd find you later." She picked up her cream and her towel. "Night, Hartsie."

"Night." I leaned in close to the mirror and looked at myself. I whispered, "You did it. You're flying again. And you're still here."

For the first time in weeks—since before my accident, before Sally—I slept through the whole night. No dreams. No waking up. No stirring around. Just sleep, quiet and deep.

June 1, 1944

Dear Velva Jean,

I got a lot of words in me I'd like you to hear, but I don't know where to start. I try to think about the Navajo, about how there's no such thing as choosing the wrong word, but how you have to say it right or you end up saying something else.

Well I ain't so good with letters. I'm better with songs. Here's one I been working on. I wrote it for you, girl.

Butch

The Bluesman

I am travelin' to Somewhere
as fast as I can go.
Just strangers on the highway,
nobody that I know.

I thought I had the Right of Way,
but then you came along,
no map, no compass, no way—
nothing but a song.

Your heart is in the music,
your soul is in the song,
your eyes are on the future—
just let me come along.

I had to know you somewhere,
maybe long ago,
on some forgotten highway
where time was movin' slow.

Or maybe on a pathway
where I knew that I was lost
or on a bridge to Somewhere
'til our footsteps crossed.

It don't matter where or when,
or who or what or why—
I'll love you forever
and on the day when we die

I'll sing "Your heart is in the music.
Your soul is in the song.
Your eyes are on the future.
Just let me come along."

FORTY-FIVE

On June 4, each WASP received a brand-new uniform. Jackie Cochran was still in Texas, but she sent a note calling them our "Santiago Blues," and telling us they had been made just for us by fashion designers at Bergdorf Goodman, a fancy department store in New York City.

The uniforms were the deepest, darkest blue, the color of the night sky—long jacket with a belt, white blouse, black tie, straight skirt that hit just below the knee (and pants too), white gloves, and a smart-looking little hat, called a "beret," designed by a place called Frederick's of Hollywood in California. The gold seal of the United States was stitched onto the beret, the winged arm patch of the Army Air Forces was stitched onto the left shoulder of the jacket, and a gold "WASP" pin, with crossed wings and a propeller, was clipped to the collar.

Janie, Helen, and the rest of the girls and me tried them on right away and marched around base where the army air force officers and cadets and Major Blackburn and Colonel Wells and, most of all, the WACs, could see us. Nothing I'd ever worn—not my dress with the bolero jacket or my blue dress with the skirt that twirled or even the gold dress Gossie borrowed for me from Gorman's—had made me feel so glamorous.

That night before bed, I was still wearing my uniform while I washed my face and brushed my teeth. I thought I might just sleep in my Santiago Blues designed by Bergdorf Goodman of New York City, because, after everything, I finally felt like an official pilot for the government, even if General Hap Arnold and the Army Air Forces still called me a civilian.

On June 5, Helen and I received orders that we were leaving the next morning. I packed my clothes and my shoes and my Mexican guitar and Daddy's old mandolin and all of my talismans. I gave Sally's banjo to Janie, who said she was going to learn to play it, and after she did she was going to pass it on to the next WASP and the next one until all the girls learned. Then she would send it home to Sally's mama.

After mess that night I sat down at my desk and typed a letter to Darlon C. Reynolds.

> Dear Mr. Reynolds,
>
> I hope you are doing well. I'm sending you this song I wrote. It's a good one. It may even be my best one. Thank you for looking at it. And thank you for telling me I could do better.
>
> I leave for Scotland tomorrow but when I'm back and this war is over, I would love to talk to you about making records. I think, after everything, singing is still my life's dream.
>
> Sincerely,
> Velva Jean Hart

~

On the morning of June 6, I dressed in my Santiago Blues and said good-bye to Janie, and then I met Helen outside the barracks. We each carried one army duffle bag. Mine had my clothes and my mandolin and my Mexican guitar and the entire contents of my hatbox— all my talismans—tied up in the bolero dress Harley bought me from the Hamlet's Mill department store. I carried Ty's compass in the pocket of my slacks and my rip cord and the wooden flying girl, the new one, in the other pocket. I was loaded down with lucky charms.

On our way to the flight line, we stopped at the PX so I could post my letter. The postmaster said, "As a matter of fact, something just came for you."

It was a letter from Beachard, dated May 24. It contained just a handful of lines: "Wanted you to know I'm okay. I'm in a place called Saipan. Biggest invasion of the Pacific so far. Using B-29s. The closest any American has come to Japan in this war." I folded up the letter, giving thanks that he was safe and wishing I could fly a B-29 to the Pacific.

Saipan—there was something about the names of these places, especially the ones in the Pacific, that unsettled me and gave me the deepest, darkest kind of spooks. Europe was one thing—a different world with different languages—but the Pacific, with its jungles and men hiding in the earth and thousands and thousands of dead soldiers washed up on beaches was enough to keep me up at night.

Tommy Collins stood by the B-17, talking to the mechanics, checking out the crew. Helen and me were pilot and copilot, but we would be flying with a squad of nine men—navigator, bombardier, flight engineer, radio operator, nose gunner, two waist gunners, a tail gunner, and a ball-turret gunner—as well as the Norden bombsight.

Tommy handed me a .45. I took it from him and strapped it on. He said, "If you're ever in England, honeybee, I'd love to take you out."

I said, "Thank you," because I didn't know what else to say. Nice as he was, I knew I would never go out with Tommy Collins.

Your heart is in the music.
Your soul is in the song.
Your eyes are on the future.
Just let me come along.

The crewmen climbed aboard one by one. Tommy said, "All right, then, we're just waiting on one more."

Helen adjusted her helmet, her goggles. She looked at me. "You sure you're ready for this?"

"I'm ready," I said.

Tommy said, "Here we go, then. All here."

I turned to see a WAC uniform and my first thought was, Oh no. But the uniform didn't fit quite as well on this girl because she was taller and wider than the other ones. Her lips and her nails were painted the brightest, raciest red you could imagine, but the rest of her looked thrown together, like she got dressed in a hurry and only just had time to get there. She was out of breath and laughing like she'd run all the way.

She said, "Shit, Mary Lou, you should see your face." Then Gossie picked me up and squeezed the breath out of me.

~

We were scheduled to fly from Camp Davis to Presque Isle, Maine, and from there to Goose Bay, Labrador, to Greenland, and then to Scotland. It took us four days to get from Camp Davis to Maine because of storms, and another three to get to Labrador. Helen and I took turns at the throttle, and as we flew from base to base I made sure to take my helmet off on landing so my hair fell around my shoulders. I wanted everyone to know that I was a girl flying this plane with another girl for my copilot and a crew of eight men and one woman.

Gossie was traveling as our radio operator. She'd joined the WAC in January after Clinton Farnham, her fiancé, was shipped out to England. It took her a while to find out I was at Camp Davis, but when she did she made up her mind to surprise me. She said they'd asked for volunteers for this trip, and before she even knew I was one of the pilots she jumped at the chance just so she could travel to Britain and maybe, just maybe, see Clinton somehow.

Somewhere over Rhode Island, I heard Gossie's voice in my earphones: "Sing us a song, Mary Lou. Do you have any new ones?"

I thought of my new song—my only new song in a long time—the one I'd just sent off to Darlon C. Reynolds. I thought of the song Butch wrote just for me. I knew all the words to "The Bluesman" by heart. I carried them around with me everywhere. I thought that Butch

Dawkins really was a code talker. He'd been talking to me in code for weeks now—through lyrics and music—only I didn't know it. I wondered if I'd ever be able to talk to a man the regular way again, and this was funny after all the time I'd spent worrying that I needed to get to know Butch Dawkins better.

Now that he was gone, I thought about him in flashes. It was never his whole face but pieces of him—his insides mostly. The things I missed about him were his words and the place in his soul where the music came from. I tried not to think of him out in the world, far from me, meeting exotic-looking women with dark hair and almond-shaped eyes and skin the color of caramel. I tried not to think of him singing them songs and telling them the hidden language of the Navajo. I tried not to think of him going to war.

What I made myself think of was what he once said to me: "I never wrote with anyone else, girl. I never showed my songs to anyone. You're the only one I ever did that with, and that one we wrote together is still one of my best songs."

I almost sang my song, Butch's song, our song, but then I thought of the men on this plane who would listen to me singing and have something smart to say after it, and I decided I didn't want to put any of those songs out there like that, not now. I started singing "Wild Blue Yonder," and one by one everyone joined in.

As I sang, I pictured myself saying good-bye to the part of me that still wore the scars from everything that had happened in my life, the part of me that was still locked away in that little black box.

We landed on what the U.S. Navy called Bluie—their code name for Greenland—on the afternoon of June 15. Greenland had a wild beauty—deep-blue water, deep-blue sky, and ice everywhere. I'd always thought ice and snow were just one color, but the snow was white and pink and blue, and the ice was the clearest blue, the color of asters. I thought the U.S. Navy was right to name it what they did.

We stayed overnight, which meant Gossie and me sat up late talking about everything that had happened since I left Nashville—Harley, the divorce, the WASP, Avenger Field, quitting Gorman's, Ty,

Camp Davis, Clinton Farnham, Sally's death, Bob Keene, Jackie Cochran, joining the WAC, my crash in the B-29. I didn't tell her about Butch because I still didn't know what that was and I didn't want to have to try to explain it to someone else, even Gossie, or to put words on it when it was more of a feeling.

We fell asleep around two in the morning, and I dreamed that I was flying the B-29 to Saipan and Duke Norris was sitting beside me, telling me to take the plane into a spin and now a stall and now a dive. Suddenly Johnny Clay came walking into the cockpit, big as life, just as full of himself as ever. He looked gold from head to toe. He said, "Don't write me, Velva Jean. I won't get it." And then he threw open the cockpit door and jumped.

I shouted, "Johnny Clay Hart! Get back in here!" We were twelve thousand feet in the air. We were much too high to go jumping out of planes.

I strained to see out the windows, to see where he'd gone, but there was nothing but empty sky. I hollered to Duke, "Did you see him? Do you see him? Where'd he go?"

Duke's mouth worked with worry. His eyes were sinking into his face. He said, "He's nowhere, Velva Jean. He's gone."

I said, "But he was just here." I leaned up and toward the window as best I could with my hand still on the throttle. The sky rolled out in each direction, unmarked, uninterrupted, never-ending blue. Suddenly the plane was going into a real dive, one I couldn't get out of. I looked over at Duke, only it wasn't Duke in the copilot's seat—it was Bob Keene.

He said, "What do you know? Engine trouble. I hope we don't have any serious mechanical issues on this flight."

"Johnny Clay!" I started yelling it. "Johnny Clay Hart!" I shouted it over and over again until Bob finally said, "Fifinella. Didn't you hear what Duke said? He's gone."

I woke up shaking, and it took me a long while before I stopped. I pressed my hand over my heart and felt it beating fast, then slowing a little, a little more. I prayed, *Jesus, if you can hear me, please let my brother be safe. Please let him be okay. Please don't ever let anything hap-*

pen to him, even if he is a fool to go off to war and try to get himself killed.
Don't you let him do it, Lord. I'll be good and true and I'll make sure he'll
be good and true too, as much as anyone can, forever and ever if only you
keep him safe.

We ate our breakfast in the officer's club, drinking coffee and eating toast and bacon. One of the officers brought in a stack of newspapers. We hadn't paid attention to the news since we'd left Camp Davis.
He said, "It's on, boys." He slammed the papers down on the table so
that the coffee cups rattled, and then he picked up one of the papers off
the top of the pile. "The invasion of France." He threw it down on the
stack and held up another. "The biggest invasion in the Pacific."

He threw that one down too, and Gossie reached for it. I read over
her shoulder. On the front page was a map of Saipan. The headline
read, "Cave Warfare in Death Valley." Thirty thousand Japanese
troops hiding in caves or burrowed in the ground, waiting for our
boys, including the 6th Marine Division—Beachard's unit—the same
men that fought in Tarawa. The paper said it was too early to count,
but there might be as many as fourteen thousand Americans killed.

At the end of the table, the bombardier looked up from the paper
he was reading. He said to me, "Isn't your brother a paratrooper?"

I had to think for a minute about what he was asking, to clear my
head from images of jungles and caves and fourteen thousand dead
soldiers. No, Beachard isn't a paratrooper. Wait. Johnny Clay. Johnny
Clay is a paratrooper. I said, "Yes," but it came out funny, like a croak.
My dream came back to me—the B-29, Duke Norris, my brother
jumping, engine trouble, the empty blue sky.

"101st Airborne?"

This time I couldn't say a word, so I just nodded.

He passed his paper down to me. It was dated June 8, 1944.

Two days ago, in Normandy, France, more than five thousand
ships and thirteen thousand aircraft took part in the invasion
of the Normandy coastline, and by the end of the day on June
6 the Allies had gained some ground. The price for the Allied
forces was more than nine thousand killed or wounded. Gen-

eral Dwight Eisenhower was in command of the invasion, which was code-named Operation Overlord.

At 3:00 a.m. on D-day, on the rugged waves of the English Channel, the Allies transferred to landing craft some twelve miles off the French coast. British units headed toward Caen, Canadians to a stretch west of Saint-Aubain-sur-Mer code-named Juno Beach, and U.S. troops directed themselves toward Utah and Omaha Beaches nearer a place called Cherbourg.

The newspaper called Omaha a suicide mission. One of the headlines said, "Bloodiest Battles Are at Omaha Beach as U.S. Forces Face Strong German Resistance." First a strong undertow carried soldiers away. After ten minutes of landing every officer and sergeant of the 116th Infantry Regiment was dead or wounded. But somehow, by 10:00 a.m., three hundred men had made it through "enemy mortar fire," across the beach covered in bodies, and up a bluff to attack the Germans. By nighttime three thousand Americans lay dead on what they called "Bloody Omaha."

Among our boys that landed on Omaha were the members of the 101st Airborne, paratroopers trained at Camp Toccoa, Georgia. One of them, a Sergeant Mickey Gorham, said in the newspaper: "It was five minutes to one when the light snapped off and a hold in the plane was opened. Under it we could see the coast of France below—and the most hellish sight it was, for flak from the coast defenses was spouting fire and flame everywhere. We were terrified by it—until we were all madly shuffling down the hold and jumping into space. As I stood up with my harness off, I knew I was lost. Suddenly there was a rip and a tear in my chute, and I flung myself to the ground as the machine guns rattled."

Mickey Gorham.

Johnny Clay wrote me once about a Mickey Gorham, back when he first got to Camp Toccoa: "This guy Mickey Gorham, from Boston, is the worst though. He was calling me 'cracker' till I told him exactly what I would do to him if I ever heard the word 'cracker' come out of his mouth again."

I got a sick feeling inside me because suddenly I couldn't feel Johnny Clay in the world, and usually I had a sense of him. I closed my eyes and tried to think of him, only not just think of him—to feel him. All I felt was empty air and the hum of engines warming up in the distance, ready to fly.

I asked to talk to the commanding officer, Colonel Bradley Burns. I stood in his office and told him about Beachard in Saipan and then I told him about Johnny Clay and how I thought he'd landed in Normandy on Omaha Beach.

He said, "Omaha Beach?" His smile faded away. I watched it go, like it was melting off in the heat, until he sat there blinking at me. He said, "I'm afraid it's impossible to know anything right now about anyone's whereabouts, young lady. No one's where they're supposed to be. Men being picked up by this unit or that one, regardless of where they belong. Scattered to all hell. It's a bloody mess."

He must have seen something in my face then because he said, "I'm sure your brother's fine," which was always the worst thing anyone could say to you when you were missing someone and worrying about them. "I'm sure he'll turn up soon." He was backtracking, trying to make it seem like maybe Johnny Clay was okay, but as I sat there, chilled from the inside out, I knew that Johnny Clay was missing and this was why I couldn't sense him anymore. He was somewhere he wasn't supposed to be, and I had to find out where.

The colonel said, "It's far too early to know anything, but I can check the preliminary reports we've gotten by telegraph. Let me see what I can find out."

"Thank you," I said. "Do you mind if I make a telephone call while you're doing that?"

Outside the colonel's office, his secretary put the call through for me and when it was connected she handed me the receiver.

"Deal's General Store," a voice said. It was a lady.

I said, "Sweet Fern, it's Velva Jean. Have you heard from Beach or Johnny Clay?"

She said, "Velva Jean? Where are you?" The line crackled.

I said, "Greenland. Have you—"

"Greenland? What on earth?"

"Listen to me. Have you heard from Johnny Clay?"

"Daddy Hoyt had a telegram from Linc. Him and some of the others in the Ranger Force invaded Rome on June 5 and faced the SS, Hitler's own personal guards. Can you believe that? Lincoln Hart Jr., quietest man in the world. He's doing good and guess who's with him? Coyle. They joined up in a place called Anzio. I can't tell you how much better it makes me feel that they're together."

I thought about the five Sullivan brothers. I said, "I'm so glad, honey, but what about Beach? What about Johnny Clay?"

"Beachard? Johnny Clay?"

"Yes."

"I haven't heard anything about them. Why?" I could hear the steam rising in her voice. "Velva Jean?"

I didn't want to worry her. She had enough to worry on. I said, "I'm just wondering where they are right now, that's all."

"Surely someone on your base can find out." There was steel in my sister's voice, and I thought, Same old Sweet Fern. I was grateful for it.

I said, "I'm trying."

"You let me know what they tell you."

"I will."

Then Sweet Fern said, "Harley Bright got himself married again. I thought you should know because I knew he wouldn't tell you himself."

My ears were ringing. My stomach turned over just like I was in an A-24 dropping into a dive or a spin or a stall. I said, "Pernilla Swan."

"Yes."

The colonel's secretary was pretending to type a letter, but I could tell she was listening. When I looked at her, she shuffled some papers around and cleared her throat and started typing faster.

I said, "I'm not surprised." The idea of Harley and Pernilla Swan hit me like a slap, even though I could have seen it coming, knowing him, knowing her. I tried to picture her up there in Harley's house, my old house, sleeping in that bed, fixing the breakfast for Levi, waiting for Harley to come home from the Little White Church, listening to his sermons, rocking with him on the porch, cleaning the floors, doing the shopping, ironing his Barathea white suit, lying under Harley at night when the moon fell in through the window while the pictures of his three dead brothers and his dead fat mama watched from the wall.

My head went foggy and I felt like I was underwater again—just like after my accident, when I woke up in the Jocassee Gorges—trying to push my way up to the surface light. I thought about the mission I was flying and about Greenland and Gossie and how I was going to be—with Helen—the second woman in the history of aviation to fly across the ocean in a bomber.

Sweet Fern said, "You done this all on your own, and I know it ain't been easy. Maybe I don't know all you been through and all you've had to do to get there, but I want you to know that I'm proud of you."

I said, "I'm proud of you too." And I was. As much as I didn't want to be Sweet Fern, she was a rock in my life and in everyone's life, and she was one of the reasons I was here in Greenland flying a B-17 bomber across the sea.

I thought she'd say, "For what? What did I do?" But instead she said, "Thank you. That's a good thing to hear sometimes."

Back in his office, Colonel Burns sat on a corner of his desk. He was holding a piece of paper and he said, "Captain Beachard S. Hart, 6th Marine Division, Saipan, has personally shot down thirteen Japanese planes before they could drop a single bomb." He looked back and forth between me and the paper. "Following that, he parachuted to shore where he captured seventeen Japanese soldiers and helped destroy eight of their battleships. He seems to be very much alive."

"And Johnny Clay?"

"He didn't drop with his unit."

"What does that mean?"

"He never landed in Normandy. His orders were changed last winter, but they don't know where he was sent or who sent him."

I said, "Has anyone seen him? Any other units? Has he reported in anywhere?"

"Not that we know of."

There was something about his tone—gentle and kind—that made me think of Darlon C. Reynolds trying to be nice to me after I sang for him at Cyclone Records. I said, "Sir, I appreciate what you're doing, but I'd rather you talk straight. I've got three brothers and I was raised on honesty. I need to know what I'm dealing with here."

He set the paper aside. He said, "Miss Hart, I wish I could help you. Truly. But I'm afraid I don't know. There's no paper trail. No record of Johnny Clay Hart past the middle of November, when he was in England, a place called Upottery."

I remembered Johnny Clay's letter: "Something big is getting ready to happen, but I can't say what. . . . Don't worry if you don't hear from me for a good long while."

The colonel said, "No one can say what his orders were." I could see he was telling the truth and this worried me. Where was Johnny Clay that no one, not even a colonel, could find him?

I said, "So he could be dead."

"Yes."

"Or he could be missing."

Colonel Bradley sighed, a sigh so heavy that I knew it wasn't just about Johnny Clay. It was a sigh about this whole horrible war. "Yes," he said.

~

I was in the pilot's seat from Greenland to Prestwick, Scotland. Helen would fly us back on the return trip. It was two thousand miles across the water. As we took off from Bluie, up through full dark clouds and pouring rain, we sailed up over the snow and the water, which was blue as a robin's egg, and the icebergs that sat off the shore like ice mountains. I felt the rush of the wind and the engine and the throttle in my hand. I felt just like I did the first time I flew with Duke Norris.

Up here, there was no looming mountainside to crash into. There wasn't any sadness or loss or even death. There was no guilt over Harley, no lost daddy, no dead mama, no dead Ty or Sally, no faraway family, no broken heart, no worries, no wondering about Butch Dawkins and when I might see him again, no fear. There was only sky and sun and wind and the earth spread out beneath me.

I could feel the .45 strapped on to my hip. There were two red buttons above the instrument panel with printed instructions to push them if you had to make a landing over enemy territory. It was hard not to look at them as I flew. I wondered if I would need them where I was going.

Even with all I'd been through since becoming a WASP, I knew that I wouldn't do anything else in this world but fly planes. Not right now at least. After the war I might go back to Nashville and try out for Darlon C. Reynolds again and also the Opry, or I might go to Hollywood and look up Mudge and try to be an actress myself. Maybe I would go to New York and be a dancer on the stage. Or maybe I would become a pilot for Pan Am or TWA. I didn't know what I was going to do, but the one thing I did know was that after the war was over, I would never go back to Devil's Kitchen or live a normal woman's life, not even if Butch Dawkins asked me to settle down with him or Ned Tyler came back from the dead and wanted me to be his wife.

If there was one thing I'd learned, it was that you were responsible for your own ship. You had to look after the engine and make sure the plane was in order and ready to be flown. You were in charge of plotting your course. When you were in the pilot's seat, it was your hand on the throttle, no one else's. If your oil ran out or you lost an engine or the engine caught fire and you had to crash, you were the one saving yourself. No one else could do it for you.

We were out over the Atlantic, the icebergs fading into the horizon behind us, nothing but blue-green ocean ahead. I thought: I am taking this bomber to Scotland. And from there I will make my way to Upottery or London or France or anywhere else I need to go to find my brother and bring him home.

I remembered something Daddy Hoyt once said about how when

love visits you don't ask how long it's going to stay. About how you should treat it kindly and give it a good welcome. And also about how you shouldn't spend all your time worrying about the love that leaves, because then you might overlook the love that was always there.

When I was little, Mama used to sing a song to me: "Mama and Daddy love Velva Jean Hart, Velva Jean Hart, Velva Jean Hart . . ." going through every person in our family and singing about how much they loved me. I thought that this was the love that stayed and men like Harley and Ty and Butch Dawkins might be momentary, even if you wanted them to be forever. You could never know if they would stay for long or if maybe they would go after only a little while.

But Johnny Clay had always been there. He was my brother and my very best friend in the world. He'd helped me learn to fly. He'd promised me just after Mama died that he would never leave me. And so I was going to find him.

I'm coming, Johnny Clay. Wherever you are, just hang on. I'm on my way.

I climbed higher and higher till we were over the clouds, up where the sun was shining—high above the overcast, ceiling and visibility unlimited.

And then I began to sing.

Beyond the Keep

Words and music by Velva Jean Hart

When I was just a girl child—
before they went away—
my mama and my daddy
kept me safe by night and day.

And when I was a girl grown—
before he went away—
I had a handsome true love
kept me safe by night and day.

Then I was a woman grown,
striving to be free.
No one else could keep me safe—
that was up to me

I learned that in the bright of day,
I learned that in the dark asleep—
I have to find my way alone
to live beyond the keep.

Sometimes the way is narrow,
sometimes the way is steep,
but you can't walk it for me.
I have to live beyond the keep.

Sometimes the river's shallow,
sometimes the river's deep,
but you can't swim it for me.
I have to live beyond the keep.

Sometimes the sky is clean and bright,
sometimes the rain clouds weep,
but you can't shield me from the storms
if I live beyond the keep.

I'm flying high above the clouds.
I'm flying swift and free.
I'm flying with my own true heart
toward my destiny.

If I'm flying in the bright of day
or dreaming in the dark asleep,
I'm living with my own true self
when I live beyond the keep.

My mama used to tell me—
before she went to Sleep—
about angels and archangels
with a lasting love so deep
that I'll feel it all around me
when I live beyond the keep.

If I'm flying in the bright of day
or dreaming in the dark asleep,
I'm living with my own true self
when I live beyond the keep.

Author's Note on the WASP

*I*n 1942, with so many young men needed at war, the United States began training women to fly military aircraft so that male pilots could be released for combat duty overseas. These were the Women Airforce Service Pilots, or WASP. Henry Harley "Hap" Arnold, commanding general of the U.S. Army Air Forces, wasn't convinced that "a slip of a girl could fight the controls of a B-17 in heavy weather," but over 25,000 women applied. The 1,074 women who were accepted—ages eighteen to thirty-five—came from the farm, the mountains, the city, and the coast, to Houston, Texas, and later to Sweetwater, Texas, to train to be pilots. They were secretaries, students, wives, mothers, but the one thing they had in common was that they loved to fly.

As WASP, they flew almost every type of military aircraft—fighter planes and bombers, including the mythical B-17 and the giant B-29 that terrified so many male pilots. They ferried new planes long distances from military base to military base. And they towed targets while ground and air gunners honed their shooting skills by firing on them with live ammunition. Through it all, they faced military ingratitude, sexism, harassment, and sabotage. In all, thirty-eight WASP lost their lives flying for their country. But they were considered a civilian program and not part of the military.

The head of the WASP was Jacqueline Cochran, then the most famous and well-respected female pilot in the world, who, on May 18, 1953, became the first woman to break the sound barrier. She campaigned doggedly to earn the WASP the military status she knew they deserved. But in December 1944, stating that the changing war situation rendered the WASP unnecessary, General Arnold deactivated the program.

Thirty-three years later, the WASP were granted military status. Then, in July 2010, sixty-five years after their service, they received the highest civilian honor given by the U.S. Congress when President Barack Obama signed a bill awarding the WASP the Congressional Gold Medal.

On December 7, 1944, General Arnold addressed the last graduating class of WASP, saying: "You, and more than nine hundred of your sisters, have shown that you can fly wingtip to wingtip with your brothers. If ever there was any doubt in anyone's mind that women can become skillful pilots, the WASP have dispelled that doubt. Certainly we haven't been able to build an airplane you can't handle. So, on this last graduation day, I salute you and all WASP. We will never forget our debt to you."

Also available from bestselling author Jennifer Niven

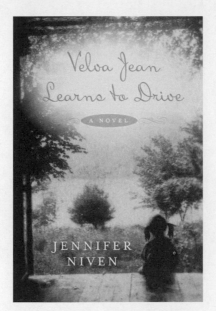

ISBN 978-0-452-28945-1

Visit www.jenniferniven.com

Available wherever books are sold.

Plume
A Member of Penguin Group (USA) Inc.
www.penguin.com